LEIA TALON

FALLING THROUGH THE WEAVING

BOOK ONE OF ROOTS AND STARS
THE WORLD TREE CHRONICLES

RHIANNON
PUBLISHING

This is a work of fiction. Names, characters, places, and incidents
are a product of the author's imagination. Locales and public names are
sometimes used for atmospheric purposes. Any resemblance to actual
people, living or dead, or to businesses, companies, events,
institutions, or locales is entirely coincidental.

Published by Rhiannon Publishing, 2021
British Columbia, Canada

www.LeiaTalon.com

Cover Design by Lara Wynter / Leia Talon
Illustrations by Glazkova Irina ~ Nutriaaa / depositphotos.com
Book Layout by Rhiannon Publishing

Falling Through the Weaving / Leia Talon ~ Second Edition
ISBN: 9780987992369

For everyone who feels music in their soul.

PART I

MAIDEN

CHAPTER 1
THE RELENTLESS SQUEEZE OF TIME

THERE WAS NO ESCAPING the bite of regret. Not when I was saying goodbye to a setup as nice as this—digs near the beach, walking distance from prime busking territory, and a pair of friends I didn't want to leave. I squinted at the distant ocean glittering in the sun, a salty breeze drifting in through the window.

With a sharp-edged blossom of sorrow in my belly, I stroked the blonde wood of my guitar, scuffed from years of playing music on the street. Stevie loved this six-string. Now it would be his. It was cowardly, not waiting for him and Jess to come home before taking off, but I sucked at saying goodbye. The note tucked between the strings was the best I could do.

> *Sweet Jess & Stevie,*
> *I can't explain why, but it's time for me to move on. Enjoy the guitar. Remember me with laughter and kisses and songs. I adore you both. ~ Shelta*

Anchor-heavy heart sinking in my chest, I adjusted my leggings and short, jagged-edged skirt. Grabbed my coat and backpack. Out the door I went, without a backward glance. Down the stairs, and onto the street.

The Pacific Ocean crashed on the beach not far from Jess and Stevie's apartment on Vancouver Island. One of the nicer spots I'd lived. Stevie had brought me home; Jess had decided to keep me. We'd had such fun, us three: jamming for tips on Government Street, waxing poetic over bottles of wine, getting tangled up in one another. Now I'd never see them again. Like so many others I'd left behind.

I had no roots. I'd fast-forwarded through eight decades in my thirty-odd years. At this point, I'd try anything to stop the pull of time.

Skirting the edge of desperation, I hoped the shimmering red dragon that kept showing up in my dreams held the key. His message last night made me pack up this morning.

Come. Find me. It's time.

I couldn't get him out of my mind. He was different from the others that frequented my dreams—small ones who curled up with me when I was lonely or cold, big ones who flew with power that made my soul soar even when I was at my lowest. I'd seen the crimson dragon before, but only from afar. Lately, he was all I dreamt about.

My long, forest-green coat flapped as I walked toward the highway; wind from passing cars blowing it open. Some vehicles were electric or solar-powered, slipping by in near silence, but every so often an old-school motorcycle or semi-truck would roar past with a rumble that went through me.

Despite being overkill on this bright summer day, my coat's weight was a comfort. I rubbed the wine-red embroidery at the cuffs in a habitual motion with my fingers. I'd slept in it more nights than I liked to admit, and had managed to hang onto it for three time jumps. Only my dragon necklace had been with me longer.

The ocean breeze was no match for the merciless heat of the sun. It beat against the buildings and radiated up from the sidewalk. I didn't let it slow my stride. I had a purpose. A problem. Somehow, I had to escape the vicious cycle that stole everyone I'd ever loved.

Not that I'd loved Stevie and Jess. Liked them a lot, yes, but love was a bad idea all around. Leaving them now was the best option. I'd disappeared too many times before, which tended to upset the people I left behind. Reading missing person searches looking for me always put me in a powerless fury, tossed into the future again, too late to go back. Nothing to do but fabricate a new identity, keep my head down, and never stop moving.

My most important rule was, "no getting attached." Life was simpler that way.

It didn't take long to reach the four-lane road out of town, and I stationed myself along the widest part of the shoulder, hoping to hitch a ride. Cars and trucks flew past, hot air and exhaust buffeting me in their wake. I only stuck my thumb out for the vehicles that looked friendly, trusting a gut feeling I'd learned to listen to back in my twenties, when I'd done more hitchhiking than was wise in an attempt to outrun fate.

Sweat was trickling down the back of my neck by the time a weathered woman in a dented pick-up gave me a lift. Friendly sort. Talker. She told me her thoughts on the latest horrors done by the usual regimes determined to rule the world. People were disappearing and murderers walked free, protected by their uniforms. Atrocities I could do nothing about.

Numb, I only half-listened.

She dropped me off at the edge of a forest that stretched halfway across the island, then pulled away in a cloud of dust. I ventured into the woods. The cool shadows were a godsend as I followed a trail north, toward the bigger trees.

After almost an hour, I ducked off the path and cut through the bush on a thin wildlife trail, letting my intuition guide me. Ferns swatted at my thighs. Leaves and moss cushioned my footsteps. On I marched, feet keeping time with the music in my head and the dragon's echoing words.

Come. Find me. It's time.

I caught myself hoping, dreaming that wherever the wormhole took me, it would be an improvement. Foolhardy optimism. Civilization was messy no matter the year. 2035 had been no different. Yes, I'd found friends. Things had worked out for me. Always did. I could never understand why.

But the state of the world? It didn't get better. My struggles were nothing compared to what so many people faced. It was devastating. Anxiety came clawing, every time I dwelled on how helpless I was to do anything about it.

I pushed the air out of my lungs. Inhaled.

Calm, Shelta. Focus.

My heart beat its relentless boom, making a drum out of my chest. Douglas fir and cedar grew all around, the air scented with golden sap and sun-warmed trees. Their thick trunks and tapering heights reminded me of ancient sentries.

When a massive fir caught my eye, I trudged through the underbrush toward it, over logs half-decomposed on the forest floor., hoping it was my ticket to a new life. A new start. One that delivered more answers than every other immeasurable span of years before.

A knot of expectation formed in my belly as I reached out to touch the reddish bark. *Take me to the red dragon. Take me somewhere where I can understand myself.*

My fingers brushed rough bark. I pressed my palm into it until bumps dug into my hand.

Nothing happened.

This wasn't the right tree.

Disappointment sparked cynical thoughts as I returned to the deer path I'd been following. Every time I'd tried to find the tree before, I'd failed. The dragon was probably a figment of my imagination; a subconscious creation to help me cope.

But what if it was a premonition? Maybe there was an actual dragon waiting for me somewhere. Beneath the jitters of anxiety that drove me on, a deeper song had called me to this specific forest. My next step forward was here. It had to be.

The portal was always a tree, every unasked-for jump, except maybe when I was born. Mother-Number-One swore I'd come from "the belly of the goddess." Whatever that meant. That was 1963. Or so. The first year I could remember was 1969 and all the hype about landing on the moon.

Every time I'd sought a way to make the time travel happen, it eluded me. Then, when I least expected it, a mere brush against the wrong branch would suck me forward a few years and plop me down in a new forest. A new city or village. A new library, full of books that didn't have the answers I was looking for.

Seventeen time-leaps in my thirty-odd years. I'd had nine foster mothers along the way. Countless friends and lovers who'd taken me in. The memories eventually blended into music. Sometimes I forgot the people on purpose, and just remembered the songs.

If I was going to keep being dragged into the future, I wanted some say in the details of my departure. I wasn't leaving this forest until I found the right tree.

It was the only move I had in a game I didn't understand.

From the place in my soul where the music came from, a pull drove me deeper into the woods. I reached for the dragon pendant at my neck, tracing the small circle of body, wings and tail, the one silver eye on its curled head a familiar notch beneath my fingertips.

At a turn in the terrain, a song welled up, and I opened my mouth to set the wordless melody free. Singing has always been my release. My salvation. The flow of notes came without thought, full of promise and mystery. Hope, even. As if something was feeding me the song.

My voice wavered as I skirted the edge of a ravine, then recovered as the wildlife trail cut away from the steep drop. When the path forked, I let the song lead me. Music enabled my intuition.

Finally, I rounded the roots of a downed giant to a massive cedar. It towered above me, emitting a subtle glow that pulsed and bled one color into another. Blue. Purple. Gold. Green.

Found the tree.

I stopped in my tracks, silence stealing my song. The humid air tasted electric. Charged. Thick with potency and power.

None of the portals I'd gone through before had *glowed*. But I didn't want to repeat the same pattern I'd been helpless to my whole life. This was different. Good.

In a desperate rush of optimism, I envisioned my version of utopia: a peaceful world where people respected each other and the earth. Twenty years into the future, maybe? However long it took for humanity to figure out that waging war and destroying the planet were awful ideas, that's when I wanted to land.

I sucked in a shaky breath. Forced myself forward. Reached both hands through the pulsing, translucent light to the soft-bark trunk of the tree. The second I touched it, everything went rainbow-black and all the music in creation streamed through my head at once in a seasick symphony. The world dropped away.

Falling.

Falling.

CHAPTER 2
AT THE ROOTS OF THE WORLD TREE

THE WORMHOLE'S CACOPHONY consumed me in a blinding onslaught of color, drowning me until I surrendered to the sparking, searing heat. Whatever this magic was, I was caught in it. Flying blind. It seemed to take longer than before. Time carried me, ferried me where it wished.

And spat me out through a wall of startling silence, into the next place.

The ground heaved like a ship's deck. Head spinning, both hands up, I staggered to my feet and blinked through blurry vision at the sight of a shaggy-haired man on his knees at the edge of a clear pool that flowed into a stream. His head was bowed, as if in prayer. I could've sworn the image of a red-haired woman glowed in his reflection, but it was gone with a swirl of water.

Seeing me, the man sprang to his feet, sword in hand and legs tense beneath a dark-green kilt. Behind him, a horse pawed the ground. Clouds lurked above a sparse canopy of trees, and a brisk wind raked leaves from the branches of a giant oak beside me. I braced myself to keep from toppling over, and squeezed my eyes shut to clear my head. Slowly, reality came into focus, and I tried to get my bearings.

The man lowered his sword and opened his mouth with a throaty sound that wasn't quite a word. "Are ye all right?" he finally asked.

I tried a smile, failed, and then tried again with more success. "I will be."

"Where did ye come from, lass?"

Scotland. I was in Scotland. But unless swords were back in fashion, something had gone terribly wrong. Backwards in time didn't appeal to me in the least. I'd only ever gone forward before. My mind stuttered. I put my hands to my head and suppressed a groan, glad the pool of water separated us for the time being. I had no idea how to explain myself.

Attempting to regain cognitive ability gave me a chance to look him over. Solid build. Sharp gaze. Unmistakably wearing a kilt. His boots were taller than mine, with buckles up the sides, their leather not quite as black as his coat. Black, blue, and white stripes crossed the forest green of his tartan, and a sword hung at his left hip, mirrored by a dagger on his right. A scar on his left temple peeked out from bits of dark hair that fell to his jaw, where another scar shot a streak of silver through a rough beard.

"Ye appeared out of thin air a moment ago." He tried again. "Singing, if I'm not mistaken."

"Singing. Yeah, I tend to do that." My gaze dropped to the flow of water between us as circuits connected in my brain. "I was walking through a forest in Canada. There was a really big tree. I touched it, and now I'm here." I didn't know what else to say, considering he'd seen me materialize. I'd never had a witness before.

"Ye travel between worlds?" His voice was little more than a whisper.

I lifted my eyes. "I guess so." Would he think me a witch?

He stayed silent, but I didn't pick up any sense of alarm, so I summoned my courage and asked an absurd question that needed sorting in order for my brain to deal. "Am I correct in thinking I'm in Scotland?"

"Aye. Ye're a long way from the New World, if that is indeed where ye came from."

"British Columbia."

"Never heard of it."

"Oh." It was a small sound. Distant. "I'm sorry I interrupted whatever you were doing here." My apology floated slack over the water. How far back had I gone? I turned around to touch the tree, the oak's bark bumpy while the cedar's had been smooth, but the portal was closed. Like always. There was no way back.

I forced my gaze back to the man across the spring.

"Ye haven't interrupted." His words were as lacking in conviction as mine.

I had interrupted something. I knew it with the same certainty that warned me I was an outrageously long way from anything familiar. "Would you be so kind as to tell me the year?"

"1753," he replied evenly. "What year was it where ye came from?"

"2035," I whispered.

His eyebrows shot up. Was that fear in his gaze? I needed him to trust me or my odds of survival would drop fast.

"I know it's hard to believe." I lifted my fingers to trace the dragon on my necklace.

He narrowed his eyes when he saw the pendant, something like recognition in the crinkle of his face. "Aye. That's a mighty long jump."

Wait. Was he accepting my freakish time-hopping thing? I held his gaze in a tense stretch of silence. His eyes were dark, with enough depth to hold the night sky. And there was something else—a sense of familiarity.

"You believe me?" My words came out entirely too vulnerable. No way did he believe me, unless he knew something I didn't.

"I've got no reason not to believe ye. That oak behind you is the World Tree. These woods are full of magic." The depths of his eyes spoke of enchantment. Of mysteries lost in time. It made me shiver as he went on. "There was nay but meself here one moment, and ye came from the tree the next. I dinna ken how ye'd come up with a story like that if it weren't true."

"Thank you," I stammered. The World Tree had come up again and again in my research, but I'd never heard someone refer to it in the context of an actual tree, like common knowledge. I accepted his outstretched hand and stepped over the narrow part of the stream, which flowed serenely through the forest.

"What's yer name, lass?"

"Shelta." I cleared my throat. "Shelta Raine."

"Ye have pretty green eyes, Shelta Raine. My name is Killian Maclean." He dipped into a regal bow, took my hand, and kissed it.

My skin flushed at his touch, and I took my hand back to play with the chunk of hair that had fallen over my shoulder. "Pleased to meet you." He looked at me with such intensity I had to drop my gaze. I gestured to the spring. "Is that good drinking water?"

"The best." Killian opened a hand, inviting me to it.

I brought my mostly-empty water bottle from my bag and knelt by the water's source, just as he'd been doing when I came through the tree. I filled the bottle, drank half of it, and filled it again.

"What is that?" Killian pointed at the bright blue canister in my hand.

"It's a flask." I handed it over for inspection.

He turned it in his big hands, opened the twist top, looked inside, closed it up again and handed it back. "That is a good flask." He eyed my pack, probably wondering what else I had in my magic pouch.

I took a mental inventory of my black backpack: minimalist toiletries, socks, underwear, a heavier shirt than the one I wore, and light clothes for sleeping or for hot days, which I wasn't sure if Scotland had. Most of my money would be useless here. I'd also packed some food, and my AIO, or All-In-One, which held the music I'd collected and created, my pictures, and years of research. I'd had the small, slim tablet for less than a month, having splurged on the solar-powered version.

That *especially* he did not need to find. I was probably breaking fifty rules of time travel having it here. Too bad I didn't know what the rules were.

At least the AIO was easily hidden. And now I was grateful I'd left my guitar with Jess and Stevie. It would be wildly out of place here, and make my *otherness* even more obvious.

The water sang its quiet song. The wind whispered in the trees and knocked leaves onto our shoulders. I worked to keep my voice even. "So, it's autumn here?"

"The first of November."

Great. Winter was on its way. I needed to find work that didn't require me to sell my body or submit to a heavy-handed boss, and arrange a safe place to sleep at night.

Killian looked toward his horse. I eyed the big animal, dark but for two white socks, and knew it was time to do the thing that did not come naturally to me. Trust.

I stowed my water bottle and hoisted my backpack. Asking for help ranked high on things I tried to avoid, but it was my best chance. Summoning a smile, I said, "It seems I am in need of assistance, Killian Maclean."

He regarded me in a considering way, the shadow of a smile beneath his beard. "Aye, it seems ye are."

Minutes later, I sat behind him as the horse picked its way down a deer path. The bedroll made a lumpy seat, and my legs draped awkwardly, with no stirrups for my feet. My temples throbbed. I gripped the sides of Killian's back, broad beneath the black wool of his jacket, the shade of my long coat a decent match to his kilt.

"Do many people visit this spring?" I asked. It didn't look it, by the overgrown trail.

"Some, but not many. Few ken it's here." His words rolled out slow, almost in time with the steps of his horse. He wasn't in a hurry.

Another thing I needed to adjust to, this far back in time. I gentled my next words in an attempt to match his pace. "Is it a sacred spot? You looked like you were praying when I first saw you."

He didn't answer. Had I misspoken? I readjusted my seat as the horse's hooves thudded on soft earth.

Finally, he said, "Aye, it is a sacred place. And ye did catch me in prayer. That's the first time I've been to the spring in a long while."

"I'm sorry. I didn't mean to trespass on your time there."

His laugh surprised me as we passed through the thinning trees. It danced up my arms and hummed in my ribcage. It was short-lived, but left me tingling.

"Ye didne trespass, lass. Rest easy."

I tried to stop fidgeting.

We came to a wider path, which led to a road, and emerged from the forest into one of those epic vistas I'd often admired in pictures but never had the chance to see. Shades of grey layered the sky, with clouds brushing the tops of rounded mountains that rose from the valley floor. A river wound its serpentine path through the browns and greens of the landscape. I half expected to find a loch around the corner and a castle on the next hill, but neither appeared.

The wind blew more fiercely now that we were out of the trees, and I fished into a pocket for my toque. Killian peered over his shoulder to see what I was doing as I pulled it onto my head, and gave me a strange look.

"What is that?" he asked.

"It's a hat." I readjusted the knitted wool cap, self-conscious. "We call it a toque in Canada."

"I've never seen the like."

"Well, I'll try to remember to take it off if we meet anyone else, so they don't think I'm too strange."

Killian chuckled. "Lass, when we meet up with others, try to keep yer coat closed so they dinna see ye've got breeks on."

"Oh. Right." Leggings and a short skirt had been a safe choice for the future. The past was a different beast altogether. At least I'd worn tall leather boots instead of sandals or sneakers. How was I going to afford a dress?

"I'll take care of ye." His voice was reassuring, like all was well in the world.

It wasn't, I knew, but I tried to relax my arms, which were squeezing Killian harder than necessary.

I'll take care of ye.

I'd been given guides before—foster mothers, friends, lovers—and maybe he was another, but I didn't like it, nor the way my body wanted to lean into him. He felt too familiar in an unfamiliar world, making my chest swirl with affection I shouldn't have for a stranger. I wanted to trust him, to be at home with him. If I did, it could only end badly.

I silenced a groan of frustration and willed my body to remember how to ride a horse. Mother-Number-Five had kept horses, though I'd spent far more time mucking stalls than getting in the saddle. I'd lived on her ranch for six seasons, then we took a trip to a National Park, I sat against a tree, and BAM! Skipped the last few years of the nineteen seventies and plunged into the eighties, where I spent my early teens in ripped jeans. On to Mother-Number-Six, inner-city Chicago, and a short stretch of hard life made better by libraries.

Enough. No sense getting nostalgic.

"Would ye like to walk a bit?" asked Killian.

"Yes." I almost groaned the word. "That would be nice."

The horse, named Lachie, slowed to the side of the road. I slid my hands from their warm place at Killian's back as he jumped down. He reached his hands up to me, and I accepted his help. It would have been a far less graceful dismount otherwise, considering the complaints from my hips and back.

We walked side by side, him leading the big black horse, me unable to keep quiet any longer. "Killian—or do I call you Mister Maclean? What do I call you?"

"Killian is fine."

"Okay, Killian, I have about three hundred questions, and I'm hoping you won't mind answering what you can."

He laughed. "I've some questions for ye also, lady. We shall trade, then?"

"Fair enough." My first priority was to establish if what I knew about the history of Scotland held up. "Does Scotland have a king?"

"Aye, we do. King James is in his castle in Edinburgh, and Prince Charles will rule when he's gone."

"So… the Jacobite uprising succeeded?"

He gave a calculating glance. "There was a successful challenge by King James in 1708."

"And in England?" I asked, my voice too high.

"England has her own king. We get along well enough. Why do ye start with this question?"

I suppressed a whimper and tried my best to explain. "In my world, the history of Scotland was filled with bloody wars, especially between Scotland and England around this time. It was heartbreaking to read about."

Something clicked in my brain, and I took several strides before I plunged on, an awed edge to my voice as I realized how much I'd broken the pattern of my life. I'd jumped tracks entirely. "I don't think I've traveled just in time and location—I think this is a different timeline altogether, like a parallel universe or something." Did any of this make sense to him?

"What was the outcome of the wars in yer history books?" The depth of his voice and the sharpness of his gaze made me sidestep away.

This man was cunning. Exceedingly so. What was I doing bringing up politics?

I tried to sound scholarly. "The books I read taught that England conquered Scotland, slaughtered many of the Highland clans, and outlawed the tartan, among other unpleasantness. That's why I thought to ask, because you're wearing your plaid in a year where it would've been punishable by prison or slavery, not to mention going around armed with a sword. That wasn't allowed either."

"Slavery? For wearing the tartan?" He sounded scandalized.

"Well, sort-of slavery. Many were shipped across the ocean to the colonies, to labor for the duration of the years they were sentenced to prison. Lots of them didn't survive the crossing, or—" Glancing up at him, I swallowed the rest of my textbook explanation. I was talking about people's lives. His people. "That's what I read, anyway."

My inability to keep my mouth shut was going to get me killed. Damn this falling backwards through time.

"Sounds like slavery." He gave me a hard look that lasted a good deal longer than comfortable. "We're certainly better off here. Scotland is too proud to fall to England, and I canna conceive of my people enslaved. King James abolished slavery years ago."

"I'm glad." I took the chance to change the subject. "The thing I've admired so much about Scotland, besides the beauty of it, has always been the fierce drive your people have for freedom—the enduring spirit of independence."

"Aye. And how do ye ken all this history ye speak of?"

"I read a lot. And I wrote a report on Scotland my third year of high school." My last year, yanked away before the first semester was finished. When I landed in the next place, I didn't bother going back to school, since I was old enough to evade the awkwardness of making up a new identity, registering as a foster child, attending classes as an outsider, and grappling with all the things I'd missed in the years between. Everything I needed could be found at the library, except the answers to understanding why I was the way I was.

Indeed. A good portion of my life had been a balance between busking and hanging out in free, warm, safe libraries, losing myself in books and research to find answers to at least some of my questions. Sadly, most everything on portals and time travel was classified as fiction, other than theories about wormholes through the fabric of space-time. There were plenty of legends about the dragons that frequented my dreams, but nothing I'd found came close to explaining my life. Generally, when dragons showed up, I was on the right path.

Maybe I'd found a world with actual magic, as Killian had mentioned back at the oak he called the World Tree. I almost laughed at my foolish hope.

Killian narrowed his eyes, head cocked sideways in a moment's assessment. With the hint of a nod, he proceeded to tell me how things had gone down in this version of history.

The key seemed to be the Scots' willingness to band together around freedom of religion, valuing each person's right to live and worship as they saw fit as long as they followed the law. Even paganism was tolerated. That tolerance was a strong reason the Stewarts were supported, and they'd negotiated so each ruler was content to represent smaller countries working together.

Perhaps I'd found a more progressive world after all. Probably not, but maybe.

"My round then." Killian walked with his left hand on the hilt of his sword. "I want two questions. First, I dinna doubt that ye've learned much from books, but ye speak of Scotland as if ye've been here before. Have ye? And second, where is this 'British Columbia, Canada?'"

I shook my head. "I've only read books about Scotland, and looked at tons of photos and videos of the landscape." Cheeks hot, I switched gears, mentally kicking myself for bringing up things like videos. "British Columbia is located in the far northwest of North America, next to the Pacific Ocean. Last I checked, anyway."

How different was this world? A map would be nice. Even better if there was a section labeled *Here, there be dragons.*

"Indeed. What are 'photos'?"

"Um…" Brain fail. I tried again. "Photographs are like paintings, except taken with a machine called a camera that captures an image on film, which you can print onto paper."

Was he satisfied with that? He paced ahead, quiet. I wasn't about to show him pictures on my AIO, so I took the opening for a question of my own. A non-political one.

"Where are we going?"

"Tonight, we go to an inn at that village 'round the bend." He lifted his hand to point.

Lanterns flickered in the distance. The sun would set soon. It shone through a break in the clouds now, setting the landscape aglow. The rolling hills lit up, the trees gilded, and the road glittered like a ribbon of light for a sparkling moment. Then the clouds shifted, and the moment was gone.

Killian gestured to the horse, and I took the hint. Soon, I sat behind him again. His warmth seeped through my hands while the heat of the horse rose up my legs.

But we didn't start forward. He turned in the saddle and eyed me, his voice a rumble of hazardous sincerity. "In a fortnight, I'll be arriving at the home of my clan. I will take ye there if ye wish."

The invitation hit my belly like lead butterflies. I stalled. "Would you be staying at an inn if I hadn't appeared?"

"No, likely not."

"Well, I'm perfectly happy to sleep outside." There was a blanket roll beneath me, so I assumed he'd be camping out if not for my appearance. I didn't want him to spend money on me that I wasn't able to repay. And it's not like I hadn't slept on the ground before, though I'd been on a good run of at least having a van to sleep in, if not a couch or an actual mattress. I pushed away thoughts of Jess and Stevie's king-sized bed with its frame draped with costumes and ropes, a pile of pillows atop the comforter when they weren't thrown to the floor.

"Nay, lass." Killian's voice snapped me back to my new reality. "No need for ye to sleep in the cold. I'll get us rooms at the inn."

The way his voice softened just about slayed me, but I kept my own even. I did not need to care for this man. "No, really. I don't want you to go through the trouble."

"It's no trouble. Would ye rather sleep outside?"

"I'm good with that." Casual. No worries. I'd be fine.

Killian's mouth twitched tighter. "Alright. We'll make camp down the road. But we'll eat at the inn." He turned forward again, and urged Lachie into a brisk walk.

As we entered the village, Killian slowed the horse near a woman who clutched a brown plaid wrap around her shoulders. He reached toward her, a coin between his fingers, and spoke words I didn't understand.

She shot a quick look at me, then took the coin and handed Killian the shawl. With a few sharp words and a twisted grin, she pocketed the money and walked away.

Killian handed me the cloth with a low warning that stopped my protests before they touched my lips. "Hide that bag ye carry, lass."

Around my shoulders went the fabric, over my slim backpack. The other woman's warmth seeped through my coat. Self-conscious now, my eyes darted around. How many people watched as we two rode one horse down the road?

"What did she say?" I leaned forward, near enough that his hair tickled my cheek. Bracing myself with hands against his back, I tried not to let my chest touch him, though the bounce of the horse didn't make that easy. Neither did the primal voice inside me that insisted I should get as close as possible to Killian—a voice I ignored. He probably emitted the same kind of pheromone that made me want Stevie on a nightly basis, which Jess didn't mind, given she was part of the fun. But there was nothing casual about Killian, and I didn't need hormones messing with my ability to think. My brain was still scrambled from the journey.

"Her mother made the wrap. She assured me her ma'd be satisfied with the price." His words rumbled through my palms on his ribcage, up my arms and into my chest.

Stone buildings with steep-sloped roofs stood on either side of the road. We passed a pair of boys chasing each other through a break in the houses and into a courtyard behind, a woman hustling along behind them. I peered up each alley and beneath stairwells, but didn't see a single sign of homelessness. Not a beggar to be found.

A small crowd stood before the inn's tavern, which we passed on our way to the stables. I kept my eyes over Killian's shoulder, but saw the stares we attracted anyway. They made my hair stand on end.

We dismounted in a small courtyard and Killian gave the stable boy a coin, leaving the horse with a kind word. I tried to calm myself, to be ready for whatever, but I was on edge. How many people would be inside? I had to trust this man, but my mind didn't want to trust a damn thing and my pulse beat fast with a spike of anxiety that was altogether too familiar.

He steered me into the dim, noisy pub, his hand warm on my arm. The hem of my coat only reached my calves, and the slit in the front opened as I kept pace with Killian. Chin level, eyes down. More than one patron turned to eye my tall brown boots. Their attention made my skin hot, and I could only imagine how strange I looked to them.

None of my jumps had set me this far outside of normal. I was in a different timeline. A different history. Every other time I'd hopped just a little bit into the future. I'd had context. Familiarity. Even if it sometimes seemed technology took larger leaps than I did, it had been easy enough to blend in and make up a plausible story for my existence.

Now, I'd dropped into another world altogether.

The noise of the tavern tore into strips of sound in my ears: heavy glass thumping on a wooden table, the slice of knife and clink of fork, a bench scraping on the floor, and the overwhelming din of voices raised above one another.

A man with a wide nose and wild hair nodded at Killian as we passed. Looked like he was working on his fifth or sixth mug of whatever he was drinking. Almost imperceptibly, Killian tipped his head in answer. My instinct told me he knew the guy. Red-rimmed eyes followed me as I passed, burning the edges of my vision as I fought to keep my focus forward. He wasn't the only one eyeing me like potential prey. Their stares gave me goosebumps, despite the heat of the room.

We stopped at a square table at the corner of the room, where I slid onto a hard, wooden bench, into the shadows. Killian sat beside me, both of us with backs to the stone-and-mud wall. He put one hand on the table, rested one casually on his dagger, and swept his lidded gaze across the room.

Before long, a woman marched toward us with dark curls framing her face, brown skirt swishing around her feet. She looked me over with one raised eyebrow before attending to Killian.

"Stew, wine, and something for the morning," he told her.

As she bustled off, I leaned toward him. "Why did you speak to her in English, and the woman with the shawl in—what was that, Gaelic?"

Killian's eyes glinted with amusement when he raised them to mine. "Aye, Gaelic. Earlier I didnae want ye interrupting."

"Ah." Fair enough.

Warmed by the heat of the fire, I began unbuttoning my coat. Killian's gaze dropped to my hands and I stopped at three buttons. If I pulled the collar back, I'd be showing more skin than I wanted in a room primarily full of men. Too warm, I slipped out of my shawl and backpack with as little movement as possible, and hid the bundle on my side of the bench, against the walls that met in our corner.

Killian's watchfulness never quit. He studied the room as if he were memorizing every face, taking stock of every exit—much the same as I did when I was playing a gig in a sketchy neighborhood. When the lights were on me and I was performing, there was only the music. The people disappeared. But before I went on stage, I liked to read the crowd. It gave me a chance to gauge what kind of music the audience might be in the mood for, and who might give me a hard time during the show. Or after.

The worst of the trouble almost always came after the music.

The server returned with wine, which went right to my head, followed by two bowls of stew and large chunks of bread. Thick slices of carrots and potatoes surrounded hunks of meat in my bowl. Venison, by the taste of it. Fresh herbs flavored the thin, salty broth.

Once the food was thoroughly devoured, Killian regarded me with narrowed eyes, his mouth drawing into a tight frown. "Wait here a moment," he said, and slid out from behind the table.

He walked out the door without a backwards glance, and I instantly felt myself being watched. My back tingled. Anxiety told me to get the hell out of there, though logic told me I was safer inside than out in the night alone. I stayed in my seat, chin level, eyes down.

Minutes crept by. What did people do to busy themselves here? My hand itched for my AIO, absurd as it was. I traced the knots in the wood tabletop and pretended the heap in the corner was only a shawl, not a backpack full of things from the future.

Next time I looked up, I caught movement from the doorway. The man Killian nodded at earlier strolled in, his hair looking something like a tumbleweed. When he passed his own table and headed toward mine, I leaned back against the wall. He stopped before me and cocked his head, close enough that I could smell the ale on his breath, eyeing me like an object he might make claim to. An interesting diversion.

I held his gaze, arms crossed over my chest, hating that he towered above me.

Finally, he muttered something I didn't understand, snorted a laugh, spun around, and walked to the bar. I stayed in position, lounging against the wall with a hard face. Nothing to see here. It took everything I had not to look around and see how many eyes watched me.

Killian returned a short time later and took his seat, the scent of outside clinging to him, smelling like freedom. Escape. I leaned close enough to talk quietly beneath the racket around us. "Who's the guy with the wild hair?"

He cocked his head, eyes dark. "Why? Did he speak to ye?"

"He said a few words I didn't get. Looked at me like a piece of meat. Nothing half the men here haven't done."

A hard look. An exhaled breath. "Ye still want to sleep outside?"

Was outside safer than the inn? Felt like it to me. A lock could be picked. Nature was more familiar than this noisy room. I was no stranger to pubs, but I didn't have an instrument. Didn't have a reason to be in this building with so many men, so far back in time.

And I didn't want to owe him money. "Absolutely."

CHAPTER 3
ON THE GROUND

WE LEFT THE LIGHT of the buildings behind and headed into the fading grey of twilight. No one followed us. I checked. The wind whipped across the road and bit at my cheeks, making me raise the hood on my coat.

The horse moved in a rhythmic cadence that set the ghost of a song through my head as I held onto Killian and tried to keep my fear from sliding into a downward spiral. He rode with confidence while I felt exposed, everything an unknown. To avoid making up disasters in my mind, I asked questions.

"Do you have a family?" I leaned forward so I didn't lose his answer to the wind.

"I've a son." Killian spoke over his shoulder, pitching his voice low. "He's nearly a man at fifteen, and lives with my brother's family since I've been away. His mother died when he was a wee child of five."

"I'm sorry. That must have been hard for you both."

He was quiet for a moment, then, "What about ye? Have ye a husband? Bairns?"

"Children?" I almost laughed. "No. Definitely not. And no husband. I'm not—I never stick around long enough to warrant getting married." Might as well tell it to him straight.

"This isn't the first time ye've traveled through time?"

"No." The free-fall of my heart came through my voice; a lifetime of being ripped away from everyone I cared about.

Did he lean back or had I leaned forward? We seemed to hold each other up.

I straightened and moved on to the next inquiry. No sense in talking about my sad, weird-ass life. "What do you do for work, that you've been away from your son?"

"My livelihood takes me traveling." A vague answer, like he didn't want me to know too much. "Mostly I carry messages and attend meetings, conducting business for Clan Maclean. I sailed into port yesterday after a visit with a relation in Ireland."

"What's your world like?" I asked, wishing I could lean into the warmth of his back. "Is it mostly peaceful? Are there wars? Do people lock their doors at night?"

"Aye, there are always wars." His hand raked through his hair. "Some are fought with armies, some with stealth. As for locking doors, most do. The more ye have, the more ye have to guard it."

"Are there any musicians?" I'd hoped for a minstrel at the inn, but there hadn't been one.

"The Macleans employ a bard. There are concerts in the cities and palaces, but most musicians earn their bread at taverns, and in the streets as they travel."

Busking. The foundation of music. I'd done my fair share, singing for meals and a bit of pay. Maybe I could find a decent patron here, enough to live. Preferably one who didn't expect me to give my body as well as my songs.

A branch cracked in the dark and I whipped my head to the right, seeking the source of the sound. Instinct pressed me close to Killian as the horse jolted into a canter.

"Easy," warned Killian. He brought Lachie down to a walk and peered into the darkness. "'Twas only a deer. All's well, lass. Ye said ye wanted to sleep outside, aye?"

"Right." How had he seen the deer? All I saw was the faint outline of the hill to our right and a stretch of darkness ahead that I guessed was a forest.

Killian's back flexed as he brought his elbow up and put his hand above my knee. "Relax, Shelta." He squeezed my leg in an encouraging way.

I let out my breath. He leaned into me and I leaned into him. The effect was entirely too comforting. I had told him I never got to stay, though. He'd been forewarned.

The horse walked on, and the dark of the forest grew closer. The night denser. We kept going until water gurgled beside us.

Finally, Killian drew Lachie to a stop, and said, "I'll get down here." I sat back, giving him space. Once his feet were on the ground, he patted the side of my calf, telling me to move forward.

I slid onto the saddle, into the heat of where he'd been sitting. Leading the horse, Killian guided us off the main road. I could hardly make out the shapes of trees three feet away, or the trail following the burbling creek.

"This'll do," he announced a few minutes later.

With a firm grip, he helped me down, then handed me his bedroll. I held the heavy blanket and listened, getting my bearings in the night. I heard the slide of leather and jingle of buckles, the thud of a saddle being placed on the ground, the low music of a man soothing his horse. Behind me, the creek's flow and bubble underscored the throaty call of an owl, the scent of damp forest in my nose.

At least the trees blocked the wind.

"Miss Shelta, the bedding ye're holding is for ye to use." Killian took the padded blanket from my arms and flapped it open, settling it on the ground.

When he draped his cloak around my shoulders, I protested. "I'm not going to take your bed from you." My words came out thin with fatigue.

"Will ye not?" I could hear his smile through the darkness. "We shall share then." At first, I thought he was trying to get me to sleep with him, but I was mistaken. "Ye'll take the blanket, I'll take my cloak. We'll do."

The weight of his cloak lifted from my shoulders, and I missed it instantly, but I was too tired to argue, and not about to give in to the part of me that wanted his comfort.

I bundled my pack into a hard pillow, placing my toque on top in a poor attempt to make it softer. Wrapping myself in my new shawl and tucking my knees into the skirt of my coat, I folded the blanket around me like a sleeping bag and completely failed to get comfortable.

Minutes after Killian spoke a soft "Good night," I was going through a list of camping equipment I wished I had. A tent would block the cold humid air. A cushion beneath the blanket would take care of whatever was digging into my hip. I cursed myself for turning down a bed at the inn, then remembered the leering looks of its patrons and decided I was better off here. The sharp nails of anxiety scratched at me, spurring my heart to race even as exhaustion weighed me down. Everything here was an unknown.

But there was nothing to be done about it now.

Eventually, the paper and wood song of the trees and the soothing sound of the creek coaxed me to relax. Sleep came in disorienting starts and stops, with dreams of small dragons cuddling close. The red dragon was markedly absent.

I kept rearranging myself, trying to get warm. At one point, I whimpered as I woke to a root under my ribs. My hips ached, and I had tremors of shivering sometime early in the morning. A typical night sleeping on the ground.

No surprise, I woke irritated, cold, and tired. Killian was already awake, had built a small fire, and was stirring something in a pot hanging over the flames.

"Feeling well-rested?" The corner of his mouth twitched.

"Yes," I lied. "I'm fine."

"That's why yer lips are blue and ye've got such a lovely scowl, is it?"

I wasn't fooling him. I wasn't fooling myself. I gave up, got as close to the fire as I could to ward off the damp, and tried to make sense of my hair with my fingers.

Killian watched me.

I pretended I didn't notice.

Once I'd warmed my body enough, I realized there were other pressing matters to attend to, and wandered off to do so. When I returned, Killian handed me my flask, cold and wet but full of water. I murmured thanks and drank.

Breakfast was hot oats, buttered bread, and a boiled egg from the inn the night before. As far as I was concerned, it was a feast.

Once I'd scraped the last of the oatmeal from the metal bowl, I said, "I'm feeling more human now, thank you." I smiled and reached a hand out for the pot he'd eaten from. "I'll do the dishes."

"That's kind of ye." He handed me a coarse cloth with his pot, and a spoon that looked a lot like the one from the inn.

"I'm going to take a bath at the creek," I warned.

"Yell if ye need help," he said with a smirk.

Before my fool mouth could betray the fact that I liked his attention, I turned away. Through the trees I went, walking along the stream until I found a secluded spot.

My hands chilled scrubbing the dishes. It took willpower to make myself strip down, clothes draped on a boulder by the stream. I tossed a look over my shoulder, but saw nothing but forest. Thus far, Killian had been a gentleman. Perhaps I was being careless, getting naked fifty feet from a man who could easily overpower me, but who knew when my next chance to get clean would be? I didn't want to smell.

My breath rushed out when I stepped into the frigid water, and I forgot my brooding thoughts. I splashed my face, ducked down to my armpits, and gave myself a thirty-second scrub with soap. Then, quick as I could, I waded over slick stones and scrambled out of the water, very much awake.

Teeth brushed, I rearranged my backpack, holding the sleek flat weight of my AIO. My thumb itched to press the little button that would wake it up so I could snap a picture of the cold creek and its secretive trees. The risk wasn't worth it. I shook my head at the absurdity of snapping a picture being dangerous, hid the device in an ultra-secret pocket of my pack, and headed back to the campsite.

Killian locked his eyes on me the second I came into sight. He stood by his horse. Everything was packed but the dishes, the fire out. Ready to go. "Feeling better?"

"Yes, thank you." I focused on brushing a leaf from my coat. His gaze was too intense.

"Tonight, we are staying at an inn," he announced, and gestured for me to come close so he could give me a leg up onto Lachie. "We'll be getting ye a horse as well. And a gown."

I settled myself on the bedroll. "Killian, I don't have much money. I'll have to find work somewhere."

"Dinna worry about money. I've enough for it."

Don't worry. Yeah, right. I was the queen of worry, especially the first few days after the portal. Maybe he was another of the many who'd adopted me along the way. Another friend. Another lover. I didn't want to count on it. Everything else had changed—glowing tree, backwards in time, a parallel reality.

Panic edged in.

If I didn't get a grip on myself, my anxiety would spike and I'd start shaking. Deliberately, I wrestled my focus to immediate senses. Killian's subtle musk. The earthy scent of horse. The sway as the animal moved beneath us. Wool warming my palms as I held onto the man before me.

The press of fear retreated in increments.

We emerged from the forest into the greyish day and started down the road. Despite Killian's easy tone earlier, a sense of debt hung over me.

"Most of the troubles in the future I came from are centered around money." Probably a bad idea to tell him more about the future, but off I went. "It's imbalanced to the extreme, to the point where governments are owned by individuals and businesses that value money over everything else—most of it isn't backed by gold or physical wealth, they just create money out of nothing."

He wouldn't be able to grasp the concept of digital currency, but surely he could understand greed. It was woven into every era of humanity.

I should've shut up, but no, I went right on talking. "Things get more expensive but wages don't go up. People and natural resources are exploited for profits. For control. It's awful and overwhelming, and it kept getting worse as I traveled into the future."

I shook my head, swallowing words that wanted to tumble out. There was no way to describe it all to him. How could I compare swords and cannons to modern-day warfare? How could I explain mass genocide and artificial intelligence and a world on track to self-destruct?

"It bothers ye, lass, this injustice ye describe." It wasn't a question.

"Yes." My throat ached.

"If ye could change it, would ye?"

"I—yes, of course. But it's so big. I did what I could; made some noise in the street, shared repressed information, tried to spend money in ways that supported good people." The familiar sense of helplessness roared in like a wave crashing over my head. "It never felt like I changed anything."

It was almost therapeutic talking about this with Killian. He was the first person who'd ever believed me about time travel. He kept riding; an ear turned toward me.

I went on, wanting him to understand the sense of obligation that weighed on me, the thought that sparked my little rant. "Most families where I grew up, women worked to earn money, as well as raising children and keeping house. I've always had to earn my keep. So, in my mind, I'd be in debt to you for buying me a horse, or a gown."

Killian brought the horse to an abrupt stop. I slid back as he turned himself sideways in the saddle, dark eyes making my breath catch.

"Let's get a thing straight right now, shall we?" He didn't wait for me to respond. "Anything I do for ye, Shelta Raine, it is done by my choice and freely. I expect nothing from ye. No payment of any kind. Ye have no obligation to me, whatsoever." He tilted his head to emphasize his words. "Is that clear?"

I nodded, swallowed, and squeaked out a "Yes."

He smiled, but still looked fearsome. Commanding. My heart raced in circles in my chest. In one fluid movement, Killian turned himself forward. Lachie took a few strides at a walk, a few strides at a trot, and then settled into a canter.

I held onto him, trying to find the rhythm in the horse and the rhythm of the man in front of me. I wanted to be able to accept his generosity and trust his intentions, but I wasn't sure if I could trust my own.

CHAPTER 4
DRESSES AND DAGGERS

WE CAME UPON a village around mid-morning. The sun played peek-a-boo through breaks in the clouds and painted the hills in light and shadow. Ahead, a ruddy-cheeked farmer leaned against a shovel, eyeing me with curiosity.

"Good day to ye." Killian tipped his head to the man.

"An' to ye." The farmer scratched his forehead.

"I'm looking to purchase a horse," Killian told him. "Would ye ken someone with a sound steed, willing to sell?"

In an accent so thick I only caught every third word, the farmer gave Killian directions to a nearby croft. Killian thanked him, and we rode at a rocking trot until we reached the farmhouse.

The stone house sat on a little rise, with a small copse of trees behind and the slope facing the sun given to garden beds, most of which had gone to seed. They looked to have as many weeds as vegetables growing in them. As we approached the cottage, a stout woman walked out to meet us, eyes squinting, greying hair blowing in the wind.

"Ye be needing another horse?" she asked, pointing from me to Killian and back again.

"Aye." Killian slid from the saddle with a barely-audible groan.

I made my way off the horse and stomped the tingles out of my toes behind him, happy to be on the ground. The woman got right to the business of listing the qualities of the horse she had for sale. She'd been widowed the year before, and no longer had need for such a fine animal. A well-mannered, hard-working mare, as she told it.

The mare in question wandered over on her own; a reddish bay with a star on her brow. She greeted me with a friendly bump of the nose when I held out my hand, then sniffed at my pockets, allowing me to stroke her dark mane. When she'd come to the conclusion that there were no carrots in my coat, she stretched her neck toward Killian's horse and flared her nostrils to get a good smell of the gelding. He tossed his head once and blew through his lips. She huffed in response.

Killian had me hold Lachie while he did a walk around of the mare, Mavie. He checked her hooves and ran his hands over her legs, and had a look at her teeth and ears. After a bit of bartering, he brought a stack of coins out of a purse. I caught a glint of sorrow in the woman's eyes as she took the money, but also saw relief in the rounding of her shoulders as she cradled it in one palm and cupped her other hand over. Almost like she was praying. The widow tucked the coins into a pocket, and leaned her head against the horse's cheek to say goodbye.

Mavie came with a well-worn saddle, which was a far cry from comfortable but better than rolling around on Killian's bedroll, bounced by his gelding's hindquarters. As I steered her behind Lachie, away from the cottage, Mavie stopped and looked back. The widow waved, then put her hand over her mouth, tears streaming down her face. I looked away, giving her privacy, and gently coaxed the mare on. She moved, obedient. Plodding along. But her head hung low, and I couldn't help but share her grief.

I stroked her neck and told her everything was going to be okay, hoping it was the truth.

We headed northeast. Killian looked over as I was readjusting my seat. Again. His horse was taller than mine, and I dragged my focus up, past his tall black boots, over the bit of knee that showed beneath his kilt, and above the curve of his shoulders, to catch his gaze.

"Ye appear to like horses well enough for someone unaccustomed to riding." He gave me a grin that lit up his eyes.

"Yes, well." I'd ridden some, at least. "It's been a while since I was on a horse. I didn't have much chance to ride where I came from. Most of the time I lived in cities where we had—other means of transportation."

"Such as?"

Oh, dear. "Cars, trains, busses, airplanes. They're like metal carriages with seating on the inside and an engine to make them go." What a terrible explanation. "They also go faster than you can probably imagine, and are a lot of fun even if they do pollute the air and use vast quantities of natural resources."

"I see." He sounded like he did not, in fact, but was willing to take my word on it. "How fast do they go?"

"Well, in a car you could get from Edinburgh to London in something like seven hours. And in an airplane, which is like a big metal car with wings that flies through the sky, you can get from New York to Scotland in about eight hours."

Killian gaped at me, then looked ahead, silent. The horses clopped along. After a minute, he seemed to have reestablished his sense of rightness in his own world, moving ever so naturally with Lachie. "Well," he said, "ye'll have lots of time to get used to riding here."

He clucked his tongue and brought his horse up to a trot. My mare followed suit, and I grimaced, forcing sore muscles to work as I tried to avoid bouncing out of my saddle.

"Where are we?" I asked. It was early afternoon, and traffic on the road had increased tenfold. Horses, carts, and people on foot.

"We're nearing Glasgow, which is where we'll stay the night." Killian's gaze swept across the road, settled on me for a brilliant breath of time, then continued to survey the surroundings—across the fields, around the houses, over the rolling hillside. Always on guard.

"Glasgow." I repeated it to myself in a whisper, trying on the accent. Throughout my life I'd learned to be a chameleon, to blend in wherever I went, but time compounded my current culture shock. I was stuck in surreal disbelief.

The traffic grew thicker as we neared a bridge. Mavie the mare seemed not to mind the busyness around us, and stuck close to Killian's horse. She'd clearly done this before.

"What river is this?" I asked in an undertone I hoped no one else would hear.

"The Clyde," replied Killian. We reached the massive stone bridge, and the horses' clomping rang louder on the rocks. A wagon rumbled past, going the other way.

I lifted my focus from the swift current of the Clyde to the buildings that dominated the view, many with dark plumes of smoke rising from their chimneys. Beside me, Killian's gaze roamed with sharp vigilance.

While the village we'd visited last night appeared free of poverty, the city had not escaped that fate. Beggars approached people on foot, and grime-streaked faces stared out of alleyways. Refuse lined the gutters, making me glad I was on a horse. The stench was awful.

Architecture drew me in with beauty rendered in bricks and stone. I tried not to look like a tourist, but my mouth hung open as we came into an area where the buildings sported carved figures and pointed turrets. The streets were cleaner here; the smell not nearly as strong.

A renegade beam of sunshine broke through the clouds and made the granite of the buildings sparkle, igniting an insistent urge to take out my AIO out and snap a photo. I itched to capture the moody light on the gardens, even if they were wilted from cold.

Eventually, we stopped at a whitewashed building with a sign declaring it the Auld Glasgow Inn. Killian slid off his horse and stood below me before I could dismount. I had half a mind to tell him I could do it myself, but I swung a leg over and let him lift me down. The momentary closeness sent warmth through my skin, into my cheeks.

It was stupid to get close like this. Wanting him could lead nowhere good. Maybe he could find a patron to employ me as a musician, or be a patron if he came from money, but those were best-case scenarios. The growing attraction was a catastrophe waiting to happen.

I stood back with my thoughts as Killian delivered the horses to the stable boy and slung the saddlebags over his shoulder, then I walked beside him to the entrance. I had a ridiculous urge to open the door for him in a play of reverse chivalry—a younger me would've done it, flirting the whole time—but this wasn't the time or place for joking around. Killian lifted his hand, leaned inside, swept the space with his eyes, and stepped back so I could pass.

The dimly-lit entrance room had a bench, a long counter, and a tapestry of a ship at sea, sailing into the sunset toward a distant island. A tangle of voices wafted down the short hallway that must have led to the tavern. With a veiled smile, Killian smoothed my hair back. It must've been a right mess. Then, he lifted the small bell on the reception desk, and gave it a ring.

"Aye," said a man by way of greeting as he came around the corner from the pub. Brown hair stuck out above reddish ears. He slid his bulk into the narrow space behind the counter. "Ye be wantin' a room, sir?"

"Two rooms, near each other if possible." Killian's voice rang with such authority that I was caught off guard. Not that he hadn't conducted himself thus far with confidence— he had, and I'd noticed—but this was something different: something that made the innkeeper snap to attention, besides the coin being handed over.

"Aye, milord, of course. My finest rooms." He placed two keys on the polished surface of the counter, other hand pocketing the coin. His gaze swept over me, eyes narrowing as he took in my unconventional attire.

I pulled my shawl closer and stood as tall as I could, resisting the desire to try to tame the disaster of tangles in my hair from riding in the wind.

Killian took the keys and escorted me up a flight of creaky stairs, where we found my room. I stepped inside.

He stayed in the hallway, and said, "Take a few minutes to refresh yerself. I'll be by shortly to collect ye. Madame Sabine is one of the best dressmakers in Scotland, and her shop is only a short distance away."

He was off before I had a chance to reply, closing the door with a soft thud and muffled click. I stared at the scuffed wood for a few seconds before forcing myself to move.

The simple room invited me with its quiet. Pitcher and basin, dresser and bed. A high-backed chair faced out the small window to a view of the city. I tossed my backpack and shawl atop the quilt with a weighty sigh. When I looked into the mirror mounted on the wall above the dressing table, the face that stared back wore a look of bewilderment. Dark circles dragged at my eyes. My hair was a frizzy mess.

As I unzipped my bag to find my comb, I realized I couldn't take my pack to the dressmaker's shop. The thought spiked my heart rate, and I dug out the thin, hand-sized AIO. The urge to open the solar-gold case prodded me, but I didn't have time. Into an inner pocket of my coat it went, its weight against my left thigh. I slipped my pocketknife into the opposite side to balance it out. Backpack stashed under blanket and pillow, I smoothed the quilt so it looked undisturbed.

Halfway through braiding my hair, a double knock made me jump. I rushed to open the door and let Killian in. I closed the door behind him with a breath, this kilted man in his black boots and jacket, armed with sword, daggers, and—yes, that was a gun at his hip now, the curved handle sticking out from a holster.

Killian noticed my attempt at a braid, and his face softened. "We shall get ye some pins for yer hair. But first, a lady's dress, so ye can feel comfortable here. Sometimes dressing the part helps a role fit better."

My mouth opened, then closed. Yes, I guess I was playing a part.

His eyes darted around the room, circled back and looked me over. "Ye've hidden yer things?"

"Yes," I breathed. "Aye."

One side of his mouth lifted, then the other. I couldn't help but grin back. He smoothed my hair again, hands falling to my coat to sweep wrinkles from the fabric on my shoulders, then down the arms. His touch made me shiver.

He stepped back in a half bow, rising to stand an arm's length away. Sobered. Something in his eyes.

Gaze down, I smoothed the skirts of my coat. My belly knotted as my hand passed over the hardly-hidden solidness of the AIO at my hip. Would it be better to leave it here?

Too late now. I draped the shawl over my shoulders. Killian opened the door with a gesture for me to go first. He locked it behind us, pocketed the key, and led me down the creaky stairs.

A little while later, we stopped in front of the dressmaker's shop. "I've some business to attend to." Killian bowed his head toward me. "I'll get ye settled, and come back before dark."

Of course he had business. It made perfect sense. But logic didn't stop my stomach from dropping out beneath me at the thought of him leaving me alone here. What if he didn't come back, armed to the teeth as he was?

Nothing to do but plunge onward and hope for the best. Up the steps we went, through the narrow door, and into the shop.

A sharp-eyed, tawny-skinned woman bustled out from behind displays of fabric to greet us, her silver hair in a neat bun. "Bonjour, may I help you?"

Killian tipped his head. "Madame Sabine."

"Monsieur Maclean." She smiled, her back straight as a board. No bow, no curtsy. This woman was queen of her domain. "Welcome."

"Thank ye. My friend from overseas requires two dresses of the finest quality ye can manage on short notice. We are only in the city the day," he explained to her furrowed brow, "and leave early in the morn."

Her thin eyebrows went back to their normal place, which seemed to be higher than necessary on her forehead. "What type of dresses do you require, Monsieur?"

"One for riding and everyday use, and one of yer finest gowns, for entertaining and society." He started adding to the list. "Also, a cloak, shoes, and a shawl if you have our hunting tartan."

I gulped as quietly as I could. He was going to spend a small fortune on me. His glance reminded me of our agreement regarding money, and I conjured a small smile I hoped gave the impression that I did this all the time.

"Oui, I have some Maclean tartan." The woman looked me over in the way of someone intimately aware of curve, line, and fashion. I admired her dress: golden-brown silk with full skirts and a low neckline. "You will pay half in advance?"

"Of course." They came to a quick agreement of price, and my stomach did a flip as he handed her a stack of notes and coins from his pouch. Madame Sabine took the money with the smallest nod of thanks, and Killian said, "I'll be back in a bit."

The heavy door creaked closed. I only caught a glimpse of him out the window before he was gone.

"Well, my dear." Madame Sabine motioned for me to follow her deeper into the store. "We must begin."

I hustled to keep up with her, struggling to shush my mind. Why did I feel like he'd abandoned me? He'd dropped a large sum of money on this; he wasn't going to just leave me here.

Shopping. I should just appreciate shopping.

"Do not look so timid." The dressmaker bustled between gowns on crude mannequins and bolts of cloth. "I will not bite you, and I'll not poke you if you stand still."

I smiled at her joke and tried to relax, but failed.

She came to an open area at the back, stopped, and positioned me on a small platform. "Take off your boots and coat then, mademoiselle."

Doing so made me a little queasy. I might as well have been naked, standing there in leggings, a pixie skirt, and my soft black shirt. But all she did was raise her acrobatic eyebrows at my attire. She gauged my size, then disappeared.

Ten minutes later, dressed in the undergarments of the time, I eyed the pile of frocks that waited on a bench. Madame Sabine held each up to my body, muttered something in French, and went on to the next one.

After a short while playing this game, I decided on two pieces that she agreed were the best of the lot. One was a riding dress with green wool skirts, a silver-grey blouse, an embroidered velvet bodice and a fitted jacket. There were oak leaves on the silver buttons, and acorns embroidered on the collar that reminded me of the tree I'd portaled through two days ago, as if some god or goddess was playing with me.

Madame Sabine fussed with adjustments until she was satisfied. Once the dress and all its pins were in the hands of her assistant—who could've been her sister or daughter, it was hard to tell—the dressmaker helped me into the blue gown.

Never in my life had I worn something so beautiful. It made my breath catch in my throat. "It's exquisite," I said, stroking the soft skirt.

"It is indeed, my dear." She laced the corset with deft hands.

As Madame worked, I looked in the mirror. The gown had dozens of yards of deep blue silk. Mother-Number-Three had given me a blue dress—nothing like this, but it had delighted me at the time, enough to distract me from the loss of Mother-Number-Two. That one had hurt.

Who was I kidding? They'd all hurt.

I brought my focus to the gorgeous garment. Gold embroidery twined in trinity knots around the scooped neckline. The sleeves flared at the elbows with a translucent layer showing beneath. Golden silk showed in the under layers of skirts, in contrast to the deep blue.

Madame Sabine stood behind me, observing my expression in the mirror through hooded eyes. "You are beautiful, ma chérie. But now you must take it off so I can make it yours."

She stitched while I sat and waited, huddled in my coat with my shawl over my lap. Time passed slowly, but at least I wasn't expected to fill the space with idle chatter, which would've required me to come up with a string of lies. The temptation of the AIO in my coat pocket was a constant reminder of how far removed I was from everything I'd known.

The dressmaker's hands moved steady, sure. Her stitches precise. Practiced. Silk shuffled through her hands as she maneuvered unending lengths of fabric with the ease of someone who had mastered their skill.

Days ago, I was in the year 2035. Clothes were mass-produced, many from dubious sources of labor who weren't paid nearly enough for the work they performed. Did Sabine and her sister-daughter assistant have a sewing machine? I couldn't comprehend making a garment like the one she held entirely by hand.

The gown was too much. It was a fairytale dress, something I'd never given myself permission to hope for, even if I envied the ones who wore them. Mother-Number-Three fed me everything Disney to keep me entertained and out of her hair with my outlandish claim that I was from the past. She fed my imagination—or used her own to escape the impossibility of my truth. She lived in the realm of fiction. Taught me to love libraries.

In that, she'd saved me.

But I didn't have a book to nose into now, nor could I use my AIO to distract me from the fact that I was farther back in time than I'd ever hoped to go in a version of history that didn't match up with mine.

I'd read about parallel universes; theories that said every possibility exists somewhere in the multiverse of quantum space-time. The thought was so big it made me shake my head.

Madame spared me a glance. I smiled at her, like I was perfectly at peace. Fine. Yes, everything's fine here. Just wrestling with existential monsters.

A rustling came from the back room, and Sabine's assistant came around the corner with the riding dress draped over her arms. She had Madame's high cheekbones, keen gaze, and smooth golden-brown skin. Her arched eyebrows told me she saw me, sitting huddled in my coat, but was too polite to voice her curiosity.

I smiled and lifted a few fingers in a wave. "Hi. Thank you for helping with my dress." My dress. These women were equipping me with my costume. My armor.

Madame extended an arm toward the younger woman. "This is my daughter, Anastasia."

"Shelta. It's nice to meet you." It was nice to give my real name, too, instead of having to come up with another false identity. There were no records of me here. No past to run from, except the past I was in.

She tipped her head, and placed the green dress on a cloth-covered bench beside me. "Thank you for your patronage."

My patronage. Killian's generosity. I had nothing but a nod for Anastasia, who Madame sent off with the blue gown and precise instructions. I folded my coat in a daze, placing it carefully on the floor with the AIO at the center of the bundle.

Sabine's hands moved so fast I could barely follow the way she tied the skirt, bunching the bottom of the silver shirt beneath it, and lacing the bodice on top. She smoothed the fitted velvet jacket with its oak-leaf buttons and wide collar, and left me staring at myself in the mirror. She returned minutes later with a green cloak made of thick wool, and a pair of heeled shoes that were not at all comfortable when I tried them on. After some obligatory pacing around to see if they fit, I pulled my feet out and eyed the shoes with apprehension.

"Now you need a shawl. I'll get the Maclean tartan." Madame Sabine clicked her tongue off the roof of her mouth, and disappeared again.

Maclean. The name echoed inside me. Weighty. Like profound music.

I gawked at my reflection for so long that I nearly got used to seeing myself in such finery. Makeup would've helped. Would've masked the haunted look to my eyes.

When Madame finally returned, she presented me with plaid fabric of deep green, dark blue, and black, with thin white stripes. The same as Killian's kilt.

"It will go well with the dress." Her eyelids dropped halfway, accompanying a content smile as she measured out a long length of the plaid for a stole.

I thought of my pack with its modern design, and said, "Could I have another length please? About this wide." I opened my arms out as far as they would go. She obliged, taking the slicing edges of her shears to the bolt of plaid once again.

Satisfied, the dressmaker sat me down and proceeded to brush my hair. The initial strangeness dissolved into something relaxing. Hypnotic. Nurturing.

Not long after Madame Sabine had finished pinning my hair into a neat updo, much like her own, the bell above the shop's door rang. I gathered my things, hoping it was Killian. Madame's eyebrows hardly even rose when I chose to wear my boots, rather than the shoes beside them.

I bundled my clothes and the brown shawl inside the length of green plaid, and followed Sabine's immaculate posture to the front of the store, where Killian stood with his black jacket and dark eyes, smelling of wood smoke and a hint of whisky.

"Is she not an exquisite beauty?" Madame asked with an impish smile.

"She is indeed." The rumble in Killian's voice sent my fingertips to seek the comfort of the dragon at my neck.

His gaze dropped to my throat as I traced the silver wing. I stopped. Put my hands by my sides. When his eyes met mine again, they held the flicker of fire.

Sabine had her daughter bring the gown to show him what he was buying, and added up the totals. Killian paid without comment, other than to compliment her skill. Madame assured him that everything would be delivered to the inn before morning, gave my jacket one more tweak, and sent us on our way.

The wind buffeted me as we left the shop, pushing my cloak and many layers of skirt against my legs. Killian gave me his arm, and I took it, coming to the conclusion that the reason women historically held onto a man's arm was to keep from landing in a pile of horse manure when they tripped on their skirts.

Historically. I was a part of history now.

Killian offered to carry my clothes, but I insisted I was fine, clutching them tight beneath my right arm, the AIO at the center. My left hand gripped the solidness of his arm, his warmth seeping through his jacket into my palm.

"Did your business go well?" I asked.

"Aye." He gazed at me with bright, mischievous eyes. "And ye seem to have gotten on with Madame Sabine."

I looked forward, his attention making me flush. "She was nice. She even did my hair."

"Aye, I see that."

I studied a fountain and tried to breathe past the tightness of the bodice and my whirlpool of emotions. "You didn't negotiate price with Madam Sabine." My tone implied a question.

"There are some items where it is customary to barter," Killian explained, "and some where it is not. Never haggle with a well-respected dressmaker or tailor. They are so because they do fine work, and are honest about the worth of their craft. Ye will, after all, live in the clothes they make to fit yer body. 'Tis not a thing to trifle with."

Such ease in his words. Like compensating someone fairly for their work was the most natural thing to do. Like it wasn't a rare thing in a future he didn't know about.

As we rounded a corner, Killian jerked to the side with a suck of breath and pulled me with him, putting himself in front of me. I braced myself as fight-or-flight mode kicked into overdrive. Something whooshed by our heads—a short knife clattered on the cobblestones behind us, glinting hard and deadly.

A man came running out of the shadows, and Killian drew his sword. I lunged out of the way, retreating with a dread-fueled surge of speed to the closest thing that resembled shelter, and hid behind the pedestal of a statue, its stone warhorse towering above me, frozen in a charge with a fierce-looking man on its back.

The attacker wore all black, his legs long in trousers that accentuated the contrast of his lunges and fast footwork against the sway of Killian's kilt. He swung his sword like he knew what he was doing. The street emptied as people hustled to get away from the fight, as if they knew what carnage looked like and wanted no part of it.

The clang of metal that echoed off the buildings sounded like cymbals being broken, their sustain shattered, their deep voices stolen. A high-pitched scrape like a knife being sharpened made me whimper, and I flinched at the force of their blows as I peered out from my cover to watch.

Killian moved with deadly skill. And respect for code of conduct, apparently. He could've drawn his gun and shot the man, but he didn't. His assailant produced another knife and let it fly with a flick of his hand. Killian dodged and drew his dagger, dueling with two blades. They fought fast. Each grunt and kick made me cringe.

With a move so swift I couldn't catch how it was done, Killian threw the other man off balance and drove his dagger into his chest. The sick, sucking noise that came from the man's mouth as he dropped to the ground made me gag.

A minute later, having cleaned his blade on the dead man's clothing, Killian strode over to where I leaned, pressed against the cold rock of the sculpture, hugging my clothes to my chest.

"Are ye alright, lass?" He gave me a once-over with sharp eyes.

"Sure." My voice shook. "What was that about?"

"'Tis a dangerous city." Killian brought his hand behind me with firm persuasion, guiding me into motion.

"What about the body?" I whispered. Were there police? Would he be in trouble?

"Best we dinna linger," he answered with a look that shut me up.

I went along with his brisk pace, hyper-aware of his touch at the small of my back, and struggled to adjust. Maybe I could question him when we got back to the inn.

He moved with a surprising amount of comfort for someone who'd just killed a man, avoiding the subject by pointing out landmarks and telling me about the city. He searched every shadow and alley with his eyes, but radiated ease. If it was an act, it was a good one.

I turned my eyes down, away from his. His hands were clean. As was his jacket. The only mark I saw was a muddy scuff on the outside of his right boot. A smudge of dirt on one of the buckles. A short laugh that was halfway to hysterics caught in my throat and escaped through my nose.

Killian turned one corner of his mouth up. "What's funny?"

My mouth opened in a ridiculous smile and I stopped him, pulling on his arm and tilting my head up to speak near his ear. "You didn't get a drop of blood on you."

He leaned back, and I sobered, my smile fading. Probably should've kept my mouth shut.

His lips twitched, head tilting a touch. "Sometimes things just work out," he said, and tugged me in the direction of the inn.

I took measured breaths, focusing on the cadence of Killian's steps. Some mechanism of survival seemed to surface from the rhythm of our walking, because by the time we reached the inn I'd calmed considerably.

The innkeeper practically fell over himself to serve us when he saw me dressed as I was, a contrast to the disheveled girl he'd seen before. He bowed when Killian requested a private room for dinner.

I lifted my skirts as we climbed the creaky stairs. As I'd hoped, Killian followed me into my room and closed the door behind him. I placed my bundle on the bed, sliding my hand to check that my pack was still under the pillows. It was.

I wanted some answers from Killian, but didn't know how to go about it. So, I plucked the plaid fabric from around my old clothes and showed it to him, stalling. "I got this to make myself a new bag, but I've just realized I have no needle and thread."

"I've got that for ye." The scar on Killian's temple made a crescent when he smiled. "For now, get ready to dine. I'm hungry enough to eat through the wall to the kitchen!"

I laughed at that, but when he moved to go, I reached out and caught his wrist, my words pitched low. "Killian, why did someone try to kill you?"

A breath. Level eyes. "I had a disagreement with his employer." The quiet bass of his voice traveled up my arm, into my chest, and I let go. "Like I said, dangerous city. But dinna worry, lass. Ye're with Clan Maclean."

CHAPTER 5
A DECK OF CARDS

THE INNKEEPER SHOWED us to a room on the first floor that held a table set for two, a worn sofa, and a small hearth. Lanterns lit the space, as did the fire crackling behind a metal screen. I sat in a simple chair and smoothed out my skirts, the velvet bodice helping me remember not to slouch and pushing my breasts toward the neckline of the shirt I wore beneath. Killian placed his gun and sword on a ledge beside him.

"This is normal for you?" I slid my eyes from the pistol to Killian. "Bringing weapons to dinner?"

"Aye." His hand went to the scar at his temple. "Not for ye?"

I shook my head no, then waved off the idea as if it were a moth dive-bombing the candle between us. "No big deal." This was his world, not mine.

A serving girl showed up with wine and bread, dark skin aglow like she'd been running food and drink for hours already. Her hair circled her head in a pretty braid, and though her dress was simple, it looked well-made. She asked our preferences on the available meals, flashed us a smile, and promptly disappeared.

Killian ate half a loaf of bread and most of the butter before she returned a few minutes later with the first course.

The creamy soup warmed me from the inside. Killian's was gone in half the time it took me to eat.

When I was finished, I sat back with my glass of wine and shifted my focus to the man sitting across from me. Studying me, it seemed.

At first, I thought he was staring at my cleavage, but no. It was my necklace he eyed; my winged dragon in the shape of a circle, hung on a silver chain.

His gaze lifted to mine. "Yer pendant—has it a story?"

"I have a thing for dragons. Dream about them constantly." No way I should've told him that. I put down the wine glass and clasped my hands on my lap.

His head tilted, candlelight sparkling in his eyes. "Fascinating."

"Why?"

He smiled and changed the subject. "What garments do people usually wear where ye come from, Shelta?"

I wanted to talk about dragons, now that he'd brought it up. And he was going to be elusive. Fine. Clothing from the future it was. I launched into descriptions of everything from jeans and t-shirts to business suits, formal dresses, platform heels, and costumes. Killian listened with interest, but we were both grateful when the food arrived.

I had grilled codfish with mashed potatoes and roasted vegetables, and Killian had a meat and vegetable pie that looked hearty enough for his Highland appetite and filled the room with the most delicious smell. He slowly polished off his meal, though I could eat little more than half of my own without feeling like I needed to untie my bodice.

"This is how you keep women skinny here," I joked, running my hands along the sides of my ribs.

Killian laughed. "This was not in the fashion you spoke of. Do ye want to loosen it?"

I was torn between the temptation of comfort and my desire to maintain a ladylike appearance, so I sidestepped the question. "Corsets and bodices are worn, but generally in costume or in—intimate settings." Fabulous. I just set myself up for discussing lingerie and Renaissance Faires.

"I see." He lowered his chin and looked at me out the tops of his eyes.

I bit my lip, relieved when the door clicked open. I studied the woman's braid as she cleared the dishes, muscles bulging on lean arms. A moment later she left with a coin from Killian, and a word of thanks from me.

"Would ye consider this an intimate setting?" Killian asked after she'd gone.

Nope, I wasn't off the hook. Could I pretend it was the wine that brought the color to my cheeks? "Yes, but a different kind of intimate."

He nodded, a teasing smile on his face, the silver patch of beard making the rest of his hair strikingly dark in the warm light. "Well, my lady Shelta, since I have ye here and alone to myself, what shall we do to pass the time?"

I said the first thing I could think of that didn't involve us touching. "Do you play cards?" Killian's eyebrows shot up. Apparently, card-playing wasn't the least bit ladylike. Go figure.

Nevertheless, Killian left the room and returned with a deck of playing cards, which he placed before me on the dark wooden table. They were more ornate than what I was used to, each face card a little different. The Jack of Diamonds had narrow eyes. The Jack of Spades had blood on his sword.

Killian sat opposite me, touching the fingertips of each hand together, eyelids at half-mast as he watched me shuffle with hands that had obvious practice. When I discovered he didn't know what poker was, I set myself the task of teaching him how to play.

"I don't have anything to gamble with, obviously." The cards made a cascading swish as I mixed them up, talking too much. At least I refrained from blurting out the existence of strip poker. "Usually, we'd have chips or something. I've never gambled with more than spare change, myself. But we can play to win hands, just for the fun of it."

"Indeed." The twist of his smile made me think he had other ideas for fun.

We played five-card draw and seven-card stud. He learned what it meant when I said "deuces are wild," and that the "Black Mariah" was the queen of spades. He caught on quickly, making up his own wild cards and rules of draw.

Laughing loud and often, I forgot all attempts of proper poise.

"Ye have a terrible poker face," said Killian, once I'd explained it to him.

"I do, it's true." I grinned.

It was getting late by the time I got around to teaching him blackjack, and I began to yawn through my description of the game.

"Let's save this one." Killian placed a hand on mine. "We ride after an early breakfast, and I would not have ye losing sleep on account of entertaining me."

"Okay." I stacked the deck of cards in a neat pile, and stood to get my jacket from the back of the chair.

Killian gathered his weapons. When we left, my arm slipped through his as if it were second nature, the closeness making my wine-thickend blood dance. A warning buzzed in the back of my mind, but I shooed it away. I'd take whatever comfort I could get.

Damn the consequences.

Killian escorted me from the dining chamber, past the unattended desk, and up the stairs.

Creak, creak, creak, creak.

As we stopped in front of my room, I turned to face him, my back to the door. Moonlight shone through the window at the end of the hall. He stood too close, and I liked it. My heart beat the quick pulse of desire straining against logic.

Without taking his eyes from mine, Killian reached in his pocket, produced my key, and unlocked my door. He came so close his heat snuck through my clothes to dance on my skin, but he did not touch me. My door squeaked open.

"Goodnight, Lady Shelta." He gave me a small bow, and handed me my key.

"Goodnight, Killian." I turned as quickly as was courteous to enter my room, shut the door, and locked it. One hand pressed against the wood; his footsteps seemed to echo in my chest as he walked to his room. His door swung open, and clicked shut.

Sleep didn't come easy, and when I finally succumbed, my dreams haunted me. It was a rare night where no dragons came to keep me company. Instead, the one woman I'd almost married appeared, asking where I was and what had happened. Evalynne. I tried to explain to her, in that scattered way of dreams, that I needed to break off the engagement, that she should live her life and let me go.

She didn't take it well. Out of nowhere, she pulled out a sword, and I was engaged in a battle I didn't want to fight.

I had no idea how I'd gotten a sword, nor what to do with it. That arm was heavy and sluggish, but the dagger in my other hand moved fast enough.

I plunged the knife into Evalynne's chest, then jerked back, shaking. Horrified by what I'd done.

Blood coated my hands. The look of betrayal on her face as she fell pierced me to my soul.

I bolted upright in bed, breathing in panicked gasps. Sweat soaked my skin. My heart seemed to want to gallop through my chest. No way was I getting back to sleep now.

The floorboards were cold beneath my feet. I wiped my face and neck with the cloth by the basin, then crossed the room and looked out the window at the grey shapes of buildings.

Glasgow was quiet like no city I'd ever been in. No cars, no sirens. The tavern below had emptied out and shut down. Most windows were dark gaps in shadows of stone.

Somewhere in this city, there were streets that didn't sleep, where the restless could find the usual pleasures they sought to fill a bottomless wanting. Drink. Gambling. Sex. Music. This world couldn't be so different—humans were the same creatures.

I'd met Evalynne on such a street, both of us reckless and hungry for something more. I could still see it clearly in my mind; the first time she'd come strutting my way in her flouncy rainbow skirt, Doc Martins laced to her knees, a ripped tank top, and gunmetal-grey arm warmers pulled up to her bare shoulders.

I was outside a bar that allowed me to busk there in hopes of luring patrons in, singing one of those songs that time seemed to compose itself. The music of the ever-changing moment flowed through me. I played my guitar as if it were several instruments at once, vocals layered on top of it all, echoing down the noisy, narrow street.

Evalynne walked right up to me, stood with her bangs hanging in her eyes and a bold smile on her cherub-dominatrix face, and said, "Your music is like gods having sex."

I laughed so hard I lost the tune. And went home with her at dawn.

Evalynne, who could play more instruments than me. The composer who'd won my heart with her music and bound it with her words. I'd been a fool to say yes when she'd asked me to marry her. And I tried to warn her. Several times. But she never believed my stories of time travel and trees. She thought they were my coping mechanism for a rough childhood.

A wormhole took me away five days before the wedding. I landed six years in the future. When I got my feet under me, I looked Evalynne up. I found an article that gave the usual story of my disappearing without a trace and the missing persons search that lasted over a year. It went on to say Evalynne had used the incident to inspire an album that went platinum, which is how she met her current wife. They had a happy family, kids and all.

After that, I always wore a hat or sunglasses when I was in public. No need for someone to recognize me and shake up her perfect life. It was better that the tree took me before we were married. Children weren't an option. I couldn't stand to lose them the way I'd lost everyone else.

CHAPTER 6
LIKE A STONE

THE HORSES' HOOVES set an offbeat rhythm as we rode through the cool, misty morning. Light rain fell on my cloak, which covered Madame Sabine's leather-wrapped package tied to the saddle behind me. My hips ached from riding. Add to that two terrible sleeps and too much wine, and my mood matched the dreary weather.

The dream last night meant nothing, of course, merely my subconscious working out the stresses of the day. Still, I couldn't shake the desperation that had saturated my sleep. My tired mind played tug of war with my heart, drawing my gaze all too often to the man riding the black horse on my left.

I'd known better than to get attached to Evalynne, and I'd done it anyway. It had broken me to be taken from her, from the life we'd had together. Mending those pieces of myself had included a vow that I wouldn't be that stupid again. I could not afford to fall in love.

And yet the tree had delivered me directly to Killian Maclean, who'd accepted my outlandish story about falling through time. He'd adopted me more quickly than several of my foster mothers. Killian, who'd flirted with me last night after killing a man in the street like it was a normal thing to do.

We weren't the only ones on the road. We rode in silence, passing carts, riders, and those on foot. I was starting to notice that breakfast had been several hours past when the wind calmed and the rain stopped. Birds sang in distant trees and nearer bushes. The sun burned a hole in the clouds bright enough to make me squint beneath my soggy hood.

As we neared a bridge, Killian pointed to a path that disappeared into the trees, parallel to the river. "This way," he said, and nudged his horse ahead.

I followed him along the narrow trail, a water song forming in my mind. Killian's head swiveled left, swiveled right. He looked behind, where the main road was quickly blocked from view. Music rose in my chest and pulled me with its own current, but Killian didn't need distraction from his surveillance. This wasn't the time or place to be singing, no matter how badly the song wanted out.

The river snaked out of sight as the woods thickened. As usual, I loved and feared the trees in equal measure. But there was no portal here, no cyclone of time hiding inside this forest, just a pathway that got darker as the clouds covered the sun again.

After a while, Killian took a side trail, and we stopped in a small, hidden meadow. When he dismounted, I followed suit, and promptly got my leg tangled in my heavy skirts and cloak. I managed to get it sorted out, but Killian helped me anyway.

His hands held my hips from behind, and I twisted to face him, eyes down, cheeks warm. My inhale carried the scent of close skin, damp wool, and cool river. "Dresses aren't the most practical clothing for riding horses," I said, relieved when he took a step back. "Pants would be nice."

He arched an eyebrow. "Where we're going, ye'll want a dress."

I gathered my skirts and followed the narrow path as it wound through the trees. Killian stopped halfway to tie the horses, but I could see the river, so I walked ahead and stood on the rocks at its edge, breathing in its misty air and quiet roar. Before me, the water swirled in a circular pattern through a narrow channel. Years of withstanding the current had carved a round chasm, a canyon that reached far below the surface.

Crunching rock told me Killian approached. I didn't turn. Kept my eyes on the water, trying to gauge the depth. It was too dark to see the bottom.

He stood to my left, and the dagger at his hip drew my attention. The dagger he'd used to kill the man in Glasgow. The same one I'd used on Evalynne in my dream. I stepped back from the edge and faced him.

"Shelta?"

I braved his eyes. "Aye?"

He gave a twitch of a smile, and held out a set of saddlebags. "Will ye put yer things in here, and leave the satchel ye came with? I think it wise, moving on, if ye didn't have it on yer back."

Ah. That's why we'd come here. To drown evidence.

Without a word, I unwound the shawl that concealed my pack and unbuckled the strap at my chest. It took some doing to get it off with all my layers, but I finally lowered it to the rocks next to the saddlebags. I crouched in slow motion, my cloak heavy around me.

Killian looked over my shoulder as I transferred each item to the leather pouches. He didn't object to my extra clothes, but the tags all got cut off with a slit of a short knife he pulled from his boot. The rest, I had to negotiate what to keep. My soap got wrapped in a scrap of leather; the pink container abandoned to the backpack. I refused to discard the clear plastic case that held my toothbrush.

It took ten minutes to explain each item in the first-aid kit to his satisfaction and convince him there was no way I was going on without it, and I fought rising frustration. After all the times I'd left everything behind, giving up my pack shouldn't have been a hardship. I knew it made sense to ditch it. Still, it stung.

When I brought out my sketchbook, I wanted to cry. I'd lost countless drawings and bits of writing through the years, and this time I'd managed to bring some with me. I hugged it close, casting my gaze toward Killian, who eyed the spiral bound book pressed against my chest.

"I'd really like to keep this." My voice wavered.

"What's in it?" His palm flipped toward the grey sky, but he didn't reach out. Didn't demand to see it. It made me trust him, despite the fact that he was asking me to sink other possessions.

I handed it over. "Songs. Drawings. A story or two."

Killian opened it with a soft swish of paper. His eyes widened at the ink illustration that covered the page—a woman dancing, wearing little more than wings. I'd drawn spiraling designs like tattoos over her body, and she arched back, arms spread wide, the feathers of her wings touching the edges of the paper.

He turned a few pages, pausing on a poem framed by a sketch of two lovers. Killian read the last lines aloud in a gruff voice. "Intimacy threads itself through you and I, weaving heart-binding breaths into a secret tapestry with smoking edges."

I ran my tongue over my teeth. The words were remembered from a song I'd lost to my jumps through time, and rewritten into something new.

Killian lifted his gaze. "Shelta, this is exquisite."

"And probably inappropriate for a lady to have," I guessed, heat rising to my cheeks.

"Aye." He handed it back to me. "But artists can break rules. Keep it."

I flashed him a tight-lipped smile, wrapped the sketchbook in one of my shirts, and tucked it into one of the saddlebags.

Digging through the front pockets yielded two bars of chocolate, which I slipped into my coat. The bag of walnuts made my mouth water, and I grabbed a handful before offering some to Killian, who quite liked them. I shoved the considerably-smaller bag of nuts into a cranny and chewed, the flavor reminding me of Jess, who Stevie had nicknamed Squirrel for her love of all things crunchy. This was my last dip into her snack stash. I washed the sorrow down with a swig of water.

A heavy sigh filled my lungs with moist air scented by rocks and trees. The river rushed past, whispering of deep places, carving into its canyon.

When I took out my velvet pouch of crystals—the one non-essential thing I'd allowed myself—I realized I'd done it all wrong and unpacked the saddlebags. Crystals in first. Nuts. Water bottle. Sketchbook, toiletries, and first-aid kit on the other side. Safer to have the clothes on top; the first visible thing, should someone look.

When everything that was coming out was transferred, I zipped up the backpack's front pocket, trapping the pink plastic soap container, equally pink razor, and the earbuds to my AIO inside. I hadn't bothered pulling the headphones out. The last thing I needed was Killian to ask for an explanation on how they worked. He was sharp enough to pick up on an untruth, and I didn't want to find out what would happen if he caught me in a lie. Better to avoid the issue entirely.

I reached my arm out. Handed Killian my pack.

He crouched by the water and filled the bag with rocks. They made a dull thud as he piled them in. It felt like they dropped through me, making me heavy and small.

Without ceremony, Killian stood and tossed the pack into the darkest part of the river.

Gone.

In an instant.

Another collection of belongings in a long line of things I'd lost to my travels. What a waste.

I closed my eyes, head twisted down, swallowing the hurt. The defeat. The stuff didn't matter so much, it was the helplessness I hated. I was as out of control of my life here as I'd ever been, and I hadn't seen the first hint of a red dragon. Not even in my dreams.

I thought I could change the cycles of my destiny—take fate into my own hands. I thought it would be different this time; that there wouldn't be so much to mourn, but there always was. Every damn time.

"Lass?"

"Aye?" It came out garbled. I cleared my throat, threw him a fake smile.

"Is there anything else ye think should go in?"

Yeah. My AIO. If I were smart, I'd throw it in the water along with everything else that could peg me as "not from around here." But then I' be stuck in the eighteen-hundreds without music—without Prince and Bob Marley. Without Tori Amos. I wouldn't have any of the notes I'd made in my effort to find clues to the mystery that was my life. My lyrics. My songs. Pictures of artwork I'd left behind.

"No," I lied. "We're good. We can go."

I led the way back to the horses, his footsteps crunching behind. The soft clink of his sword drew my attention. Did he rest his hand on the grip?

Killian added the saddlebags to my awkward throne, and I studied the way he buckled them on. Then I hiked up my heavy skirts, modesty be damned, and before Killian could offer to help me, I grabbed hold of the saddle, hooked a foot in a stirrup, and hauled myself into the horse. It was awkward, and gravity almost won out, but I got my leg over and commenced the task of rearranging my layers. By the time I was as comfortable as I was going to get, Killian sat tall upon Lachie.

There was too much in his gaze to tell what he was thinking. A small nod, and his horse moved forward.

I followed him along the trail, bobbing with the motion of my horse, talking myself down from the edge of anger that crept through my thoughts. He meant well. He was protecting me. But it grated on me that I needed protection, that I was so dependent on this man in his gray cloak. This deadly man who'd made his way into the sea of my emotions.

We rode until the trail came to a wide, shallow stretch of river with a clearing on the other side. When Killian walked his horse into the water ahead of me, I tensed, and my mare took a sideways step. "Easy," I cooed, telling myself the same thing.

She went forward with a bit of encouragement. The water only came up to the horses' knees, but I had to fight the impulse to hold my breath as we crossed the uneven stones and murmuring current. Mavie stumbled once, splashing my cloak and boots, a few cold drops landing on my face. I sucked in the scent of running water and wet horse, and held on as Mavie kept forging through. When we got to the other side, she gave a great shake and a long, unimpressed huff.

"Good girl." I stroked her neck.

Killian watched me with a keen eye. I sat up and held his gaze, knowing it was a mistake. I should look away, engage with him as little as possible, but I didn't want him to think I was scared. And, if I were honest with myself, I wanted to look at him. I forgave him the backpack. He'd outfitted me, the horse and dresses worth far more than what he'd asked me to part with.

And he fascinated me. He knew the country intimately, this gorgeous land of rolling hills and distant mountains, moody skies and enduring magic. I envied him the chance to live in one place long enough to learn its ways.

"Ye asked before where we're going, lass." Killian's horse pawed the ground beneath him.

Mavie wanted to move, too, sidestepping like she was going to go around Lachie if she had to. "To your brother's house, you said."

"The home of my brother, aye." Killian's mouth twitched. "I've a stop or two to make along the way. Ye also asked about the royals of Scotland. Well, ye're about to see the residence of our bonnie Prince Charlie."

Royalty? I had no desire to enter the gossip zone that surrounded people in power.

Killian went on, letting Lachie prance a few paces in the clearing. "We'll soon reach Stirling Castle. I have business there. We'll stay the night."

"Okay." I blew out a breath.

"Are ye alright?" He cocked his head.

I smiled. Wanted to cry. Ridiculous emotions. We were on our way to a castle I'd read about. In the history I knew, Prince Charles had laid siege to Stirling Castle in the last attempt to regain the throne from England. He'd failed. Here, it was his home.

"I'm fine," I said. "Lead the way."

Killian looked at me a moment longer, then turned his horse.

After a while, the trail widened enough for him to fall back next to me. His mouth pursed as he gazed over.

"Why are you looking at me like that?" I asked.

"I'm thinking on how to explain ye." He tipped his head. "I've an idea, but I want to run it by ye before we arrive."

Ah, yes. A cover story. "Right. What have you got?"

"Well, I've just come from Ireland, where I was visiting my mother's kin. I met ye on the ship sailing over. We enjoyed each other's company, and I yer tales of far-away Canada. Ye were traveling on yer own—a strange custom Canadian women have—and I told ye it wouldn't be right to let ye navigate Scotland alone. Which it wouldn't."

"Sure. That works." A chaperone. Just what I always wanted.

Killian went on, serious enough that I almost felt guilty for my mental sarcasm. "The part I need to ask ye about, is if ye agree to saying ye're widowed. How old are ye, lass?" His brow creased as he looked at me.

"I'm thirty-three." Or so.

"I'm thirty-seven," he said. "My son is nearly a man, and I've a wife buried. It's odd for a woman to be traveling alone, and stranger still for one as lovely as ye to be more than thirty years and without a husband."

Or a wife. I gave him a tense smile. Kept my mouth shut.

"We could say it's a cultural difference, but ye'll have questions asked about yer family. It would be easiest to say ye were widowed, without family to turn to, and so ye chose to follow yer heart across the ocean to see what ye'd find." He paused. The horses walked a steady pace. "What do ye say, lass?"

"It's logical," I answered.

The image from my dream flashed through my mind; Evalynne's stark look of betrayal while she bled from the dagger. I pushed down nausea. I never married her. She could get out of my head already.

I turned my focus to the Highlander beside me. "Tell me how we met."

Killian didn't miss a beat, like he'd already imagined it. "Ye were standing at the rail of the ship singing softly, watching the coast of Ireland get smaller as we set sail, and I stood a wee bit off, listening to yer song." He painted his picture of deceit, drawing me in. "I couldn't quite catch the words, but I didnae want the melody to stop. All too soon ye went quiet. I waited a minute longer, then I walked up beside ye and asked yer name."

His voice was like music, bass and baritone. My body swayed with the motion of the horse. I could almost smell the spray of saltwater from the hull of the ship.

Ignoring the warmth in my cheeks, I decided to play along. "That's quite good. So, I told you my name and asked you yours. I started questioning you about Scotland, which led you to ask where I was from. I told you I'm from a small mountain town on the west coast of Canada, widowed, and traveling because I'd always wanted to see the isles. My heart called me here."

"I offered to accompany ye, saying I'd be taking a route that would show ye much of Scotland, and ye'd be safe as ye went." Killian tipped his head toward me.

I pretended we were on a ship's deck discussing my future holiday. "I accepted, but only after stalling so I could get an idea of your character. We talked for a while, and I found your manner respectful, your conversation thoughtful, and your conduct most honorable." I nodded, agreeing with myself. A good lie was built on truth. "Where did we dock?"

"Portpatrick. From there we got horses and headed to Stirling via Glasgow, staying at inns along the way."

There was a pause. I swallowed the lump in my throat. "Well, Killian Maclean, I am most appreciative of your company on my visit to Scotland. I'm lucky to have such a guide."

"My pleasure, Shelta."

The sincerity in his eyes hit me like a stone, square in the chest, and my skin turned hot. I enjoyed his attention far too much. Flirting led to falling, which inevitably ended with my abandoning people and turning into a grieving mess.

Then again, every time I got sucked through a wormhole, things got messy. It would hurt no matter what I did—that was a given. All I had was the time between.

Here I was, pretending to be a widow, dependent on a generous, kind, deadly man who seemed intent on taking care of me. Things could be a lot worse—probably would be, if time hadn't landed me in front of Killian.

Maybe I should just enjoy myself and do whatever I wanted in spite of my outrageously uncertain life.

Chapter 7
A Piano and a Memory

APPROACHING THE CASTLE was like coming up on a mountain. Stirling towered in the distance with all its grey stone, giving every indication that it was invincible. The sprawl. The positioning on the hill for good defense. Its sheer mass demanded awe.

Our horses plodded up the hill, as Killian navigated the edges of the road to pass slower traffic. A man drove a cart toward us, downhill, the stench of whatever he had beneath his tarp wafting before him as the breeze blew the smell toward us. Like something dead. Killian and I moved to the trampled grass on the side and sped up in an escape to fresh air, Lachie and Mavie springing into a canter, hoofs beating in rhythm.

We slowed after a few minutes, cooling the horses down as the walls grew closer. My stomach growled as we passed through the gates and were greeted by a guard who knew Killian by name. More guards watched from atop walls and stone-slab platforms. Those not in uniform went about their business, few sparing us a glance.

A portly man met us at the stables, his face framed by long sideburns. The man insisted on carrying both Madame Sabine's package and my saddlebags, and I couldn't very well argue without seeming out of place. I said goodbye to

Mavie as she was led away, and allowed myself to be escorted toward the castle.

We entered through a door opened by a grim-faced guard whose gaze stayed focused outward, alert to any threat. As we made our way down a stone-walled corridor glowing with golden lantern light, our stout guide chatted with Killian. He said something about rooms, and mentioned the prince's schedule, carrying my saddlebags slung over his arm as if they weren't there. I was barely paying attention to his words. All I cared about was that he didn't trip and spill my futuristic paraphernalia all over the polished floor.

Up some stairs, down a corridor. The décor's posh-factor turned up exponentially as we went. Now we walked beneath chandeliers. A statue of a rearing unicorn dominated one corner, its horn reaching toward the arched ceiling, its mane and tail streaming in an imagined wind. Its eyes showed determination; one massive hoof coming down with power.

Not a creature to be trifled with.

Killian caught my awed inspection of the statue. He patted my hand on his arm, either in shared appreciation or encouragement, I wasn't sure. His saddlebags were slung over his other shoulder. They let him carry his stuff without question.

Our guide brought us to a small sitting room with a dark blue couch and wine-red chair, onto which he deposited my belongings in a neat pile. I tried not to show my sigh of relief.

"I'll have a lady's maid come an' see to ye," he said with a nod toward me. "Any requests, Sir Maclean?"

"Would ye be able to arrange a meal for us?" asked Killian.

"Of course, sir. Would ye like to take it in the hall? 'Tis quiet in there this afternoon."

"Lovely." Killian gave a small nod. "I know the way."

The man left the door open as he walked away. I wished he'd closed it so I didn't have to whisper my question, leaning toward Killian so no one would hear. "Who are you, that you get private apartments in Stirling castle?"

Silence. A thousand words behind his eyes. "That's a conversation for another time."

As usual, I didn't know when to keep my mouth shut.

Footsteps echoed in the hall. I stepped away from Killian and turned toward the pair of doors on the far wall, open to bedrooms. "Is one of these mine?"

"Take yer pick."

I heard the smile in his voice, though I didn't look to see. Either would be fine. I didn't much care. I picked up my saddlebags and entered the room that had heavy red curtains pulled back to dark bedposts. A tapestry of a garden hung on one wall, and a screen blocked off a corner, where I hoped I'd find a chamber pot. Small windows let grey light into the room.

"This one's good," I said over my shoulder.

Killian brought Madame Sabine's package in and deposited it on a table. He tapped my saddlebags, and said, "If ye put these on the top shelf of the wardrobe, they'll be left alone."

I did as he said. He left while I had my back turned.

Twenty minutes later, after a lady's maid had given me a makeover, I met Killian in the sitting room. This time the door to the hall was closed. He wore grey trousers, a fresh shirt, a black tunic, and his boots had been polished. It also seemed he'd left the sword and gun in his room.

I stared at the blue skirts and gold details of my dress. It was gorgeous enough that I could suffer the uncomfortable shoes. The lady's maid had been over-enthusiastic with the corset, which she'd called stays. Whatever it was, it pressed at my ribs beneath the dress. My heart shook a rapid rhythm inside.

"The gown looks beautiful on ye."

His voice drew my gaze up. "Thank you. The laces are a little tight."

Depth in his laugh. "Turn around. I'll help."

"It's okay." I waved him off. "I'm sure you're hungry."

"Turn 'round, lass."

Such a gentle command, I couldn't help but obey. I held onto the high back of the nearby chair, its dark-red velvet soft under my fingertips. Killian unhooked the dress to get at the corset, and pulled on the lacing to give me more space to breathe. Little tugs up and down my back made me tingle. When he finished re-hooking the dress, his hands slid down my sides, smoothing fabric. The warmth of his touch made me wish he'd do it again.

I turned to face him, flushed. "Thanks," I whispered, more breath than speech.

"Yer welcome," he answered, voice thick. He held me with his gaze one shaky breath longer, then went to the door and opened it, gesturing me through.

I slid my hand onto his offered arm in the hallway, forcing myself to calm. His touch elicited too strong a reaction. I wanted his hands on me again with the privacy of a closed door. Wanted it with unreasonable force. The elaborate tapestries and gilded decorations we passed barely registered in my mind as we walked.

Eventually, we came to a long hall with an arched ceiling and tall windows at one end, its grandeur distracting me from Killian's nearness. When I saw what occupied the back corner of the room, I let go of his arm and straight-lined over to inspect an early version of a grand piano. Its body was polished mahogany, its long keys made of cream-colored wood, the short keys shone, lacquered black.

Inviting.

Killian stood in the center of the giant room and watched me, the two of us alone.

"Do you think it would be alright if I played?" I asked, fingers itching to touch the instrument.

"Go ahead, lass. It's waiting for someone to bring it to life."

I sat, arranged my skirts on the ornate bench, and placed my hands on the keys. I did not push down, however. Not yet.

Through that touch that was barely a touch, I could feel the whole of the piano at once. The wood. The strings. The hammers. It was an intimacy I could not explain, one that had grown in intensity over the course of my life. Silence. Listening. A long moment to attune to each other: human and instrument and the spirit of music.

When that initial moment of connection passed, I began to play. Not something I'd played before. This was new to me. It belonged to this place, this time, this particular piano.

The music began low and tentative, exploring. Caught in the flow of music, allowing it to come through me, the melody grew stronger. The piano's vibrations saturated my awareness, thrumming through my body. Through my blood. I breathed the rise and fall of notes, my mind spinning in its own kind of dance.

I didn't notice when another gentleman entered the room. I didn't see the way the two men watched me. My eyes were nearly closed.

All I knew was the resonance of the instrument singing in my bones.

The song grew. It was an adventure of harmony and bass, circling round in repeated patterns that altered a little each time. When the final cycle completed, the energy coming to a natural close, my fingers settled on a low, sonorous chord.

A deep, clear breath moved through me. The spirit of the music retreated to whatever part of my soul it was where it resided.

"That," came a rich voice into my reverie, "was the finest playing this hall has ever known." The man's tone carried through the room, sure and proud.

I looked over at the first word to see a splendidly dressed figure studying me. A small flock of people gathered near the entry behind him, and applauded as if on cue. I bowed, cheeks flushed.

Killian rose from his own bow. "Yer Highness, may I present Miss Shelta Raine. Shelta, His Highness, Prince Charles Stewart."

Careful not to trip on my skirts, I rose as gracefully as possible and walked over to him. A curtsy seemed the thing to do, so I tried one and managed to pull it off without falling over.

The prince took my hand and brought it up for a gentle graze of his lips. I clasped my hands together as soon as he let go to keep them from shaking.

"A great pleasure." His eyes held sparks at their depths. "Was that from a composer I would know? I did not recognize it, nor the style."

"I—the song did not exist until now, Your Highness," I stammered. "It's what the piano gave me to play."

He looked at me differently then, eyes narrowed above a cunning smile, as if he'd just discovered something. He gave me a slow, deliberate nod, then turned toward Killian. "Ye've brought us a virtuoso, Maclean."

"It seems I have." Killian regarded me with his head tilted, like he had at the spring, when we'd first met. Like he was seeing me anew. There was a glint to his eyes that I recognized as desire.

This was the power of my music. The danger of its seduction.

"I wish I could stay," Prince Charles said in a light tone, his accent not nearly as thick as Killian's, "but I'm called to a meeting. I was going there when I heard you start playing. I will be at dinner, however. Perhaps you could grace us with another performance."

"Of course," I answered, unable to say anything else.

He smiled, turned, and left the room with his flock following behind. As soon as they cleared the large doorway, a man walked in with a tray of food.

My skirts swished, skin tingling from the aftereffects of the music as I made my way to the cloth-covered table, where Killian and I sat for tea. The server arranged sandwiches and sweet cakes before us, and set down a porcelain teapot with steam rising from its spout.

Silence stretched until we'd both eaten something, then Killian paused in his feast, dark eyes fixed on me. I finished chewing and swallowed, putting down the bread and meat.

"I dinna ken ye could do that, lass—play music like that." The curiosity in his voice made him seem younger, somehow. "How did ye learn?"

The food turned heavy in my gut. "I had a masterful teacher." True, but only part of the truth. I tried to explain what I could, and simultaneously derail thoughts of the man who first taught me to play piano. "Each instrument has a voice, a spirit. If I get my mind out of the way and feel what the instrument wants to share, the music comes naturally. It's that way when I sing, too."

My relationship with music was nothing short of supernatural. Evalynne wasn't the only one to think so. It wasn't something I could explain. Anyone who knew music, who saw me when I surrendered to the songs that came, picked up on the oddity.

Killian's face went through several expressions, each so subtle I couldn't read their meaning. Then he reached over, lifted my hand, and kissed my fingers longer than the prince had done, lips pressing with full warmth. He placed my hand back on the table with such care it made my heart twirl in my chest.

"Ye have quite a gift, Shelta." Kind words. Heavy words. His gaze shone with dangerous intimacy.

I managed a small "thank you" and tipped my head in acknowledgement. But my appetite had vanished in a dive-bombing of armored butterflies. Whatever was growing between Killian and me had just gotten serious.

It always did when someone saw through my music into my soul.

After we'd finished eating, Killian left me in the hall, inviting me to play while he attended to his business. The piano drew me. Waiting for my attention. An inner pull dragged me toward it, as if I could feel the instrument's desire for me to make it sing. So, I sat, hands on the keys again, and let the music have its way.

I didn't sing, afraid to let my voice fill the unfamiliar space. An audience filtered in, figures sitting in couches or standing near the walls, but no one interrupted me, nor did they applaud. Perhaps they fell under the same spell I did.

I kept my eyes on the keys and pretended I belonged there.

Perhaps I did belong, to the instrument at least. It entranced me, and after a while I forgot about the onlookers, forgot even about Killian and dragons and the relentlessness of time. And, in my forgetfulness, my hands wandered into the danger present each time I sat at a piano: Moonlight Sonata.

The masterpiece came as it always did, thick with memories and lust. Eyes closed, skin flushed, I saw myself as a young woman again, pulled into the memory.

I was barely eighteen. It was the first jump through time where I didn't have a foster mother to take me in. I found work in Maine as a maid at the house of a wealthy concert pianist.

I never should have wandered in the mansion after dark, but the music called to me, overruling whatever logic tried to stay my feet. Wearing only my nightgown, I lurked in the hall outside the grand room with its black piano, seduced by the song that had pulled me from my bed by vibration more than music.

Breath shallow, I inched closer to the room, and a board squeaked.

Silence. Footsteps made the floor a bass drum. The door opened with a whisper of wind, and his eyes were on mine, dark and impassioned. The pianist who'd hired me weeks earlier when I'd answered an ad in the paper. The master of the house, with his blond hair sticking up like he'd run his hand through it, his gaze as intense as the song he'd been playing.

Did he hear my heart pounding? Had my longing knocked when my fist did not?

Smooth and low, his words tempted me into his lair, where opulence draped the walls and spread herself on the floors. The instrument had center stage, cushioned by a jewel-colored carpet fortunate enough to find itself beneath the object of his obsession.

He gestured for me to come with him, and my feet sank into the soft rug, following him to the piano, where he slid into the seat like it was his home.

"You were playing Beethoven." I knew the song, but I'd never heard anyone play it like he had. With need. Lust. A touch of destiny.

His smile was an invitation. "Moonlight Sonata. Would you like me to play it again?"

"Yes." I should have said no, should have left, but I could not. "Please."

His fingers touched the keys in the first flowing notes. He knew it so well he didn't need to look down. He watched me, like he relished my reaction to his playing, but I retreated from his gaze and leaned into the mouth of the piano instead, offering myself to the music. It took my heart as its own, residing in my ribcage.

The dark resonance built until the song changed into a dance of shadow and light. I braved the pianist's blazing gaze. Another mistake.

His lips twisted up. He knew what he did to me. His fingers kept moving, faster now, urgency in his eyes. His golden mess of hair shone in the low light of the chandelier I'd cleaned that morning.

My feet took me closer, until I could see his hands flying across the keys. Such precision. Such skill. I pressed against the polished wood.

My chest felt as if it would burst, my breath deep and desperate. The song came like waves, now softer, now building to a crest. When the last wave broke, and his hands rested on the keys, the sound of our breathing mingled with the lingering notes.

"Shelta." He made my name a fleeting song. "Come. Sit. I'll teach you."

I sat beside him, astounding him with the speed at which I've always learned instruments. The uncanny way music makes me come alive.

The next night he brought me onto his lap.

He taught me Beethoven, and a great many other things. By the fifth night, he had me spread before him atop the piano, mouth on me, man and music slaying me from below.

My breath caught in my throat, pulling me out of my reminiscence. I opened my eyes to remind myself where I was, and played the sonata's last notes with trembling hands, sweat on my brow. The blue gown seemed too bright, the piano ancient compared to the one on which I'd lost my virginity.

I lifted my hands from the keys and pushed the seat back, standing on weak legs. Wanting to run. In a rush that made my jaw drop, I became aware of my audience. Killian's mystified gaze trapped mine. Behind him, a crowd of people stared. I barely heard their scattered applause.

Chapter 8
Confessions

KILLIAN STRETCHED HIS legs out, leaning back in the crimson chair in our little sitting room with a repressed groan. Maybe he was as tired as I felt, trying to hold myself together as fatigue and vulnerability ripped my confidence to shreds. I sat on the edge of the blue couch, glad the door was closed, and played with the silk of my skirts, shoes off, toes scrunched in the carpet beneath me. Unable to look him in the eyes.

"What was his name, lass?" No preamble. Killian cut straight to it.

"Was it that obvious?" Did everyone who saw me at the piano today think I was a whore?

His voice carried no threat. "Aye. To me, at least."

"I had no business playing that song here." I bit my lip. I'd lost myself in the music, so far gone that it got me into trouble. Again.

"Ye had every right to do so. Makes me curious to know the story behind it, though."

His words carried a smile, and I braved his gaze. The way the skin creased around his eyes made clear his desire to know, to understand what drove me. I'd expected accusation, but it wasn't there.

I drew a breath. "His name was Richard. He taught me that song, among other things."

"Did he compose it?"

A nervous giggle snuck from my throat. "No, that was Beethoven. It's an old song—well, not to you, I guess. It won't be written for another half-century, or so."

Killian said nothing, tipping his head.

I took it as my cue to keep talking. My tone came out wry. Disillusioned. "Richard was my first. Where I come from, being a virgin when you're wed is rare." I should've stopped there, but, of course, I didn't. "I wasn't married, but he was. He and his wife appeared to loathe each other, so I told myself it was okay to give myself to him like I'd given myself over to the music."

Killian listened like a priest taking confession. Still. Serious. Patient.

"His wife found us one night," I blundered on, "after my piano practice, when we'd moved on to more lustful lessons. I cowered beneath the piano as she threw everything breakable within reach and screeched such that the walls shuddered." I remembered it clearly, huddling naked on the ornate rug. Slinking out to get my clothes when she left. Richard had looked as broken as the shards of porcelain littering the floor. "I did that. My fault."

"No." Killian's growl made me slide further from him on the couch. "Not your fault. His."

"I didn't protest." I gave a shrug. "I liked it. I was the one who kept going to him, until that night. Then I headed into the forest and sought a tree to take me somewhere else." What a dark night that had been.

"Did ye find what ye sought?" asked Killian.

"No." I swallowed against the lump in my throat. "I went to the next city and found different work. And more trouble."

My mind buzzed with memories of giving myself to men. They expected it. As if sex were a form of payment for the work they'd offered.

"I felt powerless." Saying it aloud, I knew I'd found the truth.

I'd retreated to the far side of the sofa. My body curled in. Defensive. Protective. I'd done the same after sex—not those first times with Richard, but many times thereafter, until I'd turned to female companions.

Nurturing friendships and uninhibited lovers had helped me shed old patterns, but now the wounded reaction gripped me again. By the standards of the time I was in, there was no question that I'd be called a whore and treated as such.

What a terrible thing, shame. I shrank further into myself, the corset pressing into my flesh.

Killian leaned toward me. "Shelta, look at me."

"I don't think I can."

"Ye can," he said, quiet but firm. He moved onto the couch next to me, brought his hand under my chin, and lifted my head from where it was trying to burrow into my chest. I still looked down, away. Surely he wouldn't want me to accompany him now.

"Shelta." Such tenderness in his voice.

With effort, I raised my eyes to his. His fingers slid across my cheek, kindling feelings that were best stomped out.

"I do not judge ye, and I'll not share yer secrets." He spoke formally, so carefully I trusted him on instinct. "What ye've done in another world is none of my concern. I know ye as kind, honest, and brave. I'll not dishonor yer confidence."

I nodded. Put my head in my hands. All the shame I'd swept into dark corners of my heart rose like a tide to choke me. I couldn't speak past the ball of tension in my throat. Tears started down my cheeks. Saltwater atonement.

He gathered me into his arms with words of comfort. "It's alright, lass. Ye're safe. Ye've done nothing wrong."

Killian gave me his handkerchief. A soft thing. I dabbed my eyes, pulled myself together, and went to the basin in my bedroom to wash my face. He followed, stopping halfway through my door.

"I'll have them bring your dinner up," he offered. "I think a formal gathering would not be a kindness for ye now."

I put the towel down, my skin still damp. "Thank you, but I promised the prince a song."

Killian shook his head. "Ye gave him one already, and a concert for his guests besides. Rest. He'll not mind."

"But I'm in my gown and everything, Killian." I smoothed the silk, preparing to suck it up and go to dinner. "You bought it so I could attend the prince."

With swift strides, he crossed the room to stand before me, gaze so serious it stole my breath. Hand under my jaw, his thumb stroked my cheek. "I bought ye that gown because ye need a fine dress. Not for any one person or occasion, but because ye deserve to be adorned beautifully and not feel at a disadvantage to those around ye."

"Thank you." I spoke in a small voice. He insisted on the only thing that made sense. I did not need go to dinner with raw emotions and red eyes.

"My pleasure." Killian bowed his head, sliding a hand behind my waist, and my gaze dropped to his mouth.

Heart thundering in my ears, I almost tilted my head up. Instead, I froze. As his lips brushed my cheek, I wanted to lean into him, to put my nose in the curve of his neck and breathe in his subtle musk, but I couldn't move.

He stepped back, said goodbye with a careful nod, and went to dinner without me.

Fear and desire surged inside. My blood raced with the residual warmth of Killian's closeness and an awareness that something dangerous lurked beneath mere attraction. It lured my heart into the dark waters where love grows. I was in the shallows yet, but I knew the sheer drop would come.

Thoughts crumbling in on themselves, I stood like a fragile statue. My hands played with the fabric of my sleeves, but the rest of my body had frozen in place. My eyes stared unseeing at the fire in the fireplace. The memories our conversation brought up threw shadows across my mind; memories I thought I'd made peace with.

Apparently, I had not.

When I realized I was barely treading water in the black deep of regret, I shook myself to break the spell.

All I could do was hope my confession had done some good for my psyche without damaging my relationship with Killian. He seemed so willing to accept me. The way he looked at me? We could play this thing out and end up in a world of hurt the next time I dropped through a window in the World Tree.

Or I could try to stop it now. If that was even possible.

I needed Killian to not want me as much as I wanted him. Maybe what I'd shared would throw him off.

Then again, maybe it turned him on.

Desperate for distraction, it took every ounce of willpower I had not to pull out my AIO to take a selfie in my lavish gown, or put on some music. I wanted to watch a movie or read a book to escape. I could do none of those things.

It wasn't long before a girl showed up with a tray of food that made my mouth water: savory soup, herb-roasted root vegetables, juicy roast beef, and creamed potatoes.

After I'd eaten, a maid came to help me out of my dress and ready myself for bed. She took the dinner tray away, but left my glass of wine. Walking to the window, I leaned one arm on the cold ledge and sipped the velvety liquid until I'd numbed thoughts of past and future.

The countryside was dark, with stars glittering between the clouds. Moonlight reflected in the ribbon of water that was the river below.

The night's beauty combined with the weight of time to make everything seem surreal—but beyond the wine and sheer fatigue, a sharp urgency sang in my bones.

This was real. As real as it got.

My gaze traversed the river below, seeking escape in shadows of forest. Even if I wanted to run, I couldn't. I was in a guarded fortress. And I had nowhere to go.

Sticking with Killian was my best chance of survival, regardless of what it ended up doing to my heart.

That night, in the swirling world of dreams, dragons staked their claim on the castle towers, including the crimson friend I'd been missing. Little ones played, flying and tumbling through stone-framed windows while their massive cousin perched on the heights.

I watched from the battlements of the highest turret, the red dragon roosting above me with wings that gleamed with veins of gold. A pair of dragons zoomed past, streaks of blue-green and pearly-grey that spiraled through breaks in the walls and whatever other obstacles they could find.

A gown would have suited the scene, but instead I wore the jeans and leather jacket that had been my everyday gear in a part of my past best left forgotten. I shoved my hands in my pockets to ward off the chill, and frowned as my fingers brushed a soft scrap of cloth in the right pocket. I knew what it was before I pulled it out and let it flap in the wind.

The blue bandana didn't belong to me. Not really. I earned the taking of it after all the times I'd gone to bed with its former owner. Jesse, who'd taken me on a first date I'd never forget, teaching me how to ride his motorcycle and sitting behind me all night as I opened the throttle and tasted freedom. As the sun came up over the field where we'd parked, I let him have me, naked on his Harley, reveling in a different kind of bliss. And I liked it at first.

Then it got scary.

Jesse had punched through the wall when he found me packing my stuff, whisky on his breath. I'd lied my way out that night. Said I was only going for a few days. Snuck out when he was snoring and never looked back.

But I decided to put a sting into leaving him, having finally convinced myself to do it. The bandana was his trademark accessory. I knew he'd miss it. It was a petty thing, really. I wanted to take a piece of him after letting him take so much of me.

I burned the damn thing two time-jumps later in a campfire by the ocean, around which I danced and drank and sang and screamed.

I was not happy to see it again.

Movement made me look down. Killian strode below on the wide walkway of the main castle roof, his cloak billowing, carrying himself like a rogue king. His eyes found me on the battlement, but they didn't shine with kindness like they usually did. He glared at me.

Of course, he would distance himself from me. Push me away. He should. But I wasn't up for goodbyes with undertones of shame. No dismissals for me.

I clenched the bandana in a defiant fist. I wouldn't give him the chance.

"So I've forsaken my innocence." I spoke in an undertone, to myself. "What's it worth, anyway? Everything gets dirty at some point. Nothing stays clean and young forever."

Disappointment narrowed Killian's eyes, annoyance pinching his mouth. Like he'd heard my whispers on the wind.

Humiliation burned my skin, searing through the walls around my heart. I dropped my gaze to the bandana, faded and threadbare with a rip on one corner.

Turning away from Killian, I threw the fabric into the whipping wind. I sprinted four strides to the other side of the battlement, brought my foot high, and leaped off the saw-toothed wall with everything I had. In an instant, I was in the quick flight of a fall, arms out, uncaring of what the end might be, but trusting. Trusting.

The crimson dragon dove beneath me and spread his wings in an angle that lifted us away from the world below. Killian gazed up as we cleared the castle, but I didn't seek his gaze.

The clouds were pink and orange, the sky deep blue. The dragon and I soared on a thermal, and left everything else behind.

CHAPTER 9
A CARRIAGE RIDE

IN THE DARK BEFORE dawn, as rain pelted the windows, I stared at myself in a small mirror. A maid had woken me up, gotten me into my green dress and tamed my mess of hair, but I wasn't remotely awake. All I wanted was to burrow into the bed and sleep the morning away.

Killian knocked at the door, and I made myself join him in the sitting room. We stood, facing each other across the small space, where a table set for two waited with food I had no appetite for. Bread. Cheese. Apples. Cold meat.

At least there was tea, its steam rising like the fog in my mind.

"Good morning." Killian gestured for me to have a seat. "How are ye feeling?"

I sat on a hard, wooden chair, avoiding the couch from the night before, and tried not to groan. "The rain makes me want to sleep through the day."

"Aye, that would be nice, but we'll be heading out after breakfast." There was an edge to his voice that hadn't been there yesterday; a pinch between his eyebrows, a tightness to his eyes.

"In this weather?" I tried to sound like I didn't really care.

"Aye." He gave a wry grin. "It's Scotland, lass. It rains here. We won't be waiting for it to stop. My plans have changed. We can't delay for the rain, ye understand?"

"Of course." I imagined myself a drowned rat on a miserable horse trudging through the mud.

We ate little and said less. Soon, I gathered my things, slipped my boots on under my dress, and covered up with coat and cloak. What had happened that we were leaving before dawn? Was he sneaking us out, afraid to be seen with me?

Killian led the way down the stairs, carrying the leather package with my gown. The saddlebags weighed on my right shoulder, both hands necessary to lift my skirts high enough that I could match Killian's pace without tripping. He strode sure and swift to the massive doors of the main entrance of the castle, where tall lanterns lit white walls and shimmered on the weapons of the guards. A somber soldier opened one heavy door. It was still dark outside.

As I took a step toward the inevitability of being soaked to the bone, Prince Charles strode toward us. He wore red in cheery opposition to the weather outside, making me think of my dragon friend, and carried himself with vitality; a royal of the land, certain of his place. My heart gave a twist. In my world, this man had been defeated in a failed revolution.

"A carriage awaits," said the prince, stopping before Killian. "May the land carry you swiftly and God watch over your keep. Send a messenger if you need anything at all."

"Much appreciated." Killian gave a parting bow.

"Thank you for your hospitality." I curtsied, grateful to hear I'd be inside a dry carriage, rather than on a drenched horse.

"You're most welcome, Lady." The prince dipped his head. "Come back sometime and play music for us again."

"I'd like that." I doubted it would happen.

I made it to the carriage at a run behind Killian, and ducked inside as he pulled me up by my arm. When I looked back, it was to see the prince wave, framed in golden light and flanked by armed men. Then the carriage door was closed, and the driver cracked the whip.

Killian sat across from me in the dark, both of us bobbing and swaying with the motion of the carriage. Water dripped down my cloak, infusing the air with the musk of wet wool. I was tempted to pretend to sleep, but was too on edge to close my eyes.

It wasn't long before the darkness dimmed to a dull gray that made its way through the coach's small, curved windows. Killian studied me in the low light. I struggled to hold his gaze.

"Prince Charles enjoyed the story of our meeting," he said, breaking the silence.

"Your business went well, then?" I didn't know what kind of business he had, and wasn't up to questioning him about it.

He didn't answer anyway. "Here." He leaned forward and undid the clasp of my cloak. "Take this off and let it dry. There's a blanket to warm yerself."

Several thick blankets were folded in a basket below my seat. I arranged one around me, draped in warmth, and looked down at the pattern of the weave, tracing the lines with my fingers.

"Lass." Killian coaxed my gaze to him with his voice, dark eyes intent. "Ye're hiding from me."

"Aye." I was too tired to lie. My walls were up. Shoulders forward, chest collapsed. I desperately wanted a dragon to fly me away.

He sat back, patience smoothing his features, and said, "Let me tell ye a story."

I cocked my head, silent, listening hard to catch his words over the noise of the wheels and hoofbeats, and the squeak of the carriage's suspension.

"When I had newly come into manhood," Killian began, "my uncle brought me a woman. He said that she was mine to do with as I pleased. What he thought I would do—that I would use her and be done with her—I didnae do. She taught me the art of making love; instructed me so I would know how to please my future lovers. She was older than me by a few years, yet still young. A kind, beautiful, trusting woman who bared herself to me and allowed me to do the same. I grew to care about her, looking forward to the time we shared for more than the physical rush and release."

He fell quiet. The rain filled the space, drumming on the roof until Killian started speaking again. "When my uncle learned I was still seeing her, observed that I had feelings for her, she was taken away—gone without goodbye."

"That's awful." Rage and compassion pricked the backs of my eyes.

Killian's mouth twisted into a frown. "My uncle told me that men do not trouble themselves with the affections of whores. To him, my companion and any like her were good for only one thing. I thought otherwise." His lips turned up, the creases around his eyes softening. "To me, she was no less worthy than anyone else. She was a lovely, caring woman. She never made me feel awkward or unwanted. We laughed together, shared stories. I trusted her in my most vulnerable moments."

I didn't know what to say. My smile would have to suffice. As Killian fell silent, distant, I realized he didn't need me to respond. He only needed me to hear him.

The carriage continued its rolling rhythm. Killian stared out the window. I watched him without the pressure of his gaze on mine, and it gave me a chance to really study his face. The width of his brow and curve of his cheeks softened the hard lines of his nose and jaw. His black hair fell forward, and I wanted to reach across and push it back from his face, maybe trace the crescent shape of his scar with my thumb.

Killian trusted me. Confided in me. In that crystalized moment, I didn't want to be anywhere else. I was in Scotland, way back in time in some sort of alternate realty, in the company of a man I wanted badly—a man who had stacks of secrets he wasn't telling me. And some unnamable song of truth told me I was exactly where I was meant to be.

"It is assumed by much of society," Killian said, his voice subdued, "that a man is stronger and more capable than a woman. I dinna agree. Strength and courage appear in many ways. For a woman to teach me such an intimate art, to instruct me without impatience or annoyance as I fumbled through, to share stories of sacred rites and respect for the existence of lovers—I found her conduct most honorable. Women are the nurturers. They shape our world as much as men. We would not be whole without the influence of mothers, grandmothers, sisters and lovers. Women give birth. Men bring death."

"Men create as well." My voice carried over the sounds of our travel. "Men conceive of ideas and build all kinds of things."

"Of course." Killian focused on me. "People are never so easily defined. I merely wanted ye to understand that I see things differently than perhaps ye may think."

I nodded, my mouth pulling together. I hoped he could see how much I appreciated the reflection of what I'd bared the night before: trust of a most intimate nature.

"I'm told," he went on, "that the priestesses of old used to teach young ladies as they came into womanhood—that the power of feminine sexuality was celebrated and held sacred."

I thought about the difference it would have made to me—and countless other girls, for that matter—if I'd been supported, guided, taught to hold sexuality as sacred from the start, instead of it being an unknown thing to conquer.

"You're a good man, Killian Maclean."

"And ye're a fine woman, Shelta Raine."

It had never been easy for me to look people in the eyes. It made me feel exposed. I didn't want to be seen so fully, opened to the depths of me. Yet here I was, eyes locked with Killian's. There was no discomfort. I didn't have to will my gaze to stay. It was the natural place for it to rest, as if I'd forgotten to be self-conscious in the hypnotic swaying of the carriage. There was only us in that infinite moment. Nothing else held any importance.

"Shelta," Killian spoke after so much silence, "will ye sing me a song?"

I smiled. There was already a rhythm in the rocking, a cadence to the hoof beats. Even a subtle chord in the sound of the rain. With the smell of damp horse and wood and wool in my nose, I started to sing.

> *There once was a wish for adventure,*
> *That led me to worlds unknown,*
> *And now that I'm on this adventure,*
> *I need to choose which way to go.*
>
> *To ride through the woods to the castle,*
> *Each heartbeat, hoof and stride,*
> *To enter the doors and waltz 'round the halls,*
> *Riches await inside.*
>
> *To live in a mountain cabin,*
> *Tend to the hearth and fire.*
> *It's magic I seek with all its mystique,*
> *Revealing my desire.*
>
> *To sail the seas in a proud ship,*
> *The wind in the sails wide,*
> *To run my hand 'long the polished wood rail,*
> *And watch the dolphins glide.*
>
> *Yet none of it has quite the appeal,*
> *If I see myself there alone.*
> *I much prefer a journey that brings,*
> *Us together home.*

The last three words began on a high note, falling like a many-pooled waterfall to rest on the single note of "home." The rocking, the rain, and the horses kept on.

I'd closed my eyes. I usually did when the music came through. What surprised me was that Killian had closed his own, and they were still shut. Finally, once the afterglow of the song had dissolved, his eyelids opened and he looked straight at me.

"That's some magic, lass." His voice scraped.

I swallowed, chest heavy, cheeks flushed by whatever was growing between us.

He studied me for another minute, then said, "I think I will tell ye now that I'm taking ye to my own home. The home of my clan. We will be with my family sooner than the two weeks I spoke of. There will be no detours for business along the way."

I wasn't sure what he meant. "Killian, where are we going?"

"We ride to Duart, lass. We ride to Duart Castle."

CHAPTER 10
HEADING FOR HOME

THE CARRIAGE SLOWED, rumbling and swaying to a stop. Though the rain still fell, the sky was lighter. It must've been well into morning.

"We'll change horses here." Killian lifted his chin, the silver streak in his beard showing in the dull light, and I wondered about the scar beneath it, and the one at his temple. A story I didn't dare ask him about now.

While he helped our driver and two stable hands swap out the horses, I ran through the rain to use the outhouse. We set off straight away when I returned, fresh horses eased into a quick, maintainable pace.

"I did quite like my mare," I half-joked to Killian. I'd only had her a couple of days.

"We shall find ye another," he said. "She will be well-tended in the prince's stables."

She was probably happier where she was than out in the mud and rain. "What's the hurry?" I asked. There must be something pressing if we left before dawn and were stopping only to change horses.

He looked at me as if considering what to say. When he spoke, it was in a deep, enduring voice, touched with a hint of sadness. "Some believe there should only be one crown to rule."

"Why?" Of course, there was unrest here. Same humans, different world.

"To control people, resources, and land within a single organization of power," Killian explained. "Many of those who oppose the triple crowns trade in human lives, which is illegal. To them, it's not so important who is king or queen, but that the monarch is under their influence, and that they are free to do whatever they wish in the name of the governing organization."

I frowned. "Sounds familiar."

"The lust for power runs deep in those it claims."

It seemed to stretch through time, too. "So, does this party you speak of have a name?"

Instead of answering, Killian moved to sit beside me. I lifted the blanket on my lap and draped it so it covered his legs as well. I was cold just looking at him in his kilt, even if his boots did come up to his knees. The move earned me a smile.

"Thank ye, lass." His quiet tone reverberated through his body, into mine. "The group I speak of would be the Union Party, but its members do not give their names publicly. They operate in shadow, and behind closed doors. Part of my business—what I do as I travel or as others travel for me—is to gather information that assists those of us who want Scotland and her people to remain free. I give this knowledge to the Stewart spymaster. It was a warning given by the prince last night that drives us now, though he sent a messenger to my father straight away."

"So, you're a spy?"

"Of sorts. I am other things, as well."

"Of course." I started connecting dots. "That's what the fight was about in Glasgow?"

"Aye." Killian touched the fingertips of one hand to the other. "My business there included collecting a letter that contained vital information. It was meant to be intercepted."

"But they failed." They died. Failed meant dead in this instance.

"Aye." His eyes were as serious as I'd ever seen them. "It will be late when we arrive, but we travel with haste so I can be home before those I've been warned against arrive—visitors who come unannounced and uninvited to my castle."

"Your castle?" I repeated.

"The castle of my family, of Clan Maclean."

"And what, exactly, is your place in Clan Maclean, Killian?" He was obviously wealthy, well connected, a gentleman to be sure, but it was the way he spoke about the castle in a proprietary manner that made me ask.

"I am the heir." His tone suggested he was simply talking about the weather, that it wasn't a big deal, yet his eyes held insurmountable strength. "I'm the eldest son to Sir Malcolm Lorne Maclean, the chief."

"Ah." So much about him made sense, now. "And you let me sleep on the ground?"

Laughter felt good. His warmed me with its bass. "It seemed the least I could do, seeing as ye clearly wanted to sleep outside. And what better way to acclimatize yerself to Scotland than to sleep on her soil?"

He had a point. "You're right, you know." I lifted a hand, gesturing as I spoke. "I didn't actually get a lot of sleep, but it was grounding. To breathe the fresh air of this place, to rest on the earth and bathe in the stream in the morning—it was probably the best thing for me. Besides, staying at Stirling made up for any discomfort I may have endured."

Killian looked like he'd fit a puzzle piece together; like something had clicked into place in his personal picture of who I was. "Ye understand then," his voice rolled through me, "the deep connection that can be made with the earth."

It wasn't a question, but I nodded.

"The old Celtic kings used to be crowned in a marriage to the land. Some say they were the children of pagan gods." The corner of his mouth twitched. "The ceremony reminded them of their duty to protect the earth and all her creatures, the bond between lord and land. Clan chiefs still follow this tradition, for we are descended from those ancient kings."

I let his words sink in. "So, at some point you'll be taking part in that ritual marriage to your homeland?"

"Aye." His sharp eyes, the set of his mouth, the crease of his brow showed determination and dignity easy enough, but there was something more that ran back to the kings of old. A presence. Perhaps it was the surety of knowing his place, that he came from those ancient kings, following the most primal law of the land: take care of the earth, and she will take care of you.

"In my previous life," I spoke quiet, leaning toward him, "one of the most difficult things for me to accept was the devastation of the environment. For many, profit was the only importance. I'm sure everyone's quality of life would've been different if the state of the earth was a priority for those who wielded power." I looked down. "All leaders should have to marry the land."

"Indeed." His breath warmed my face.

I moved back, circling around to the original subject. "So, these unannounced visitors are?"

"All I was told," he said, "is that a group of men with a small army behind them ride for Duart. And they're not friendly."

The changing rhythm of the carriage woke me. I'd been sleeping with my head on Killian's shoulder. I straightened into my own space on the bench we shared.

"Sorry." I brought a hand up to block my yawn.

He placed a hand on my thigh. "Not at all. 'Twas comforting. I was thinking in twisted channels. Sometimes the warmth of another helps to lessen the shadows of concern."

"Glad I could help." I stretched my arms up. "Is there food?"

"Aye." Killian retrieved a basket from beneath the bench, and we ate apples, cheese, and bread in easy silence.

"It's a pity we don't have cards," I said after we'd finished our snack.

"Ah." Killian flashed a mischievous grin. "Interesting ye should mention that." He slid a hand into his saddlebags, and produced the deck we'd played with at the Glasgow inn. He must've snagged it before we left.

I clapped my hands like a giddy girl, reached for the deck, and began shuffling on my lap in a movement that was second nature. The carriage bumped along. Killian sat beside me, his attention a palpable thing.

A tiny space on the padded bench between us served as a table. He drew two, I drew three, and in the end his three kings beat my queens and sixes.

"Five cards." He called the terms of his game. "Two draws, and sevens are wild."

On it went, through the afternoon and into the evening after another change in horses. At some point, we switched to Blackjack, and he taught me a game as well. Finally, it grew too dark to see the cards in the dim of the coach.

"Sleep if ye can, lass." Killian packed the deck away. "At the next stop, we'll take a ferry across the Firth of Lorn. I would that ye could see my home from the water in the morning's light, but that must wait. I hope instead the moon will come out to shine on the walls of Duart Castle."

"You're proud of your home."

"Aye. It's in my blood. It is part of me."

How different to have been raised on land that he knew from childhood. The exact opposite of my life. I wanted his sense of security. Roots. An unreachable desire.

Did Duart have a library? Killian accepted my ridiculous time-hopping; maybe I'd find some answers there; some clue to help me control my traveling, or at least understand it. I closed my eyes and leaned back against the wall of the carriage, a familiar frustration simmering in my belly. Better not to think about it.

Killian was an easy distraction. Heir to the chief. The surety that belonged to the man beside me was absolute.

I caught myself idealizing him and grimaced inwardly. Did I really think he was immune to doubt, always steady in himself? Everyone was human. Expectations were dangerous. Best to remember such hard-earned wisdom.

I willed the motion of the carriage to rock me to sleep, but my head jostled around awkwardly. Giving up, I leaned against Killian's shoulder as if it were the most natural thing in the world for me to do, and didn't pull my hand away when he wrapped his fingers around my own.

Killian squeezed my hand. I woke with an indrawn breath and a crick in my neck. I'd slept badly, wedged between him and the wall.

"We're nearly at the water." He drew back the curtain so I could see.

The rain had stopped. We passed houses lit from within, and street lamps hung along the road. Ahead, black water held rippling reflections of the lanterns on the ferry.

When we stopped, I climbed down from the carriage and stretched. Small waves lapped at the shore; the air was salty and the breeze crisp. The driver coaxed the animals up the ramp to the flat deck, and soon the coach and four horses were secure on the wide ship.

My All-In-One was still in the secret pocket of my coat, which I'd insisted on wearing beneath the cloak to block the chill wind. I had the terrible, sinking feeling that I should let it fall into the water and be done with it. I was about to enter a castle crawling with people. What if someone found it? What if Killian felt it in my pocket and asked what it was? He'd tell me to dispose of it, of that I was certain.

But I'd lose so much. My songs. My list of all the places and dates I'd traveled to, my endless records trying to make sense of it all. I'd found patterns, but no reason; there was no logic to my jolted path through time.

Maybe I'd find the missing pieces here. Maybe there was no answer. But I couldn't give up all that research, all those notes and midnight-inspiration sketches. I'd just make sure the AIO stayed hidden.

The ferry set off. There were rowers and a sail, with the wind at our backs. Killian said a few words to the captain as he led me to the prow of the ship.

I came fully awake in the crisp of the night, the swish of water on the ferry's hull and whoosh of wind across the loch singing in my ears. The reflection of the lanterns wavered in the dark liquid beneath us, and a silver gleam lit the water as the clouds parted above us.

I tilted my head toward Killian. "You have your wish. Here's the moon."

His face lit up, not from moonlight, but something from within—as if, traveling over that water, we entered his domain. With an exhale through rounded lips, he moved behind me and cupped his hands around my upper arms. His warmth went through my layers to ignite my blood.

Each breath came deep in the cool night air. Killian slid one arm across my chest in line with my shoulders, as if he were claiming me. Could he feel my heart thundering away as we crossed black water to a fortress by the sea?

The island grew large ahead of us. Silver light glowed on a distant castle, torch fire flickering on its walls.

"Your bonnie home?" I asked.

"Aye." Killian spoke low, his mouth near my ear. "I hope ye feel rested enough for a late night. My brother will be surprised that I have in my company a lady, and—forgive me, but it's the truth—he'll want to know that ye're not a spy."

"Oh, excellent." If I was a spy, I had a weak cover story. Maybe I didn't need to be worried about someone thinking I was a witch; they'd think I was a spy. I thought of my AIO again and—despite the loss it would be—wished I'd dropped it in the water with my backpack. I couldn't do it now, with his arms around me. "Why would he be surprised to find you in the company of a woman?"

"My wife died ten years ago, Shelta. I have not taken another."

"You loved her?"

"I did." The words came out gentle. "I'm blessed that she left me a son, and that she lives on in him."

I wrapped my hands around the thick forearm below my throat and swallowed, knowing the way his arm draped across me was not a casual thing. "I'm looking forward to meeting your son. And your brother. What are their names?"

"My son's name is Charles." A father's pride honeyed his voice. "Charlie, we call him. And my brother is Wallace Bruce Maclean."

I leaned back to speak into his ear. "Wallace and Bruce, both," I whispered, aware of his eyes on my throat. "I hope he doesn't think I'm a spy. He must be very fierce indeed."

The rumble of Killian's quiet laugh jolted through me, and I looked forward, more turned on than I wanted to admit. "Aye, he can be fierce, for certain, and will likely be intimidating from the first. Dinna let him fool ye. If ye saw him with his three-year-old daughter, ye'd ken him truly."

Perhaps. Or maybe seeing him in battle would show me his true nature. If Wallace was anything like Killian, I wouldn't want to be on his bad side.

The ship turned to the right. "The landing for the ferry is north a wee bit." Killian pointed. A lone lantern shone dead ahead.

Finally, the boat bumped into the dock and men from shore secured the lines. There were many hands to take the hobbles from the horses and untie the coach from the deck. On land, we climbed into the carriage one last time, and wound up the short road to the castle.

Killian said only one thing to me while we sat, side by side, swaying in the darkness. "I'm glad ye're here, Miss Shelta Raine. This may be a strange world for ye, but be unafraid. I will be at yer side."

"Thank you." I took his hand in mine and squeezed. My other hand rested on my AIO, too aware of its solid shape beneath the velvet of my cloak.

I was glad of Killian's arm as I exited the carriage and walked toward the inner walls of the castle. The layers of skirts grabbed at my ankles. People stared. Guards stood at attention everywhere I looked, most in the same green plaid Killian wore, though some wore red kilts or dark pants instead.

In the torchlight beneath a mighty stone arch, a broad man waited, arms crossed at his chest. He was shorter than Killian, but wider, bulkier, and obviously related.

"Brother." Killian extended a hand as we reached him. "May I present Miss Shelta Raine. My lady, this is my brother, Wallace Maclean."

"Welcome, Miss Raine." Wallace gave a small nod, his face like stone. He snapped his gaze back to Killian. "Brother, welcome home. We have much to discuss this night."

"Aye," Killian agreed.

I kept up with the men as we crossed the courtyard, towed along by the strength of Killian's arm. The air carried scents of cold stone, torch smoke, and a chill sea breeze. As we reached the stairs to the castle entrance, a clipped shout echoed off the walls and a tall teenager leapt down the stairs. I stepped away, seeing what was coming. The embrace would have knocked me over, but barely rocked

Killian. The young man pulled back and regained some composure as he realized I was standing there.

Killian grinned at his boy. "My lady Shelta, may I present Charles Malcolm Maclean. My son."

I made a small curtsy. "Very glad to meet you."

The boy took my hand, bowed to kiss it, and forgot to let it go. "Be welcome, my lady, to Duart Castle." He spoke with surprising weight despite his cheeks coloring as he finally released my hand. "It is a pleasure to have yer beauty grace our halls."

"Thank you kindly, Charles." I wished I could see Killian's reaction to the courtly manner of his son. I didn't want to turn my head to look.

"Charlie, milady," he corrected gently, turning his attention back to his father. He was clearly about to launch into questions when Killian's brother stepped in with a firm look.

"It'll have to wait, lad." Wallace's tone allowed no argument. "Yer father and I have much to discuss, and the night is no longer young."

CHAPTER 11
INTERROGATION

WE'D BEEN INSIDE the castle for all of a minute when a woman appeared at my side. She was near my age, with a long braid down her back, and full lips that widened in a kind smile. Something about the tilt of her cheekbones and glow of her bronze skin reminded me of my first female lover. Maybe it was the spark in her amber-flecked eyes.

"My name is Annelle, milady." She made a curtsy, and drew me away from the men, who strode down the hall. "I'll be yer lady's maid, so please tell me anything ye need."

I wanted to tell her not to curtsy to me, for starters, but that would peg me as strange right off the bat, so I kept my mouth shut for once and thanked her with a smile. She led me up a flight of stairs, down a corridor, and through a small sitting room into a bedroom. There was even a bathtub in a room in the far corner. Annelle caught me looking longingly at it, and offered to have hot water prepared.

"Not now." I shook my head. "But thank you. I think tonight is not yet over for me, and I wouldn't want to ruin such a luxury, nor cause so much work when it can't be enjoyed."

Annelle smiled and took my cloak. She reached for the coat, but I walked to the wardrobe and hung it up myself, praying no one would go through my pockets before I found a better place to hide the AIO.

"There were saddlebags and a gown in the carriage." I tried to keep my voice casual. Should I have grabbed them? Killian had left his things behind.

"Someone will bring them up." She steered me into a chair and worked on taming my hair.

I studied her focused expression in the mirror, amazed at how much she looked like Amy, who'd taken me into her tiny apartment in Brooklyn and helped me find a sense of equal footing in a relationship. I missed her scratchy singing voice, sometimes falling out of tune, sometimes in perfect harmony. I'd left her with a lie when we started to get too close. A lie was better than gone with no goodbye.

Annelle met my eyes in the reflection. I dropped my gaze to my face in the mirror, and saw a woman pretending to be something she was not. When Annelle asked how I came to be here, I told her the story of meeting Killian, such as we'd discussed.

"Canada." She spoke with unconcealed awe. "That's a mighty long distance. Ye never hear of Canada, only of the Americas. What's it like?"

I painted her verbal pictures of rugged wilderness, impossibly high mountains and endless plains.

"Was the ocean crossing frightening?" She pinned my hair with sure hands. "I'd be wary to do such a thing."

I thought of the spinning pressure and cacophony of sound that always accompanied a trip through a wormhole, but that wasn't going to help. Imagining what it would be like to cross from North America to Ireland in those days, I recalled the one time I'd been far enough out on the ocean to feel completely insignificant, at the mercy of the sea.

"It was frightening in some ways," I answered, weaving a tapestry of lies. "The ocean is so big, the sky so endless, that the ship seems such a small thing in comparison. But fate was kind, and brought us over without heavy storms or sickness. And there were so many beautiful sunrises, and sunsets, and dolphins, and starry nights."

The sense of displacement flooded me, my racing heart thudding in my ears. I was so far back in time. I'd have to hide well to blend in. Hopefully I could pull it off.

This wasn't like the summer I spent working as a roving minstrel at a Renaissance Faire, pretending to be from the past for the tips of tourists, this was life-and-death acting. If Wallace thought I was a spy, would Annelle be reporting to him? Would she go through my coat?

I shot Annelle a smile in the mirror as she finished with my hair. She was brushing off my dress, cleaning splatters of mud from my skirts, when a knock sounded at the door. I followed her to the entrance and grabbed the saddlebags from the man who held them out, letting her carry the package from Madame Sabine.

I stowed them on the top shelf of the wardrobe with a terrible thought blooming. Had they snooped through my stuff? With Annelle standing too close for comfort, I opened each flap quickly. Everything as I'd left it. If they'd inspected my luggage, they'd put things back carefully. Good thing I'd had the AIO on me.

If only I could hide it better. Did I put it in the saddlebags, or leave it in my coat pocket?

Annelle cleared her throat behind me, and I turned away from the wardrobe, striding back to her. Muddy as my boots were, I had no excuse to keep her from wiping them down, and hoped she wouldn't look too closely at the design of the soles. Though she exclaimed, "These are curious boots indeed!" she took the questioning no further.

"I'm sorry for the mess." I stared at the pile of dried mud on the wood floor.

"Ach." She waved her hand once. "'Tis no fuss, milady. A quick sweep and it'll be gone. At least it is no longer on yerself."

I had to agree.

As I paced from one side of the room to the other, Annelle unwrapped the package from Madame Sabine, accompanied by oohs and ahhs over the lush gown. She swished the layers of silk into her arms, arranged them in the wardrobe, then took the plaid stole from the leather wrappings that spilled over the sides of the table.

Annelle draped the wool around my shoulders with motherly motions, saying. "It gets drafty in the halls."

I was grateful for the kindness in her hands as she arranged the fabric. The warmth hugged me, lending a much-needed measure of comfort, but it was the way she touched me that gave me confidence.

A knock came at the door, and a red-kilted man stepped in when Annelle opened it. "Yer presence has been requested, milady." He gave a formal bow and an apologetic look.

Killian's brother wanted to speak to me. I'd been warned, but I was nowhere near ready. Flame butterflies burned wispy lines inside my belly as I moved toward the door.

Stiff-backed, chin lifted, I followed the red-kilted man down stone stairs. Halfway down, we passed a tapestry that stole my breath. Lit by a lantern in a sconce, the scene on the weaving showed the oak that had delivered me to this world, with the pool of water spread before the giant tree. Even in the shadowy corridor, I could make out the face in the water. A woman's face—one that made my heart tumble down the stairs, though my feet didn't falter.

The man kept his pace, not hearing my silent gasp, not looking back to see my eyes widen, or my chest rise and fall. It was all I could do to control my breathing and not turn claustrophobic in my bodice.

Eventually, we stopped at a door near the front entrance. The man knocked, then opened it for me with a quiet creaking of hinges. He nodded as I passed him on my way into the room, where Killian and Wallace waited.

I almost tripped when I saw the bronze dragon hanging on the far wall, my dreamlike-disconnect from reality doing a nosedive. The circular shape was almost exactly like the dragon that curled around the pendant at my throat, but this one was nearly four feet wide and had what appeared to be a ruby shining in its eye. Maybe I was on the right path to find the red dragon after all. It took a tremendous amount of willpower to pull my focus away from the sculpture and face Killian's brother.

Though I clutched my skirts to restrain myself from touching my necklace, Wallace's glance went there anyway. Half-sitting on a massive wooden desk that dominated the room, he tipped his head sideways. I turned to Killian, who gestured to a seat by the fire. He lowered into the leather chair next to me, leaning back in a relaxed manner, even as his gaze remained sharp on his brother.

"Ye'll forgive the lateness of the hour," Wallace leaned forward, "but there are things that must be understood before the morn."

I nodded. All I wanted to do was study the dragon on the wall. I could sense something from it, like a kind of music I couldn't quite hear.

"Whisky?" Wallace gestured toward a bottle set on a side table. Both men had glasses of the amber liquid.

I shook my head with a polite smile, and the questions began.

"Killian said ye come from a place called British Columbia." Wallace frowned at me. "I've never heard of it, and I am a learned man. What is it like there, in yer home?"

"It's wild and beautiful." I caught myself about to wring my hands and clasped them instead. "Much like your Highlands, but with fir, cedar, and poplar trees rather than the oak, ash, and pine I've seen here. The mountains are taller and sharper." My cheeks flushed with his penetrating look. I pressed on, pure fiction tumbling from my mouth. "There are few settlements that far west, as most of the cities are in the eastern portion of the country, but my family was part of an expedition that reached all the way to the Pacific Ocean, on the far side of the continent, and we settled there when I was a young girl. Last year, I lost my husband to the sea, and my parents passed away two years prior from sickness."

Lies. They tasted like flat notes as I wove my words in a forced sort of music that had no melody. A story made of need, because the truth was too bizarre and dangerous.

Killian shifted in his seat and brought his whisky to his lips. Wallace stared me down like an inquisitor. My dragon necklace drew my hand like a magnet. I traced the crisscrossing lines on my stole, my voice strange in my ears, witnessing my own performance.

"I had nothing to comfort me there but the trees, so I set off on a pilgrimage to the east. I wanted to cross the ocean and see the isles I'd been told of in my childhood. My mother's grandfather was a Scot—a Sinclair." I pulled a name from the hazy clan-map in my mind, which I'd studied for my last school report, and hoped the clan both existed here and was far enough away that Wallace didn't send me packing. "I don't know much about his family, though. I was raised far from relatives, other than my parents."

I was definitely talking too much.

"So ye braved the ocean crossing yerself, and came alone to Ireland, and from there to Scotland?" Wallace's inquiring tone was laced with suspicion.

"I did." I gave a curt nod. "It was an adventure."

"Where did ye stay in Ireland?"

I panicked inwardly and answered in vague sweeps of untruths. "I stayed in many places. The folk I met were kind, and the endless shades of green in the countryside had me in awe."

Wallace narrowed his eyes. "What is yer intention here in Scotland, in Duart?"

"Intention?" I looked at the dragon behind him, taking strength from it, from a piercing intuition that said there was more to my being brought here than chance. I calmed my voice. "I am here by invitation from your brother."

I'm here because I appeared before him by the oak in the tapestry in the stairwell, stepping through time to answer the call of a dragon.

Killian nodded and gave his brother a hard look. "She is, indeed."

"And yer intentions with my brother then?" There was the hint of a growl in Wallace's voice.

Fighting fatigue and annoyance, I drew myself taller in my seat. Surely Killian had explained it to him. "Your brother has been respectful, generous, and exceptionally pleasant company."

"She didnae ken, Wallace." Killian finally spoke. "Be at peace. I didnae tell her who I was until this morn. Once ye have time to spend with her, ye'll discover Shelta has truly traveled from a far land, for she knows little of our customs and has strange ones of her own. Her dream of finding a new life led her to Scotland, and her courage drew me."

The brothers stared each other down. After a minute, Wallace looked at me. Though his eyes still held suspicion, the fierceness faded. He gestured to my stole. "Ye wear Maclean tartan."

"Yes." I stroked the wool. "It's lovely."

"It was a gift." Killian stood up. "And now, brother, it's time we let the lady retire. She's traveled far, and we'd a long day in the coach." The set of his jaw left no question that the interrogation was over.

I rose, taking the hand he offered.

"Very well." Wallace seemed to concede, but he leaned forward again. "One more question, if ye'd be so kind."

I eyed him, waiting.

"Where'd ye get that necklace?" Wallace pointed with his eyes to the pendant at my neck.

All I could do was exhale. I finally let myself trace the familiar pattern—the wings, the tail, the turned head and notched eye. I'd never thought much about the necklace until now, other than feeling drawn to it. I'd come across it newly through a wormhole four jumps back, taking it at first as something I could use to barter. But I'd kept it, becoming attached to it as my dragon dreams came more and more frequently.

I opted for the truth. "I found it many years ago on the branch of a tree, and thought it was beautiful. I couldn't help but notice you have a match on your wall." I glanced at the bronze dragon with its ruby eye.

"Aye," rumbled Wallace. "Curious, that."

Killian led me back through the castle in silence. I slowed before the tapestry on the stairs, but he gave a slight shake of his head and marched forward, carrying me along, my hand on his arm.

We didn't speak until we'd entered my room, the door left open behind us. I wanted it closed, wanted to question him. I missed the reassuring closeness we'd had in the carriage.

"Ye did well, lass." He brought my hand up for the brush of a kiss. When he let go, he took a step back. "I should leave ye to get some rest."

"The tapestry." I whispered the words, head tilted, questions in my eyes. "The dragon?"

"Shelta." He spoke my name low, an apology in the twist of his mouth. "There are many things I will tell you in time."

I pressed my lips together and took a step away from him, my chin lowered though I didn't mean to let it. Tired and fragile, overwhelmed by a whirlwind of thoughts that had no answers, I couldn't look at him.

"Of course. Good night, Killian."

He hesitated. His hand rose, upturned, but it only came a short way toward me before his fingers curled in and he dropped his arm to his side. "Good night, Shelta."

Chapter 12
Uninvited Guests

HOWEVER MUCH SLEEP I'd gotten, it wasn't enough. Annelle placed a tray on the small table, then went to the windows and drew the heavy curtains back. Light streamed in, making her dark, coiled hair shine. My mouth watered at the smell of cinnamon.

"Morning," I managed.

"Good morning, milady. I've brought ye some breakfast." She crossed the room with a dressing robe as I slid out of bed. "And there's water heating for yer bath. We'll be bringing it up in a little while, so keep the door to the bath closet closed once ye're finished in there."

"There's another entrance to it?" I imagined secret doorways and winding passageways.

"Aye, milady. We wouldn't want to carry water buckets through the halls proper." She smiled. "Now if ye'll just come see if the food is to yer liking, I'll leave ye for a bit so ye can wake up."

On the tray was an apple, a pretty clay pot with a lid to keep the porridge warm within, a boiled egg, and a large slice of fresh bread with butter. I assured her I would be quite happy with the food, and watched her disappear through the door, dark skirts swishing around her legs.

If Jess and Stevie were here, we'd be having coffee and joking about sleep deprivation superpowers. But they weren't here, and there wasn't any coffee. I reached for the teacup and sipped, trying to ground myself in my new reality.

The bath, filled by unseen hands, was divine. The warmth soothed the aches from so much sitting and riding. Annelle appeared not long after I dried and slipped into the dressing robe. I wished I could wear the clothing I'd been accustomed to—the clothes in the saddlebags on the top shelf of the wardrobe.

"Would ye like me to unpack for ye, milady?" She'd caught me looking at my luggage.

"No, thank you." No elaborating. The less I said on the subject, the better.

She carried on as if nothing weird had happened. "We'll find ye another dress, I'm sure, but this one is quite nice."

Her expert hands dressed me, layer by confounding layer of clothing, and soon I was outfitted in green again. Annelle draped the long plaid around me, bunching it in a fashionable way instead of looking as if I had a blanket hanging around my shoulders. When she produced a gold brooch from her pocket and used it to fasten the wrap at my chest, my mouth fell open.

The dragon. Again.

"It matches yer necklace." Her eyes darted to mine for a split second. "Killian chose it for ye."

"Oh." The sound barely made it out of my mouth. I cleared my throat. "That was very kind of him."

She watched me in the mirror as I touched the brooch. "Are ye alright, milady?"

I looked like a deer caught in headlights. "Oh, it's just that it's all so different." I gave a breath of a laugh, playing the *I'm from Canada* card. "In the mountains where I lived, we worked the land and walked the wilderness. It was rugged and uncultivated, and I guess so were the customs. This dress, the way you pin my hair so perfect—having someone to help me at all—this is new to me."

She smiled wide, showing two crooked teeth that didn't detract from her beauty one bit. "Well, ye've followed your heart to Scotland, and now here ye are in a castle, with a lady's maid, wearing a beautiful dress which, though ye might feel it strange, looks wonderful on ye. And so, what would ye like to do? My lord Killian said I should show ye around, this morn. Would that suit ye?"

She spoke like a friend, making me relax a degree or two. "That would be wonderful." My fingers traced the tail of the dragon on the brooch. Its diamond eye caught the light and made my throat tighten, like the hand of fate was around my neck, squeezing.

I forced myself to lift my head, and followed Annelle out the door.

She led me through the corridor, and I peered through pillar-framed openings down to the main hall below. My eyes roamed woven landscapes and battle scenes, fingers sliding along the cold marble top of a table or the smooth wood frame of a painting.

Having exhausted the top level, we headed down the wide stone stairs where I'd seen the tapestry the night before. When we came to the landing midway, seeing no one at the bottom and no one above, I stopped in my tracks and stared at the weaving.

A shaft of morning light illuminated the scene. A woman's face shone in the water, her hair like copper ablaze. Surrounded by banks of moss, the spring flowed into its creek while the mighty oak tree towered behind, crowned in the colors of fall. Embroidered ropes of gold and red ran around the border of the tapestry, intertwined in complex knots. At each corner were runes.

The perspective was impossibly close to what Killian would've seen when I came through the portal, making a tingle stretch from my spine out through every nerve in my body. Otherworldly recognition. Déjà vu times a thousand.

Annelle hovered behind me, her voice a hush. "Milady?"

"Annelle, this place, does it have a story?" I murmured the question.

"Aye." She stepped closer, not to be overheard. "'Tis the Spring of Brighid, the goddess. Her magic regenerates, bringing life anew. The World Tree connects sky and earth." She gestured toward the oak in a small movement. "It represents the cycles of life, of lifetimes, and the transformations we have as we live."

She paused, still at my side. Was she deciding how much to tell me? "What are the symbols in the corners?" I asked. "The significance of the knotwork?"

There was a pause so long I didn't think she would answer, but she was waiting. Listening. Someone came around the corner and started up the stairs. Annelle turned to face me, fussing with my brooch and shawl. The man nodded as he passed, I nodded back, and he continued on. I didn't breathe properly until his footsteps faded. Voices carried up from somewhere on the first floor. I wondered if one of them was Killian's.

Annelle lowered her head and spoke quickly. "The runes are of the elements: air, fire, water, and earth. The lines intertwine to represent how all things are interconnected, and the unending flow of time."

The unending flow of time.

"How do you know all this?" I asked, knowing I shouldn't. The World Tree was an accepted thing to these people. Alive. Real. Shards of puzzle pieces fell into place, and a dangerous hope bloomed in my chest.

"It's a clan legend." Annelle's mouth drew together, telling me I'd pressed far enough. "A very old legend."

Reluctantly, I followed her down the stairs. The sense of power that emanated from the tapestry diminished as I left it behind.

Annelle toured me around the first floor, giving me the lay of the land. When we entered the library, the smell of leather, paper, wood, and dust made me smile. Light shone in through the biggest windows I'd seen in the castle, illuminating chairs and a large table at the center of the room. Hide-bound books made my fingers dance when I ran them tenderly over the spines.

"Do you mind if we stay awhile?" I asked, tearing my eyes away from the shelves.

"As long as ye like." She smiled and retrieved a book. A minute later she'd settled into a chair, shoes off, feet curled beneath her, grinning at me over the top of her book, and I liked her all the more.

Facing the shelves again, I wrestled with the weight of time. I was used to entire buildings filled with books, but here, now, they were rare enough that a castle this grand only had four tall bookshelves.

Starting at the top left, I systematically worked my way through. I skipped over copies of the Bible, other religious texts, history and war, and a whole collection of tomes that reeked of law. There were books in Latin, French, German, Spanish, and other languages I couldn't identify, mixed in like they were organized according to subject.

Some had plain leather covers, with lettering on the spines only, while others were richly decorated, their thick hide worked with symbols or knotwork, flowers and vines framing ornate titles. Shakespearean tomes dominated one shelf, with multiple copies of several dramas as if they were used for live readings.

I fell into a book of ballads for a bit, but returned it to the shelf after skimming a third of the pages and finding no mention of dragons or time travel. Most of the songs were about love, loss, sailing, and deceit.

Philosophy. Mythology. Maritime pursuits. Part of me wanted to open each book to taste the words, the voice of the writer, the essence of story or subject, but I sensed Annelle, and glanced over my shoulder to find her watching me.

If she was reporting to Wallace, it would look like I was rifling through every book looking for something. Which was exactly what I was doing.

I picked a collection of Celtic mythology, the only title I saw in English amidst several in what I guessed were Gaelic and Norse. Choosing a chair kitty-corner from Annelle, I slipped my boots off, tucked them to the side, and curled up as best I could in the bodice and layers of skirts.

Though the writing proved dry, a section about goddesses caught my attention. Brighid was one of those mentioned, associated with hearth, home, childbirth, and springs.

The author recounted a story handed down through oral tradition. It was said that Brighid once fell in love with a mortal, a king of men who befriended dragons as easily as the goddess. They'd had less than a year together before he was betrayed by someone close to him. Pierced by an arrow, he died out of reach of his immortal lover. When Brighid found out, she destroyed her lover's killer, and buried her beloved in a ritual that called on the World Tree. She planted an acorn above his body, its sapling consuming the mortal king's flesh and bones until it became a mighty oak.

As Brighid mourned, her tears cut a hole through the earth, plummeting into an underground cavern. Her grief turned the cavern into a lake, filling it until water spilled over, carving out a pool and a creek that cut through several worlds. At the roots of her beloved, submerged in sweet water laced with sorrow, the goddess gave birth, and bound her child to the World Tree.

My mouth hung open as I read the next paragraph, which explained the magic of Brighid's spring. If someone knelt before the water with a pure heart and deep desire, and spoke with love in their words, the goddess would grant them a wish.

I stared at the page, thoughts racing, the oak and spring clear in my mind. Killian had been kneeling, and there had been a woman's face in the water. The goddess. She existed.

She had to.

I'd come through this World Tree—the one in this legend.

Hoping for more, I turned the page. At the top, a trinity knot curled its three loops, drawn in ink, shaded as if it shimmered like the embroidery on my blue gown. Below, it read:

> *The trinity knot symbolizes the cycles of life: maiden, mother, and crone. Earth, sea, and sky. Life, death, and rebirth. Mind, body, and soul. God, Goddess, and creation.*
>
> *The sacred trinity of maiden, mother, and crone exists in all humans, woman and man. The maiden is freedom, growth, and beauty. She is dawn. The blooming of spring. A maiden's innocence is at once wonderous and dangerous, as confidence can give way to recklessness.*
>
> *The mother is nurturing and manifestation. The fullness of summer. A mother gives life, but she also takes on great responsibility and personal sacrifice.*
>
> *The crone is the night in winter. Wisdom. Visions. Prophecy. Death and rebirth. She has a kind of freedom that only comes with perspective and loss, acceptance and humility. When the crone speaks, listen.*

I read the page twice, its words like the ringing of a bell that tolled in my soul.

The next chapter launched into a different subject entirely. An hour later, my stomach growled as I finished a story about a trio of warrior goddesses that reigned over a bloody battle. I closed the book with a long breath, still thinking about Brighid.

My boots padded over the floor as I returned the book to its shelf, sliding it carefully into place, and stroked the leather. I'd come back here another time and keep searching.

"Annelle, would you please show me the kitchen?" A snack was as good an excuse as any to see behind the scenes of the castle, perhaps a secret passageway or two. Always better to know my way around and have places to hide. Never knew when they might come in handy.

Annelle's eyes widened ever so slightly at my request. "Of course, milady."

She shelved her book, and led me to a door hidden behind a tapestry on the far wall, where we entered a hallway wide enough for two people to pass if they were friendly about it. The dim corridor widened as we descended a set of stairs and moved toward the sound of voices.

The kitchen was big and bright, orderly and chaotic at the same time. The cook instructed two helpers on what must've been the makings of lunch or dinner. One chopped garlic on a large wooden cutting board, the other stirred a tablespoon of something peppery into whatever was bubbling away in the large pan.

"Whatever you're making," I said to the cook when she turned her sharp eyes on me, "it smells wonderful." I knew I'd walked into her domain, so I gave her a cautious grin, questioning whether this had been a good idea.

"Milady." Her capped head bobbed in a curt nod. She was tall, and looked down her nose at me through squinted eyes. "Can I get ye something?"

I breathed a nervous laugh, deciding I probably shouldn't have interrupted her. "That would be lovely. I mostly wanted to see the kitchen and thank you, but I'd love another piece of that bread I had at breakfast, if there's any left."

"Thank me?" She put one hand on her ample hips and added a handful of green leaves to a giant pot on the back burner of the stove. "For what?"

"You and your staff." I gestured toward them. "For the food."

"All ye've had yet is a simple breakfast." Her mouth made a skeptical rainbow shape.

"Think of it as thanks in advance for everything I'll eat while I'm here." My hands went out, palms up. "I'm Shelta Raine, from Canada, but you probably know that already."

"Aye, and they call me the Cook, but my name's Malva. Ye want bread only? How 'bout a berry scone? I've made 'em for tea later."

I was tempted, but shook my head. "Just a slice of bread for now, if it's easy. I look forward to teatime, though."

She produced a loaf, cut a thick slice onto a plate and slid over a dish of butter. "Ye want milk? Or ale, or wine?"

"Water would be great, if there's drinking water handy." I scooped butter with my knife, spreading it on the bread.

She eyed me like the stranger I was, then walked away, returning with a cup of clear, cold water that sloshed as she put it down before me. "Ye come to my kitchen, and all ye want is bread and water?" As an afterthought, she added, "Milady."

I smiled again, hoping to win her over with kindness. "I love bread, what can I say?"

She squinted at me, shook her head, then walked away to orchestrate her craft. A few minutes later, halfway through my piece of bread, a bell rang in a series of quick bursts. Everyone tensed, myself included.

The cook barked at her assistants, who resumed their work with vigor. Three people ran through the hallway past the kitchen door. "Ye might be missed, milady," said Malva, before turning her back and getting on with lunch.

I finished chewing in a hurry and downed the water. The part of me that had gone hungry before wanted to pocket the remainder of the bread. I left it on the plate and let Annelle lead me out, through the narrow passages.

"The bell means we have visitors," she said, and quickened our pace.

We emerged into the library, panting a little. Annelle immediately fixed my hair and smoothed my clothes. I studied her furrowed brow, hoping I hadn't gotten her in trouble with my strange requests.

"Thank you." I dropped my voice low, like when we'd talked by the tapestry.

She stopped fussing and held my gaze. After a moment she inclined her head, the hint of a smile at the corners of her mouth. "Milady."

We entered the main hall together. There were a good deal more people in it than the last time we'd walked through. Guards stood along the walls clad in red tartans and stiff jackets, swords at their belts, battle-axes at their sides. With a gust of wind and the creaking song of heavy wood, the front doors opened. In strode Killian and Wallace, followed by six strangers and more Maclean guards.

Charlie materialized next to me, smelling of outside, curiosity brightening his eyes. He was taller than me, though he was less than half my age. Without a word, he inclined his head. I tipped mine in hello. Annelle retreated, giving us space.

The entourage of men marched straight toward us. Killian saw me standing next to his son, slowed his stride, and beckoned with a small gesture. Charlie stepped forward, and I went with him, my stomach clenching as the group stopped before us.

"May I present my son," said Killian, "Charles Maclean, and Lady Shelta Raine." He moved to my side.

I gave a small nod. A sense of unease snaked through the castle.

"This is Sir Seann Lynch, a distant relation, and his companions." Killian gestured as he introduced them. "They're on pilgrimage to Iona, transporting an important relic to the monastery."

I saw the mistrust in Wallace's face, his eyes narrowed far more dangerously than they'd been last night. The group of men gave brief greetings, speaking to Charlie and Killian. I was expected to keep quiet, apparently. Fine by me.

A minute later, Wallace led them farther into the hall.

Killian turned his back to the strangers, standing before me. His fingers touched the dragon brooch lightly. "That looks good on ye."

"Thank you," I answered, utterly aware of his son, who hadn't moved from my side.

A splendid old gentleman strode down the lower part of the stairs and into the hall. He had a crooked smile, a penetrating gaze, and a fierce pride. Chest lifted, he rested one hand on the sword at his hip. He wore a bright red tartan, a dark grey jacket, and a calculating expression I'd seen before on Killian's face.

"Seann Lynch." The older gentleman lifted his chin toward the new arrival. "Ye've not been to this castle since ye were a boy of nine and getting into trouble in every corner." Without waiting for an answer, he turned his head, his gaze swinging toward me. "Ye, however, I've not met in my castle before."

"Hello." My smile betrayed my sense of awe. The man had such presence; the whole room was attuned to him. And, therefore, me.

Killian stood so I was sandwiched between him and his son. "Shelta, may I present ye to the chief of this clan and castle, Sir Malcolm Maclean."

I curtsied as carefully as I had for Prince Charles.

"Lady Shelta, all the way from Canada, I've heard." Sir Malcolm approached with a sparkle in his eye. "I look forward to hearing of yer adventures, my dear. It seems, however, that I have other guests to attend to at the moment." He kissed my hand lightly, then walked toward the gathering of men standing beneath his roof.

Killian stayed by my side. Charlie took a step away from us, alert and still as a guard as he watched his grandfather. I slipped my hand into Killian's offered arm and tried not to look nervous.

Sir Malcolm addressed the eldest priest, introduced as Father Galloway. "What is it ye carry, Father?"

"We bring the rosary and altar cross of Saint Fianaí back to their proper resting places on Iona." The priest's voice carried sincerity, his words hinting at music.

"Our beloved ancient abbot." The chief patted the priest's arm. "Good of ye to bring his things home." He turned to the other men. "Do ye ride to Iona the day?"

Lynch raised his cleft chin and spoke. "Sir, I have a message for you from my mother. I had hoped to stay long enough for you to respond, and ask your hospitality to ride out in the morn, so we may come to Iona in good light."

Something about him made the hair on my neck stand up.

"I see. In that case, we shall make our table ready for ye." The chief held out his hand. "The message?"

Lynch pulled a sealed envelope from his jacket pocket. The chief took it, glanced at me with a sideways nod, then strode off and left the newcomers in the care of Wallace, who proceeded to guide them away, saying something about lodging in the barracks.

Killian slid his hand behind my back, leaning toward me. His touch was warm, hidden beneath the draped plaid of my stole. "Charlie," he addressed his son, though he looked at me, "would ye be so kind as to walk Shelta through the gardens?"

"Aye, Da, easy enough."

Killian's thumb rubbed the velvet of my bodice, secrets in his eyes. "I think ye'll enjoy it." Turning his gaze to Charlie, he spoke in the quiet tone of a father saying nice things to his son. "Take her to meet Rodric, lad. Find her a dirk, and show her a few things to do with it."

One of Charlie's eyebrows twitched. Otherwise, he had an excellent poker face. "Aye, Da."

I shut my mouth, which had fallen open again.

Killian turned serious as he addressed me, close. "I want ye to have a blade at all times, Shelta. Do ye understand?"

I gave a small nod. What was I going to do with a dagger? I had a pocket knife in my first-aid kit, but that was for cutting things, not people.

"It seems I'll be occupied much of the afternoon, but Charlie is good company. Tell him if there's anything ye need." As a sort of afterthought, he added, "Wear the blue gown to dinner."

I smiled, thinking of the dress. "Killian?"

"Aye, lass?"

"I like your father."

"Aye. I thought ye might." He gave me a wink, directed a nod toward his son, and was gone in a few long strides.

Aware of the absence of warmth on my back where Killian's hand had been, I turned my attention to Charlie. He was a little taller than me, with dark hair and chocolate-colored eyes that held more than a little mischief in them, much like his father's. There was a difference in the structure of his nose, though, the curve of his brow and lips. His mother showing through.

My smile reached my eyes, but felt tight on my lips. I liked the boy; I just didn't know how to be around him. "It seems you've become my guide."

His smile wavered. "Aye, my lady."

Either overhearing the conversation or reading minds, Annelle appeared with my cloak. She draped it around my shoulders, and Charlie gestured for us to go. I matched his stride as we walked through a set of doors at the back of the castle and went outside, into the courtyard garden.

Wind blew at my hair, and I raised the hood on my cloak to block the chill. The walkways were tended, the perennials cut back. Branches and not-yet-fallen leaves rustled in the trees at the edge of the courtyard, where benches were tucked into corners, positioned to view the sculpture that dominated the center of the circle and made my blood thunder through me.

Despite the brooch, despite the dragon art on the wall last night, I had a hard time believing what I saw. The statue's wingspan was at least fifteen feet wide.

I walked over as if entranced. White stone had been carved into a dragon that looked at once fierce and protective, its wings arching above my head. Its tail circled around, held aloft before its feet, one of which grasped an enormous stone battle-axe. It stood upon a wide platform of rock, un-carved but for the knotwork that twined around its base with the same elemental runes I'd seen in the tapestry.

The dragon's words from my dream the night before I'd left Jess and Stevie's echoed in my mind. Come. Find me. It's time.

Charlie stopped next to me. "Do ye like him?"

"He's magnificent," I whispered.

"This is Gillean's Treasure," Charlie explained with the tone of a tutor. "He's the guardian of our clan and this land. Dragons are movers of power and energy, gatekeepers to other worlds. They possess universal wisdom."

Gatekeepers to other worlds. My heart migrated to my throat. "What's the significance of the axe?"

"It is the sacred weapon of Clan Maclean. Gillean of the Battle Axe is our namefather, the king from which we descended."

"Ah." That explained why the guards carried axes. It did not explain why I dreamed of dragons almost every night, or why my blood sang as I stared at the figure before me, my fingers going first to my pendant, then to the brooch pinned atop my heart.

I hadn't found a live dragon yet, but it seemed I was on the right track.

CHAPTER 13
BORROWED BLADES

CHARLIE WALKED NEXT to me as we made a slow tour of the garden courtyard. He kept the conversation going with the bearing of an ambassador and the quirkiness of a fifteen-year-old.

Trying for truth when I could, I spun stories for Charlie as we meandered into a different section of the estate. I warmed my hands in the folds of my cloak and tried to avoid personal details. The likeness of the garden statue to the red dragon in my dreams distracted me to the point where I barely heard Charlie's response to my fabricated tales of "home."

As if I'd ever had a proper home.

He led me through the archway of an outside wall, into a large courtyard. "The barracks are there." He pointed to a long building on the far side of the field. "And if ye'll come this way, I'll take ye to meet the armourer, Rodric."

I tried to look interested, but my fingers kept tracing the circle shape of the dragon at my chest. I wanted desperately to understand. Was there more here than legends? Did dragons exist this far back in time? Every instinct and thrum of music in my soul told me that the red dragon from my dreams could help me control the time travel.

I had to find him.

A thick wooden door opened as we walked toward the stone building that hugged one side of the castle, and out stepped a shrewd-looking, wiry man. He was not as large as the guards standing to either side of the blocky entrance, but the way he moved captivated me. He emanated prowess.

"Charlie, lad." The man inclined his head, brown hair not quite long enough to fall in his dusk-colored eyes.

"Rodric." Charlie made a subtle bow. "May I present Shelta Raine, come to Scotland from Canada."

Rodric executed a catlike bow without taking his gaze off mine. "Milady."

"Lady Shelta met my father on her travels," Charlie went on. "He's asked that I take her to ye for a blade, and an idea of what to do with it."

Rodric looked me over. Without a word, he gestured for us to follow him inside.

Swords, axes, muskets and crossbows lined the walls in orderly rows, with an assortment of other deadly instruments scattered around like accessories. Charlie and I went to a long, scarred wooden table, while Rodric crossed to a rack that held a collection of daggers, and returned with a handful of choices.

He slid a small, sheathed dagger toward me. "This one, ye can hide just about anywhere. It's wise to have a blade on ye at all times, and handy for it not to be seen."

I gripped the smooth wooden hilt and slid the dagger out of the sheath. It was a touch longer than my hand, and the blade glinted in the low light.

"It's called a sgian-dubh," Charlie informed me in his tutor's voice, standing to my left.

"It's lovely." I repeated the sounds he'd made in my head so I'd remember the word. *Ski-en-doo, ski-en-doo.* "I don't know that I'd be able to do anything with it, other than cut food or flowers, but I quite like it."

Rodric graced me with his version of a smile, wry but real. "Ye'll do what ye have to with it, lass, and hopefully it willnae be more than that. Now, try this." He held a much larger blade, arm extended with the dagger's handle toward me.

"A dirk," Charlie said quietly.

The hilt was carved antler, polished beautifully. There was a small, sleek metal guard and matching round pommel. The blade was long, its edge was keen, and it frightened me a little.

"This I definitely don't know what to do with." Its weight felt wrong in my hand.

"Try a few more. Get used to the feel of them."

He gave me four more dirks. I chose one with a hilt of rose-colored wood, a trinity knot carved into each side, and a scabbard of thick leather that matched.

Rodric spent the next hour instructing me in the art of knife fighting. My lesson was conducted inside the armory, because, as Charlie said, "It wouldn't do to have our guests see a lady with a blade."

I struggled to accept the fact that I was being trained to kill another person. Cloak off, face flushed, I focused on things that seemed important—the need to thrust powerfully in order to break through tissue, where to stab to avoid bones, and which vital arteries could be slashed with the small knife—but it all seemed surreal.

Finally, I reached the limit of what I was able to take in and put up a hand, closing my eyes against a surge of nausea. "I'm sorry, I think I need a break."

"That's enough for now." Rodric gave a quick nod, as if agreeing with himself. "Let's find places for ye to hide yer blades."

Both men were pleased to discover that I wore tall boots. I sat in a chair, my breath shallow, while Rodric stitched loops of leather on the inside of my brown boots to hold the daggers. He told me to hide the sgian-dubh "elsewhere" if I was wearing slippers, and to ask Annelle to sew pockets in my skirts for the blades.

I agreed, but my head spun and it was all I could do keep a pleasant expression on my face. My fingers circled the dragon at my chest. It calmed me, somehow, that simple act of touching the smooth gold, an adornment that was worth more than anything I'd ever owned. Other than the AIO, which was, at this point, priceless.

Better not to think of that.

Eventually, with daggers pressing against the outsides of my calves and weighing each step, Charlie and I emerged from the weapons room into the grey day. I sucked in fresh air, but the bodice prevented my ribs from full expansion. Dizzy, I grabbed onto Charlie's arm. "I think we missed lunch by a long shot."

His stuttering reaction told me it hadn't even occurred to him.

"It's alright." I wasn't going to pass out. Probably. "I do need to eat, though."

"Of course, my lady. My apologies." Charlie cut across the courtyard in the shortest possible route to the kitchen.

"Ach!" Malva raised a large wooden spoon as we entered her domain and its torrent of delicious smells. "Now ye bring me his young lordship for bread and water?"

She put a mug of water in front of me, all I asked for at first. I sank into a stool and sipped it, leaning against a wall.

"Actually, I brought her. It seemed the fastest way." Charlie spoke respectfully to the cook. "It's my fault she missed lunch."

Malva shook her head, but smiled. "Well, milord, let's say I give ye a bite here so the lass doesn't swoon on us, then have a proper tea brought up?"

We left the kitchen after I'd had a boiled egg and another slice of bread and butter. Charlie navigated the maze of servants' corridors with ease, finally taking me through the hidden entrance of a sitting room on the second floor. It had a low table set between pastel-colored chairs and sofas, and a commanding view of the gardens below. Tea was served within minutes of our arrival, accompanied by sandwiches and scones.

"My mother loved this room." Charlie's eyes softened.

"I can see why." I took a sip of honeyed tea. "What was her name?"

"Aislin." His voice carried a mix of sorrow and pride. "Her portrait is just there, if ye'd like to see it."

I put down my teacup and followed him to a framed canvas on the wall opposite the window, positioned as if to allow the woman in the painting to look out over the gardens. She had blue eyes, bright hair, and fine features, which I could see subtly in her son, though his coloring matched Killian's. I wondered at the boy who'd lost his mother when he was only five, and how he'd turned into the young man who'd given me tips on how to best use my daggers.

"She was very beautiful," I said softly.

"Yes, she was," Charlie agreed.

He stood quiet, next to me. I studied the design of Aislin's dress and the skill of the artist who'd captured her likeness, but mostly I thought of how horrible it would be to let myself get close to this family, only to disappear on them.

What choice did I have?

Back at the table by the window, I sipped my tea. A large bird sped across the sky, making me think of dragons.

"My father—" Charlie said, then stopped. He tried again. "Da speaks highly of ye."

"I think highly of him as well."

"Ye traveled here from Canada." Charlie's tone was casual, but I could tell he was fishing for something. "Was it to Scotland specifically that ye wanted to come?"

"Yes." No. Not even a little bit. I was supposed to go forward in time.

"Do ye plan to remain here? In Scotland, I mean."

"I really don't know." Damn. What was I supposed tell him? "I guess I didn't think past the point of getting here and finding whatever I found."

He nodded, still searching. "What have ye enjoyed most so far in yer visit?"

"I don't think I could choose any one thing, Charlie." I hoped my smile looked natural, hoped my eyes didn't give away my uncertainty. "Stirling Castle was a treat, and the land is beautiful. But the magic has been in the discovery along the way, I think. And in your father's company."

That was what he wanted. I could see it in the flash of his eyes. He wanted to know how I felt about Killian. Of course he did.

How did I feel, exactly? I had no right to give this boy hope that I could become his father's next wife, yet here I was. The danger of my existence bit at my mind like the daggers that pressed against my legs.

Chapter 14
Double-edged Surprises

ANNELLE ENTERED MY room with a snicker, observing me sprawled sideways across the bed with complete disregard of proper orientation, blankets bunched under my head for a pillow.

"I'm here to help ye with yer gown for dinner," she said.

I groaned. Twilight had darkened into night outside the narrow windows. Annelle had brought me back to my room "for a wee rest" hours ago. I could've slept 'til morning.

Then I remembered the men who'd arrived earlier, and the daggers in my boots on the floor, and came awake in a hurry. "Right. Just a minute." I made my way to the basin to splash water on my face.

A short while later I stared at myself in the mirror, sparkling in blue and gold silk.

"This is one of the finest gowns I've seen. Ye wear it well." Annelle stood behind me, her words gentle. She double-checked that my hair was up to her standards of perfection, then went to the wardrobe to take the shawl that matched the dress from where it was folded on the shelf.

Too close to the pile of my belongings.

I watched in horror as the blue fabric caught on the saddlebags, which caught on my coat below, and everything came tumbling to the floor with a thud that echoed in my gut. One of the buckles was open, and my clothes spilled out, the velvet bag of crystals following.

Fists full of skirts, I almost tripped trying to get there, but wasn't fast enough to stop Annelle from starting to repack the leather bags. "Milady, I'll put it right," she insisted.

"It's okay." I took over. "It's just some old clothes." I stuffed them in, crystals beneath, glad my first-aid kit hadn't tumbled out, then pushed the bag all the way back on the top shelf.

Annelle picked up my jacket and went to hang it.

"Here, I'll get that," I said, and grabbed the coat out of her hands, my hand sliding to the pocket where my AIO was hidden.

Except when I squeezed for its familiar rectangular shape, it wasn't there.

Lightheaded, stomach plummeting as if I'd jumped from a great height, I shook the coat out and hung it up. A quick search of the secret pocket confirmed that my All-In-One device was indeed missing. Someone had taken it.

Sick to my stomach, I swallowed. Hung the coat. Walked to my boots in a daze. Knowing I needed to divert Annelle, whose confused expression told me she knew nothing about a missing piece of advanced technology, I brought out the daggers. "I almost forgot, I've been instructed to wear these, or at least one of them, at all times. I was to ask if you're able to sew pockets into my dresses for them."

"Aye, milady," Annelle answered with a raised brow. She placed the dirk in the slim drawer at the dressing table with hands that clearly knew how to handle blades. "Ye'll only have room for the wee one tonight, but I'll be sure the dirk finds its place in the green."

I clasped my hands so she didn't see that they shook, allowing her to secure the sgian-dubh in the garter that held up my left stocking. I felt like some kind of glamorous assassin, except for the fact that I didn't believe myself capable of killing anyone, and the missing AIO had me right rattled.

A knock made me jump. Annelle gave me a pat on the shoulder and a reassuring glance in the mirror before going to open the door. She slipped out as Killian stepped in.

He wore a red tartan and black jacket that made his dark hair even more striking than usual. His beard was neatly trimmed. The hilt of his dagger shone like it had been polished. My breath caught as his eyes narrowed and his mouth curled as he looked at me.

Killian crossed the space between us, and kissed my hand. "Ye look enchanting," he said, and took hold of my waist, standing close. Bold.

I drew as deep a breath as I could, blowing out through my lips. There was something electric about him, distracting me from what I knew I had to do. "Thank ye," I said, trying on the accent, then giving it up and leaning in, knowing full well my breasts were all but spilling over the top of the dress. "Killian, did you take something from my wardrobe?" If it wasn't him, I was in real trouble.

"Aye." He moved a breath closer, voice a warning rumble. "Ye hid it from me, Shelta. Ye lied to me." His grip was hot through the dress, and it crossed my mind how easily he could kill me if he wanted. What was the punishment for lying to a spy?

"I'm sorry," I whispered. "I should've thrown it into the river."

He cocked his head. "Why didn't ye? What was it?"

For a few seconds I couldn't say anything. Time warped my thoughts. I tried to breathe, ran out of space, and exhaled. Tried again. "Killian, that little device has thousands of songs on it and hundreds of images I've captured in the last few years of my life." Not to mention my research. My head swiveled back and forth as I spoke, as if my body didn't like where my mind was going. "All the songs I've written, every record of where I've come from— it's like giving up my entire history."

His hands slid behind me, almost lifting me off the floor as he leaned his mouth close to my ear. "A history that hasn't yet happened."

"Right." I couldn't pretend otherwise. "What did you do with it?"

"I threw it into the sea." His face hovered an inch from mine, creases at the corners of his eyes deepening as my face crumpled.

I fought to keep the anger from my voice. "Please tell me you're lying."

He shook his head. "I'm sorry, Shelta, but ye're lucky I found it and not Wallace."

"I'm sure I am," I managed, not feeling lucky at all. "But Killian—" I broke off, unable to find words for my frustration. The last tether to my previous life had been severed. I was falling into the sea with the AIO.

Killian's thumb traced my cheekbone. "I'm trying to keep ye safe, lass."

I forced something that resembled a smile.

He straightened and offered me his arm. "We'll be missed if we don't go to dinner."

"Of course." I tried to hide my devastation. My pulse pounded in my throat. He was my friend, was trying to protect me. So why did it feel like a betrayal? He could have at least asked me about it. Maybe I could have showed him how it worked, gone through pictures and listened to music—

I shook my head, cutting off the runaway thought. As far back in time as I was, the device was probably better at the bottom of the ocean, no matter how much I missed it, or how pissed off I was that he'd thrown it away.

Gathering my wits so I didn't show how upset I was, I slid a hand over the wool of Killian's jacket and let him lead me through the castle. My thudding heart seemed to take up too much space. Down the stairs we went, past the tapestry with the image of a goddess in the water. We were the last to arrive to dinner, and my cheeks burned as all eyes turned our way. Killian sat me next to him, with the hearth at our back. The heat of it hit me immediately.

The chief held court at the head of the table with Killian to his right and Wallace to his left. Opposite me sat Cristina, Wallace's wife. Charlie was to my right, and Wallace and Cristina's eldest daughter, Fione, sat across from him. Seann Lynch and the priest faced each other at the other end of the table. Father Galloway seemed to be the most relaxed one there.

I wanted to be forgotten, but I felt eyes constantly on me—many glances aimed at my breasts, which was understandable, considering how the corset pushed them into a shelf. I started on my bowl of soup, content to keep out of the conversation, half of which was lost to me in thick accents and fast words.

Every time I looked at Killian I imagined him standing on a cliff, tossing the AIO into deep water. I pushed food around on my plate when it came, unable to stomach more than a few bites.

Sweat started to bead at the nape of my neck, and I slipped the shawl from my shoulders, pretending not to notice Killian's glance at my cleavage, the glow of the fire flickering on his face.

Sir Malcolm tossed a question across the table. "How did ye come to assist the monastery with its delivery of the relics, Seann?"

Lynch paused in his eating, picking something from his teeth before speaking. "When the abbot learned of our relation, he asked me to come with my companions as guards for the relics. He knew I'd wanted to make the pilgrimage to Iona for years. It was an easy fit."

With a nod, the chief turned his fatherly gaze on me. "Tell me about Canada, Shelta. What kind of game do ye have there?"

"Well," a whole list of animals came to mind, "there are deer, elk and moose, which are the largest of the lot: bigger than a horse with an enormous rack of antlers on the males." I opened my arms as wide as they could go to demonstrate. He looked impressed. "And then we have different types of bears, mountain lions and bobcats, coyotes and wolves. The bigger and wilder the mountains, the bigger and more dangerous the wildlife.

"In one lake I visited, a very deep lake, there's a legend of an ancient creature of massive size that lives there. I thought of it more often than I should when I swam in the lake." I wondered if the legend of Nessie had begun yet.

"Ye swam in the lake?" Lynch's tone reeked of disapproval.

"Well, yes. Why wouldn't I?" I ignored the scattered laughter and went on without waiting for his answer, hoping the fire could be blamed for the heat in my cheeks. "There's quite a variety of birds, as well, from tiny jewel-colored hummingbirds, to eagles whose wingspan would be at least as large as your reach, Sir Malcolm."

"My, my." The chief brought his arms out for comparison.

"It sounds like a wild land indeed," said Cristina with a smile.

"It is, yes." I nodded, wondering how to turn the spotlight to someone else.

"Do ye plan to return?" asked Lynch.

"I—I don't think so," I stuttered. "It would be a lonely life for me there now, and a treacherous journey to return."

"You braved it once to come here," he persisted.

"Yes." My reply was sharp, annoyed by the man, irritated that I had to make up more lies. "I was lucky I didn't encounter misfortune on the way here. I believe a return trip would be tempting fate." I turned to the priest, anxious to be out of the limelight and all-too aware of Wallace's suspicious gaze. "Please forgive my ignorance, Father, but what faith do you practice?"

"Christianity, my dear." The priest's face wrinkled in kindly creases. His voice was friendly, devoid of the holier-than-thou tone Lynch had used. "A kind of Christianity that aims at unity of faith, rather than its division."

"That's rather lovely," I told him, hoping he was telling the truth.

"I'm glad ye think so." He gave me a soft smile. "And what faith do ye follow?"

Well, that was stupid. I'd dug myself a hole.

"I confess there was no church in our small mountain settlement," I answered, hoping the lie landed well. "My family had more need to tend to the tasks of survival than to teach me any particular faith."

The priest's bushy eyebrows rose, along with several other pairs around the table.

"I've read the Bible, of course." Would that redeem me? They didn't need to know I'd read the book with severe skepticism, or how much the politics of the Church had influenced its modern-day versions. "I suppose I have my own way of connecting with the divine, my own relationship with prayer. I do believe in God, in Christ, in Mother Mary." In divine feminine as well as divine masculine. Do you believe in the goddess, Father?

"Ah, but ye need a priest to speak on yer behalf to God." Lynch used a voice that was meant to put me in my place. Or what he thought was my place.

Oh, the words I'd spill if he used that tone with me on the streets of Victoria. Jess would've given him an earful, had he pulled this misogynistic snobbery on our turf, and then Stevie would've hacked and drained the weasel's wallet.

"Do you really believe that?" The words left my mouth before I thought about them, and I plunged on, hoping I wouldn't say anything too damning. "It may be true that some people need the services of the church, but I don't believe God would ignore any of his children if they reached out with sincerity."

"Well said, my dear." Father Galloway gave me a tip of his head.

"Thank you." I forced a small smile, like I wasn't bothered, like the whole discussion had interested me in a pleasant way instead of making me want to flee the room or toss wine in the face of the irritating man who sat across from the priest.

Thankfully, Killian took the reins of the conversation, steering the subject into nonthreatening waters. I ate in silence, or tried to eat. The corset didn't leave much space for my stomach, nor did my roiling emotions.

After the meal, we moved to a sitting area decorated in reds and earth tones, where I was delighted to find a minstrel. I settled on a pine green sofa next to Killian to watch.

The musician, Gavin, had several instruments with him, and a strange-looking guitar cradled in his arms. It had a smaller body than I was used to, strung with five courses, or ten strings. I was so captivated by his music and the way his expressive mouth delivered the stories he told that I almost forgot about the knife pressing into my thigh and the fact that I might never see a photograph again, or listen to punk rock.

"Shelta has a rare gift in music," Killian announced after the third song. Instantly, all eyes were on me.

"Aye?" Killian's father leaned forward in his chair. "Will ye play for us?"

I didn't see how I could decline. These people had welcomed me into their home, and Killian had taken care of my every need. At least I could give back with my music. I smiled at the minstrel, who held the instrument out to me.

It was heavier than a modern guitar, the round body both awkward and comforting against my belly. I ran my hands over the carefully-shaped wood, touched the strings and took a breath, feeling into it, getting to know its spirit.

"I've never played a five-course guitar before." I spoke mostly to the musician who watched me with the fire flickering in his eyes, trying to pretend my audience wasn't there. "I'm used to six strings, or two courses of six to make a twelve string. But let me see what I can do."

The tuning was different, but I'd watched the bard's hands as he played, and my instinct guided me. Trying out a few chords, a melody took shape. Soon my voice and the resonance of the guitar filled the room.

Singing was like coming home to myself. Only once did I look up to see Killian's face bright with the spell of the music, his eyes full of affection. My fingers stumbled on the strings, and I closed my eyes, not wanting to lose the thread of ability that came without knowing, the rush of tapping into whatever magic made the music.

I finished the tune, letting the strings vibrate with the last chord. When I opened my eyes, it was to a murmur of appreciation and applause. Sir Malcolm leaned over and squeezed my hand. "Splendid, my dear. And ye've never played this instrument, truly?"

I shook my head. "I have not."

"Then it must be a fine treat to hear ye play one you know well." The chief tapped his fingers together. "Perhaps we should have an instrument made for ye."

The minstrel lit up, saying something about a luthier in Edinburgh, and next thing I knew we were having an in-depth discussion about the adjustments needed to make a six-string guitar. Once we wrapped that up, he produced a violin and asked if I played.

"No." I shook my head. "That's one instrument I've not yet taken time to master, and one that certainly needs devotion to do so."

"Well, lady," Gavin said in his musical voice, "perhaps ye can play another tune, and I will accompany ye?"

We made lovely music together: the little guitar and the clear, soaring voice of the violin. But as the night drew on, the tension in the room grew taught. Cristina and Fione excused themselves, and I found myself the only woman surrounded by men.

A guard approached Sir Malcolm and spoke something in his ear that made the chief's lips draw together. Killian's expression hardened around the edges of his eyes, his gaze moving to Lynch. Wallace looked like he was readying himself for war. The priest continued to enjoy the music, seemingly unaware.

As soon as we ended the next song, the chief stood and bid everyone goodnight. I gave the minstrel a smile as I handed his guitar back.

Fingers tingling from pressing down such thick strings, I leaned on Killian more than I wanted to going up the stairs, my ridiculous shoes rubbing blisters on the backs of my heels. Halfway up, I made him stop so I could take them off. He spared me a smile, but his eyes darted up and down the stairwell. I knew better than to ask him about the tapestry. Not now.

When we reached my room, Killian stepped inside and shut the door behind us. The click of the latch relaxed some small part of me, but all I wanted was to breathe a full breath.

He drew me to the center of the room and came as close as he'd been when we spoke before dinner, hands around my waist, his mouth near my ear. "There will be fighting, this night."

It shouldn't have surprised me, considering the warning the prince had given and the tension I'd felt between the men, especially with Lynch. Where had the others who'd come with him been this whole time?

"Lock the door and do not come out until I come for ye," warned Killian. "Two ships were spotted on the horizon. We expect their aim is Duart. We hold valuable secrets and a strategic position."

Two ships full? "Killian—"

"We're ready for them, Shelta. They think they're unexpected, but they're not. We're well armed with traps set. Our visitors are an unknown element, however. There'll be a guard outside yer door."

I held his eyes for a long moment. He was going to leave me in this room. Alone. Maybe I'd be safe; maybe I'd be trapped. Maybe I was hyperventilating.

Killian brought me close with one hand at my cheek. Then he straightened and began pulling pins from my hair as if it were the most natural thing for him to do.

"Killian?" I had to say something.

"Shelta?" His breath warmed my neck.

I lowered my voice. "I really wish you hadn't destroyed my AIO."

He stepped around to face me, skin creased at the edges of his eyes. "I'm sorry it hurt ye, lass." My lips pressed together as he added, "I wish ye hadn't lied to me."

I squished my toes into the rug. "I'm sorry I lied."

He brushed my cheek with the back of his fingers, and said, "I forgive ye."

Without waiting for me to respond, he stepped away to place the pins in the dish on the dressing table. My hair fell down around my shoulders. He moved like a predator as he came back, but I wasn't afraid. Well, maybe a little.

Killian closed the distance between us, hands warm on my waist. "Will ye forgive me for taking yer device?"

Such sincerity. I couldn't resist melting into it. "Yes," I whispered. My hands slid between the black wool of his jacket and his soft shirt, pulling him in. He responded to my touch, drawing me flush against him with a rumble that went through my chest.

"I do not want to leave ye right now." He tipped his forehead to mine. "But I must. Do not fear."

I made a sound between a growl and a whimper. "Keep yourself safe."

He brought his lips to mine, spiking my blood with fire. He surrounded me, crushing me with great care for far too brief a time.

I drew a bottomless breath, wanting more. Much more. I wanted him despite the fact that he'd destroyed my AIO, despite the fact that this was impossible.

I knew I shouldn't, but I wrapped my arms around his neck and guided his face back to mine. I pressed into him, opening my mouth to taste him. Fire. Want. Need. The man evoked desire on levels that surpassed any memory I had to compare, like flight and free fall at the same time. Exquisite torture.

Before letting myself get too far gone, I turned my head and placed it on his chest.

"Is that how ye feel then?" Killian's breath was hot on my neck.

"It is."

His eyes pinned mine for a long moment, then he stepped back and bowed. "I wish ye a good night, my lady." Killian kissed my fingers. My palm. My wrist. "I said I would protect ye, and I shall."

Speechless, I nodded. Each step he took away from me ripped the walls around my heart a little more; searing me with the knowing that any love I was fool enough to indulge in would inevitably be torn away.

Chapter 15
A Scare in the Night

I COULDN'T SLEEP.

Of course, I couldn't sleep. There were probably a few hundred warriors sneaking up on the castle, plus betrayal from within. And I wanted Killian, badly. I tried to distract myself with fantasies of what we'd be doing if there weren't a threat to be dealt with, but the quiet of the night made me edgy.

Worrying was a waste of time, fretting over something out of my control, but I couldn't help it. My mind ran in circles, resisting my efforts to meditate on my breath, relax my body, or repeat a mantra—techniques I'd learned from doing yoga in an attempt to rein in my anxiety.

With the dirk under my pillow and the sgian-dhub on the bedside table, I had weapons at hand, but I couldn't imagine myself using them against another person. My mind kept replaying the fight in Glasgow and the sound the man made when Killian's dagger took his life.

Enough with the tossing and turning. I slid out of bed and began to pace.

Wrapped in my dressing robe, I slipped the smaller knife into a pocket. I gripped the dirk in my right hand—sheath and all—and started to wear a trail in the large rug at the foot of the bed. Every so often I would walk, bare feet across the cold wood floor, to peek out the narrow window.

I could see nothing, could hear nothing, but the castle hummed with anticipation, as if the stone walls held a song. That was new, hearing music from a structure. If I'd had a piano, I could've translated it into actual sound. Instead, it formed in my head: a secret serenade marching into the dark, cloudy night.

The hair on the back of my neck rose as an acute sense of dread cut through the morphing melody that circled my mind. Time crystalized, and instinct required me to find out what danger lurked in the hall. It compelled me.

Without thought, my feet carried me through the bedchamber. Shaky fingers touched the lock. The music of the castle pounded in my head as I slowly slid open the bolt. Reaching past the noise in my mind, I listened hard. Heard nothing.

As soundlessly as I could, I eased open the heavy door.

My guard swung his gaze toward me. Behind him, the face of one of Lynch's men appeared in the shadows. He wrapped an arm around the guard, brought a knife to his throat and made a swift, deep cut. A scream tore from my mouth as an awful garble of blood and air escaped the guard's lungs. As he crumpled to the floor, another of Lynch's companions appeared, coming out of a hidden door in the hall. They rushed at me.

I scrambled back, putting all my weight on the door to close it, but the men were through before I could send home the bolt. Unsheathed dagger in hand, I stumbled across my room. Outside, the roar of cannon fire erupted with a cacophony of shouting.

The first man circled toward me, dirty blond hair and light-grey eyes shining as he neared the fireplace. "Ye're going to bring a pretty penny from some rich bastard who wants a new toy." He grinned, like he was letting me in on a delicious secret. "I wanted ye as soon as we met."

The second man bolted the door and sneered, talking to his friend without taking his gaze off me. "We've ships full of men to take this castle. Let's wait out the fight here. Have some fun while we're at it."

Grey Eyes agreed with a barked laugh devoid of mirth.

Nowhere to run, I did the only thing I could think of: I sang. I bared my teeth and snarled a war-song in a language I didn't know. As if the castle was singing through my bones.

The men split up, advancing on me slow. The song spooked them. I chanted louder.

"Ye're a witch!" Grey Eyes spat at my feet.

The other man circled me with a broken-toothed snarl. I dodged his first attempt to grab me, but lost the chant in a poorly-executed effort to defend myself. Grey Eyes came up behind me and ripped the dirk out of my hand.

I took the small blade from my pocket, twisted in his grip and slashed at his inner thigh.

His yowl, followed by a backhanded hit that made my ears ring, told me I may have made a mistake. I'd ripped his pants and drawn some blood, but it didn't appear to be serious, considering he was still standing. His partner snatched the blade from my hand, crushed me in his grip, and growled.

I screamed, thrashed, bit, kneed, kicked, elbowed, and generally panicked. I regained the chant, shouting in their faces, feeling as if I were harnessing the strength of the land, but despite my efforts to keep them off me, I ended up on my back on the cold, hard floor.

Grey Eyes kneeled on my thighs, his weight pushing down to bone and making me whimper. The broken-toothed man knelt on my hands, his palm over my mouth. Unsure what was stronger, rage or fear, I refocused my efforts on kicking and twisting. The boom of cannon fire thundered through my chest.

Bleeding on my robe, Grey Eyes ripped it open and tore the top of my nightgown. I screamed beneath the other man's hand, tried biting him, and thrashed as hard as I could.

With a curse, he brought the edge of my own dagger to my right breast. I stopped moving.

"Aye, now, there's a lass," he said in a thick voice, and shoved his other hand down his pants to stroke himself. The blade stung as it cut into my skin. Grey Eyes straddled me, undoing his laces as my breath came shallow and quick.

Then the door to the bath closet shot open with a bang louder than the cannons, making everyone jump. Killian ran in, his roar filling the room. The men sprang to their feet, and I rolled out of the way. With a savage chop, Killian severed Grey Eyes' head.

The other man drew his sword and blocked Killian's attack. He kept up with the first few swings, but Killian's fury overpowered him in a hurry. He fell. Impaled. And bled profusely on the floor where they'd had me on my back.

The room filled with a metallic scent that made my mouth water and turned my stomach, blood rushing in my ears. On my feet, I backed away from the gore, hands trembling as I closed my robe.

Killian laid his sword on the floor and came to me, searching my body with his hands. "Are ye hurt lass?"

My voice didn't work. I was afraid if I opened my mouth I'd start screaming and not stop. I shook my head, arms crossed to cover myself.

Killian's eyes locked on mine. He waited until I met his gaze. "Shelta, are ye bleeding?"

His concern made me answer. "Just a scratch."

"Where?"

I looked down. "It'll be fine."

He drew a breath. "Did they harm ye?"

I swallowed. Knew what he meant. "No. You came in time."

Killian brought me to the chair by the hearth and sat me on his lap, arms circling me. "What happened?" He buried his face in my hair. "I told ye to lock the door. How did they get in?"

Like my body, my voice shook. "Something drove me to look. The hall was quiet, and then I opened the door and they were there."

"Dammit, Shelta."

The grumble in his words made me curl in. "It was stupid. I'm sorry." Tears welled up but I choked them back. "I'm so, so sorry."

"Aye. I suppose ye are at that." He rocked me like I was a child. "As am I." His voice caught.

"What made you come?"

He cleared his throat, cannons rumbling in the background. "Wallace has the battle well in hand. I came looking for these two, and then I heard ye singing." He took my face in his hand. "Did ye sing?"

The memory of the chant was still on my tongue. "Yes. I sang. I don't even know what the words meant."

"I *felt* it, Shelta, felt ye calling me. I heard ye clear, though I was on the other side of the keep. Ye sang an ancient song. How did ye know it?"

My head shook side-to-side, tears spilling over. "I don't know." I wiped my cheeks with the back of one hand. "The castle gave me the song. I've never done anything like that before."

He kissed my temple. Crushed me close. Then he lifted me to my feet, and strode across the room to ring the bell pull.

The fabric at my legs hung heavy with a dead man's blood. I checked the cut on my breast while Killian was turned away. It bled, but didn't look too deep. At least the wound was cleaning itself. I hugged my arms, pressing on the cut, and tried to ignore the bodies bleeding out on the floor.

Killian grabbed a blanket from the bed and wrapped me in warmth. His arms circled me, trapping my arms against his chest. Still, I shivered.

"Ah, lass." He spoke into my hair again, head bowed, breath hot near my ear.

Outside, the explosions stopped. I pushed back so I could see Killian's eyes, and started babbling. "Is everything all right out there? Is any of this blood yours? I've never heard cannon fire, except in movies."

"Nay, all is well." He didn't bother questioning me about movies. I'd probably have to cover that another time. "Most of the cannons were our own, fired afore the ships could get their guns into range. Those that came by land are either slain or retreated, along with the ships, which have reversed course, by the sounds of things. I've that betrayer Seann Lynch locked up for questioning and transport to Stirling, along with Father Galloway. The other two masquerading as priests were slain—one by my father's own dirk."

"Were many of your clan killed?"

"Only a few that I know of, one being the guard in the hall there."

My fault. "Killian, I'm so sorry."

"Ye've more than paid the price of foolishness."

"But the guard, I watched him fall. I opened the door at the same time they came up, and it distracted him, and—" His sigh spoke volumes. My heart did a free fall into my knotted stomach. "I'm so sorry," I whispered again.

"Stop." He lifted my chin. "Don't blame yerself."

"But, Killian—"

"Nay, lass. One of these men held the blade that took his life, aye?" He gestured to the bodies on the floor.

I sniffed, swallowing tears. "Aye. That one." I pointed my chin toward the one whose grey eyes were now covered with a mess of blood and brains, the front of his pants open to pale skin.

"They are to blame. Dinna think on it again."

"That might be hard." My voice rasped. The cut on my breast reminded me of the hands that had been there, the sharp sting of the dagger, the weight on my thighs that would likely leave bruises. It could've been so much worse.

Killian rocked me, sending a comforting rumble through my ribcage as he spoke. "Ye'll feel better once ye've cleaned up."

Right. Sure.

Annelle showed up with a small shriek, standing in the doorway to the washroom. "God above, are ye hurt?"

"I think a bath and a good scrub of the room will set most things right," answered Killian. His voice did something to me, soothing the frayed edges. I no longer shook quite as badly.

"I'll have water readied for a bath, and some help to get this cleaned straight away."

"She'll have my chamber, Annelle." It was an order.

"Aye, milord." She slipped away with a nod.

I closed my eyes. He was moving me into his bedroom. He'd heard my chant, my cry for help, and he'd killed to protect me. He was claiming me in every action, and I wanted to be claimed. Wanted to belong to him.

A thread of hope whispered through my mind. Maybe I wouldn't be pulled through the tree again. Everything about this time was different. Maybe the rules had changed. Maybe I could belong with him. Maybe I could stay.

Killian's chamber wasn't far. Down the hall and around a corner. He sat me on his lap by the fire as we waited, and I melted into him. Every time my mind tried rehashing the events of the night or making up possible futures, I reminded myself that all I had was this moment.

He didn't let go until the bath had been readied, and even then he was disinclined to release me. But I wanted to wash the blood off. Annelle pointed out that Killian could do with a bath himself. He left muttering something about Wallace, and I followed Annelle into the bathroom, which had clearly just been cleaned.

Annelle took my bloody nightgown, promising to burn it, which I agreed to wholeheartedly. I lowered myself into the warm water of the tub, where I quietly cried.

Annelle returned with soft sounds of comfort. "I've built up the fire," she said. "Let me wash yer hair. I don't mind if ye weep."

Weep I did. She held space, massaging my scalp. She ran her hands down my neck and worked on my shoulders, her touch a healing thing. The tears cleansed me. Annelle soothed me. And by the time I got out of the bath, I was empty. Clean.

As clean as I'd ever be.

Annelle ran a brush through my hair, and talked to me like a best friend. Like she'd have my back if I needed to bury a body. "The fears of this night are nothing compared to the light that shines from ye. Don't give the memories power. When they try to come, send them into the fire. Think instead of Killian, who has clearly taken ye into his heart. He is a good man, milady."

"He is." Guilt twisted in my chest. Every lie was a small betrayal. Each time I pretended I could stay, I dug deeper.

"I'm glad to see he's found it in his heart to love again," she confessed.

I thought of how many years she must've known him. How long would I have before I disappeared? A year? Two at most, if the pattern of my life continued. Would she hate me for leaving, even though I wouldn't have a choice?

CHAPTER 16
PICKING UP THE PIECES

I HALF-EXPECTED KILLIAN to be next to me in the morning, but he must've slept somewhere else. The bed had an empty feel. My hand went to my pendant, seeking comfort in the circular shape and the ridges of the wings, wishing my dragon friends were real.

I got up with a stretch, groaned, and checked the bandage over my breast. The wound had closed. That was good. It made me shiver to think how I'd gotten it, but I was safe. Or functioning under the illusion of safety, at least.

On the earth-toned carpet at the center of the room, I dropped into a forward bend. My body needed to move and my mind needed to chill out. I had to work hard to keep from dwelling on how reckless I'd been to open the door, but each stretch made me feel stronger, and the intensity of the fear began to fade.

After I'd had a bite to eat, Annelle surprised me with a new dress. The light-pink top was soft, the brown wool skirt warm. Chocolate-colored ribbons laced through the pink bodice. A sensible riding jacket completed the outfit, embroidered with roses on the cuffs and collar.

"The dress belonged to Aislin." Annelle adjusted the jacket, smoothing the fabric. "We can alter others of hers easily enough, so ye have more choices in yer wardrobe while ye wait for dresses of yer own. Milord has asked that it be done."

I nodded, not trusting my voice. Was the dress a favorite of Killian's? Would he see Aislin's ghost when he looked at me? I didn't like the thought of him bending over a trunk, pulling out his late wife's clothes.

"Is it closer to lunch or breakfast?" I asked, tugging my brain away from worry.

"Mid-day, milady." She smiled. "I have instructions to deliver ye to milord once ye're ready."

And so, with a new sgian-dubh tucked into the pocket of my jacket, the dirk pressing into the outside of my right calf, and my cloak carried by my lady's maid, I followed Annelle past the library with its beckoning books to the office where Wallace had questioned me the night we'd arrived. Killian sat behind the colossal desk with a letter. He put it aside with a quiet rustle of paper, standing as I entered. Annelle draped my cloak over a chair and closed the door as she left.

"Did ye sleep?" Killian asked, coming around the desk to study me.

"I did. Did you?" I tried to smile, but it didn't come out right and I dropped my gaze to the desk.

"Aye." He lifted my chin with one finger, concern deepening the lines around his eyes and tightening the scar at his temple. "Would ye walk with me in the garden?"

"That would be nice."

He wrapped my cloak around my shoulders, then offered me his arm. We took the back door into the courtyard where I'd walked with Charlie the day before. The sun shone, and the castle walls blocked some of the wind. The air smelled of salt water and wood smoke and dying leaves.

"I love the dragon," I commented as we walked past the massive statue, not quite brave enough to ask him about it. My fingers rose to stroke my necklace. "Charlie was an excellent guide yesterday."

"I'm glad to hear it."

"Is everything—cleaned up?"

"Aye. Nearly. There will be a service for the warriors we lost. The enemies' bodies are being burned near the water. The prisoners have been questioned by Wallace, who ye ken to be a good interrogator, though ye dinna ken the half of it. The priest seems innocent, but they're in a carriage on their way to Stirling for the prince and his lawmen to deal with."

"When is the service?" I asked. "I'd like to attend, if that's okay."

"Aye. It will be soon, just over an hour from now."

"Do I need to wear black?" I studied the delicate pink flowers on my jacket.

"Nay, lass. Come as ye are."

"You really don't mind me wearing Aislin's clothes?" I tipped my head to look at him. "I mean, thank you. I'm honored. I just don't want to feel like I'm bringing up sad memories, or—taking her place."

He walked on, quiet. Leaves rustled on the ground. Heat seeped through his coat where my left hand wrapped around his elbow.

Finally, Killian stopped, face to the wind, eyes locked on mine. "Shelta, yer presence clears the sadness from my heart. Ye're quite different from who she was, and—I hope we can create new memories. Together."

Throat tight, I slid my hands into his.

Killian's eyelids closed at my touch. The wind blew at my cloak, but I barely felt it.

The service was held in a small church within the castle's walls. There was a burial ground outside, but those close to the fallen were brought into the sanctuary of the chapel for the service, out of the wind. The room was packed. I should've stayed outside, should've given my place to someone else who knew the fallen, but I couldn't leave now.

I blamed my stupidity for the death of the guard who'd been assigned to me. If I hadn't opened my door, he might've heard the men who'd snuck up on him through the secret passage. If I hadn't opened my door, I wouldn't have the memory of two men leaning over me, my back to a cold floor. It chilled me from the inside, made me impervious to the warmth of so many people in one room.

No tears touched my cheeks. I had no right to share these people's grief. I stood straight and still next to Killian, barely understanding the priest's words through his thick accent. This was only the second funeral I'd ever attended. I had never been anywhere long enough to have someone to mourn. If I did mourn them, it was finding out after the fact, when I'd looked up those who had felt like family and discovered they'd succumbed to the passage of time.

Eventually, the procession wound out to the graveyard. Killian and Wallace were among the men who carried the coffins over the windblown hill to the final resting place of the fallen. I walked next to Cristina and Fione. Charlie was somewhere in the mass of red kilts marching up the slope. The dead were lowered into graves with blessings, flowers, and tears.

In the distance, thick black smoke of a pyre rose into the sky, the bodies of the enemy burning. The wind carried the smoke off to sea.

Killian and I spent the afternoon in the garden view sitting room with my length of plaid fabric, needle, and thread. We moved the low table out of the way, and I showed him how I thought to make a simple purse. It was nothing more than a sling with a pouch at the bottom, but my sewing skills were rather lacking. He helped me pin the rough design and use the heavy scissors.

"Annelle can sew a pocket or two in it for ye," he offered. "Perhaps ye can find a button ye like to fasten it shut." He handed me a bowl of buttons to look through, then deftly put green thread through the eye of a needle, tied the ends together with his big fingers, and started to sew.

I gaped at him, impressed at how easily he started the stitch. "You're much better at that than I am."

"Ye need the practice then." He handed it to me with a twist of his mouth.

Killian offered a few tips here and there, but mostly he kept me company, lounging on the sofa telling me stories of Clan Maclean. The tale of a chief who spent his whole life at sea. The generation that survived the three-year storm. Beltane celebrations that stretched all through the night until dawn.

The stitching was nearly finished when I found the courage to ask the question I'd been sitting on since we'd arrived at the castle. "Can you tell me more about the dragons? Why are they significant to you?"

Killian's eyes narrowed as he straightened in his seat. I stopped sewing. The possibility of truth hung thick between us.

His deep voice carried an edge of warning. "It is said that Gillean of the Battle Axe journeyed across the sea, and in a place where midnight skies dance with fire, he became a god." Killian's gaze told me we were treading in dangerous waters, but he went on. "He befriended a dragon, who won him many battles and carried him away upon his death. This legend promises our clan protection. It tells us the dragons are our guardians."

I pressed on, needing to know more. "Are they? Has anyone seen dragons, besides in sculptures and legends?"

"The legend is enough. In time of great need, Gillean's treasure will protect us."

I nodded, wishing for better news. Live dragons. A map to find them. "Are there books in the library that tell the legend?" I hadn't found any, but I wanted to be sure.

He shook his head. "It is a guarded secret, Shelta. I trust ye to keep it as such."

"Of course." I nodded, and gave a strained smile.

A few hours later, I stood with Killian in his room, saying goodnight. His warmth was a comfort I didn't want to be without.

"You could sleep in here, you know." I caught his hand in mine. "It's your bed."

"Tempting." He stepped closer; one hand warm on my hip. He slid his other hand behind my head, into my hair, making me tilt my chin up as he lowered his face.

His lips brushed my neck once. Twice. My breath rushed past his ear.

Fist tightening around the hair at the base of my skull, he spoke with his mouth an inch from mine. "I want ye, Shelta, with everything I am."

There was a "but" coming, and I didn't want to hear it. I closed the distance, tasting the wine on his lips. His kiss was consuming, his presence a welcome intoxication. As wrong as it was to get involved, nothing had ever felt so right.

Killian pushed back, holding me by my shoulders. He panted, like it was taking all his willpower to stop. His next kiss was barely there. A brush of lips. "Not yet," he said, and backed away. "Goodnight."

My voice cracked as I answered. "Goodnight, Killian."

He left, closing the door. Leaving me alone.

Restless energy moved my feet. I paced the room, mind wound up to breakneck speeds. Outside, snowflakes fell through the dark night. I had no movies to entertain me, no music to plug into my ears and take me away.

Finally, I sank into the chair by the hearth. Staring into the flames, I decided to do what Annelle suggested the previous night: toss the thoughts in the fire. I moved the screen to the side and dropped to my knees before the blaze.

Trusting my instinct, I started incinerating the memories of the men who'd attacked me. The scene replayed in my mind for the hundredth time, and I breathed deep, clawing at the space before my chest with fingers that grasped invisible thought-forms. With a forceful exhale, I thrust my hands toward the flames as if I could physically throw the fear into the fire.

When I leaned back, I felt a little clearer. A little lighter. So I did it again, and again, and again, until the ritual cleared my mind of horror, guilt, and the rage that came when I thought about how helpless I was to stop the pattern of my life.

Chapter 17
Lessons

THE NEXT MORNING, I made my way down to the dining room wrapped in my plaid stole, dragon brooch pinning it together at my chest. The voice of a young girl rang out in protest as I approached.

"But Ma, the boys go play outside afore breakfast! Why can't I?"

Entering, I recognized Cristina and Fione, but not the young girl.

"Who would keep me company, if ye went?" Cristina replied to her youngest charge. The little one looked much like her mother, with red curls and green eyes. Fione took after her father, Wallace, with darker coloring and a gaze that showed sharp intelligence.

"Hello, I don't believe we've met." I stopped in front of the young girl. "My name is Shelta."

"My name is Rheanna." She eyed me with wary fascination.

I joined Cristina and Fione at the table. "Is there another?" I asked, knowing Cristina had three children.

"Aye." Her smile made a little twist that suggested pride and a fair bit of work behind the raising of the boy. "Young Bruce is out in the field with the men, practicing his swordplay."

"He's eleven." Fione shook her head. "Insists on training each day with Charlie."

"Ah." I grinned. "And that leaves us with an all-girls' breakfast?"

"Most of the time," Cristina replied. "The odd day we've the chief as well, but it's rare he misses his morning round."

"I'd like to see that." I imagined the chief could hold his own on the battlefield.

"Aye!" Rheanna agreed with enthusiasm. I made a face. I'd brought up the subject of contention, but Cristina waved me off, asking Rheanna what she thought she was going to do in the midst of all that clashing and moving about. "Play in the snow!" the girl said, as if it were obvious.

"Well, ye can play in the gardens after ye've eaten." Cristina pointed at her daughter's plate, which she'd barely touched.

I did actually want to see the men in training. How was I going to pull that off?

Fione watched me. "There's a good view from the tower."

I flashed her a grin. "Which tower?"

A short while later, my breath came heavy as I ascended yet another floor of spiral staircase. Near the top, Fione turned into a small room stocked with several bows and quivers of arrows. We crossed to an open window, where I could see the courtyard near the armory alive with the movements of men, grass and mud showing through the thin layer of snow.

"There's Charlie and Bruce." She pointed at two forms less bulky than the rest. "Charlie is quite good, and Bruce tries to match him. He'll be a fine fighter by the time he's my age."

I squinted. We were too far up to see as well as I would've liked. "Is that Killian with Sir Malcolm?"

"Aye." Fione nodded. "Da, Uncle Killian, and Grandpapa have a tradition of sorts, always challenging each other on the field. It helps keep them from doing so elsewhere."

Charlie and Bruce finished their bout. I was pleased to see Wallace step in to work with his son. His movements were sure, but his patience and care were clear from all the way up here.

"Father and son always take a turn on the field," Fione informed me. "I'm sure Killian and Charlie started the morn that way. That is their routine."

I couldn't tell who won the contest between Killian and his father, but the ferocity with which they fought made me shiver. As exciting as it was to watch, it was another reminder that the world I'd entered was a dangerous one. The cut on my breast had only begun to heal, and a dagger rested heavy in my right boot. Killian's role as spymaster put him in harm's way; frequently, it would seem.

A chill wind drove us away from the window and down the stairs. I gave Fione's trailing skirts lots of space so I didn't step on them, fists full of my own dress so I didn't trip. "What's at the top of the tower?" I asked.

"It's a bit of a lookout, a bit of a hideaway." Her voice bounced dull off the circular space.

"Does the minstrel reside in the castle?" I asked, hoping to take my mind off the man who trained with his clan in the courtyard below.

"Aye. Much of the time. He goes on trips often enough, but he's here now. Would ye like me to show ye the way to his music room?"

"That would be wonderful." Just the distraction I needed.

We followed a series of hallways, and ended up in a different building altogether. Fione left me in the good company of the bard, whose home consisted of a small bedroom behind a closed curtain, and a large room filled with instruments, sheets of music, and comfortable chairs.

"Welcome, Miss Shelta." Gavin steered me to a seat by his little hearth, which had a kettle hanging above the fire. "Let me get ye a cup of tea."

I sat, grateful, and wrapped my hands around the earthen mug when it was handed to me, letting the warmth seep in. Instead of small talk, the minstrel took up his violin and said, "I was just composing something. Would ye like to hear it?"

"That would be lovely," I answered with a smile.

The morning unraveled into the joy of music. I jumped at the chance when Gavin offered to teach me the violin, and lost myself in the discovery of the strings. At first, I made awful noises with the bow, screeches and rough notes, but after a while something clicked, and the instrument opened itself to me, or I opened myself to the instrument, more like.

The strings quivered through my body, the resonance of the violin's song seeping into my soul. Eyes closed, I let go of my mind as the music raced through my blood.

I played the melody Gavin had composed earlier, knowing I shouldn't have that kind of skill so quickly, only vaguely aware of the minstrel's awed murmur. Completely unable to stop myself, my body swayed, breath filling with the scent of resin and wood. The vibration seemed to delve through the floorboards and into the land.

Like flying, it was.

A presence brought me out of my reverie, and I pulled back, taking the bow off the strings. Killian stood in Gavin's doorway with his mouth half open.

"That was remarkable playing." Gavin's head tilted sideways, wonder and suspicion glinting in his eyes.

"Indeed." Killian stepped into the room, coming to stand with us, making my pulse pound. "Ye've never studied the fiddle before?"

"No." My mouth split into an apologetic grin. "I've always been this way. I listen to the instrument and it teaches me. I know that probably sounds crazy."

"Nay, lass." The intimacy of Killian's tone made me tingle. "'Tis a blessing."

"Aye. I hope ye'll come visit me again and play some more." Gavin took the violin and bow that I handed him.

"I'd love to." My cheeks burned hot.

A few minutes later, I held onto Killian's arm as we negotiated the winding way back to the main hall. His words were warm, but dangerous. "Ye've some magic, Shelta."

"I don't know that everyone views magic as a good thing." I pitched my voice quiet. "I'm not sure it's magic, anyway. More like instinct."

"Maybe." He didn't sound convinced. He smelled of outside, of wood smoke and fresh air. "Would ye care to take a ride this afternoon? I'd like to show ye some of the countryside."

"Sounds like fun." I hoped the sun would come out and warm the wind.

Killian squeezed my hand. "Fione said she took ye up for a look at the practice field."

"She did, though I would like a closer look." We reached another door, and I was pleased to see a part of the castle I recognized.

"Perhaps we should arrange a lesson for ye. Then ye'd have reason to be on the field and we'd see how many of the men could stay focused with ye there." He smiled at his joke.

"Um," I stammered, ever so eloquent. "You're sure I wouldn't be getting in the way?"

"Nay, lass. Ye'd not be in the way at all."

The thought of a sword lesson wasn't an issue. That might be fun. But being a complete novice and getting schooled in front of a field of warriors who wielded swords like it was second nature? Talk about intimidating.

We reached the dining room, and I didn't have time to wiggle out of the lesson before greetings were underway and I found myself sitting between the chief and Killian.

"How was yer morning with the minstrel?" Cristina asked me from across the table.

"Really lovely, thanks." I lowered my water glass. "He's teaching me the violin."

"How excellent!" Sir Malcolm flashed me a smile.

"She'll be taking up the sword tomorrow." Killian grinned at me.

"I—" I was going to say I hadn't actually agreed to it yet, but was interrupted.

"Aye? And who will be teachin' ye?" Wallace entered the room and sat next to his wife with a wry grin.

I raised my eyebrows and tried a smile. What had I gotten myself into?

Killian ignored my silent plea for help. "I reckon Rodric will have some ideas."

A flush rose hot on my face and neck as the men spoke about my training with no input from me at all. Bending forward, I busied myself with my meal. At this point, I couldn't back out without looking like a coward. I'd just have to suck it up and look like a fool instead.

After lunch, I wound my way up to Killian's room, wanting my coat and gloves for riding. Annelle was there, dusting the dresser.

"Annelle!" I crossed the room, fighting the urge to hug her. "I'm so glad to see you. I've gotten myself into sword training in the morning." Her eyes widened, but she waited for the rest. "Is it possible to have skirts made that only come down to my shins? I want to be able to move without tripping."

"Aye, I could do that tonight." A sly smile spread across her face, making her cheeks round and deepening the lines around her eyes.

"What?"

"I've an idea, is all." She took some twine from her pocket, measured the right length, tied a small knot, and slipped it back into her pocket.

Killian was on his way to get me as I walked downstairs, and we met at the landing where the tapestry of Brighid's spring hung against grey stone.

"I've been meaning to ask you about this." I eyed the image of the place where we met. Where the goddess Brighid allegedly turned her tears into an enchanted spring.

"Curious, isn't it?"

Is that all you're going to say?

The play went out of his smile. "Ye want to ken why I went, is that it?"

I nodded.

"I sought the blessing of the goddess." He looked at me for a long time before going on. "And ye appeared from a light in the oak with a song on the wind."

He left out a whole story between those two sentences, I was certain, but it didn't seem the rest was forthcoming. The legend carried weight enough for Killian to visit the sacred spring. Did the goddess have anything to do with my crossing? Did she actually exist?

A full-body tingle made me think that she did.

We walked outside to the stables, where I inhaled the smell of horses and sweet-talked the beautiful creatures as we passed them. Killian brought me to the stall of a handsome white Arabian and introduced him as Taj. The stable hand came at Killian's call to saddle him for me.

Not long later, the guards bowed as we rode through the castle gates, turning away from where pyre smoke had risen only yesterday.

The vista stole my breath with craggy hills, far-off mountains, endless rolling water, and sky layered with clouds and patches of blue. We hadn't gone far before I asked my horse to stop, mesmerized.

"It's so beautiful." My voice was an awed whisper.

"Aye. I'm glad ye think so." Pride in his words.

The horses only gave me a minute to enjoy the scenery, frisky in the crisp air. Killian moved with ease on his tall chestnut gelding. We came up to a trot on the trail that ran parallel to the bay below, hooves clopping out a steady rhythm. When the road opened wider, Killian turned to me with a roguish grin.

"Have ye done much riding at a gallop, Shelta?"

"No." His question made me wary. My foster mother who had the horse had forbidden me to gallop, and I'd only dared try a few times when she'd gone off to do something and none of my foster siblings were around.

"Well, all ye do is find yer balance by leaning a wee bit forward, then let the horse move beneath ye."

"Right." Just smile and nod, and hold on tight.

We went from a walk to a canter, then launched into a sprint. Killian and his gelding became a blur of color to my left and the road sped toward me. I focused past the flying white mane and curved ears of my horse, heart going at least as fast as his hooves.

Then my balance shifted. Off-kilter. I pulled on the reins until the horse relented and pranced his way into a trot, but I was still getting bounced around, my grip on the saddle the only thing keeping me on the horse. I slowed him to a walk, finally getting my legs even. Killian trotted back to me, grinning, and we walked the horses with the coastline on our left.

"Killian, are you testing me—the galloping and the swords and all?"

He flashed a playful smile. "Nay, lass. I wouldna want ye to feel life here is dull."

"Not likely!"

We did a loop back toward the castle, stopping for a few minutes above a long stretch of dark blue water. The sun hung low, painting brilliant shades of pink and orange on rolling land, sea, and sky.

In that moment of perfection, I realized what Killian was trying to do. He wanted to keep me from thinking about the attack two nights before. I'd certainly been busy enough, and in good company. The dread had barely surfaced since I'd thrown it into the fire.

But another fear rose up, and being near Killian intensified my unease. None of this was more than a fleeting dream.

I did a happy dance the next morning as Annelle presented me with my fighting attire.

"You wonderful woman!" I fought to stand still as her deft hands laced the red ribbon of the black bodice, which layered over a black blouse. I thought of the dragon who'd visited me again last night, and how handsome we'd look together in my new outfit.

If only I could find him.

The genius was in the skirt of red Maclean plaid, pleated like the warrior's kilts, but longer. On one side, the plaid was raised to reveal the black petticoats below; a touch that added a whole lot of sass. I hoped I could live up to it while being schooled by whichever poor Highlander was given the duty of training me. Or Killian. Which might be worse.

With the dirk in a sheath on the belt at my hip, I walked to the entrance of the armory, and approached Rodric alone. "I was told to come for a lesson." I hoped I sounded casual, not like I was already sweating under my wool jacket.

"Aye." Rodric eyed me. "Killian has gone to fetch ye, I thought."

"Oh. Well, here I am." Good. I'd beaten him here.

Rodric snatched two wooden swords in one large hand and gestured for me to follow him outside. I stretched my small frame as tall as I could as we walked. Gaze forward. The men on the field traded snickers.

"Ah, excellent." Killian strode up behind me. "Ye found yer way."

His smile was larger than it had any business being as he made a show of looking me up and down. I tried to be annoyed with him, but couldn't quite pull it off.

"Do you like my new dress?" I kicked one leg higher than necessary, making the skirts fluff up. They wanted a show; I was a performer.

Rodric cleared his throat.

Killian smirked. "Aye. I'll leave ye to it then." Off he went, the grin still on his face.

Charlie and Killian squared off not far away. Rodric drew me to a corner of the field, and allowed me a few moments to watch, then we launched into the basics of swordplay. Footwork, strikes, and blocks. I practiced over and over, until I no longer had to think about the moves.

When I had that down, Rodric surprised me with an attack. I tried to keep up and block, but found the wooden point of his sword at my shoulder.

"Next." He began teaching me how to deal with what he'd just done.

Off came the wool jacket, my body hot from constant movement. I was too busy trying to keep my sword up to wonder how the men thought I looked in my red-ribboned bodice. Rodric certainly didn't care, coming in faster once I'd gotten the hang of the movements. He had me continuously on edge, making me scramble to keep up.

"Aye." He finally let me catch my breath. "Ye'll do."

"I'm so pleased," I panted, "that I measure up to your standards."

Rodric flashed a lopsided grin at the sarcasm and came at me before I was ready. He tested everything he'd taught me, switching up the order, attacking from new angles. When he bashed my wooden sword with a hit that vibrated up my arm and echoed in my ears, I lost my grip. The sword flew out of my hand. As it did, I noticed that Killian, Wallace, and Sir Malcolm were watching.

I let out a breath through rounded lips, and went to retrieve my weapon. Killian got there before me, picked up the practice sword and presented it hilt first. Wisely, he didn't comment on the way my hand shook when I took it, nor did I thank him before I stalked back to the armourer.

The wooden sword was a lot heavier now than when we'd started. "I don't think my arm will take much more of this," I told Rodric in an undertone, struggling to keep a grip on the handle out of sheer fatigue.

"Good." He swapped his sword to the other hand. "Let's switch to the left."

Learning the same moves on my left side progressed more slowly, which was somewhat of a relief because he wasn't hitting as hard.

When Rodric finally relented, he held his hand out for the sword, saying, "That's enough for the day."

I handed it over gladly. When I turned to recover my jacket, I found Wallace waiting for me. Killian was nowhere to be seen.

Wallace gave a nod and gestured with an open hand toward the castle. "Ye did well."

My smile came out as more of a wince. "Thank you. Between this and galloping across the countryside yesterday, every part of my body is going to be sore."

"Ye said ye wanted Scotland." He laughed, but when I flashed my gaze to his eyes, he was sizing me up. "I hear ye have a gift for learning instruments so well ye go from novice to master in a day."

"I don't know about *master*." I tried to downplay my ability. "I do catch on quickly, especially with string instruments. I've always been this way with music."

"Ye'll have to give us a concert tonight."

"I don't know that I'll be able to lift a violin this evening." I was glad we'd reached the castle, hoping he'd let me off easy.

"A song then." Wallace's eyes bored into me. "Ye've enchanted my brother, Shelta Raine. I want to know that ye've done so honestly, and not with some magic in yer music. How does a girl growing up in the wild have access to instruments?"

I shut my mouth with a click of teeth, took a breath, and composed another lie. "My father was a musician before moving west. He brought instruments with us and taught me from an early age."

"I dinna believe ye." He leaned in, spoke quiet. "Ye're lying, but I dinna ken why."

"I'm sorry," I stammered. "I don't know what I could say to make you believe me. I only hope you'll see my sincerity."

"That's what doesn't match up." He cocked his head. "I dinna doubt yer sincerity, yer heart. But ye lie all the same."

CHAPTER 18
QUESTIONS IN THE TOWER

"OH, GOD." I stared at the wooden ceiling, lying on my back on the rug in Killian's room, fatigue and fear weighing down my body.

Annelle had helped me freshen up after Wallace let me go, his suspicions clear. With nothing to do about it, I'd stretched my muscles as well as I could in the dress that had belonged to Killian's wife, then sprawled out on the rug, cursing the time travel that had made a liar out of me my whole damn life.

Exhausted, the urge to fall asleep pulled hard. It would be nice to forget about everything for a while. Maybe a dragon would come keep me company. The fire crackled in a mellow sort of way. Birds twittered outside the window.

Then came footsteps I felt through the floorboards, and a knock at the door.

I was not getting up. No way. I took a deep breath and called, "Come in."

The door creaked open, shut with a dull thud, and Killian started across the room. "Shelta? Are ye alright?"

"I'm fine." My voice flowed soft, trance-like. "I'm relaxing."

"I see."

"You seem to ask me that a lot," I said dreamily, "if I'm okay."

He came closer. "Ye seem to need to be asked frequently enough."

I hadn't moved, other than opening one eye for half a moment.

"Do ye want me to go?"

"No." I sighed. "I'll get up, if you don't mind waiting for me to do it slowly."

He sat by the hearth. I took a deep, full breath, then rolled to one side, pushed up, and sat cross-legged in my skirts. I brought my palms together in front of my heart, something that had inexplicably helped me through rough times. Finally, I released my hands and opened my eyes.

"Hello." I smiled up at him.

"Hello." He grinned down at me. "What was that ye just did?"

"It's called yoga. I stretch and work on my balance, that kind of thing."

"Were you praying at the end?" He brought his hands together, mirroring what I'd done.

"Sort of. It was more bringing my energy back to center, and basically acknowledging that all things are one in the grand scheme of things. It makes me feel more grounded."

"Is it yer faith?"

"Hmmm. Some of the philosophy makes sense to me. I use pieces of it, pieces of other traditions, weaving my own beliefs together."

He nodded. "Like a tapestry. One God or many?"

"Both. The overriding principle is that there's one energy that encompasses all that is." My hands went wide, making large, roundish shapes in the air. "You and I, everything around us, we're all part of that one divine consciousness. So, in that sense, there's only one God." I shifted in my skirts, hoping I wasn't damning myself by telling him all this. "At the same time, there's divine feminine to balance divine masculine, and the one becomes many. Other gods and goddesses represent different elements of life and the universe, yet they're all of the one God. Each archetype can help us focus on something specific. Like saints, in a way."

"That's very interesting." Killian placed his hands on his thighs. "I look forward to further discussion on the subject."

I smiled, stood, and slid into his lap. He knew my secrets. I might as well give him another. "Your brother knows I'm feeding him lies." My words were a quiet confession. "I know I have no choice, but I hate it."

"He'll come around." Killian's fingers brushed my cheek, his head tilting closer to mine.

I kissed him. Fatigue sapped my ability to hold back. All I knew was how badly I wanted the escape of his touch.

Killian drew me in, arms crushing me close. Finally, he pushed back with a heavy breath and slid me off his lap. "We better stop afore I toss ye on the bed."

"I wouldn't mind you tossing me on the bed." Too bold, but what the hell.

He stood tall and offered me his arm. "There's something I want to show ye afore dinner."

"Okay." I slipped my hand onto the wool of his jacket and let him guide me out of the room, and through the castle. When we reached a tower, I broke the silence. "Where are we going, Killian?"

"Up." He gestured for me to lead the way.

Our footfalls set an off-tempo beat on the long spiral staircase. I had to stop once to catch my breath, leaning into the wall as Killian gazed at me, one side of his mouth curled up. We kept going past the place where Fione and I had looked down on the practice field, to the room at the very top.

Opposite the highest step was a window, open to the elements, with a long view of the sea. Cold air drifted through, scented by rain. The sun was low in the sky behind the clouds.

Killian produced a key and turned it in the lock. When we'd stepped in and the door was shut behind us, the circular room was actually cozy. Glass windows let light in from each of the four directions, and tapestries hung on the walls between. Against one wall was a long, wide couch that looked like it served as a bed, with a desk and some shelves on the other side of the room. A man-cave watchtower.

We sat on that couch that was really a bed, and Killian wrapped a fur-lined mantle around my shoulders. "Is this where you've been sleeping?" I asked.

"Aye." He swept his hand in a semi-circle, gesturing to the space. "'Tis my hideout. This is the place I come to think, or to find peace in my heart."

The gravity of his gaze plummeted through me. "It's something special that you've chosen to share it with me, then."

"Aye, and for something special that I've brought ye here." He kissed my hand, and then my wrist, but said nothing until he lit a few candles, the natural light rapidly diminishing.

Once the room was aglow, he settled in next to me.

My heart beat inside my throat. He looked way too serious for comfort. "What is it?"

His voice rumbled into my bones. "Shelta, I want ye to be my wife. Will ye marry me?"

My mouth fell open. Of all the things, I hadn't expected that. "Killian—I can't. I'll just disappear into another world. How is that fair to you, or your family?"

"I dinna care if it's fair, and I'll take whatever time I get with ye. Shelta, the goddess brought us together, and there's a wanting between us that deserves to be fulfilled."

"There is." I squeezed his hands. "But we could fulfill it without being married."

He ran his fingers up my arm, over my shoulder, to touch my throat. "We could, but people will have less respect for ye, and it wouldn't look good for me, either."

"So, we get married just for appearances?" I reminded myself how far back in time I'd gone. Of course, this was the way here.

"Nay." He pulled me close and spoke into my throat. "I want ye as my wife. There's magic in the marriage, in the bond. Even if ye leave me, I'll still be tied to ye."

I'll still be tied to ye. If only.

My lips were too close to his. Everything in my body told me to kiss him, to say yes, to let him have whatever he wanted. But it was all a lie. "And when I fall into another time, another world, am I to be faithful to you, alone for the rest of my life?"

He turned his face away, jaw clenched. When he brought his eyes back to mine, they had a sheen to them. "Nay. Ye are free to do as ye choose. I ask only that ye remember me."

"Like I could ever forget you." I tangled my fingers in his hair.

"If ye love me, marry me, Shelta." His thumb ran across my lips. "I ken what I'm getting into. I want ye as my wife even if only for a day. Say yes."

I didn't stand a chance against the flood of need in my blood. "Yes." My heart cracked open with the word, knowing I was breaking my most important rule: never get attached. Falling in love was bad enough. Marriage was pure stupidity.

But I couldn't tell him no.

We met with such passion that the room seemed to spin, our mouths hot against each other. Hands in hair, on faces, sliding down. My fingers traced the muscles of his neck, dipped beneath his shirt to the skin on his chest, the curves of his shoulders.

"Shelta." He breathed my name, cheek on mine.

I panted with him. I didn't want to leave the tower, the strength of his embrace, but there were others in this castle. "Did you talk to your family?"

"Aye." He touched the dragon hanging around my neck. "The friend ye keep here helped to convince Wallace, even if he suspects ye aren't all ye say."

"I dream of dragons nearly every night, Killian. I have since I was a child. Sometimes, there's a red dragon that looks very much like the statue in your courtyard. That dragon called me to find the tree that brought me to you." We were all this way up, yet still I dropped my voice, my cheeks burning as I told him.

Come. Find me. It's time.

Maybe the dragon's call had been to find this clan. The statue could be the dragon I was supposed to find, not an actual living creature. Could I just love this man who descended from a dragon rider and live out the rest of my life here?

"Dragons." Killian swept a strand of hair from my face. "I believe in magic, Shelta. It runs in your blood, and in mine. We might not understand it now, but maybe one day we will."

"Maybe. One day." My fingers threaded between his. Better not to think about what I'd have to give for that understanding. Probably this man. Likely more. I wanted to sleep here with him and forget about time and trees.

Killian brought me back to reality. "We should probably go down to dinner."

"Can't we stay here all night?" I buried my face in his neck.

"Nay, lass. Not yet." He drew me in for a long breath, then pulled back and slid from the bed, taking me with him.

I slipped my feet back into my boots, thinking about who I'd see downstairs. "Killian…" My voice was a warning. "We're not just setting ourselves up for heartbreak, but your family—they won't understand."

"I'll tell them when the time comes." His eyes told me he didn't expect to do any such thing. "If the time comes."

Chapter 19

Perfection Never Lasts

KILLIAN SURROUNDED ME, kissing at least four different parts of my face and neck. "Ye're so beautiful, Shelta. My wife."

A door separated us from the crowd coming inside from the wedding in the chapel. The hall rang with voices, people I'd have to face in a matter of minutes, pretending forever really meant forever. I stood in my blue gown, a gold and sapphire ring around my finger, my heart pounding and melting at the same time.

"Thank you." I pulled him in, trying to get as close as possible, and whispered a word I never thought I'd say. "Husband." I saw what it meant to him, that I was his wife. There was more to the gaze, more to the touch, more to the being with one another. "We have roots now." A thrumming sensation seemed to reach down into the earth, twining with his energy, his world. "It's like we've grown roots into each other. Do you feel that?"

"Aye." His hand cradled my head. "Ye say those words, stand in sacrament, and it calls a great power. The bond is woven by the fire within us, and a magic beyond our understanding."

I nodded, breathing him in. Then Killian took my hand, and we walked out to receive our guests. My breath tightened with the awareness of so many eyes turned my way.

I'd never stood in a reception line before. Killian was first, then me, then Sir Malcolm and Wallace, with Cristina at the end. Prince Charles was the first in line, a woman with curly hair and a pleasant smile on his arm. No pressure. To Killian, he gave his congratulations and a hearty handshake.

"My dear Lady Shelta, you are the picture of loveliness." The prince took my hand and lifted me up from the curtsy I'd begun. "No curtsies, now," he said with mock seriousness. "Today you are a princess! May I present my own princess, this is Clementina, my wife."

"Thank you both so much for coming." Though I would say those words at least fifty times more, they were heartfelt. "It means a lot that you're here."

"We'll speak again later." Prince Charles gave me a wink. "I've brought you something I think you'll quite enjoy." He moved on to greet Sir Malcolm with an air of kinship and camaraderie.

"Thank ye again for that last wee message," I overheard the chief say with an easy smile. "Proved mighty useful."

"Glad to be of help," replied the prince, and then I heard no more, occupied by meeting too many people to ever remember their names, clans, positions, or in what way we were now related.

After everyone had a chance to share their enthusiasm for our happiness, we went into the hall for a feast. Killian kept kissing my hand, touching my back, and wrapping his arm around me. People surrounded us, but above it all, beneath it all, through it all, I sensed him like a pulse.

My husband.

The lie was there, too, lurking beneath the current of happiness that buzzed through the room. Which of them saw through me?

After we'd eaten, a pair of cellists began to play, and I was irrepressibly drawn to the resonance. I walked over to stand near the players, Killian warm behind me. Closing my eyes, I leaned into him and let the music make its way into my being.

A voice came to me then, in my mind, deeply female and wide as the sky. She crept into my awareness so softly I almost didn't flinch when she spoke.

It is a bright thread you weave with this love. Know that you have my blessings.

Thank you, Goddess, I managed. Who else could it be?

You've sparked a new pattern in the Tapestry of the World Tree. It shall be a wonder to watch how it grows.

I fought to breathe normally. *Are you Brighid?*

I am. Such surety in two words, as if she'd never once questioned her existence, while I'd spent my whole life wondering why.

Will you stop the time travel, Goddess? I want to stay with Killian. Impossible hope flooded my heart, wetting my eyelashes.

There is much to come, my daughter. She was already retreating.

My throat tightened. *Goddess, please, let this love survive. Don't separate us.*

Your life is linked to the World Tree. But, as you wish. This love will ever be with you. There was a touch like a kiss at my brow, and she was gone.

Something shifted in my soul. Her words went round and round my mind, swirling with the sound of the cellos.

"What is it?" Killian whispered.

I softened, with difficulty, and wiped my cheeks. "Just the music." I stroked his arm at my chest, fingertips tingling. The musicians finished playing. I forced my smile to reach my eyes. "That was heavenly. So mysterious and sweet."

They received the praise with grace. When I turned to walk back to the table, I found Prince Charles standing next to us. The brightness of his eyes drove the words of the goddess to the back of my mind.

"I think," he said with a look at my husband, "that this is a good time." Killian nodded in agreement. What were they up to?

Next thing I knew, my husband and the Prince of Scotland were escorting me through the room. My skin crawled as all eyes followed us.

When we stopped, Prince Charles addressed me in a voice that carried. "Shelta Maclean." The name hit hard, making me swallow tears. "May I present you with a gift for your wedding. I could not wish you a better man. I hope this day brings joy to Clan Maclean for generations to come."

Maclean. I had an actual last name. Shelta Raine was the name I'd clung to when I'd been flung through time at the age of three and a nice lady found me wandering the woods on the edge of her property. I'd never had my own surname; I'd only ever borrowed them from temporary mothers and fake IDs.

Behind the prince, men moved potted plants to reveal a large, odd-shaped object draped with green hunting tartan. The shape, to me, was unmistakable. Killian removed the sheet of wool, and revealed the piano.

"Oh, Your Highness!" Emotions raced through me in rapid succession. Surprise. Awe. Elation. And a shadow of guilt.

"I'm glad you're pleased." He grinned, clearly proud of himself.

"Am I allowed to hug you?" What was the procedure was for touching royal persons?

He laughed and opened his arms. I dove in. He squeezed me firm, for just a moment, the scent of jasmine and rose sliding through my breath.

I pushed back with an immense smile. "How did you get it here?"

"It took quite a few men, quite a few horses, and a sturdy cart."

People gathered as we spoke, including a group of minstrels, excited to be around an instrument that was rare to encounter.

I ran my hand over the wood and moved to lift the cover, to touch the keys. "But this is the same one I played when I was at your palace." I raised my gaze in disbelief. "You've given me your piano!"

"Aye." The prince's head tilted a touch. "I've another on order to replace it. A new one would never have arrived in time. Besides, you seemed to like this one so much, I thought you should have it."

I nearly cried. I'd never had a piano of my own, I'd only ever borrowed them. And from a prince, no less. "How can I ever thank you?"

"Play, Lady Shelta." Prince Charles stroked a curve of the instrument. "Enjoy it. Let your music and the music of this instrument ring through these halls evermore."

Evermore. Not my music. Not likely. But Gavin would play it. Maybe he'd play my songs when I was gone.

Eyelashes wet with suppressed tears, I arranged myself on the bench and placed my hands on the keys. Slowly, the surge came in. I let the music move me as it wished.

The song that came through was joy and gratitude, beauty and eternity, uncertainty and longing. It built in waves of mystery, trust, willingness and love. And it allowed me, in the only way I could, to give the people listening a glimpse into my soul.

I tried not to let notes of loss creep in, tried not to let my thoughts turn to the World Tree, but my fingers strayed to minor keys, keeping the piece honest. No love was without sadness.

It was some of the most beautiful music I'd ever made. I played on and on, imagining the song would weave my love through the worlds, distilling the belonging I'd found with Killian into sound. I forged my own bond, using the magic of music, lifting my eyes to my husband's as I willed the goddess to keep us together.

Finally, the melody shifted into a tender finale. When I reached up to wipe my tear-streaked face, there were few surrounding me who did not do the same.

Hand in hand, Killian and I walked through the corridor toward his room—our room—leaving the din of dancers and drunkards behind us. My lips tasted of red wine and Killian's kisses, having received a long one as soon we'd been out of eyeshot from the party.

His footsteps echoed up my legs, my feet moving in time with his. Our breathing layered together; every sensation laced with wanting that pulsed like the warning of something destined to explode.

True to the wondrous, self-destructing fantasy I'd fallen into, Killian lifted me into his arms to cross the threshold of the chamber. I wondered if he'd given me his bedroom so I was already comfortable with the scent of him, his clothes in the wardrobe next to mine, his daggers on the dresser.

Planned like a true strategist. I loved him for it.

Wasting no time, he walked straight to the bed, sat me on the edge, and took my mouth with his. I arched over his arm, leaning back, lifting toward the hand that slid from my face to my throat, to my chest.

Shelta. Shelta. Shelta. He chanted my name like a prayer between kisses. His breath warmed my neck, the brush of teeth on my shoulder making me gasp as he drew the dress down.

I wrapped my legs around him, half-supported by the bed, but mostly by his hold. Blindly, fumbling, we removed the layers between us.

Only when we pressed warm and naked together did I remember the danger. The thing I hadn't told him.

"Killian, please don't get me pregnant." The words spilled out, hanging awkwardly between us.

He stopped kissing the inside of my wrist, lips still rounded as his dark eyes locked on mine. "Ye dinna want bairns?"

"I can't." My voice cracked at the struggle in his eyes. "I can't be responsible for a child if the World Tree takes me again."

"I would care for the child if ye were to leave, Shelta." He frowned. "The loss would hurt more, but at least one of us would have part of the other with them."

I closed my eyes. He'd already raised a son alone; it would probably be a comfort to have a piece of me in our child. "But if the child came with me, Killian, the tree could take us anywhere."

"I have faith that our love surpasses time." He kissed the tear that ran down the side of my face. "It's bigger than whatever might take ye, and—if ye go—it will draw ye back to me. I want a child with ye, Shelta. If the goddess wills it, she will care for us."

"The same goddess I heard in my head tonight?" More tears fell, fat and hot, into a cavern in my soul.

"She spoke to ye?" His eyes widened with the whispered words.

I nodded.

Killian kissed my forehead, exactly where I'd felt her touch when the voice came with the song of the cellos. "Then ye have nothing to fear, Shelta. She will watch over us. Over our child."

His words sank into my heart. I wanted to believe him so badly that I deceived myself, my resolution cracking. Maybe a child would bond us more fully. Maybe it would help me find Killian again should I be ripped away. "Okay," I whispered, nodding. "I trust you."

He lowered his face to my neck. I tipped my head back, surrendering everything for him, giving over to whatever magic existed between us. That magic would keep us together.

Somehow.

My blood turned into a current of fire, his kisses leaving me panting, chanting his name.

It was the most primal and ancient of songs. Wet and wanting, I met him with my hips. He slipped into me with a groan that came from both of our throats. We pressed together, muscle and skin and breath and moans. His mouth kept coming back to mine, open to his tongue, letting him enter me in two ways at once.

I wrapped myself around him, need and something deeper sparking through us. Each stroke was a merging that shone in my mind as impossibly bright light. Pain and pleasure, the danger of yielding to him ripped through me, an edge that sliced seductively through every illusion I'd clung to before.

Such exquisite vulnerability and power. I drank him in, pulsations rocked every part of me. I gasped as I drew the ecstasy up, that light that was Killian and more than Killian, the glory of what it meant to be husband and wife.

Trembling in the aftermath, I gazed into my husband's eyes and saw my own reflection alight.

He gave a soft laugh. "Ye glow, Shelta." With a shake of his head, he leaned closer. "Every day ye amaze me more."

Unable to speak, I stared at my luminescent skin and had no doubt we'd done something extraordinary.

Chapter 20
Caught in the Truth

I REALLY DIDN'T want to accept the fact that I was pregnant, but it couldn't be helped any longer. Blaming the wet morning and feeling under the weather, I told Killian I needed the day off of warrior training. He left me with an assessing squint, shutting the door behind himself. As soon as he left, I launched across the room to kneel before the chamber pot that still had piss in it from the night before.

Annelle found me sweating, back against the wall, ready to dry heave again from the smell. "Lady Shelta, are ye alright?" She produced a cloth and gave it to me to wipe my face.

I groaned in answer, wanting to swear, but sure it would shock my friend to find I wasn't excited to be pregnant.

"Ye haven't bled in over a moon, milady." She helped me away from the stinky chamber pot, back onto the bed.

"I know," I admitted mournfully.

"Does he ken? Have ye told him?" She looked so happy.

I moaned again. "No, not yet."

She stroked my hair, patted my shoulder. "Ye'll be alright. Ye need to eat. Milord will be thrilled."

"Mmmm." I couldn't be less thrilled, berating myself for getting into this mess.

I closed my eyes and curled into a fetal position until she returned with food, choking it down at her insistence that it would make me feel better. It did, eventually. A bath helped as well, but nothing took away the sharp words in my mind and the weight in my chest.

I had no business bringing another life onto the twisted path of my own. I would either drag the child through wormholes or unwillingly abandon it somewhere along the way. I was a horrible person to even allow it to happen.

The fact that my searches in the library had turned up nothing new about the World Tree, or dragons, or anything else useful somehow made me feel worse. And the goddess hadn't spoken to me since the wedding, despite all the times I pleaded and prayed for her to answer my questions.

I was no closer to my fool's hope of finding dragons or a way to control my time jumps. Add a child to the mix? So much trouble.

Killian came back from training to find me in bed. I'd been there all morning, partially because moving made me nauseous, but also because the thought of becoming a mother still had me paralyzed.

"Shelta, are ye ill?" The smell of him nearly overpowered me as he approached.

"Nope." I sighed. "I'm pregnant. Please come back when you've bathed."

His laugh was a waterfall of light. I couldn't help but smile. "That's wonderful news!"

I closed my eyes as he planted a kiss on my cheek. Kept them closed while his footsteps crossed to the basin by the fresh set of chamber pots. Annelle had put a particularly clean one by the bed earlier, and hovered until I'd sent her away.

Dozing in the jumble of my thoughts, I didn't hear him undress or rinse off, but woke to his body behind me on the bed. He fit himself around me, his arms a comforting weight. Without words, he reassured me, stroking my hair, kissing my neck. He made me feel worshipped like a goddess, but part of me knew the truth. I was a woman lost, and inside me grew a child that would inevitably lose one of its parents.

Forbidden by my husband from the training field and from riding horses, I spent long hours in the company of music and books. Sometimes I'd draw with black ink on thick paper, sketching faeries, dragons, mountains, and trees. My imagination kept me busy, which was welcome when Killian was away. He wouldn't let me accompany him on his travels.

I met with Charlie every few days, sitting for tea. The portrait of his mother watched us, and the lad's kindness made the ravine of guilt growing inside me deepen. When I disappeared, I'd be breaking his trust. I betrayed him each time I pretended everything was fine.

After coming home from a trip with bruises and cuts, Killian went overboard on my security. He left the next day for Stirling, unsure when he'd be back. Refused to tell me anything. I worried for four days straight, until one morning I heard a cough outside the secret door in my bathroom and opened it to find a warrior I'd trained with. He was mildly embarrassed to be caught there, but insisted he was following orders and could not leave his post. I slammed the door, furious.

That afternoon, when I'd finally convinced myself to confront him about the unnecessary guards, Killian arrived home with a surprise that eclipsed my annoyance. With a grin so wide I couldn't be mad at him, he led me to the sitting room. Sir Malcolm waited for us, beaming, with a long, rounded case stretching across the table where I often took tea with the family.

"What's this?" I asked, face growing hot.

"This is the guitar we had made for ye." Sir Malcolm gestured toward the leather case.

I'd completely forgotten the conversation we'd had the first time I met Gavin. "I didn't realize you'd actually had it commissioned."

"Indeed." Killian pushed it toward me. "Open it."

Excitement unfurled like wings inside me as I undid the latches and lifted the top. Cradled in padded cloth lay a six-string guitar with a compact, rounded body, and silver pegs. I ran my fingers over the lacquered wood, tracing the trinity knot at the base of the neck, silver frets beneath the strings. In the wood at the top, where the tuning pegs shone, was a carving. A dragon spread his mighty wings to soar.

The two of them, father and son, radiated pride.

"It's exquisite." I cradled the instrument. "The artisan did an exceptional job."

"He made three," Killian informed me, "before deeming this one worthy."

"Do ye like it, my dear?" The chief's smile couldn't get much wider.

"The dragon is magnificent," I gushed. "The whole thing is amazing. Thank you ever so much!" I put the guitar back in the case and got up to hug them both.

They trailed me downstairs to the piano. After tuning the guitar three times, the strings held, and I tried out a few chords. It sang bright and clear, with a decent bit of bass. I couldn't help but stomp and twirl around, my laugh echoing through the hall.

"Will you give us a wee concert?" Killian asked.

"Of course!" I couldn't wait to play. "Should we get the others?"

In short order, the big room was nearly full. The family gathered in the chairs and sofas with their backs to the fire. Gavin came, and Annelle, and quite a few others. Even little Rheanna was sitting still, big eyes locked on the new instrument in my arms.

"Okay." I figured I should give them some sort of warning. "The guitar lends itself to a wide variety of music, but some of the most fun is likely going to be new to you. I'll play some folk songs, and some that would be categorized as rock 'n roll."

"Rock 'n roll?" Charlie repeated, curious and skeptical at the same time.

"Yeah." I spoke with a sideways grin and a little country drawl.

Oh, it sounded so good. It felt so good to play! I hadn't realized how much I'd missed having a guitar in my arms, the resonance of familiar songs vibrating through my chest.

I warmed up with a folk song and a little raggae, then picked it up a bit. I grinned through a tune by the Beatles, and for the grand finale, I chose *Me and Bobby McGee* by Janis Joplin, which was hands-down one of my favorites to sing. I was sure there were a few references lost to them, but by the loud, blues infused vocals at the end, it was clear the Macleans dug rock 'n roll.

The applause came with cheers. Charlie's yell would've fit in well at a rock concert. Fione joined him with a trill of her own.

"Again!" Young Rheanna clapped her hands.

I laughed. "I'm glad you liked it."

"That was indeed different." Sir Malcolm's eyes were wider than usual.

"What was the third one ye played?" asked Cristina.

I thought back and told her the name. "Ripple."

"I liked that one."

I tried to keep my composure as I imagined Cristina at a Grateful Dead show.

"What was the song about the guitar weeping?" Gavin asked.

"Ah. That is called *While my Guitar Gently Weeps*, by one of the greatest bands ever—to have danced around a fire on Victoria beach." I stumbled through the lie, and instantly knew I was caught. My cheeks burned. Wallace eyed me with skepticism. "Surely it's time for dinner," I said, turning to put the guitar in its case.

Killian and I walked to our room for a brief respite before the evening meal. I placed the guitar in a safe place, and steeled myself to face him.

His eyes were narrow, his mouth twisted into a smirk. "Does 'busted flat' mean ye got beat in a fight, ye have no money, or something else?"

"It, ah, actually is referring to a blown car tire, I believe." I grimaced, thinking of how many references to modern culture I'd just sung. "Though it might refer to being down on your luck. Now that you mention it, I'm not entirely sure. Perhaps I should keep those kinds of songs out of my public performances."

"They may invite questions that would be difficult to answer."

It was a valid observation. My lies were unravelling.

Later that night, Wallace approached as we took our leave from the group after dinner. He leaned close to me, and asked, "Might I have a word?"

I gave him a sideways nod, interlacing my hand in my husband's. Killian's mild expression belied his air of protectiveness. Safe. I was safe with him.

Wallace wore a polite smile beneath calculating eyes, and turned toward the office. Inside, we took the same positions we'd taken the first night, when Wallace thought I might be a spy. I sat in the green chair by the hearth, with Killian next to me in a seat of worn brown leather. Wallace leaned against the massive desk. Moisture gathered on my forehead and neck as the fire crackled its wood-and-flame song.

"Shelta, I think there's more to ye than what we've been told." Wallace's eyes held an obvious request for honesty. "Are ye truly from a small mountain town in Canada?"

My gaze flicked to Killian, who gave a subtle nod. I drew a deep breath, and blew it out. I'd never told anyone but Evalynne—in my adult life, anyway—and she'd never believed me. None of my foster mothers had understood. None of my fleeting friends. Now Killian *and* Wallace would know. Would they tell Sir Malcolm? Cristina? Would everyone know I was a freak from another time?

It would almost be better. Even if they thought differently of me. At least then they'd understand when I inevitably disappeared.

"I am from Canada," I began, "and other places, but the circumstances are rather different. You're right, there's a lot more than what I've told you, but for good reason. The truth is rather hard to believe."

Wallace looked at me, asking with his silence. My gaze drifted to Killian.

He leaned toward me. My husband. The man who'd gone to Brighid's spring and watched me emerge from the World Tree. "I think," he said, "that if anyone can believe ye, it would be my brother. Ye also have me to vouch for ye, mind."

Throat tight, I had to force myself to speak. "I traveled from another time, Wallace. There was this big tree, glowing, and I touched it and found myself standing before your brother in a different time and place."

My tongue tripped over my words. I was doing a terrible job explaining. Should I tell him I'd always fallen through time? Probably better to give him as little information as possible.

"She came out of the World Tree at the spring." Killian's voice was even. Deep. A secret surrendered. "I was paying my respects to the goddess."

Wallace was quiet for a long beat, eyes narrowed as he studied his brother. Then he returned his focus to me. "What was the year from whence ye came?"

"2035." Just shy of three centuries forward. The staggering weight of time pressed on the room.

Wallace nodded, his eyebrows high. "That explains the music. Explains quite a few things."

"You believe me?"

"Aye." The word came out in a wavering note. "If Killian says ye came from the World Tree, I believe him, and I detect no dishonesty in ye. It's not something ye would want to tempt without reason anyhow, the work of the goddess." He turned a sharp eye to his brother.

Killian tilted his head, his expression unreadable.

The two of them stared at each other for long enough that I cleared my throat. Both brothers snapped their focus to me, and I smiled at Wallace, heart pounding, hands out. "So, are we good?"

Wallace snickered. Shook his head. "Aye, sister from another time. We're good."

Killian stood, and I looked down to grab hold of my skirts. By the time I was standing, the brothers were engaged in another silent battle of slightly narrowed eyes and grim almost-smiles. Whatever was going on between them would be fought out on the field the next day. I made a mental note to go and watch.

The corridors were quiet as Killian and I walked back to our bedchamber, me in a sort of shell-shocked daze. I'd told Wallace who I was. What I was. And he believed me.

Safe inside the sanctuary of our room, my husband helped me out of the layers of my dress. His hands progressively touched my body more and the laces less. "Ye're the gift of the goddess," he whispered in my ear. "Did it feel good to tell Wallace?"

"It did," I admitted. "He's a good man. Better that he knows the truth, rather than there always being something about me that doesn't seem right to him, but it's still a lot for anyone to handle."

"Aye, but he'd prefer the truth." Killian removed more of my dress. Soon he had me in my shift, one hand rubbing my swollen belly, another wrapped around my ribs, climbing higher.

I had to ask before he carried me away from thought entirely. "Killian?"

"Shelta?" His gaze bored into me.

"What did you do at Brighid's spring? What did you ask of her? There's something you haven't told me."

He stopped his advances and drew a long, even breath. "I gave the goddess an offering, and a confession. I told her that I was ready to love again—that I wanted to love again." He smiled easy, unashamed. "My brother would say I tempted fate by involving Brighid, but this is the old way, being in tune with the land and the powers that guide life."

I nodded, unsure how the man and the goddess could pull me so far back in time. How much did my charging into a portal on purpose change the rules? How much could my will bend the branches of the World Tree?

"Hey." I grabbed his hand. I needed to make a promise. Needed to believe in it. "If I disappear, I want you to know that I will do everything I possibly can to come back to you. I'll find a way."

"Ye will." He moved closer. Slid a hand behind my head. "We will. Ye came to me, Shelta. My wife." His voice thickened with power. "If I must, I'll reach through time to find ye."

My head bobbed in an awed nod. My soul seemed to float. Expansive. Aware.

Like the goddess was listening.

Chapter 21
So Precious, So Fleeting

SUMMER CAME TO the Isle of Mull in shades of green and grey and the occasional burst of glorious sunshine. By the first week of August, my belly was round, the child within so strong it sometimes kicked the breath from my lungs. The midwife assured me all was well, but I had to talk myself out of pure panic when I thought about giving birth without modern medicine.

I woke one morning to sunlight streaming through narrow windows, and my husband readying himself for training. Killian pulled on a jacket as black as his hair.

"Good day, my wife." He gave me a bow.

"Good morning." I stretched my arms up.

"We've a clear sky. Would ye care for a walk?"

I nodded. "Aye. I'll take my guitar and play by the sea." A nearby viewpoint had become a favorite spot of mine, outside the castle walls, overlooking the ocean.

Killian came close to catch me in a kiss. His beard scratched me gently, his touch sending a thrill through me that never got old.

I smiled up at him. "I'll stop by the field and get you on my way out?"

"Aye." He gave my belly a rub, kissed me again, and walked out the door.

A little while later, I slung my plaid purse over one shoulder, laden with four berry scones, a chunk of cheese, a flask of water, and the few things I didn't dare leave the castle without. I might've fooled myself into not dwelling on the fear of a wormhole snatching me away, but I still kept necessities with me at all times.

My daggers were a comforting weight in my boots as I made my way outside, guitar in one hand, rose colored skirts swishing beneath my cloak. As I neared the dragon statue that dominated the garden courtyard, I recalled the dream I'd had the night before. There'd been a wide valley with steep mountains and dragons flying amongst the rocky peaks. The red dragon had been trying to tell me something, but I couldn't remember the message.

The clang of metal on the other side of the wall lured me toward the practice field. As always, my heart gave a little leap as I passed through the stone archway to the sight of Maclean warriors sparring with axes and swords.

I picked a favorite spot in the shade and settled onto an empty bench to observe the brothers. They were well matched; Killian and Wallace, sons of the chief. They'd been trying to best each other their whole lives.

Both men had discarded their jackets, and their arms bulged beneath their linen tunics. The muscles in their legs tensed, kilts swaying as they circled and lunged. They moved with deadly speed, making my pulse quicken.

Beat, thrust, parry, swipe, pull, step, lunge, slice. There was music in their dance-like combat, though the moves varied constantly. Then came a shift in the rhythm—Wallace's sword went a hair wide. Killian took his chance, stopping with the point of his blade near his brother's chest. I held my breath.

Both of them panted as Wallace stepped back with a small bow of admission. They clasped arms, then Killian saw me and came over.

I beamed at him. "That was well done."

The compliment earned me a grin. "Thank ye. It was not easily done."

"No. It didn't look it." I leaned against the wall, following him with my eyes.

He sheathed his sword, splashed his face and neck with water from a nearby bucket, and took a long drink from a separate barrel. Droplets fell from his hair, catching in the light as his gaze sought mine. The moment drew out, like time slowed down, a picture etched into my mind by the brazen sunlight. Then Killian walked toward me, and held a hand out to help me up.

We strode across the courtyard, turned the corner, and went out the main gate of the castle, where a strong breeze tugged at my cloak. The weight of my body slowed me down, but the walk felt good. Being outside the castle walls was strangely freeing.

Killian carried my guitar, and soon I could see the tall pine tree with its wooden bench and spectacular view. I'd touched the tree before. It was safe. The ocean air sharpened my senses and the sun warmed my face.

When we reached the viewpoint and settled on the log bench, I marveled at the loch that stretched into the mainland, dark blue water sparkling in the sunlight. Distant mountains rose above like gods surveying their domain.

In that epic setting, I brought my guitar out of its case and tuned the strings. As I did, the baby kicked hard enough to make me wince.

"Strong little one." I rubbed my belly.

Killian slid a hand on top of mine. If the child was a boy, we'd name him Brendan, after the saint known for his navigation—in hopes that the child would be safe voyaging through time. If it was a girl, Killian was adamant that one of her names be Brighid. After the goddess. For the thousandth time, I wondered which it would be.

Hormones surging, I fell into Killian's gaze, overcome by how much I loved him. "Thank you for this life, Killian." I leaned forward, and he tilted his head down so I could reach him with my kiss. So much within that intimate touch couldn't be expressed in words.

Finally, I turned my attention to the guitar and began to play. Music drifted in waves of clear notes, melody, and ocean breeze. It wasn't a song I'd played before; this was one of Time's compositions. It lilted on gusts of wind and reached for the mist coming off rocks far below.

Haunting. Enchanting.

The rhythm rolled through me, making me sway.

I leaned back against the bench, tipping my head to look at the tree that towered behind me, its branches green beneath the blue of the sky.

The wind picked up, pulling at my hair and blowing in my skirts. One of the tree's branches reached toward me, grazing the crown of my head, and all at once I realized I'd been a fool. There was no safe tree.

The world sucked in on itself. Killian drew a sharp breath and reached for me, but the brush of his hand against my arm burnt into oblivion with a blinding flash of singing light.

PART II

MOTHER

Chapter 22

Into the Wilderness

MY BREATH LEFT me in a wordless, primal sound.

Every wormhole came with a different soundtrack, all of them ridiculously complex. This one was smoky, like a heavenly choir headbanging to dark country. The portal squeezed me, and I glimpsed silver starlight, but was pulled toward a swath of bright blue sky.

All at once, the spinning stopped and the deafening light dimmed. I shook, my sight slowly adjusting to my new surroundings. My mind felt as if it'd been liquefied. The usual symptoms of being sucked through a wormhole.

I had one hand gripped around the neck of my guitar and the case was still beside me, tucked against my leg. Somehow that was reassuring. The dark green of my cloak spread beneath my pink skirts, and my purse hung on a branch to my right.

There was, however, no ring on my finger.

Oh, Killian. My eyes stung. I rested my head on the body of my guitar.

Holding onto the branch beside me for balance, I looked down. I was sitting in a tree, seven feet in the air.

Surprise overtook the grief. Was this Brighid's idea of a joke?

I wasn't sure how I was going to get down without a great deal of trouble, and gaped at the roundness of my belly. The trunk beside me spanned wider than my arms. Carefully tilting my head back, I followed the tree up so far I started to get dizzy.

Where and when had I gone now?

Rugged wilderness surrounded me, with a ridge of pointed mountains on either side of a wide valley. Forests crept up the hillsides. Rocky heights reached far into the afternoon-blue sky, and I had a blast of déjà vu. It was the scene from my dream the night before. The dragons had been trying to warn me, and I'd been too dense to get the message.

Beneath me, a path wound through the high grass of a meadow that stretched across the valley floor. A fresh, green scent hung in the air, and a creek burbled in the distance. Birds sang their songs, the sun low in the sky.

All of this seemed quite pleasant, except for the fact that my guts were being pulled through a black hole, my heart having disintegrated. The anxiety I generally kept at bay raged out of control. I turned to the goddess that had spoken once in my mind to the music of cellos. Would she answer me now?

Goddess, why? Surely she knew the rest of the question.

It was time for the next step of your journey.

The hair on the back of my neck stood up in response to the enormity of her attention. *I was happy, Brighid. Please take me back.*

Your path is not tied to one world, Shelta. You must keep growing. Could the goddess feel sorrow? I thought I heard it in her voice. It came through like the scent of rain.

Why? What is it I'm supposed to be? I was desperate to understand, but her presence faded.

Trust, she whispered, and left me alone in the wilderness.

There was no going back. And I was stuck in a tree.

With hurricane-force emotions whirling and my brain a numb wreck, I absentmindedly strummed minor chords on my guitar. Through tears, I opened my voice to release the pressure building inside.

I was about to go into another round of the raw, soaring melody, when a soft whicker made me look up. I had an audience.

"Don't stop," said the man on the horse who crossed the clearing.

My hands froze. I stared at the stranger who'd found me, desperate for a clue about where I'd been transported this time.

He rode as if it were more natural than walking, wearing a black, wide-brimmed hat, tan leather coat, and bone-white handled pistols strapped to each thigh. Like I'd landed in the Wild West or something. He rode a palomino, golden and blonde. The animal eyed me with intelligence. I took a big breath, in and out, and the horse responded in kind, proceeding toward me with its ears facing forward.

"Hello." The man stopped beneath the tree. He had to look up to see my face.

I wiped my cheeks with my hands. Sniffed. "Hello."

He flashed a brief smile beneath his beard. "You sing beautifully."

"Thank you." I tried a hesitant smile.

"How did you get up there?" He had an American drawl with a touch of an accent. Spanish, maybe? His skin was a shade or two darker than mine.

"You probably wouldn't believe me if I told you." How, indeed, did I get up in this tree?

"Would you tell me truthfully?" His hazel eyes were unbelievably clear. Steady. Something in them reminded me of Killian.

"Yes." Stupid, stupid answer.

"Then I'll do my best to believe you." His black hat concealed half of his face as he tilted his head in a nod. When he looked at me again, waiting, all I could do was exhale and brace myself.

It would sound outrageous. Killian had seen me come through, and Wallace had his brother to believe. This man had no reason to trust me. I didn't know how to start, or what to say. Yet he looked at me with sincerity that deserved an answer.

"Alright." I nodded. "You asked for the truth, I'll give it to you. I have the troubling tendency of falling through time and space. Up until a short while ago I was in Scotland, in the year 1754. Before that, I was in Canada, in the year 2035. Perhaps a quarter of an hour ago the world spun around me, and suddenly I was sitting in this tree. I'm not sure how or why it happens, but it's quite disorienting."

"I can imagine." He arched an eyebrow over stormy eyes, like he was wrestling with my confession. "So, you decided to sing a song?"

"Yes, well. I wasn't sure what else to do, and I was already holding my guitar, so…" I trailed off, knowing how ridiculous I sounded. I'd had a death grip on the instrument since I came out of the spinning. I brought it to my side to put it in its case, and the man saw my belly.

His eyes widened. "You're with child!"

"Rather far along, I'm afraid." I swallowed. "I really don't know where I am. Or when."

Holding his gaze took all my effort, and for a split second my scattered thoughts silenced. He studied me, seeking honesty or deception. I had no idea if he actually believed me—it didn't show in his face. Only intense assessment. Reluctance.

I needed him to believe me.

Finally, he held up his hand, and I reached down to feel the worn leather of his glove. His voice was kind and steady, like his grip.

"My name is Troy Sanchez. It is the fifth day of August in the year 1887, and we are in the Territory of Wyoming, in the United States of America."

I nodded as a wave of heat went through me. My eyes stung. The child would be due any day. A child Killian would never meet.

"I suppose you're going to need some help." Troy's tone was friendly, but his eyes told me he would've preferred if this whole awkward situation hadn't occurred. "Would you like me to help you down?"

I frowned at my tree branch. "That would be much appreciated."

I packed up the guitar and handed him the case, holding the trunk for balance each time my belly tried to tip me forward. With a death grip on Troy's hand, I stepped down as gently as possible, bringing my cloak with me and crouching on the furs of his bedroll, grateful the horse didn't try to shimmy me off its hindquarters. My purse banged against my belly.

Troy slid to the ground, giving me the saddle. I arranged my skirts as best I could while the horse waited for me to get it together. The saddle was scuffed, with dust clinging to the creases. Well worn.

Troy attached my guitar case to the back, pulled a rifle bag from his saddlebags, and slung it over his shoulder. He caught my hand as I teetered, trying to get my feet in the stirrups, and a wave of recognition washed over me as I looked down at his face. It jolted through my chest and sunk into my belly like a bolder. I pulled my hand away.

"Here." He lifted the stirrup to get to the buckles beneath. "I'll shorten these."

His hat hid his face as he worked, but when he looked up again, a chill shivered through me despite the warmth of the day. His face was sculpted differently than Killian's, his chin broader, his nose wider, his hair longer. And still there was a sense of Killian's presence, totally unexplainable and utterly confusing.

Troy's eyes showed a shadow of hesitation, his posture rigid. "You look strangely familiar. What's your name?"

Familiar? Was he reading my mind? "Shelta Maclean."

"Well, Miss Maclean—or is it Mrs. Maclean?"

"Shelta, please." Tears leaked from my eyes. Damn pregnancy hormones.

"Alright, Miss Shelta, whatever's happened to you, you've had a shock, but you're safe now. Cry if you must, but know that I will help you." He said it like a promise that had poisoned edges, a commitment made but not wanted.

All I wanted was Killian.

Chapter 23

The Horse Whisperer

THE HORSE MOVED beneath me, following Troy without guidance. I let the rope reins hang on its sloping neck and focused on trying to breathe. It took everything I had not to fall to pieces and start sobbing on its golden mane.

What a terrible feeling, helplessness. Who was going to help me give birth? My child was about to be born into a world surrounded by strangers. The World Tree abducted me at my most vulnerable moment, and I'd all but given up on finding the red dragon.

Riding behind my reluctant hero, who walked in long strides with pistols at his thighs, I struggled with the practice of trust. An ocean of uncertainty, a relentless rain of loss, and an ever-rising edge of panic threatened to drown me.

And then the baby kicked. Three times. When I pressed my hand over my belly, the child poked at my palm. The warmth of the horse rose through my skirts. I willed myself to calm with the steady rocking, bringing myself into the moment, into my senses. I couldn't panic. I had to keep it together for the baby.

The path followed a stream through grasses and brush, cool water scenting the air. The sky was a painter's dream of pink clouds against a deep gradient of blue. Colossal mountains rose from the far side of the forest like a wall of granite and went so high it was easy to imagine them as the home of gods and mythical creatures. If dragons were real, surely they lived in mountains like these. But I didn't dare hope.

I drew a shaky breath, and broke the long silence. "This valley's beautiful."

"Yes." Troy's hat angled as he lifted his head to gaze at the ridge. "It still strikes me to the bone with wonder."

"Have you lived here all your life?"

"No." He didn't elaborate.

"Where did you grow up?" I coaxed, needing to talk, to keep my focus present. My thoughts kept trying to derail into worrying about what Killian was going through. Was he walking through the courtyard alone? Was he stoic? Was he on his knees by the edge of the ocean, praying to the goddess in vain?

"On the prairies." Troy didn't look at me, but he dropped back to walk near the horse's neck. Like he didn't want the sound to carry. "My father was from Mexico. He met my mother in Indiana, and I spent the first part of my life on a farm, until the railroad forced my parents to sell their land. Then I headed west. I spent a few years in Santa Fe, and helped build half the town of Columbia—little place in the mountains of Colorado. Mining town. I took what money I made there and left to find a place away from everything. I like to live quietly."

"You're a carpenter?"

"Sometimes."

"Did you find that place of peace you were looking for?" I asked, knowing I was invading his quiet.

"This is it." He lifted a hand and swept it around. "Or part of it. My house lies at the base of those mountains." His voice dropped even lower, as if it were a secret.

"That sounds lovely." And lonely. "Do others live there with you?"

"No. I live alone, mostly."

"Mostly?"

"Sometimes I have visitors."

"Ah."

"Would you like to walk for a while?" He looked up, but didn't meet my eyes. My giant belly drew his gaze.

"That would be great." Either he'd noticed my fidgeting in the saddle, trying to find a position where my hips didn't complain, or he wanted to talk without making so much noise.

Getting off the horse was an awkward half-fall into Troy, who caught me under my arms and blushed furiously when his hands inadvertently brushed the sides of my milk-swollen boobs. Better than putting pressure on my belly. I thanked him, heat in my own cheeks, and set my feet on the soil of Wyoming for the first time since a road trip I'd taken in 1994. What a mindfuck.

Troy adjusted my guitar case on the saddle and gave the horse's head a rub. The beautiful creature followed as we began to walk. I studied him over my shoulder.

"I have another question." I had a thousand questions.

Troy chuckled. "Let me guess, you want to know why my horse doesn't run off."

"Yes." I tried to keep up with his steps, but my heavy body made me slow.

"Well, that's a bit of a story." He paced beside me, gaze darting around, so much like Killian. Alert. Constantly surveying the surroundings.

"Would you be willing to tell it?" I spoke low. Perhaps we weren't the only ones out in this wilderness. Was he watchful for wildlife, or something else?

"I was thinking about how to start." Troy flashed a wary smile. "The first time was when I was a boy. I helped my older brother care for the horses we had: two big drafts and a gelding for riding. It was one of the drafts that began it."

"Do you have other brothers or sisters?" I asked.

"No." He met my eyes for a heartbeat. "Do you want to hear this story?"

"Yes, sorry. Please go on." I nearly tripped on a rock, and scrambled to steady myself.

"Well the draft—her name was Maggie—she was my favorite. I talked to her like I talked to the other horses, but one day she talked back."

I pressed my lips together so I wouldn't interrupt. The name Maggie reminded me of my mare, back in the field behind Duart. Would she wonder why I wasn't bringing her my apple cores? Would she miss the way I brushed her?

"She talked to me," Troy went on. "Not out loud. I heard her distinctly in my mind. Different words than I would've chosen. She thanked me for the meal of hay, and asked if there would also be oats."

Troy's face broadened, brightening, showing a glimpse of the child he'd been. Our eyes met, and it was like a glimpse into his soul. Recognition socked me in the gut. I looked away, reeling. I was losing it, making him into Killian in my mind. He wasn't. He was a stranger.

"I was so young, I didn't really think anything of it." Troy flipped his palms up, talking with his hands. "I brought her a helping of oats and left her munching contentedly in the stables. It went on from there. Not with every horse, mind you, but a good number of them. Our little chats became actual conversations while I rode west, since I had so much time with only my horse as a friend."

Out of nowhere, I heard Killian's voice in my mind. *I believe in magic, Shelta. I think it runs in your blood, and in mine.*

"You talk to horses?" I blurted stupidly to Troy, off-kilter.

"You fall through time and space?" Troy cast me a dubious glance.

"Right." If he could believe me, I could certainly believe him. "That must be nice, being able to communicate with them. Horses are incredible animals. This one is particularly beautiful." I tossed a glance at the palomino clip-clopping behind us.

Troy's chest rose with obvious pride. "He is, isn't he? Well, Miss Shelta, it's my pleasure to introduce you to Sundance."

"Should I curtsy or something?" I joked.

"You could, but it would go straight to his head." Troy smiled sideways at me.

I turned to get a good look at the horse behind us. He stopped, both ears forward. I was again taken by the intelligence I sensed in him. A thin white stripe started above his eyes and nearly reached his nose, otherwise his hair shone golden, mane and tail champagne blonde.

"You're magnificent," I murmured.

A velvety voice spoke in my mind. *You're not too bad looking yourself, for a two-legger.*

I let out a small yelp.

"Did you hear him?" Troy's expression teetered between disbelief and suppressed hilarity.

"Yes." My insides tickled with the strangest sensation of giddiness. "He's laughing at me now, isn't he?"

"Can you hear him laugh?" With a hand on my arm, Troy drew me around. He gazed at me with something like awe.

"It's not a sound, really. I think I feel him laughing." I broke into a huge grin.

Troy turned toward the horse. "Well, Sundance, what do you think of that?"

I didn't hear the answer. Evidently Sundance wasn't letting me in on that bit of conversation.

Our shadows grew long. I couldn't walk very fast, and Troy wanted to cover some ground before dark, so I had to ride again. He grunted as he helped me onto Sundance. I tried to pull myself up on the saddle, but my belly got in the way of everything, with a restless child inside.

The horse's hooves clopped a steady rhythm on the dirt trail. Troy's footfalls were nearly silent beneath the whisper of grasses and trees swaying in the wind. The creak of leather rubbing on the saddle underscored my labored breath. It didn't take long for my hips and legs to ache.

As we rounded a bend in the road, the mountains blocked the sun. Not ten feet down the trail, in the cool of the shadows, a huge bear turned its head toward us. My breath came in sharp. Troy had a gun drawn in an instant, his body still, the barrel of the pistol pointed down.

Sundance stopped beneath me. I clutched the reins and took a fistful of mane, careful not to pull. I didn't want to fall off if he spooked. I was spooked. I'd seen bears before, but none so close, and always much smaller than this one. It had the rounded shoulders of a grizzly.

"Hello, bear." Troy spoke in a low voice. "We're headed up the trail here. If you'd care to get on into the bushes and put us behind you that would be just fine."

The bear sat on its haunches as if considering the suggestion, but leaned forward as leaves rustled and two cubs emerged from the foliage, one of them behind us. My blood turned icy as the grizzly rose to tower above Troy.

"You don't want to do that, now." Troy cocked the gun. "We don't mean you any harm."

Sundance backed up, step by measured step. I never knew a horse could be so calm. He made space for the young bear to sidle past us, and Troy sidestepped to give it more room. The mother now had both cubs with her, but she didn't back down. A growl rumbled in her throat, sharp teeth showing.

The moment she moved to attack, Troy shot a bullet into the ground at her feet. I flinched at the sharp crack, but Sundance did not. The cubs took off into the brush. Momma bear jumped back, her face scrunched like she wasn't sure if she should run or be offended.

Troy didn't give her time to think. Two more shots went off in rapid succession, dirt exploding a few feet from the bear, and she went barreling through the bushes after her cubs.

We stayed still until the sounds of the grizzly's retreat were too far away to hear. My heart pounded in my chest, the child in my belly pushing painfully against my organs.

Troy slid his pistol back into its holster and looked at me. He didn't say anything, and the best I could do was nod. I guess he decided that was enough, because he started walking down the path again. Sundance followed, my fists still entwined in his mane.

The night choir came out in layers of music around us. I watched the road closely, but wasn't as jumpy as I'd been an hour ago, when we'd seen the grizzly. Nature's serenade put me at ease.

Crickets thrummed, frogs croaked, and birds trilled their evening songs. Every so often an owl would sound its throaty call, to be answered by another several trees away. Twilight gave over to starlight.

Troy led me off the trail to an area sheltered by small trees and large shrubs. A fire pit waited, ringed by rocks.

"We're stopping?" My voice croaked after so much silence.

"Yes. We won't reach the cabin until tomorrow, and it's a good night to sleep beneath the sky. The moon is almost full." Troy helped me down, and started unsaddling Sundance.

I turned around to see the moon rising huge and bright above a mountain range to the east. It lit up the faces of the peaks towering above us. Goosebumps rose on my arms. There was no doubt in my mind that the goddess watched, her beauty cutting through the night.

Troy walked up behind me, only a foot away. Too near. As if realizing it, he stepped back, but my heart still pounded. Cocooned in my cloak as if it could shelter me from the intensity of my feelings, I turned from the moon, my stomach a knot of confusion with a small child adding to the mix.

Chapter 24
Songs by the Fire

FLAMES DANCED RED and orange. Wood crackled, smoke swirling up into the night. I stared unblinking into the fire, my thoughts haunting and painful. My fingers searched in vain for my wedding ring. I'd taken to playing with it as often as I touched the dragon at my throat.

Troy noticed. "I think it may be your turn to answer some questions, Miss Shelta, if you're willing." His voice was at once a new song and an old one, low, with an edge of caution.

I gave a moan so quiet I doubted he heard it. He'd allowed me the entire day without anything further than the explanation in the tree. He'd shared personal stories of his own, carried me on his horse, fed me dinner, and set me up with a bed of thick fur under the bright moon, insisting he'd be fine sleeping on the sandy soil with only a thin blanket and his coat as a pillow.

I adjusted myself, eventually accepted that no position was going to be comfortable, and aimed a pleasant look his way. "You deserve some answers. What would you like to know?"

He looked hesitant to ask, but came out with it anyway. "Should there be a ring on that finger?"

"Should?" I sighed. "I don't know about should. There was earlier today. It didn't make it through the World Tree, apparently, though my other belongings did. I don't understand why." He kept quiet. I thanked him inwardly, and went on. "The last time I fell through a portal, I appeared at a sacred spring in front of a Highlander in eighteenth-century Scotland. Killian Maclean." I had to stop to swallow. "He saw me appear from thin air."

"Scotland?" Troy's voice had a dreamy feel to it, like he was trying to imagine it.

"Aye." I cast him a smile steeped in sorrow. "I lived in a castle on an isle by the sea. Beautiful, rugged, and in a parallel reality from the world where I grew up. Wars that were the basis of the history I'd learned hadn't happened in the Scotland I found." The whole thing still made my mind spin.

"And this Killian asked you to marry him?" Troy watched the fire, his face unreadable.

"He did." I rubbed my belly and fell silent. Throat thick. Emotions far too raw.

Troy turned to me, gaze level with mine. "Well, Miss Shelta—" He shook his head. "Mrs. Maclean. I don't know what magic brought you here, but it placed you directly in my path. I will do what I can to help you and your child."

"Thank you." My voice was barely a whisper. Troy's words sent a crack through me. Mrs. Maclean. If the goddess was behind this, why take me now? Why here?

"Are you alright?" Troy asked, ever so gently. The compassion alone was heartbreaking.

"No." I cracked a smile. "I'll be fine, all the same."

He leaned against a rock. "I expect you're tired."

"I am. But you deserve a song—as long as you don't mind if I play." I reached for my guitar case and unbuckled the straps on the side.

"I don't mind, but you owe me nothing. Do you understand?" Troy's voice required me to look at him, his words an echo of Killian's.

"Thank you," I answered, knowing it was not enough, could never be enough. "Thank you ever so much. But music is a gift I'm able to give. I'm sure rescuing a pregnant woman wasn't on your list of things to do today."

He made a sound that wasn't quite a laugh. "Not exactly."

"Besides." I tuned the strings. "It would be a terrible loss to have a night this perfect, with a campfire so close and an instrument at hand, and *not* play some music."

He smiled at that, though his eyes were still guarded. There was nothing of the easy acceptance Killian had welcomed me with—but then, by his own admission, Killian had *asked* for me.

I didn't know if I could trust my voice, so I played the strings softly, letting the guitar sing for me. Eventually, the music brought me an inner calm, and I swayed, letting my voice sneak into the night, pitching it close, so the sound wouldn't carry too far.

Ocean Mama sings me a lullaby
Waves crash me to sleep
A hypnotic serenade
Offered from the deep

Ocean, I feel you
In my blood, in my bones

In the space within my heart
That my soul calls home

Shining in the moonlight
Swallowing the sun
Birthing the stars
Ocean Mama, bring me home

I rocked as I sang, waves crashing inside of me, comforted by the rhythm even as remembrance of the seas around Scotland wrung my heart. The child within was still. A lullaby for the baby, therapy for mommy. Bittersweet, I ended the song on a minor chord, and let the resonance ring.

Troy waited until the last note had drifted into the night before he spoke. "I've never seen the ocean. What's it like?"

"It's vast. Nurturing. Dangerous. And beautiful enough to take your breath away every time."

"Like these mountains."

"Yes."

"Will you play another song, Miss Shelta?"

I did. I played several—easy, sweet songs that I knew by heart. They flowed out of me, through the guitar in ripples of sound that stretched subtle roots into the wilderness. I felt the earth beneath me listening, the fire dancing in time, the breeze adding a whisper of harmony through the leaves of the trees.

Troy banked the fire while I played, spread out his blanket, and settled in, eyes closed. I thought perhaps I'd sung him to sleep, and put my guitar quietly in its case when I finished the last song.

Every bone in my body gave a collective sigh when I laid down on my side. As I covered myself with my cloak, I noticed Troy had opened his eyes. If we both reached out, we wouldn't have been able to touch, and yet the closeness was as much as I could bear.

"That was the most beautiful music I've ever heard," he murmured. "Thank you, Shelta."

Not "Miss Shelta" or "Mrs. Maclean," just my first name, spoken with incredible care. I smiled as kindly as I knew how, whispered, "You're welcome," and closed my eyes. I couldn't handle looking into his any longer.

CHAPTER 25
TO THE CABIN

MY DREAMS TOOK me back to Scotland, into Killian's tower room, where we lay together with soft furs beneath. His words were a chant at near-whisper, arms encircling me, breath on my skin. "Shelta, my wife. Gift of the goddess. Our love spans time and space."

He rested a hand on my enormous belly, his face giving way to sweetness.

"I have your ring," he said. "I'll keep it safe. Every time I touch it, I'm sending you courage. Sending you love."

Tears spilled over. I tried to tell him how much I loved him, how afraid I was, but the dream denied me words. I had no voice.

As the vision of Killian faded and I half-woke in a tide of sorrow, a small green dragon emerged from the forest. It climbed my legs and curled up in the space above my hip, near the child. The little creature purred contentment as my breath made it rise and fall.

Deep in the night, when the cat-dragon had faded away and the stars shone in my dreams, the red dragon came. I stood with him on a mountain ledge, overlooking the wide, moonlit valley. His scales were like fire, silver shimmering on gold and crimson.

"Where are you?" I restrained my urge to reach out and touch him, afraid he'd disappear.

Waiting for you. The dragon spoke in my mind. *It will be some time before you reach me.*

"Why?" I asked. "Tell me how to find you."

You're not ready. You have a child.

Frustration rose. I never should've listened to Killian and let myself get pregnant. "I'm ready."

You're ready for the next step in your journey, but not for me. Not yet.

Why? I slid into my mind with my words. Could he feel how much I wanted this? *Can you take me back to Scotland? Help me navigate the World Tree?*

First you must cross the threshold into motherhood.

The dream twisted, and the ledge melted into nothingness. The dragon was gone, no ground beneath my feet. I fell from the tall cliffs near Killian's castle, into the cold, dark sea.

The sky was just beginning to lighten when I woke to strong jabs from the baby and an urgent need to pee. Stars were still visible; the sun was a long way behind the mountains. When I walked awkwardly back to my bed and sank into the furs, Troy sat up, blinking at me.

"Good morning." His voice was scratchy.

"Good morning." I wished the dragon was still here, the discussion on the ledge in my dream at the forefront of my mind. It made sense that I had to be a mother first, but I didn't want to wait to meet the crimson dragon. He was the key to traveling the World Tree. Had to be.

The baby kicked, making me wince.

Troy's mouth pulled to one side, like he didn't know what to do about me. "Do you need more rest?" His eyes slid to my belly. "It's early yet."

"I'm too awake to sleep now." My body was very much in control, all needs focused on the child within. A child I would meet soon.

The birds sang and the sky grew lighter. I took deep breaths of crisp morning air. Troy produced a breakfast of apples and cheese from his saddlebags, I contributed the last of my scones, and we ate in silence, listening to the music of dawn.

As I gave my apple core to Sundance, I let out an audible "Ooof!" The kid was most definitely awake.

"Are you alright?" Troy sounded alarmed.

"Yes, but there's a party happening in there right now." I held out my hand. "Do you want to feel the baby?"

He lifted one side of his mouth and stepped closer. I placed his palm where most of the action was taking place. Holding my hand over his, I assured him, without words, that everything was okay.

"Whoa!" Troy exclaimed, surprised at the strength of the kick.

"I know!" I lifted my hand.

He dropped his away. "You're really close to giving birth, aren't you?" It was more a statement than a question.

"Honestly, it could be any day now." I tried to sound calm about it, but considering we seemed to be in the middle of the wilderness and I had no idea how to give birth on my own, I was borderline terrified. I hoped I could at least find a midwife.

Troy packed his things and my guitar onto Sundance. "We should get to the cabin. It's not far from here. And then I'll go for help."

He flashed a reassuring smile, but a shadow of alarm showed in the strain of his eyes.

We crossed a wider road before entering a thick forest that stretched up the side of the mountain. Troy strode ahead while Sundance moved beneath me, climbing the narrow trail into the shelter of the trees.

A few minutes later, as we turned a switchback above the road, I heard the whinny of a horse and men's voices from below. Troy retreated into the shadows. Sundance hustled into thicker cover where the sun didn't shine on his golden hair. I wrapped my fingers in his mane, chest pounding as if I were sprinting though I'd frozen in place, as still as the horse beneath me.

A patch between the bows of an evergreen tree gave me a narrow view of the road below. Dust rose as man after man passed on their horses, every one armed to the teeth. Bits of conversation wafted up over the sound of so many hoof beats, but I couldn't make out the words.

Lightheaded, I realized I was holding my breath. I exhaled as silently as possible, loathe to give away our hiding place above them. The last man in the pack looked up, but no sign of suspicion showed on his face. He continued whistling his off-key tune until it was lost in the cloud of dust that followed them.

We waited until the riders were well past. Finally, Troy came over to where I sat with bunches of mane in white-knuckled fists.

I made myself relax, and stroked the horse's neck.

Troy's gaze was a silent question.

I nodded, not wanting him to see how scared I was of the world I'd entered, the condition I was in, and the fact that everyone I loved was gone. I think he saw it anyway.

He reached up and touched my hand, rubbing his thumb over the back of my fingers like one of Killian's kisses. Then he turned away, and began his long strides up the path. Sundance followed. I clutched the saddle in an attempt to keep myself from falling apart.

"We're nearly there, Shelta." Troy turned around to check on me. "Can you ride a bit longer?"

"Yes." All I wanted was to lie down.

The trees opened up to reveal a large clearing ringed by forest. A cabin sat on a rise in the clearing, and a lake shone blue to the north.

"It's lovely," I said. "Did you build it yourself?" I took in the log walls, the covered porch, and what looked like a garden on the side surrounded by a tall fence. A mountain towered above in the distance.

"I did, with some help." A wolf-like dog bounded up to us with a deep bark. Troy squatted down to greet him. "This is Damien."

I grinned in the way you can't help when a dog is wiggling with joy from head to tail. Troy began walking again, and Damien bounded along.

"Is he young?" I recognized the puppy-like bounce.

"Two." Troy threw me a sideways smile. "He's got a bit of wolf in him, which is handy, as he catches his own meals easy enough. I brought him home after visiting my Nwetaka friends." He looked at me with a watchful expression.

"Are they the tribe native to this area?"

"They are. I see more of them than I do of the folk in the nearest town."

I nodded. "What's the situation between those settling this country and the natives? It wasn't a pretty time in the history I learned."

Troy shook his head. "It isn't good. Most settlers have an irrational fear of people who are different—though there are more similarities than differences if you pay attention. And the natives don't understand how we can claim ownership of land they've roamed for as long as their people have been here. It isn't right to deny them their territories, to push them out or make them live by rules that don't apply to their way of life."

I agreed with him, but held my tongue, not wanting to voice the atrocities that came to mind. I'd never heard of the tribe he named, which made me think I might be in another parallel timeline.

"At least the tribes have allies in Mexico," Troy went on, "especially Alta California. There was a war forty-odd years ago that the United States lost. It's kept the Indigenous people in the west from being forced onto reservations. Unfortunately, the tribes farther east haven't been as lucky."

My jaw dropped. Yep, definitely a parallel reality. "California is still part of Mexico?"

"It is." He eyed me from beneath his black brim. "That surprises you?"

I huffed a breath. "Where I'm from, Mexico lost that war. What about Utah? Arizona?"

"What's Utah?"

I looked at him aghast. "It was a state." I'd lived there for a year in my twenties. Even when I tried to hide in the desert, I couldn't escape the World Tree. I'd been walking down the street in downtown Moab when someone passed me in a hurry, jostled me to the side, and my shoulder hit one of the trees that lined the sidewalk. Boom. Gone from one state, reappeared eight hundred miles away in San Diego, three years into the future.

Troy shook his head. "Colorado is the last territory south of Wyoming—that land was won in the war. Everything Southwest is Mexico."

I focused on not falling off the horse as my mind spun with the new information.

"It will be to the Nwetaka that I go for help, for you and the child." Troy's assessing look was back.

"Thank you." I tipped my head toward him. "They have a midwife?"

"They have two healing women who attend childbirth. The elder may not make the journey, but her daughter is more than capable."

There was something in the way his eyes softened then. "Troy, do you have someone of your own with the Nwetaka?" I felt awkward saying it, but the words were already out.

He looked away. "There was a love there once." The grass swished around his legs. "She took a different path than the one I walk."

I really needed to learn how to keep my mouth shut. I clenched my jaw, wiped sweat from my brow, and inhaled the mingled scent of horse, grass, and mountain air.

An upward-facing cone of wooden poles showed over one section of the roof. "Is there a teepee behind your cabin?"

"There is, yes. My friends use it. I spend some nights out there, too." His friends. The Nwetaka. He side-eyed me again like he wasn't sure how I would react.

I smiled, trying to reassure him, but he looked away again, and my mouth curved into a grimace as pain shot through my hips from being in the saddle so long.

I lost view of the teepee as we reached the house. Sundance stopped beside the porch, where Troy helped me down to the wood deck. Exhausted, I made a beeline to the chair by the door and sank into it with an unladylike groan. My hands gripped the curved, pine-yellow armrests. Leaning back, I tried to open the front of my chest so there was more space for my lungs. Troy told Damien to wait behind him and fixed me with a cautious expression.

"I'm alright." Another half-truth.

He mumbled something encouraging that I didn't quite get, and disappeared around the side of the cabin. The big dog stayed where Troy put him, panting contentedly. I closed my eyes.

Dream dragons were starting to gather when the brush of clothing and nearness of warmth sent them scattering.

"Here." Troy knelt next to me with a glass bottle of water.

"Oh, lovely," I struggled to sit up straighter, took the bottle and drank a third of it in one go. It tasted cold and the slightest bit sweet, cooling my body and easing a degree of shock from my mind. "Can I meet Damien now?" It seemed rude not to acknowledge the happy creature that surely counted as part of Troy's family.

"Of course." He called the pup over.

After giving me a good, wet sniff, the dog put his nose to my belly, both ears forward. Kick went the baby, right where his muzzle was, and Damien jumped back. I giggled. The dog's incredulous expression drew laughter even from Troy.

"Alright you," Troy told the dog, "go on." Damien went to his spot, made a circle, and huffed onto his side. Troy held out his hand. "Can I offer you a bed to rest for a while?"

"Yes, please." I summoned the strength to stand.

The inside of the cabin was sparse, but spacious enough. It smelled of wood, leather, and long-cold ashes in the hearth. A kitchen dominated the back corner, with a fireplace at the center of the right wall and a sitting area directly to the right of the front door. To the left side of the kitchen lay a back door with an area that held boots, jackets and gear.

Troy led me through an opening, where a heavy curtain was tied to one side with a strip of leather, into a tidy bedroom behind a plank wall. He stood at the doorway as I tucked away my boots with their hidden daggers, and half-crashed into his bed. Too tired to worry about his drawn expression.

The curtain unfurled with a quiet whoosh. No goodbye, no words of comfort, just footsteps retreating to the front, where a horse waited to be unsaddled. I was a burden to this man, and there was nothing I could do about it.

Sometime later, I rolled my oversized body off the bed and onto my feet, a moan escaping each time I moved. The scent of broth wafted from a pot hanging over the fire as I waddled into the main part of the cabin, and I added "unreasonably hungry" to my list of bodily functions needing to be addressed.

Not finding Troy inside, I headed out the back door in hopes of an outhouse. It wasn't far, tucked away near the trees past the teepee. On my way back, I found Troy kneeling in the garden on the side of the cabin.

"Feeling better?" he asked.

"Much, thank you."

"Hungry?" He had a fistful of dark green leaves.

"I'm starving." I gave him an apologetic smile. Now he had to cook for me, too.

"It won't be long." He came out through the gate with thyme and chives beneath what looked like spinach.

"I think I'll stay out here and stretch until it's ready, if that's alright."

"Of course. You're welcome to go inside the teepee if you'd like." Without a backwards glance, he climbed two steps to the short back porch, and went through the door.

I lifted the flap of the teepee entrance, and let myself in. Light filtered down from above. The space was quiet. Peaceful. A fire ring sat in the center, beds of fur rolled up along the sides as if waiting for company. One pallet stretched open on the floor, deer hide beneath thick sheepskin, and dark-brown fur pushed to one side. Maybe bear.

I stood on the earth in bare feet and shushed the tide of emotions that waited to pull at me. Thinking about Killian made me want to cry, thinking about giving birth made me want to panic, and I wasn't interested in doing either right now.

Methodically, counting in my head, I slowed my breath. A groan escaped as I reached to the ground in a wide forward bend. My whole body ached with the weight of the child.

Maybe ten minutes later, Troy stuck his head into the teepee as I was doing a side stretch. He cocked his head to match the tilted level of my eyes.

"There's food when you're ready for it."

"I'm ready." So hungry. I brought myself upright, ducked out of the teepee, and huffed my way up the stairs behind him, into the cabin.

Dinner was rabbit stew with veggies from Troy's garden. He'd even baked flatbread, which was rather dense, but welcome.

I hadn't cooked anything since I'd entered Scotland, and I'd never cooked over a hearth fire, something that was second nature to Troy. I wanted Malva's fluffy bread and thick-spread butter. I wanted Annelle, who would've put my feet in a warm soak before bed and told me stories of births she'd attended, assuring me everything would be fine. Excited to meet the child. My steadfast friend.

Here, I'd be cooking over flames. On my own, starting tomorrow. One more thing I'd have to get used to in a hurry, as Troy informed me he'd be leaving at dawn to visit the Nwetaka and get some help.

"There's honey and cheese for the bread." Troy opened a cabinet and pointed out sacks of grain, a hand grinder, and jars of honey. Another cabinet, far from the fire, held cheese wrapped in waxed paper. Next to it, more packages of tightly-wrapped paper and leather. "Smoked meat is here." He stood, opened another polished wood door. "You can get apples from the tree, eggs if you visit the chickens by the stable, anything you want from the garden." Troy turned to face me, pointing toward the back door with his thumb. "I'll bring in some water from the spring. The trail is to the left of the teepee, if you need more. The pool below the spring is good for bathing."

I blinked away tears. "You're very kind, Troy. Thank you for everything you're doing for me."

He brushed it off as if it were nothing, and kept showing me where to find things. Kindling and wood. Matches. Cooking pots. He gave me a tutorial on how to use his spare rifle, as well, which sent my mind spiraling into scenarios where I'd have to use it: a bear banging down the door, a cougar after the horses, the men who passed us on the trail riding up the rise…

Finally, we sat down in chairs next to each other. His eyes went to my belly, where I rested my hands. My enormous, ready-to-burst belly.

"I think it's time for me to tell you it will be okay." I played it off like my stomach wasn't a knot of worry. The idea of giving birth without help scared me more than being on my own, though. I wanted a midwife. As long as they got here before the baby came.

Troy gave a ghost of a smile. "I want to be sure you'll be all right. I'll leave Damien to keep you company, and to keep guard."

I counted my breath. One. Two. Three. Four. Slowed it down to fight the rising fear.

"I may be three days gone if the elder medicine woman chooses to travel." Troy played with the little jar of salt on the table. "If your time comes before I return, send Damien to get me. He'll know where to go, and he'll understand if you speak in his mind." He locked his eyes to mine. Serious.

"So, you speak with other animals besides horses?" I steered the subject away from my going into labor alone. "What about people?"

Troy stared at the small fire in the hearth. "I've spoken with many animals, but I don't reach lightly into a mind where there is no heart connection. Once, I tried with a bear that was set on my demise. It saved me, but it left behind a wildness—an imprint, if you will. It took some time to heal from that. In the end, I needed help."

Silence stretched out. The fire crackled in the hearth. I kept my mouth shut on instinct. Troy valued quiet. Listening was a gift I could give.

He shifted his gaze to me. "This way of speaking can be done between people. I think we once used it regularly as humans, but that was long ago. I've spent a fair amount of time with the healers of the Nwetaka. They're able to see beyond what most would consider the edges of reality. They have legends that include records of this ability. It was common in ancient cultures more advanced than what we have today."

I thought of the legends of Atlantis and Lemuria. "Telepathy. Being able to speak mind-to-mind."

"It's not just mind-to-mind." He tilted his head, gaze intense. "There is also the heart. There must be the heart, or the connection isn't stable, isn't safe."

I wondered what Troy had been through with the bear. It had been bad. I could see that much.

An instinct of nurturing made me want to ease the worry from his face, and I reached for my guitar.

I played only three songs that night. Lullabies, really. I was tired and Troy was withdrawn. Still, the music was a nice way to sit together without needing to talk.

The dragon carved into the guitar made me think of Killian, and of Charlie, who'd have to watch his father mourn again. It made me think of the sculpture in the garden, and the dragon in my dream telling me I was here to become a mother. In this isolated wilderness, this quiet man was looking out for me, taking care of me.

As Killian had done.

Choking back emotion, I finished playing, and bid Troy goodnight. Something about him reminded me of Killian. I couldn't reconcile the connection. They were two men from different worlds, but it was stronger than mere likeness. Something deeper. Unexplainable.

Troy left to sleep in the teepee. I rested the weight of my head on a pillow that smelled of horse and pine. My eyes closed, but the child squirmed inside, a child who waited to make its entrance into a world that was vastly different from the one in which it had been conceived.

This was no castle full of music and family. The cabin was silent, and I was alone. Too tired to cry again.

Eventually, grief gave way to prayer—the only thing I could do to stop the fearful thoughts. I trusted Brighid could hear me, even if she didn't respond.

Goddess, take care of me. Take care of Killian. And if it's possible, please, I wish for this child to know its father, and for Killian to know his child. Let us see him again.

Over and over I prayed, crossing the boundaries between waking and sleeping upon the wings of faith. That night, the red dragon spoke to me in whispers of hope and play, inviting me to fly in these new mountains I'd discovered. There was no mention of the conversation on the ledge, and I left off my questions. Flight was enough. The illusion of freedom.

Yet even as my dream-self soared to moonlit heights, the ache of loss persisted. My heart chanted one name:

Killian Maclean.

Chapter 26
Humility

DAMIEN FOLLOWED ME everywhere the next morning, nudging me with his shiny black nose so I'd brush my hands through his thick, cream-and-grey fur. I was glad for his company, but as I stood on the front porch, an alien aloneness struck me. A reminder of how far out of my element I'd fallen. I was at a homestead on the side of a mountain, pregnant as pregnant could get, responsible for giving birth to a child and keeping it alive.

Everything familiar was gone.

Humbled by the vastness of the mountains, I wondered how far I was from the nearest person. Probably a long, long way. Just me and the dog, a couple of horses, some chickens, and a black cat that ran off the deck when I opened the door. And a rifle.

Damien put his head into the palm of my hand. I scratched behind one of his ears and decided I couldn't imagine a more awe-inspiring location, even if it was on the far side of scary to be here alone.

The front door of the cabin faced east, where a range of craggy mountains—some snow-capped—stretched across one of the widest valleys I'd ever seen. The sun beat down, not quite at its apex, and illuminated a thousand shades of green, shining on the great river that snaked its way along the valley floor. To the north lay a deep blue lake, and I turned my chair so I could see it as I rested.

"Wow," I said to no one in particular.

Damien gave a low "woof," then plopped down on the wooden boards and scratched himself.

I sat until my body demanded I move. A walk sounded nice, but first, I headed into the bedroom where all of my belongings lay. "I am not," I informed Damien, who watched me from the door, "going anywhere empty handed."

I slipped on my boots, a dagger in each, slung my pouch over my shoulder, and grabbed a snack from the kitchen before I left. Cloak on, I emerged into the bright yard feeling incredibly over packed, but as prepared as possible in case I found myself falling through reality, or deciding to camp out in the forest for a few hours.

I was glad for the dog as I left the cabin behind, anxious mind offering up images of bears and outlaws. Maybe I should've brought the gun.

The path to the spring wound past the teepee, into the forest, and through the trees. It wasn't far; maybe seven minutes for an overdressed pregnant woman. More like three minutes for Troy to get water with his long strides.

When I entered the small meadow where clear water bubbled up from the earth, my heart flipped over. It was almost exactly like Brighid's spring, minus the massive oak. The source gushed out of an opening in a large rock and spilled into a pool that was perhaps ten feet wide. From there, the water made its merry way through the forest and toward the big river in the valley.

I stood for a long minute, dumbfounded by the likeness of the spring, then piled my things on the moss near the pool and stripped down to skin. I was here, I might as well enjoy it.

But before I stepped into the pool, I knelt before it, remembering the legend about Brighid granting wishes at her enchanted spring. Closing my eyes, I imagined the red-haired goddess in the tapestry at Duart.

Goddess Brighid, I wish to find a way back to Killian. Help me find him again.

The water flowed past. Leaves sang their quiet song. No hint of a goddess. Trying to keep my frustration at bay, I prayed again, this time out loud, addressing the omniscient silence. "Goddess, please. Answer me. If you won't talk to me about Killian, tell me about the dragons. Why am I so tied to them?"

A wind picked up, her whisper barely there. *It is your birthright.*

And that was all I was going to get.

I lowered myself into the pool. It was cold, but not icy, a welcome relief from the sweat I'd worked up on my walk to the water. I moved into the center, ducked under the surface, and came up with a shout. The current rushed past me, strong. The baby danced inside like it was enjoying the swim.

Well washed and starting to get cold, I climbed onto the bank, and lowered down to my cloak on a patch of grass, naked in the warm sunshine. My arm became a pillow, and my eyelids slid shut.

Heart heavy despite the soft whisper of trees and birdsong, I didn't really sleep, I just basked in the sun thinking of Killian. Flirting over a game of poker. The way he'd looked at me when I played the piano at Stirling Castle. The love in his eyes the last time I'd seen him.

When the sun started to sink, I packed up and headed back. I cried myself to sleep.

The second day was much like the first, though a pair of horses came to say hello in the early afternoon. The tall bay barely lifted her gaze to me before setting to work on the grass by the stairs, but the other, a Clydesdale-like draft, wandered up to introduce himself.

"Would you be so kind as to tell me your name?" I stroked the softness of his nose from the top of the steps.

Brogan, came the sturdy voice in my head and heart. That was all he'd say, though, and after a while of me sweet-talking him, he wandered off to graze by the stable.

The brief contact made me feel even more alone. I had a pressing urge to pass the time with a movie or a game, but my AIO was beyond gone. I wished Annelle was around so I could tell her how much Troy reminded me of Killian.

There were no distractions, only the wilderness humming its earthly song and the persistent ache of my pregnant body.

On the third day, I woke with a gasp to intense tightness in my belly. The contraction lasted half a minute. Not long after, another came.

"I will not panic." I forced my mind to calm, taking a deep breath. Still, I called Damien. He trotted over to me. *Go get Troy,* I told him. *Please.*

The dog gave a sharp bark and went to the door. I rubbed his head and let him outside. He shot off to the north. I watched, riding insistent contractions, until he'd loped across the rise above the lake and disappeared into the forest.

Now I was really, truly alone.

I went through the motions of taking care of myself. Between intervals of increasing discomfort, I made tea and ate the last of the bread with honey. I tried to rest, but the tightening didn't back off.

On the way back from a trip to the outhouse, I yelped at pain sharp enough to make me hold onto a pole of the teepee for support. After it passed, I crawled through the teepee entrance to collapse in the pallet of fur. It was closest to the outhouse, after all.

Laying on my side, I touched cool earth. The bellows of my breath seemed to circle around the space. The clean scent of soil filled my nose, my focus narrowing as the intensity of contractions stepped up a notch.

In a lull between rushes, as I closed my eyes and tried to relax, I saw the trail in my mind where Damien had run. Troy would come back by that trail. Without thinking whether it would work or not, I sent a prayer in that direction. *Come back, Troy. Please. Come soon.*

Shelta, I hear you. I'm coming.

His answer was a current that flowed from my heart to my mind—communication on a level of consciousness that eclipsed mere words. I reeled at the concern that abruptly cut away.

My heart squeezed as hard as my belly on the next round. When I crested over the edge, where the pain receded, I concentrated on Killian with every ounce of my will.

Killian, our child is about to be born. I love you. I wish you were here.

Silence. Emptiness. What did I expect? We were worlds apart.

Shelta? My heart leapt, but it was Troy. *Are you alright?*

I will be if you're bringing help soon.

We're nearly there. This time, instead of near-panic, Troy's words came with a wave of affection. The connection faded, a soft withdrawal this time, with a lingering presence like a whisper of listening.

And then the strangest thing happened: the contractions backed off.

My belly gave a few less-painful spells of tightening, and took a rest. When nothing came for several minutes, I finally relaxed and my eyelids dropped.

I was sound asleep when Damien barged in and woke me with his wet nose. "Hi." I put my hands up to fend him off. "Good boy. Help me up."

I grabbed the scruff of his neck, pushed into one arm to sit, got lightheaded, and went horizontal again. Dog breath in my face, I willed my blood pressure to figure itself out, and gave it another try. It took three stages of varying support before I was able to stand, but I finally ducked out of the teepee and walked barefoot around to the front of the cabin, with Damien panting at my side.

Sundance shone as he trotted along the path above the lake. Troy sat astride in his wide brimmed hat, with two riders behind him, hustling up the hill.

It's okay, Troy. I sent the thought across the distance. *You don't have to push the horses.*

I waved. He raised a hand in return. I dropped my arm and laced my fingers beneath my belly as the baby did exercises of its own. "Hey, little one, ease up." I pressed my hand against the point where it pushed, hard. "You'll be out soon enough."

Troy gained the field ahead of his companions and cantered the rest of the way to meet me.

"Hi, Troy." I raised a hand to greet the horse, who gave me a bump with his nose, nostrils flaring. "Hi, Sundance."

Troy swung down, took off his hat and scratched his head. "You seem like you're doing well. I thought you were in trouble."

"Me too." I shrugged. "I had contractions all morning, but they stopped after I talked to you."

"Nemonte, the medicine woman—she and B'alam are behind us—she sent some energy through the connection when you called, to calm your body." He leaned forward as if to touch me, then stood straight again. His half-lifted hand dropped to his side. "I was quite a ways off when I heard you. I've never spoken at a distance like that."

"I've never spoken with *anyone* like that." I frowned. Maybe that wasn't true. What were my conversations with the goddess, if not telepathy? Assuming they weren't figments of my imagination.

"What?" He looked at me beneath the brim of his hat.

I shook my head. He might believe me if I told him, but now wasn't the time.

Troy turned to Sundance. As he took down his saddle and gear, two more people rode up.

The man and woman were strong-limbed and sharp-eyed, with light brown skin and black hair. His was straight and bound in a ponytail, hers loose and wavy, shining in the sun. They dismounted, took the leads of their horses, and walked over.

Both wore pants and cloth shirts, and the woman had a leather vest decorated with bones and stones, feathers, and bits of fabric. I knew by the careful, artful way each piece had been attached that each one had a story.

Troy spoke in his unhurried way. "I'd like to introduce you to Sarina and Diego. Sarina is a midwife and daughter of Nemonte, who is coming along at a walk with the seer of the tribe. Diego is a close friend, and wanted to meet you."

"Thank you for coming." I made a little bow with my head.

Damien sat by me and nudged my hand for more attention. I didn't miss the glance Troy gave him, somewhere between pride and amusement.

The woman, who seemed to be about my age, looked me over with kind eyes that creased at the edges. "What are you feeling?" she asked. "When did you last eat? When did you last sleep?"

"Right now, I only feel a slight pressure." I rubbed the underside of my belly. "I had intense contractions this morning, but they stopped. I've just had a nap, but it's been hours since I've eaten."

"Food, then." Sarina wrapped her hand around mine and brought me up the stairs, into the cabin.

Troy saw to the horses while Diego packed saddlebags into the kitchen. He had a long scar that reached from his right elbow to his hand. When he looked at Sarina, his gaze held unshakable loyalty. They were clearly at home with each other.

Sarina took over the kitchen, whipping up a soup of greens, herbs, and poached eggs.

I ate as much as I could, but my stomach was rather crowded. Mostly, I drank the broth and watched Sarina move with surety and grace. And familiarity. As if she knew the house intimately. The way she and Troy worked together, I guessed they knew each other intimately, as well. His eyes would follow her, then flick away. He anticipated her needs, the two of them negotiating the small kitchen with the ease of people who have shared space before.

When I couldn't eat another mouthful, I handed my bowl to Sarina with thanks, and retreated to one of the fur-covered chairs by the front window. There I had a good view of the three of them.

They were a family. I was the stranger.

Troy stood against the wall near the bedroom door, while Diego leaned against the counter. The two treated each other like brothers, Sarina captivating them both.

When Troy's head swiveled toward me, I dropped my gaze to the sheepskins that covered the floor around my chair, and curled my toes in the wool.

I found sly eyes on me when I glanced up. "You need to walk," declared Sarina. "Troy, help Shelta outside. Bare feet on earth."

Apparently, he took her order to mean both of us, for he removed his boots and socks before offering an arm to escort me down the front stairs. The wood was smooth beneath my swollen feet, the grass cool beneath my toes.

His sure steps steadied me as I lumbered away from the cabin, a breeze ruffling my hair as it blew waves in the grass and played in the trees. We didn't speak, but no matter how I tried to contain them, the sounds of pregnancy seeped out of me in labored breaths and moans.

If Sarina was grace and ease, I was slow and heavy. She was sleek and powerful while I was puffy and cumbersome.

And then there was the man beside me, who wore pistols on his thighs and nothing on his feet. Living all the way out here, alone.

I stumbled on an uneven bit of ground, and Troy caught my arm with quick strength. "You alright?"

"Yes." I looked down. "I'm sorry for the inconvenience, Troy. I've intruded on your sanctuary here."

He laughed—a bright, rare sound. "You haven't intruded, Shelta."

"Of course, I have." Another arduous breath, another heavy step.

"I brought you here as my guest."

"What choice did you have? You're too much of a gentleman to leave a pregnant woman stuck in a tree." I smiled, but the sentiment was serious.

"You are welcome here, Shelta." His eyes drove the message home, with that inexplicable sense of Killian at their depths.

He patted my hand on his arm, and the gears in my heart shifted, lining up with a click of knowing that sent irrational fear through my blood.

A horse whinnied on the path in the distance. "Here come the elders."

I followed his gaze to see a pair of riders emerge from the forest beyond the lake. We made our way toward them, meeting at the cabin.

A man with silver in his long hair helped an old woman down from her horse. One of his eyes was milky, his skin spotted with age over wiry muscles. Sarina and Diego came out of the house, and I recognized the similarities in the women, mother and daughter with wide, heart-shaped faces and a hint of mischief in their eyes.

"Shelta, this is Nemonte," said Troy, his hand warm on my back. "And B'alam is the seer of the tribe."

"It's very good to meet you." I bowed my head to them. "Thank you for making the journey." My words fell short of the gratitude that flooded my chest.

Nemonte held out wrinkled hands. Her curly hair escaped its braids. "May I touch?" she asked.

I nodded, and she placed her hands on either side of my belly. Feet wide in a steady stance, her eyelids went heavy. I studied the creases and folds of her skin, the curl of her lips as she listened to whatever music she heard in her own way. After a short while, she began speaking in a lyrical language that was like music I couldn't quite understand.

"She says the child is ready," Sarina translated. "The baby is strong. Full of will to live."

Nemonte beamed at me, and I couldn't help but smile back. She looked like a wise, wrinkly child. I liked her immensely.

Soon, I was back in the cabin, sitting in a chair with my toes in soft wool. Sarina kept busy in the kitchen, while Diego, B'alam, and Nemonte sat at the table and drank the same tea that was in my cup. The taste of roots and honey danced on my tongue.

Troy sat near me, catching my gaze. "You're going to be a mother."

"I am." Something I'd promised myself I'd never do.

"Are you excited?"

"I'm terrified." I laughed, trying to lighten the confession.

He grinned. "I would be, too, if it were me. You'll have help, though."

All I could do was smile at him. Nothing I could say would make up for my barging in on his life like this.

I'd barely finished my tea when Sarina came over. Troy shifted his gaze to her, and a trace of envy snaked through my fragile emotions. She held her hands toward mine, and said, "Walk with me?"

Tired, I waddled next to her along the path to the spring, hands clasped beneath my belly, careful not to touch any trees. Sarina stepped lightly next to me. When we reached the spring, I lowered my huge self onto the grass. She sat down with ease and grinned in her welcoming way.

"I like you," I announced, not planning to. The envy had evaporated in the absence of Troy.

She laughed. "I like *you*. I like this place. And the man who brought us to you, I like him as well."

Nope. There it was again. Jealousy. I wanted the comfort she had with Troy, and the realization staggered me. I had no right to him, no right to want whatever affection he had for this woman, even if there *was* something inexplicable about him, as if a piece of Killian existed in this world.

Sarina reached out, closed her eyes, and held my belly like her medicine-woman mother had done. Her voice made me think of light through amber. "Your child has a deep, true spirit."

She took her hands away and studied me with dark, clever eyes. I looked at the water flowing past, rubbed my belly, and tried not to squirm under her gaze. Finally, she seemed satisfied, for she leaned back and gave a little nod.

"Troy says you were born to this world through the tree magic." She said it straight as fact. "He told a story of walking with you, of heart-light and music."

I wasn't sure what to say.

"You were given to Troy." She flashed me a wide, curling smile that made me think of a fox. "Or maybe he was given to you. You are not lost."

"Do you read minds?" Did she know how torn my heart was? My throat swelled. I looked across the pool where once I'd seen a dark-haired man holding a sword. No, that was another pool. Another world. Denial fought a battle that started a dull ache in my head.

She shook her head. "I am the daughter of two spiritual healers. Some things are clear to me."

"Oh." Maybe anyone could look at me and see that I felt lost.

"Troy told me you had a husband. That you were taken away." Her face tightened. "You have choices now. There will be a child soon. As a mother, you will bend yourself to his needs with love. That will be easy for you." She waved a hand, dismissing something that made me feel actual horror. "For yourself you must choose. Who will be your family? Who will you allow to take care of *you*?" She stared at me pointedly.

"I really don't know." I did, of course. I just didn't feel right about it. None of this was anything but shocking.

"You do not need to know yet." She shrugged off my indecision. "But when it is time to choose, use this." She touched my chest with two fingertips. "Don't listen to this." She flapped her hands around her head as if swatting a dozen mosquitos at once.

Easy for her to say. I turned my gaze to the pool and began a silent prayer.

Goddess, show me the way. Help me to be a mother. Help me to know the right choices. Give me the courage to make them.

Not two seconds after I'd finished the thought, a bird with vivid blue feathers dove down to land on the opposite side of the spring. It looked directly at me. Then it waded into the water, dunked under, shook itself, preened a few times, and flew off.

Sarina wore an enormous grin. "I like you," she said, then threw her head back and laughed.

After dinner, Sarina and her family retired to the teepee. Troy and I sat in the padded chairs by the fire. I hadn't had a contraction for hours. I was supposed to get as much sleep as I could, but I wasn't ready to move yet.

Troy broke the silence. "I would've slept in the teepee, but I was instructed to sleep in here." He indicated a spot near the hearth. "When the healer tells you to do something, it's generally a good idea to listen."

His words triggered a memory of what I'd read in Duart's library:

When the crone speaks, listen.

"I'm glad for your company," I said. "You should sleep in here anyway, it's your house." That, and I really didn't want to be on my own again. Being near him brought comfort. It also felt like a crushing betrayal to Killian, and for that I was sorry, but when I sought the truth—needing to know and not wanting to be mistaken—I found that I wasn't trying to make Troy into Killian. It wasn't substitution; it ran deeper than that.

"Was it hard to be alone?" Troy's question was a low, soft snippet of a song.

"It was." I drew a too-shallow breath, the baby taking up space that my lungs were accustomed to occupying. "Damien helped, though. And the horses, and a black cat came around a couple of times."

Troy smiled, so much kindness mixed with hesitation. Warmth at a distance. "How was your time with Sarina?"

"She told me I would need to choose who would become my family here." The light from the fire flickered on our faces. Troy waited for me to continue, but my heart was lodged in my throat. My words hung in the air and twisted into an unspoken question.

"You have choices," he said. "The Nwetaka have invited you to live with them. I suppose you could go into town if you wanted, or move somewhere else entirely. But you're welcome to stay here and make this your home. I'd be happy for your company. Your music is lovely, and—as much as I like solitude, it does get lonely."

My heart wanted it, but I saw fear in his eyes, too.

"I asked B'alam and Nemonte if there is any way for you to go back to where you came from." He gave me an apologetic headshake. "They said no, and said it with certainty."

I was about to become a mother. The World Tree had placed me directly in Troy's path, and there was something inexplicable between us—I couldn't pretend otherwise. Not to mention the replica of Brighid's Spring.

Still, my words were heavy with debt I had no way to repay. "Are you sure you'd want me to stay? This is your sanctuary."

"I wouldn't have offered if I wasn't sure." He leaned toward me in his seat. "This is your home, if you want it. Yours as much as it is mine."

I held his gaze and struggled to reconcile my battered heart as my head bobbed three times, slow. I rasped out my answer. "Then I'd like to stay."

Late that night, Killian visited me in a dream. He walked through the cabin like a ghost, stopping to look at Troy for a long time with an unreadable face.

The mattress gave as Killian sat beside me, and held both of my hands in one of his. He stroked my hair. Caressed my face. Touched my belly where his child waited to be born.

When he bent to kiss my forehead, my eyes flew open. I was alone in the room again.

Was this Killian's magic? Being able to visit me like the dragons did, in dreams that were more real than illusion? What did he think of me, already living with another man?

As silently as I could, I got out of bed and tiptoed past Troy, out the door, tears running down my face. Damien came along. I was glad for his company, stumbling into the field, away from the sleepers in the teepee, trying to contain the sounds of my grief.

I wept on my knees in a patch of clover. Before long, the front door opened, and Troy made his way over with soft footfalls on cool grass. He didn't ask what was wrong. He didn't tell me to come inside. He lowered himself to the dew-wet ground and enveloped me in his arms, rocking me.

Side to side, over and over, we swayed together.

When we finally headed back to the cabin, my fingers traced the dragon at my throat.

Chapter 27
Crossing the Threshold of Motherhood

THE NEXT DAY, after a late breakfast, Sarina brought me through the drizzling rain to the teepee. Nemonte waved a flour-covered hand at me from the kitchen window when I glanced back at her, making bread in the quiet of the cabin. I ducked my head and stepped into the teepee.

I hadn't seen Troy since the night before, and my heart started an unreasonably strong bit of pounding at the sight of him sitting near Diego inside the sheltered space. B'alam sat on furs opposite the door. The seer looked at me with one dark eye, one milky white, and gestured for me to sit before him.

Diego spoke for the elder. "He will see for you, if you wish."

"Sure. Thank you." I didn't know if I wanted someone to tell me my fate, but it seemed rude to refuse, and I needed all the help I could get. I lowered myself to soft fur. It was warm, as if someone had been sitting there before I'd arrived.

I pressed my lips together to suppress the moans wanted to accompany the task of positioning myself cross-legged. My body protested the weight, the fullness, the unreasonable effort it took to do the simplest things. Dirt smudged the pink fabric of my dress.

Troy sat next to me, with Diego beside the elder. Sarina cozied into a fur on the other side. Rain drummed soft on the skin of the teepee, the scent of cedar wafting from the small fire surrounded by stones in the center of the space. Smoke swirled up to a narrow vent above.

I braved B'alam's gaze for all of two seconds, then focused on the leather pouch at his chest. The old man reached out and put his hands on either side of my head, his palms warm on my cheeks. After a moment, he took his hands away and began to speak.

"You are one who journeys." Diego translated in his rich tenor voice. "Do not be tricked into thinking time is real. Your path winds through worlds, but you resist because you focus so much on time."

He paused, waiting for the seer to continue. My mind spun in circles that churned up a host of emotions, and a question that needed answering. The old man went on.

"If you resist the journey, you will bring yourself misery. Do not fight your heart. For you, love comes with many faces. You must be brave enough to see that love is boundless. Without it, you will become lost." B'alam closed his eyes.

Cheeks burning, hyper-aware of Troy, I asked, "Can I learn to control the time travel?" I told myself not to hope, but I needed to know.

The seer's mouth made a crooked line before he spoke. "Control is an illusion."

I swallowed a groan. *I am one who journeys. Meaning I'm not done journeying. Meaning there are more worlds ahead for me as I tumble helplessly through time. Great.*

Diego's steady voice mingled with the lilting language of the seer. "You must not cling to time, to places, to people. If you are willing, you will know a love present in all worlds."

I practiced my poker face, trying not to show the free-fall happening inside of me.

Diego looked at my belly. "Love is also being a mother. Your children will be world-weavers, as you are."

"Children?" One was scary enough. More than one? Maybe I shouldn't have let him see for me.

"Yes." Diego nodded. "They will hold the secrets of the great winged ones."

"Dragons?" I couldn't help interrupting.

"Yes." B'alam answered me himself.

"The red dragon," I blurted out. "Is he the key to controlling the time travel?"

The seer's eyes narrowed, one dark, one milky, both shadowed. "The key is inside of you. Your dragon will help, when you're ready."

"I want to be ready now." My voice cracked. "Why am I here? Why did the Tree take me now?"

"You are here to learn to trust yourself."

Couldn't I have done that in Scotland? My heart seemed to fall a thousand feet into Brighid's underground cavern.

"Remember, as you journey, that children deserve to have a father, even if he is not the one who sired them. The father would want that for you, would want that for the child."

Killian would want his child to have a father. The words seeped into me. I sighed, fighting tears.

B'alam's laughter came from deep in his throat. "Do not worry." He spoke in English, shaking a finger at me. "You fly with eagles and sing with stars!" He reached his hands to the sky, then let them fall. "No need to worry."

I managed a small smile. Too many feelings crashed against the rocky shores of my heart. "Thank you." I bowed my head to him, sensing the reading was over.

When I moved to rise, Troy helped me up. He wrapped his hand around mine and escorted me outside, where I discovered the rain had stopped. We walked in silence, the wet ground a strange comfort beneath my sore feet. Troy led me clockwise on a path that circled the clearing. He moved with me, stopping whenever I needed to catch my breath, taking more of my weight when I stumbled.

I contemplated the seer's message. *You will know a love that is present in all worlds.* What was I supposed to do with that?

The man next to me kept his peace. The grass swished around our legs. The horses in the distance watched as we made our way toward the lake. I wondered if Troy had been the one who'd warmed the furs before me.

I finally broke the silence. "Did B'alam see for you as well?"

"Yes." Troy took a long, audible breath, like he was working up the will to say something. A breeze picked up as he exhaled, and I brushed my hair back, looking at him through the corners of my eyes. He pointed. "We can stop for a rest just over there."

The trail turned and followed the ridge above the lake, where a simple log bench gave a sweeping view of the water and the mountains beyond. My skirts brushed against one of his pistols as we sat together, and my cheeks flushed when he took my hand.

"I'm still coming to terms with the things the seer told me this morning. I imagine you're feeling much the same." He mirrored my tentative smile.

I forced myself to hold his gaze as my heart thundered along.

"Shelta," he said, "I know you're hurting, that you miss your husband. I see in your eyes that you're frightened, but I also see confirmation of what B'alam told me today, and what I feel—what I've felt since I saw you sitting in that tree and heard you sing. The seer said that you and I belong to each other."

Troy looked toward the lake for a long time before he went on. "I don't understand it, but apparently my spirit has more than one incarnation in more than one world." He brought his gaze back to mine. "B'alam said I've already married you once."

My breath caught as doubts shattered against the knowing of my heart. I closed my eyes and opened my mind. *You twined us together after all, didn't you, Goddess?*

Such love in the sentience of the breeze. *You sparked this magic. This is your weaving.*

My hand was so tiny in his. My gaze roamed over the bone-white handle of his gun, up his arm to the roundness of his shoulder and the hollow of his throat. My eyes tripped over his lips. He'd shaved this morning.

"What else did he tell you?" I had to ask, even if I was afraid of what he'd say.

"That you would save my life one day."

I shook my head, studying the play of green and brown in Troy's eyes, the same colors of the forest that climbed up the jagged mountains he'd chosen as his sanctuary. Finally,

I fell into the black of his pupils, and the pull of our spirits to be together.

I couldn't speak the truth yet, and I definitely didn't know how to proceed. My gaze was drawn to the water below, where a blue patch in the cloudy sky shone in reflection.

"What is its name?" I pointed to the lake.

"Depends who you ask," said Troy. "I call it Silver Lake because of the way it shines in the moonlight, and because of the silvery skin of the fish. Sometimes you can see the heavens in it. I'll take you there one night."

"I'd like that." Fatigue came on without warning, coupled with a kick to my ribs. "And now I think I need to lie down."

"Come on." Troy helped me back to the cabin and into his bed. When I asked, he covered me in the plaid stole that still smelled of Scotland.

The way his hand caressed my cheek could've easily been Killian, and in the complete surrender of exhaustion, I accepted that they shared something in their essence, and that at least part of this was my doing.

This is your weaving. The words of the goddess floated through my mind. I held fast to the discovery that I wasn't entirely at the mercy of fate, and faded to black.

After dinner, I found myself in bed again with orders to enjoy the quiet while everyone else went outside to the teepee. I tried to get comfortable, but no matter how I positioned myself, my body ached and my restless child kicked and punched and winded me. I wanted the little earthling out, but desperately wished I could skip the whole giving birth thing.

The rain had returned, drumming on the roof. I focused on the sound, reaching for the sense of peace it usually brought me, and hummed a short song in hopes that the baby would get with the program. We were supposed to be resting.

No such luck.

The hearth had made the house so hot I was lying in my shift and nothing more, window wide open. The cabin was still, dark outside and in, but for the flickering shadows that danced on the fabric between the bedroom and the banked fire.

Then the back door opened and closed, making the curtain flutter. The long, quiet strides belonged to Troy. I thought he would go to his bed on the floor, but instead he drew back the cloth with a lantern in his hand. I pushed up on my arm.

The light glowed on the curl of his lips, the round of his cheeks. "I hope I don't offend you when I say this." He paused to open his mouth with the hint of a laugh. "Nemonte told me to come to your bed. She said the energy that brings the baby into being also encourages it to come out."

My mouth watered. I wanted his company, wanted his touch. I didn't want to wait for the unknown of birth alone.

Troy cleared the distance between us with slow steps. He placed the lantern on the dresser, kneeled before me, and brought his hand to the side of my head. "I want to hold you, Shelta." Such strength in a whisper. "I want to be here for you, to be with you."

I pushed up, making space for him on the bed. The first few buttons of his shirt were open, chest bare beneath. I leaned into him, into the sanctuary of his arms, into the impossibility of our souls being bound through time. His breath was a wave on the shore of my hearing.

"It may sound crazy," his words scraped, raw with emotion, "but I feel as if your child is my own. I want to care for you as my own." His voice vibrated through my bones as if laced with magic, and the ache in my body eased. The child stopped kicking. "Will you allow it, Shelta? Will you let me love you while you're here?"

I felt like I was on the edge of a cliff, about to jump off. "Yes."

"Does it feel too fast?" He moved his hand up my arm.

"Oh, aye. Yes." I closed my eyes. My blood burned. "Far too fast. But it also feels right."

I heard the smile in his words. "It's said that God created the universe in six days."

"I think that's meant to be a metaphor." My reply was more breath than voice.

"I think it's meant to show us that great things are not bound by time." Troy moved closer, touched his forehead to mine. He wound his hand into my hair.

My fingertips moved to his face, my gaze to his lips. Heart pounding.

"I don't know what magic is at play," Killian's voice rumbled through Troy's, "but I know we are meant to be together. I know it as surely as I've ever known anything."

He kissed me. Tender. Tentative, at first. But as I kissed him back, Troy's touch blazed into a passion that matched Killian's. I knew him in the kiss, knew the song of the same soul.

Troy's hands roamed over my round form. He lifted my breasts and held their weight. His kisses were deep. Driving. Intoxicating.

Swept in the current of wanting, I relieved him of his shirt. My palms moved over the hardness of his chest, the curves of his shoulders. Our fingers interlaced like the knotwork around the tapestry of Brighid's spring that hung in the stairwell of Duart castle.

When Troy lifted my shift over my head, my hands went to my belly, and I looked down, self-conscious.

"You're beautiful, Shelta." Killian's voice again beneath Troy's.

My eyes blurred, and it was Killian's hand in my hair, Killian's mouth on mine, Killian's thumb grazing my breast. I gasped and blinked my sight clear. Not Killian. This was Troy. The love felt the same, but even if they shared the same soul, they were different men.

He laid me back on the pillows. My nipples tightened beneath his touch. All I could do was rest my hands on him and breathe out a symphony of moans. Something inside of me shifted, and it went far beyond the physical.

I drowned in sensations born of primal need. His tongue in my mouth. His mouth on my breasts. Fingers below. It wasn't the explosive climax that had created the child, but it was ecstasy nonetheless. He didn't stop until I cried out, having ridden the wave to its end, and wrapped my hand around his.

And then, as Troy cradled me, the aftershocks of orgasm turned into the beginnings of a contraction. "Oh." I panted, catching my breath. "I think that got things started."

Troy laughed. "I think that was the point of my being sent in here. Sarina said you were to rest until the rushes get strong, then move around the cabin."

He fit himself behind me, drawing a light blanket over us both. He still wore his pants, but his chest was bare and comforting against my back. I started to say something to the effect that I owed him one, but he cut me off.

"It wasn't my pleasure I wanted tonight," he whispered. "It was yours. I am more than satisfied to hold you."

Hold me he did, until I pushed him away in a sharp bout of pain. The contractions ramped up. My breath went deep in response.

Troy put his hand on my shoulder. "Are you alright?"

"I think so?" Another round moved through me. I counted to fifty before it subsided. "It's intense."

After the next contraction, I decided to get up and move around. Troy came with me, tossing his shirt on.

We paced through the small cabin, pausing whenever contractions came. I had to hold onto something while they rocked me, usually him. At one point, Troy left me clutching the table and built up the fire. He came back and held me, an embrace between the squeeze of labor.

His eyes shone in the firelight. "Shelta, I'd like to stay with you through the birth."

"That's a gallant offer, but I don't recommend it." I shook my head. "There'll be sweat and screaming and blood, and—I won't be at my prettiest." I sucked a breath and started riding the oncoming contraction.

Troy moved to support me better. "I'm not afraid. I want to see you in such a powerful act of life." He kissed my temple. "And I would like to welcome the child."

In the space between agony and breath, his words helped me recognize the power inherent in becoming a mother. As scary as it was to know he'd see me at my most vulnerable, I wanted him by my side.

And maybe, just maybe, whatever connection Troy shared with Killian would let him know his child was coming into the world.

"Okay," I yielded. "You can stay. I want you to stay."

Three contractions later, Troy went to get the midwives. Sarina came in grinning, her gaze darting between me and the man who crossed the room to his place beside me. While she poured water into the largest pot over the fire, I was in too much pain to wonder if it was weird for them, this change in their relationship.

Nemonte put her hands on my belly, gave a satisfied nod, and reached up to pat Troy on the shoulder. The corners of his lips tugged up, and the elder cackled. She did send him to my bed. I smiled, though it probably came out as a grimace. All I could do was breathe.

Hours blurred as the labor progressed. The women said only what they needed to, coaching me with encouraging words and touch. Sarina put one hand on each side of my hips and squeezed during the contractions, which lessened the pain some. Nemonte hummed a low, soothing song.

I tried every position—sitting, squatting, walking, hanging onto the man who didn't leave my side. Most of the time I was happiest on my hands and knees, a dark sheepskin cushioning the floor beneath me, crushing Troy's fingers with my grip. I don't remember when my shift disappeared, but I found myself naked and sweating, the cool breeze coming through the bedroom window my only respite.

Modesty evaporated. Pain and primal instinct took over completely.

Light crept into the sky as I labored. The oil lamps were no longer needed, but they burned on. Gaze focused on a flickering flame, I whimpered, overwhelmed by effort and exhaustion. Finally, I reached an apex of agony.

Troy leaned toward me. "You're so strong, Shelta. Don't hold back."

With a roar, I pushed with everything I had. My body pulsed in great waves, cried out in raw, deep moans. Troy kneeled before me. Sarina pressed on my hips, and Nemonte guided the child out. I looked down to see the red, wriggling infant in the medicine woman's hands.

A boy.

My son's cries tugged at me as I took him into my arms. "Hi baby." The child opened his tiny eyelids to look at me. I laughed and cried, softly, gazing at him. "Brendan Malcolm Maclean," I named him, my love for Killian and his family making saltwater tracks down my cheeks.

The infant wriggled up my chest. Sarina helped him latch onto my breast, and a surge of gratitude flooded my hormone-rich veins as he drank.

Troy helped the midwives clean up. When they retreated from the room, he joined me on the bed.

As the sun rose above the mountains, we three breathed together. Little Brendan looked to Troy's face behind me in a clear connection of father and son. It was beautiful, but on the edge of sleep, as a watercolor dragon snuggled up to the baby and the red dragon watched from an outcropping on the mountain above, I remembered that none of this was for keeps.

Now that I had a child, I could lose him.

CHAPTER 28
FEAR LURKS BENEATH

MOTHERHOOD'S LINEAGE might've been coded into the blood and being of women, but I would've been lost if I'd hadn't had help. Instinct and intuition provided some of what I needed to know; the midwives taught me the rest.

My body was a wreck, sore and awkward and weak. Troy and Sarina helped me do everything for the first few days. And beneath the joy and hurt and healing was the dull ache of missing Killian. His essence was with me through Troy, and in little Brendan, but the man I'd broken all my rules for was not there. I imagined the way his face would soften as he gazed at his son, how Charlie would bond with his brother, how proud Sir Malcolm would be of his new grandson. I wished they could see the beautiful baby I held in my arms, wished Brendan could know his family.

Did they mourn me? Did they think less of Killian for having chosen me, the woman who disappeared and took his child with her?

Troy amazed me by how fully he embraced the role of fatherhood. There was no indication that the child was not his own. Quite the contrary, to see the two of them together was to know all was well in the world.

For now.

Though it was still midsummer, Troy worked hard to prepare us for winter. He and Diego went out several days in a row with the big draft horse, Brogan, hauling deadwood back to the cabin and sawing it into smaller sections that were then chopped for firewood. B'alam helped with the stacking, filling the woodshed. I held my child and watched them, thinking of the battle-axes of the Macleans. How old would Brendan be when he first wielded an axe?

Somehow, I was going to find my way back to Scotland, but not now. I was here to become a mother. To trust myself. As much as I wanted to go off searching for dragons, I had an infant to care for. There would be time later to contemplate time travel.

When our Nwetaka friends left, riding off one early morning as the sun crested the mountains, the house seemed smaller. The valley wider.

A few weeks later, I sat at the table with Troy as he wrote up a list of supplies we'd need from the nearby town, a trip he planned to make when I was strong enough to ride. Brendan slept nearby in a cradle Troy had made him.

"Laundry soap," I said. Troy added it to the list. I repressed the desire to tell him about modern washing machines again. I'd already lamented the hand washing of diapers several times.

He hadn't protested once about our disrupting his life. I had no right to complain, even if I wanted to sometimes. So I had to hand-wash the laundry, big deal. Troy helped, and at least it was still summer. In the winter, the mess would move inside. I imagined myself elbows-deep in a wash-pot of suds and poop on the kitchen floor, splashing water as I put the diapers in the rinse pot, hanging cloths like stained prayer-flags by the hearth.

The inconveniences of homesteading were also empowering. It was cumbersome to get our water from the spring, but that water was clean and cost only the energy it took to collect it and carry it to the cabin. There was no utility bill, or plumbing to fix. I might not want to hand-wash diapers, but even that task left me with a faint glow of pride.

Troy finished his list as I built up the fire. The nights were already getting cold. He rose from the table, stretched his arms nearly to the ceiling, and heaved a sigh. "I think that's everything."

I lowered myself into a chair by the hearth and gave him a smile. "I'm looking forward to seeing what town's like."

The way he cocked his head gave me pause, made me wary. The chair squeaked as he sat across from me. The only reason I could imagine Troy not wanting to go into town was some kind of danger, and my mind flashed a scene of the outlaws we'd seen on the road over a month ago.

"Troy," I began, unable to leave him in his silence, "what's in town that makes you hesitant? You never go anywhere without guns. I'm guessing you're armed for more than the odd bear."

The warning in his eyes reminded me how little I knew about the world I was living in. How little I knew of this man I'd come to trust.

"When I was in Santa Fe," he said, "I worked as a hired gun." His flat tone hinted at hidden pain. "It was just a job at first, protecting bank deliveries back and forth across the border, but I'd take whatever work came up. I was young, it was exciting. Paid good money."

I waited, hands in my lap, eyes on the child who slept in his cradle near my feet.

"Things started to get out of control. The outlaws outnumbered the lawmen, and the comandante—which is something like a sheriff—started recruiting deputies. Really, we were vigilantes. We took the law into our own hands to protect people from violence that had escalated to a point where something needed to be done."

The fire crackled in the hearth while he went quiet. I bit my tongue, hoping he'd tell me more if I gave him time, knowing he didn't like to be rushed.

"I made myself some enemies," Troy finally said. "We would rarely get a whole gang under control—there were always some who got away. We captured and tried many, killed others, and it became ever more dangerous for those of us who were doing our best to uphold a sense of order."

I'd never ask, but I wondered how many men he'd killed, how many he'd seen die around him. If it were me, would I be able to kill to survive?

"They hunted us as we hunted them." He stared into the fire. "My friends started turning up dead. They had wives, children, families. I didn't have anyone but my horse, and the men who had become my family." Time drew out. The creases around Troy's eyes deepened. "Eventually, I rode off in the dead of night like an outlaw myself. I couldn't live in constant fear anymore. I thought leaving would fix that."

He was quiet for so long that I asked, "Did it?"

"No." He gave a sad smile. "Fear followed me. I found work in the mountains of Colorado as a carpenter. Thought a change of trade would help. It did, for a while. I lived simply, saving all the money I could, adding to what I'd made in Santa Fe. Being a gunslinger paid more, especially when we'd brought in men with prices on their heads, but I was happy with a humble life of building things instead of constantly confronting death.

"Then a band of outlaws came to see what trouble they could cause. I would've been fine if I'd kept my head down, but the instincts I'd developed in Santa Fe took over and I found myself in a gunfight, defending a small-town sheriff who was in over his head. After the smoke cleared and the corpses were lined up for a body count—one being the sheriff—I realized I couldn't stop them. There would always be more."

He shook his head, and my heart twisted to see the defeat in his eyes.

"They wanted me to be sheriff, those people, to continue the same path I'd tried to run from. But I couldn't. That wasn't what I wanted in life. So off I rode in the dead of night, this time with enough money that I didn't need to go looking for another job as long as I lived simply. It took over a year to make my way here, but I was called to this valley, to this particular stretch of forest—to this meadow with its magical spring. When I found it, I knew I'd come home."

I shivered, thinking of Brighid's spring. Like Killian, Troy was a warrior, but he had no comrades to train with. They'd all been taken from him.

"It was lonely until I met the Nwetaka." He tilted his head, the fire reflecting in his eyes. "I've been happy here, but there are still men who know my face, who've put a price on my head for what I've done."

I crossed the space between us, sat on his lap and slid my hands across his chest. My words pushed past the tension in my throat. "I love you."

His sorrow retreated into a lopsided smile as I leaned in for a kiss. When I lifted my head to look in his eyes, he whispered, "I love you too, Shelta," and kissed me again.

Six weeks after Brendan was born, I had a horrific dream.

I sat astride the crimson dragon, flying on gilded wings. Below, white men invaded the Nwetaka village. Gunshots echoed off the mountains, a chorus of screams rising from below. The invading force wore navy-blue jackets. They killed women, children, and elders as often as the men who fought against them.

I wanted to intervene, to stop the madness, but I couldn't. The dragon wouldn't talk to me, or respond to my requests, he simply carried me along. Helpless. Forced to bear witness. Frustration leaked from my heart like gasoline and blazed like fury through my blood.

A streak of gold raced across the ground. Sundance galloping in. Troy raised his rifle and pulled the trigger even as he rode. Every bullet he fired hit its target. Soldier after soldier went down, the diversion giving the Nwetaka a chance to sink more arrows and bullets into their attackers. The cacophony had a choppy rhythm; a disorienting, life-halting, gut-wrenching cadence that made me sick.

Again and again Troy shot, using his pistols when he got close enough. It seemed the battle was turning in favor of the Nwetaka. But then, as if in slow motion, the captain of the troops aimed his rifle at Troy. I saw what was coming and panicked.

"No!" I shouted at the top of my lungs. "Help him!" I kicked the dragon beneath me in rage. Why didn't he dive down? Why didn't he breathe fire and melt the bullet in its flight? Why was I forced to see this without being able to do anything?

No answer came. The shot ripped into Troy's chest. His mouth opened with a breathy groan I somehow heard from so far above, and he slumped forward onto Sundance, whose flaxen mane turned dark as blood came gushing out.

My roar ripped through the sky. I shrieked angry words at the goddess and tried to jump off the dragon, but the big creature lifted me away, humming a sad song as I pounded my fists against his crimson back.

"Shelta!" Troy woke me, his voice raspy and sharp. He grabbed my hand, blocking my punch to his shoulder.

"Sorry!" I pulled back, gasping for breath. I pushed both hands against my chest as if I could slow my hammering heart. I could do no such thing. My whole body trembled.

"What did you dream?" Troy drew me into the safety of his arms.

All I could do was shake my head. I was convinced I'd seen his death. Didn't think I should tell him. But Troy pressed me, coaxed me, until finally the horrors spilled from my lips in a blubbering mess of half-explained fears.

Gathering myself, I went over the dream again, this time more clearly, imprinting the details in my memory by saying it aloud. Troy cradled my body with his, and, through that telepathic connection we barely used, wrapped me in love. The wash of energy soothed me, but I couldn't stem the urgent need to find the dragons and make them real.

Did they live in these massive mountains, or did I have to go farther back in time to find them?

My heart plunged, recognizing the truth and hating the knowing. But in the aftermath of the nightmare, I was more determined than ever to find the red dragon who dominated my dreams.

He was real.

I knew it in my soul.

Chapter 29
Threads of Love

MY SON WAS pure joy, irresistibly cute. He was part of me, and a complete stranger at the same time. His weight was a sweet comfort when I held him, his tiny feet and hands a wonder.

But sometimes he'd fuss and nothing could calm him. The noise of his cries split through my hormone-enhanced hearing and, in my most tired moments, I wished I could run away. Sometimes I hated myself for choosing to have a child, then hated myself more for thinking such things.

I'd walk Brendan outside or rock him by the hearth until he finally quieted, worrying about what would happen the next time I met the World Tree. How could I care for a child when my own path was so uncertain? I knew the answer—day by day, with trust—but that didn't end the dull notes of dread that gathered in the back of my mind.

I managed my anxiety. Kept it at bay. I drowned it out by enjoying Troy's company and staying busy. Tend to the child. Tend to the fire. Tend to the garden. Wash the diapers. But it was always there, waiting, spiking with fearful thoughts anytime I let my guard down.

Troy was absolutely Brendan's father. I'd never seen a man so in love, so devoted. The joy of it made me laugh. The tragic beauty made me cry.

On a Monday in October, I came into the cabin from a bath at the spring to find my two boys napping. Brendan's little hand curled around one of Troy's fingers.

For the gazillionth time, I wished for my AIO, or just a simple camera. This moment, so crisp and perfect, would fade in my mind. Eight weeks had flown by since Brendan's birth, and the first month was a blur already. I didn't have a single photograph of him. Not one video. Nothing to look back on but my memories.

Maybe it was just as well. If I had pictures, I wouldn't have anywhere to send them. Killian and his family were all out of reach. Better to focus on the two I had, the man and the child before me.

A board creaked beneath my foot. Troy turned his head, hair falling across his face. I smiled, and he rolled out of bed, positioning a pillow to keep the child safe.

In the front room, Troy wrapped himself around me for a kiss, and the fire of wanting rekindled in my body, taking me by surprise. Until now, I'd been too tired, too sore, too focused on the newness of being a mother. Troy had been nothing but nurturing.

But I remembered the night I'd given birth to Brendan, and how Troy had touched me. There was no child between us now. My body was my own again. I pressed into him, told him with my mouth and hands what I wanted.

Eyes afire, Troy traced his fingers from my throat to my heart.

And then the baby woke. Of course.

I bit my lip. Troy laughed as I spun around and went to nurse Brendan.

That evening, I sang my son to sleep. Troy rocked the cradle with his foot, sitting in the chair beside me, sheepskins spread between us on the floor. The fire crackled over a thick bed of coals in the hearth.

When Brendan fell asleep, I shifted from a lullaby to a love song. My fingers plucked a complex pattern. Mysterious. Seductive. The vibration of the guitar buzzed through me, my voice a low resonance in my bones. Troy watched me, the fire behind him casting shadows across his face.

When I finally stowed my guitar, Troy lifted Brendan—cradle and all—and moved him into the dark of the bedroom. As Troy walked back to me, I drank in the curve of his shoulders, the length of his legs, the strength of his stride.

Firelight dancing in his eyes, he dropped to one knee on the sheepskin at my feet, took my hands into his own, and kissed me with every ounce of feeling in his heart. I slid down so we knelt on the sheepskins, facing each other.

He pressed his palms against mine. The firelight danced, a warm play of light and shadow. I was in my shift, white and soft and worn. He knelt in a loose shirt and doeskin pants, hair framing his face.

I love you, Shelta. He spoke inside me, even as he kissed me.

I love you, Troy. Such intimacy.

Desire rose like a flood, and his mouth began to roam. My shoulder. My collarbone. My throat. He tasted my fingers, the centers of my palms, the skin inside my wrists and elbows.

Beneath him on the sheepskins, his weight felt good all the way to my bones. When he pushed back and looked at me from above, I reached to touch his hair. Slid my fingertips along his jaw. His hand came across my face, and

I opened my mouth to wet one of his fingers before he took it away.

His hands wrapped around my ribs, slid to my waist and hips. His kisses traced a line down the center of me, through the white cotton I wore. A moan welled from deep in my throat.

Troy bent my leg toward his mouth, kissing behind my ankle. He placed my foot on his shoulder as he moved up the inside of my calf. My shift fell around my hips, and my hand glided over the soft leather of his breeches.

He stopped and looked at me, eyes bright.

"Want." I pulled myself up to sit astride his thighs.

"Yes." He brought my shift over my head, and tossed his own shirt to the ground. I got the laces of his pants undone in a hurry. He brought me back to his lap, eyes hungry.

The overlap of our breath wove a music of sorts, groaning sighs like a song. His hands scooped beneath my thighs and lifted me—brought my breasts to his face. With a moan, he lowered me down. I opened my mouth in a hot exhale and took him in. Delicious. Needed.

He laid me back on the padded floor. I wanted him closer, reaching toward him with my thoughts.

Troy, open your mind to me.

His eyes went wide, still for a breath of time. Then his consciousness entered, and the two of us melded together, our minds as intertwined as our bodies.

Love flooded me in a rush that heightened every sensation. Every kiss was amplified, everywhere we touched. We moved together, and I pulsed around him, swimming in the illumination of our souls like two fires blazing as one.

Our breathing came in gasps, ecstasy an explosion within.

Afterwards, I could do nothing but breathe and cling to Troy with the barest effort possible. He brought himself out, body and mind, and kissed me before letting his head fall back.

It didn't take long for him to succumb to sleep, his arm heavy and protective around my hips, his body pressed against mine. I slipped out of his hold and covered him with a blanket.

Outside, my breath showed in puffs of air as I stood beneath the stars in only my cloak and boots. Reaching toward the goddess, I sent out a pulse of gratitude that looked, to the eye of my imagination, like a sphere of light bursting from my heart to ripple through the universe with my prayer.

Goddess, thank you for this gift, this time. Let me stay with him for a while. Please. I will cherish every moment.

Chapter 30

Showdown in the Wild West

A WEEK LATER, morning sunshine shone through the window as I gave Brendan a fresh diaper. He squirmed on the bed, and my stomach turned with nervous energy. In a few minutes, we'd mount up and ride to Jackson, the nearest town.

The day was cold enough to warrant my cloak and plaid stole, remnants of a different time, which I threw on over a pair of pants and a sweater Sarina had left me. I wished I had my coat instead of the cloak, but that was in Scotland. Had Killian packed my dresses away with his last wife's, or did they still hang in the wardrobe in his bedroom, waiting for me?

Wrestling my focus to the present, I slipped into dagger-loaded boots, scooped up my brown-eyed baby, and went outside. Troy was leading the horses across the field from the stable, his level gaze on me, the big animals following his long, measured strides. Tall and wide, with thick muscles rippling under his chestnut coat, Brogan carried the goods we had for trade in bags strapped to his saddle.

Troy saw me looking at the draft horse with my head tilted, and said, "He doesn't mind playing pack horse every so often, though he prefers hauling logs out of the forest."

He gestured toward the spry palomino beside the draft. "I want you to ride Sundance."

I raised my eyebrows—I'd thought I'd be riding the mare.

I made sure Brendan was securely wrapped at my chest in the carrier Sarina had given me, and mounted Sundance. Troy swung himself up on Roxanne and led us all forward.

Sundance? I reached tentatively to the horse with my mind, sensing an openness on the other end. *It's an honor to ride you, of course, I'm just wondering why Troy has me in your saddle. You're his horse. I thought I'd be riding Roxanne.*

He chose me because I have a smoother gait. His velvety voice carried a tremor of falsehood. He was hiding something.

Is there anything else he told you about carrying me today?

A mental shrug, as if he decided it didn't matter. *I have specific instructions, should any danger arise.* He withdrew from my consciousness. Conversation over.

I gave him a pat and rode on, my mind making up scenarios that all ended with wild, galloping getaways.

Stop, I told myself. *I am safe. All is well.*

I made the words a mantra as we rode southeast, away from the lake, down the hill and through the forest. Coming out of the trees, the horses turned south. We followed the valley with the grandeur of the mountains towering above us, making me feel so very small.

The sun was high as we rode into Jackson, Wyoming, and my hips were sore from hours in the saddle. The town reminded me of an old western movie, its dusty main street lined with awning-covered buildings and hard-faced locals who were all a bit rough around the edges.

"The general store is just up a bit farther." Troy sat astride the bay mare to my right, turning his head so he didn't have to raise his voice. Brogan walked, large and proud behind us, his lead rope loose in Troy's hand.

I nodded, holding onto Sundance's reigns for show as I took in the town. We rode past the sheriff's office, the shoemaker, the tailor and the post office. The bank sat on its own in a brick building on the other side of the street.

As we passed the saloon, three ugly characters stumbled through the door, piling into each other as the doorman pushed the last man out. I averted my gaze when one of them, red-eyed and filthy, looked toward Troy and me. His head turned to follow our path.

Unease straightened my back with prickly fingers. Did they recognize Troy? Did they know about the price on his head?

We reached the general store and tied the horses out front. Inside, it smelled of spices and kerosene, soap and wool, with shelves of everything from fabric to canned goods. Baskets of produce covered one table, while blankets, sheets and pillows were stacked on another.

The keen-eyed shopkeeper inspected the goods we had for trade: leather pouches and gun cases, fur-lined boots and antler carved buttons, dried herbs and jars of salve, a few knives, and several sets of carved bowls and plates like the ones we ate from each day, polished smooth under Troy's expert hands.

The merchant and Troy agreed on a price, and I set to work finding some of the items on our list while the merchant assisted with the bulk of the order. He and Troy slipped into Spanish, so quiet I only caught a few words, *problemas* and *bandidos* among them.

We were there for an hour, collecting a variety of smaller supplies as well as large bags of grain. Cotton flannel, whisky, salt, spices, cheeses and other ingredients all went into canvas or leather bags, as did an assortment of things for the Nwetaka. We took the goods outside, and the merchant helped Troy strap them onto the giant horse, one by one.

Troy was shaking hands with the shopkeeper when those three dirty men walked up, reeking of trouble and booze. Sundance moved into my space, making me sidestep closer to Brogan. The merchant disappeared into his store.

I froze, arms wrapped around the child at my chest, itching to draw my dagger.

"Troy Sanchez. Look at my luck." The man's disrespectful drawl carried down the street. Scraggly hair plastered to the side of his face, he was missing several teeth, which did nothing to help his slur. "I think you owe me a new shirt, seeing as you bloodied the last one up good and ruined."

Troy put himself between me and the other men. "I owe you nothing, Monroe. You got exactly what you asked for."

Evidently, Monroe didn't agree. He spat on the ground at Troy's feet. "How 'bout the lady then." He peeked around Troy to sneer at me. "If you don't wanna buy me a new shirt, I'll settle for a turn with your woman."

"Monroe, walk away now." Troy's words were cool as a glacier.

"Or what?" Monroe spurred.

People shifted in the shadows near the shops. Some retreated, wanting no part in the fight. Some came closer. Every movement was made in awareness of the confrontation.

Troy looked back and pointed me toward the general store with eyes that shifted to a man on the wooden walkway. By the look of his badge, that man appeared to be the sheriff. He nodded as I stepped onto the wooden walkway.

"Ma'am." The sheriff tipped his hat and walked past me into the street.

Monroe leered at me. "I bet she tastes mighty nice," he taunted, swinging his gaze to Troy. "If I take her, then give her to Boar and Grun here, I'd say that 'bout counts 'fer a shirt."

The sheriff swore quietly as Troy's fist collided with Monroe's right eye. His second hit was a jab to the stomach, producing a sickened grunt from Monroe, who doubled over. As Monroe staggered back, the other two came on, one slashing with a knife.

Troy sidestepped, drew his gun, and struck a blow to the man's temple with the bone handle. Boar or Grun, whichever it was, crumpled to the ground, his knife beside him.

In a fluid motion, Troy holstered his gun and spun to throw a punch at the second man, who ducked. Monroe spat blood onto the ground behind them. Troy took a blow that snapped his head to the side, but he didn't slow. With rapid jabs and a well-placed kick, the second man was down. Writhing in the road.

Monroe stood several paces away, raw hatred in his eyes. His hand hovered over the gun at his hip.

I slid my right foot up the wall and retrieved the dirk from my boot, wishing I'd had more practice throwing knives. Hatred surged through my veins. I wasn't sure I'd hit him, but damn, was I tempted to try.

Monroe started backing down the street, and Troy moved clear of the horses. My gaze narrowed to the six-shooters strapped to his thighs. I was in the Wild West for real, and it was my man in the gunfight. I suppressed a wave of nausea and gripped my dagger. Helpless. Enraged.

In my heart, I heard Troy's voice. *Have no fear, my love.*

Both men drew their guns, and the air split with a booming crack that echoed off the storefronts and made me jump. Blood sprouted from Monroe's chest, and he fell to the road with a fleshy thud.

As Brendan screamed, emotions rolled through me, one after another. First came a thrilling sense of pride in Troy's ability to wear the role of hero so well. Then the horror hit me. The sight of blood pooling around the dead man seared into my brain and triggered flashbacks of the man Killian killed in Glasgow, and the ones who'd attacked me at Duart. Did he always incarnate as a warrior?

Troy had come to the mountains seeking a place of peace, trying to get away from this exact thing. He holstered his gun. Beneath his hard expression, I thought I saw regret.

I rocked Brendan, comforting both of us with the motion, the dirk still in my hand in case one of the other two men got up and gave me an excuse to use it. When I stepped down to the road to go to Troy, the sheriff came along, his long strides slow beside me, dark hair framing a sun-browned face.

"Troy." The sheriff tipped his hat in greeting.

"Tom." Troy gave a nod. "Sorry about the mess."

"Wasn't your fault." The sheriff gave a sigh. "I apologize for the trouble, ma'am. This isn't usually how we greet folks in Jackson." He held out his hand. "Tom Thompson, Sheriff."

I hid my dagger in a fold of my cloak. Unable to shake, I gave him a nod. "Shelta," I replied, my other arm wrapped around Brendan, who had stopped crying and was now staring at Tom with his mouth open.

"Pleasure to meet you, ma'am." He turned back to Troy. "You're probably ready to get home. We'll clean up."

"Thanks, Tom." Troy touched his hat.

The sheriff turned to the bodies on the ground: one dead, one unconscious, and one rolling around moaning.

Troy guided me to the horses, his inquiry a quiet one. "Are you alright?"

I angled my body so no one else could see, and sheathed my dagger. He raised his eyebrows at the sight of my blade. I squeezed his hand and tried to look more confident than I felt. "I'm alright. Are you?"

He looked to the sky for half a breath. "I'll be better when we leave."

We'd been riding for a while when the shaking started, as if the shock had been biding its time and decided now was the right moment to kick in. I couldn't stop replaying the scene in my mind. It could've been Troy in a pool of blood in the road.

Troy hadn't had any doubt, hadn't flinched as he pulled the trigger. I remembered Killian roaring into my room, swinging his sword. Blood on my nightgown. Fear surged.

I shook harder, unable to do anything about it.

Troy stopped, pulled me off the horse and engulfed me in his arms. He wrapped around Brendan and me like a shelter. "You're safe, Shelta. It's alright." He stroked my hair, my back.

With effort, I slowed my breathing. Finally, the shaking subsided.

"I want you to feel safe with me." His voice was deep with sorrow.

"I do. It's not that." I rocked the fussing baby, eyes down, shoulders forward.

He lifted my chin with his hand, reassurance in his gaze. Killian's soul showed through the black of his eyes. His consciousness poured into me like a widening of my mind, and I felt him seek the hurt, the fear. He soothed it away, a balm within me.

Troy held me, withdrawing from my mind, and Brendan cooed in his wrappings.

I lifted my eyes. "How did you do that?"

"I just loved you." Troy placed a kiss on my lips.

A tremor of energy shot through my body; fathomless recognition at the soul level. Troy was part of me, and within him was Killian. It was absolute knowing, absolute intimacy. There was something more, though, something I couldn't name.

He released me with a caress, and we started walking with the horses behind us. I was glad to move, to feel my feet on the earth, to move through some of the nervous energy.

Troy shot me a sideways smile. "You wear daggers in your boots."

"You should see me with a sword." I smirked.

I'd never told him about my time with the Maclean warriors. It was something I'd pushed to the back of my mind as I met the needs of my baby. I missed swinging a sword in my sassy red-and-black dress.

"Have you ever had to use them?" Troy asked.

"Not really. The only time I tried, I botched it up badly." I shuddered. "It was the same day I got the daggers, when I didn't think I'd have it in me to use them. Today, I wanted to bury my dirk in Monroe's head."

"When you have need, instinct takes over. You use the weapon because it's required to survive. It's as simple as that." He shrugged, though I could see in his eyes it wasn't that simple. I knew his memories haunted him if he gave them thought.

I looked to the road, my stride long, and said, "I think it's time you taught me how to shoot that rifle."

CHAPTER 31
THUNDER IN THE MOUNTAINS

THE NEXT DAY, Troy and I made time for weapons practice. He guided me through the workings of his rifle and showed me four different places where ammunition was stored in the cabin.

I practiced loading the gun over and over, until I could do it quickly. Then we went out to a wide, bullet-ridden stump for target practice. It lay to the north, between the lake and the house—away from the trail that led toward town. Troy warned me how strong the kickback would be, but the first time I shot the rifle the force of it jarred my shoulder something fierce. Once I knew what to expect, I was able to brace myself better, but I'd have a bruise, no question.

There was a thrill to shooting. And a rising fear. Loud. Lethal. The sharp explosions echoed off the mountains, violating the peace of the wilderness, and set Brendan crying in his little bed on the porch, guarded by Damien. Troy went and consoled him. He slid his hands over the child's ears and looked at me with command in his eyes.

Keep shooting.

We hadn't discussed it, but I knew why Troy was edgy. Three men had recognized him in the street yesterday. Only one was dead. Would they find us, hidden up here? If they did, our only chance was to kill them before they killed us.

After my session with the rifle, I walked closer to the stump I'd been shooting at and took out my daggers. I gripped the small one, tried to remember Rodric's instructions, and tossed the blade at the stump. It went wide and fell short. I tried again with the dirk.

Troy watched me, saying nothing for a while. When I'd retrieved the knives for the second time and still hadn't stuck one in the stump, he left Brendan with the dog and came over.

"Try it like this." He showed me a different hold. Talking through his motions, he threw both daggers. He taught me how to brace my shoulder, how to change the flick of my wrist depending on the weight of the blade.

I stepped into position and tried again. After a more successful round, Troy produced a pair of his own knives.

My eyebrows went up. "I didn't know you carried daggers."

"I'm armed more heavily than usual." Troy's eyes darkened.

"And you have the horses on perimeter patrol?" Brogan and Sundance grazed warily near the trail that wound through the forest to the road below.

"I do, yes." His blade sunk into the stump with a thud.

A little while later, with a fed child in my arms, Troy led me through the cabin to the back door with a secret in his eyes.

"It's time I showed you something." He turned to the wall and guided my hand to a latch that held the wood in place. A portion of the wall swung open on hinges hidden behind a long coat. The opening was narrow, only a couple of feet wide, with a wooden platform and a ladder leading down. Troy went in first and held Brendan while I stepped down, rung by rung.

The room was as long as the cabin, but not as wide. Meager light drifted in through a small window. A frame of wood held earthen walls in place, with a chest on the dirt floor to side, and a sturdy chair by the wall with the window.

"This goes to the root cellar." Troy opened a narrow door in the subterranean wall. "It's another way out. If something should happen, grab this bag," Troy pointed to a canvas backpack that had a blanket roll at the top, "and go to the spring. Beyond it, to the north, is a deer trail that goes around the other side of the lake and meets up with the road to the Nwetaka. Tell Sundance to meet you down the trail, he'll know where. The village is a long day's ride, maybe three days on foot."

He showed me the chest next, which had a blanket, a fur, a flask of water and a pouch of venison jerky. Troy lifted the false bottom of the chest to reveal ten sacks of coins, and looked at me with gravity. "Shelta, if anything should happen to me, this is yours. There's more buried at the foot of the largest rock on the west side of the spring, closest to the water."

"Nothing is going to happen to you." My words had an edge.

"No, it isn't." Troy's voice was calm. Assured. "I have a lot of practice evading death. But everyone dies sometime. I'm not afraid. I want to know you're taken care of; that you would live well, and have the means to do so." He brushed his fingers over my pinched forehead.

I refused to entertain the possibility of him dying.

Troy smiled, lines of concern melting away. "Shelta, we're going to be fine. But it's good to have a back-up plan."

I squeezed his hand. "Yes, it is."

We went to the chair below the window, where Troy showed me an extra rifle and a full box of ammunition. Standing on the wooden seat, I peered out from under the porch with a grounds-eye view of the field.

"If we should have unfriendly visitors," Troy's words were grave, "you come down and stay here until it's safe. You can shoot from this spot and not be seen, but you still need to duck if someone's firing this way, as the bullet could go astray."

I nodded, not trusting my voice to answer.

He showed me where I could find candles and matches, but warned me against using them since the light could be seen from outside. Then he followed me back up the ladder, and we had lunch. That was all that was said about it.

Late afternoon, three days later, the horses came galloping up the rise all a-whinny and a-wail. Damien joined in, sounding the alarm in his booming voice while the horses raced past the cabin—manes and tails streaming—and ran behind the stables, out of sight.

Troy called in the dog, then bolted the door. "Go below." He grabbed his rifle and escorted me to the hidden passage.

I climbed down. He handed Brendan to me, and shut me in.

No goodbye, no I love you. My heart twisted in a complex knot of fear.

As Troy's footsteps moved toward the front window, I hurried to make Brendan safe on the floor behind the chest. I wedged him between folds of fur so he couldn't roll, tucked a blanket over him, and kissed his cheek. Then I went to the chair and took the rifle out of its box.

With shaking hands, I made sure it was loaded, grabbed several cartridges—each holding fifteen rounds—and put them in my pockets. The chair stayed steady when I stood on it to tilt the window open.

I looked out from beneath the porch. Watching. Waiting. Blood rushed in my ears and my skin rose like a thousand pinpricks. Damien's growl traveled through the floorboards as men came snaking through the grass on their bellies.

I couldn't see much more than their hats, but that was enough of a target for me. I sighted down the barrel at one of them, rifle butted up to my shoulder, finger on the trigger.

A gun cocked out in the field. An indistinguishable word, and they started firing.

A window shattered above, where Troy returned fire. I swore under my breath, braced myself against the wall, took aim, and squeezed the trigger. The man I'd aimed at still fired.

Ears ringing, I cocked the gun, ignored the fact that there were bullets flying in my general direction, took more careful aim, and fired again. He dropped.

Every shot had its own sound. It varied from the deafening blast of my rifle, to Troy shooting through the window above, to the snap-crack of the pistols far afield. Peppered between the bullets were curses and shouts. Somewhere behind me—sounding far away in my adrenaline-soaked hearing—my son screamed.

I shot again and again, vaguely aware that my shoulder ached from the pounding of the rifle. *Two.* An indifferent voice in the back of my head tallied my hits.

Three. Another shape disappeared behind the tall grass and did not reemerge.

When I heard a stifled cry above me, my instinct was to go to Troy, but I aimed again, firing at the last man I could see from my narrow view.

Four. The gunfire stopped. I ducked down and sucked in a breath.

Distant words reached my ringing ears above the rhythmic pounding of two or three horses galloping away. Troy shot at them as they tried to retreat, but I couldn't see what had happened. I just knew they were gone.

Window closed, I put down the gun, grabbed Brendan, and was up the ladder in a hurry. The hidden door banged as I bumped my shoulder on it in my haste to get out. I found Troy leaning against the front door, blood gushing from his arm.

"It's nothing," he lied.

"Oh, really?" I put Brendan in his cradle, and wrapped my hands over my husband's arm to apply more pressure to the wound.

"It's a clean shot," Troy insisted. "Just a graze."

"Good. Keep pressure on it." I ducked out the door and grabbed a handful of yarrow. Gagging from my aversion to blood, I put the yarrow on the wound and wrapped his arm with a cloth so he didn't bleed to death while I got what we needed.

Brendan started to settle as he watched me move around. I set water to boil over the fire, tore up an old flannel kitchen cloth and tossed it into the pot. Next, I brought out the whisky.

"Get the needle and sinew thread." Troy told me where to look. My stomach churned as I tried to wrap my head around what I was about to do.

I cleaned the wound with the hot, wet rags, and sanitized the needle in the boiling water and the fire both. "I'm not qualified to do this," I said. I was lightheaded, the sinew-threaded needle shaking in my hand.

He smiled at me, hurt and bleeding, total trust in his eyes. "You'll do fine. Just draw the skin back together like you're patching a tear in your clothes."

"Right." Now wasn't the time to tell him how bad a seamstress I was. Troy took a swig of whisky, then passed the bottle to me. I splashed the wound to disinfect it. He hissed through his teeth, and set his jaw as I leaned in.

Pushing down the repulsion in my gut, I forced myself to make the stitches carefully and quickly. Needle through skin. Through the other side. Back again. Stich by tiny stich, I pulled flesh together.

Numb, I reached the end and tied the thread off. Troy produced a knife to cut it. I then wrapped it with fresh yarrow under a clean bandage.

"That was wonderful." Troy's color was off. Pale. At least he was sitting down.

"I think I'm going to throw up." I ran out the back door to retch in the bushes.

After a bit, I ducked inside for a cup of water, made sure Troy hadn't passed out, then went back outside to rinse my mouth. Sitting on the back step, head in my hands, I tried to slow my breath so I wouldn't be sick again.

Troy came out and put his uninjured arm around me. "You did amazing, Shelta. It's over now."

"You go back and sit in the chair," I ordered.

A brief bit of laughter sounded in his throat. "I'll be fine. I've been shot before."

"Of course you have." I let him lead me back inside. Sitting on the floor, baby at my breast, I asked, "How many were there?"

"More than a dozen." Troy leaned back in a chair next to me, his color still off. He took a swig of whiskey, then another before he put the bottle down.

"I think I got four of them." My insides went cold. I'd killed people.

Troy nodded. "I think you did, too. I got at least seven. Two got away."

"Do you think they'll be back?"

"Maybe, but not today."

Troy stroked my head as I leaned against his legs. Brendan held onto the long ends of my hair, giving gentle tugs. The dog came and curled up by my thigh, leaning into me with his thick fur. Even the black cat appeared, jumping through the broken window to curl up in a corner by the fire.

After a while, Troy sighed. "Unfortunately, I need to go out there and gather the bodies. Make sure they're all dead."

I closed my eyes. He could only use one arm. I was going to have to help him. Taking a deep breath, I started to stand up.

Troy put his hand on my shoulder. "No. I can do it. Brogan will help me. This isn't something you want to see."

His color had improved, at least. I watched in silence as Troy took another swallow of whiskey, and chased it with some water. He walked out to the field with his arm in a sling, and Brogan trotted up with a rope in his mouth to meet him.

With Brendan strapped to my back, I took the broom and swept up broken glass. Much of the front window had broken, and I did my best to get every shard, using a moist cloth when the broom was no longer doing any good. I collected spent bullets in the dustpan and broken pieces of porcelain that had been shot in the kitchen, then busied myself shaking out sheepskins and scrubbing blood from in front of the door. One stubborn piece of lead had to be pried out of the wall with the tip of my dirk.

Finally, there was nothing left for me to do. I found myself standing before the gaping hole that was formerly our window, looking out to a field filled with dead men.

Troy tied his rope around an arm or leg, and Brogan pulled the corpse to an area downwind of the cabin. They walked back, repeating the process over and over again. When Troy pulled out his gun and shot a man who had apparently not been entirely dead, Brendan started crying again. I turned to pace by the fire, trying to console my child and myself.

A long while later, when the sky was dark, Troy knocked on the back door with his foot. "Can I have the soap, please?" His tired voice came through the wood. I brought it to him, and was glad when I saw Brogan follow him down the path toward the spring.

In a daze, I got a fresh pot of water hanging over the fire and tossed in handfuls of vegetables and herbs, along with some smoked meat. I didn't feel like eating, but we'd both need something to sustain us.

Sometime later, I heard Brogan whicker, and Troy came in the back door naked. I hung his wet clothes while he went to the bedroom for clean ones.

"Can you eat?" I asked when he came back. He nodded, but didn't look at me. He stood before the fire with a haunted, hollow stare.

We ate in silence. Brendan watched from his cradle.

Troy smiled at me tiredly as I took his empty bowl. Leaving the dishes for later, I stood behind him, massaging his neck and running my fingers through his still-damp hair.

After a while, he put his hand up to mine and squeezed it. *Thank you*, he said within me, and I knew he'd be okay.

Before we went to bed, Troy wrote out a message and tucked it into a pouch tied to a rope around Damien's neck. "He'll run through the night," he said as Damien bounded through the hole where the window had been. "Diego will be here tomorrow, then I'll go for the sheriff. He'll need to come out and see, but I won't leave you here alone."

For that I was grateful. The part of me that wasn't terrified of what I'd done wished for a dragon so I could catch the two that got away and make sure they never came back.

CHAPTER 32
QUIET AFTER THE STORM

DIEGO DID INDEED arrive the next day, at dusk, with a hunting party. They trotted up on weary horses who put their heads to the ground and started tearing grass as soon as their riders dismounted.

Sarina was the only female. She marched to the house with drawn eyebrows and tense lips, more serious than I'd ever seen her. The other five men were armed with rifles, knives, bows and arrows.

Damien flopped onto the porch. I held Brendan and knelt down, stroking the dog's fur as Troy greeted our guests.

He told them about the attack, and that he needed to have the sheriff come out before burning the bodies, and that he didn't want to leave the house unguarded. All eyes went to my child and me. I glanced up, their attention a tingle at my neck, but lowered my gaze to the dog again.

The men walked around to put their belongings in the teepee. Troy went to follow them, but Sarina caught the wrist of his injured arm. Troy winced, and her eyes went wide.

"You're hurt. Let me see," she insisted.

"It's fine." He didn't fight as she removed his shirt. "Shelta stitched it up."

Sarina pulled her lips to one side in a scowl as she unwrapped the bandage and inspected my work. Her face softened when she saw my apprehension. I was sure I'd botched it up.

"You did well." A hint of her smile returned, but I could see she was shaken.

Lying in bed with Troy that night, I whispered my question into his ear. "Were you and Sarina lovers?" I smiled to show him I was okay with it.

Troy took my hand and kissed it. "Yes. She chose Diego, and I'm glad she did. I could only ever be yours."

My heart stumbled as he said it, the impermanence of my existence crashing over me. The threat of falling through the World Tree scratched its nails at the base of my skull. "You know I'm probably not here for good. I'd want you to find love again if I have to go."

"No. For me, there is only you."

"Troy—"

"Don't, Shelta. Please don't worry about it now." He crushed me to his chest and kissed me with something that bordered on desperation.

Before we slept, he told me he'd be leaving before dawn. Diego and two more men would go with him in case of an ambush, and would wait outside the town while he got the sheriff. Sarina and the others would stay with me. They'd be back before dark, Troy assured me, then covered me with kisses and held me with one arm the whole night through.

When he slipped out of bed in the morning, I trailed my hand over his chest and croaked out three words that were both an order and a prayer. "Come home safely."

He leaned in for one more kiss. "I will."

After he left, I opened the curtain and peered into the darkness. Dim shapes of men checking saddles were all I could see of Troy and his friends. Then four horses tromped along the trail to the south.

I was still awake when the first rays of light crept into the sky, nursing my son as the mountains held fast to their shadows. Quiet had reclaimed our homestead, but I couldn't forget the pile of bodies that lay across the field, nor the red dragon that had come in my dream with a message.

This was only the first of my battles.

The day was one of waiting and listening.

My consciousness rode with Troy, willing him home safely. I was in good company, but I still felt vulnerable with him gone. A dull, creeping fear riddled my mind with holes of mistrust and dread of my time with Troy being cut short.

In the afternoon, Sarina watched Brendan. The faraway surge of the ocean pulled at me while I washed in the pool beneath the spring. It rocked my body, clearing my mind. I'd been surrounded by water in Scotland, and in Canada—in many places I'd lived. The mountains were stunning, but I missed the ocean, and the family I'd left behind.

Still, I didn't want to go back. Even to Killian, not now. I wanted to stay with Troy, to live in our home in the wilderness and be his wife. I wanted the simple pleasure of tending the fire, cooking food, and watching the way Brendan made Troy light up every time. I didn't want the connection between us to end.

In the fading light of dusk, I went out to the porch for the hundredth time to see five horses climb the rise from the forest. They left the path to stop at the pile of bodies, but Troy and his companions stayed mounted. The sheriff's tall silhouette bent his head, then his big hat tilted in a nod, and they continued up the path to the cabin.

I stood on the stairs and watched them ride up, my hair and skirts stirring in the wind. Reluctantly, I took my eyes from Troy to greet the sheriff.

"Ma'am." Sheriff Tom tipped his hat to me, stopping at the house while the Nwetaka dismounted to the side of the cabin. Tom gave his horse to Troy, who proceeded to strip the gear off, then rub the animal down with a brush he must've had in his saddlebags. Sundance waited his turn.

"Sheriff." I forced a smile. "Can I offer you some tea? Whisky perhaps?"

"Ah. Whisky would be the thing for today, I think." He handed me a package. "This is from my wife, Betty."

"Please thank her for me." I sniffed baked goods and spiced meat from the cloth bundle. But I didn't go inside with it; I went down the steps to Troy.

"Will do." The sheriff took his saddlebags and walked them back to the teepee.

I said hello to the horses as I approached, stroking Sundance's nose, but all I wanted was Troy. He pulled me in with one arm when I got to him, lowering his forehead to mine, his fingers in my hair.

"Troy, are you—is everything okay?"

"Yes." He sounded rough. "Everything's going to be fine." He turned his nose to the package in my arm. "That smells delicious."

"Are you hungry?"

"Take it to our friends first." He lifted his chin toward the teepee. "And whisky for me, please. I'll be up in a bit."

"Okay." I turned and climbed the stairs to go inside.

The warmth of the fire welcomed me as I shrugged off my cloak. Brendan was on his back on a sheepskin, smiling as Sarina played with his feet.

I ran two glasses of whisky out front, then unwrapped the parcel. Tom's wife had sent a pile of rolls baked with spiced sausage. I grabbed the one on top, bit into it, and moaned.

"You have got to try one of these." I held one out to Sarina.

She took the pastry and hummed appreciatively as she chewed.

I went out the back door with a plate full of food, making sure everyone got some of the treats. When I came around front to deliver the last few rolls, Troy was sitting on the steps with Tom.

The sheriff nodded at me, his words easing some of my worries. "I've got the two men that got away locked up. They'll be tried for attempted murder, and a number of other things. More than likely they'll hang within the month. You can rest easy knowing they won't be able to bother you again."

"Thank you." Strange, finding relief at the thought of someone's execution.

"That's what I do." The sheriff drained his whisky and gave a sigh. "I suppose we should get on with burning the bodies."

The men roped up bundles of wood. Tom worked with them, helping to load the horses. When they were ready, Troy rode in front with a lantern, over to the pile of corpses. Sarina went, too.

Damien stood guard at the front door, and I watched out the bedroom window, my son sleeping beside me. The memory of the pyre in Scotland brushed my mind. Turning away, I lay down, exhausted, and let the bed hold my weight. The warmth of Brendan's hand became my comfort. I should be out there with them, facing the demise of the men I'd killed, but I stayed here with my child, sheltered. Wrestling between sharp pangs of guilt and hot flares of anger.

A while later, a flicker caught my attention through the window, and I crawled from the bed and went outside. The pyre was huge, even from a distance. I wrapped my cloak closer, watching the flames reach high into the sky.

I'd shot four men. It seemed so removed, closer to a video game than real life, which was twisted. Wrong. But I hadn't actually seen them dead. Hadn't seen their blood, not even their faces—just a threatening shape I'd managed to sight and take out with a lucky shot.

The fire blazed into the night as my thoughts circled on shadowed wings. I'd taken lives defending my family. In a way, I was okay with it. And yet, I wondered what it meant, what it changed in my life and the path I would walk.

Chapter 33
Leather and Fur

TOM LEFT EARLY in the morning, with only a cup of coffee before he rode off. "Betty packed me some goodies too," he said when I tried to insist he have breakfast first. I relented, and waved as he turned his horse.

Most of the Nwetaka rode off as well, everyone except Sarina and Diego. The others went with the goods we'd brought them from Jackson, strapped to some of the horses that had recently belonged to dead men, all saddled up and roped together.

And then we were four. Well, five with Brendan.

We spent much of the day inside the teepee, drawn into a project that involved a good deal of leather and fur. A winter coat. My cloak wouldn't be enough for the deep cold of these mountains. Sarina, sweet woman that she was, had already made most of it, and unrolled the soft, reddish-brown leather, showing me how the cloak-like garment could be buttoned in various positions that allowed me to wear it with or without the baby.

The task was to sew an inner lining made of rabbit fur. And as grateful as I was for the company and the gift, my anxiety didn't fade. Were all the outlaws accounted for, or had the men we'd killed told others before they came to threaten our home? And what had the red dragon been trying to tell me as it flew over a wild ocean in my dreams last night?

Each time Sarina noticed my face drawn up, she distracted me with a new part of the sewing project, or a story filled with laughter. Troy, who couldn't sew very well with one arm, watched over our son.

That evening, when the creation was finished, I modeled it for everyone to see, enfolded in a warm sense of safety. "It's amazing. Thank you," I gushed, and hugged my friend.

"This gift is not only from us." Sarina's eyes glittered. "It comes also from my parents."

I raised my eyebrows. What magical garment had I received?

"They have blessed it—blessed you—with safe travels in all worlds." Sarina brushed her hands down my arms. "This blessing of safe passage is for you and your children. It is yours no matter if you wear the coat or not."

I blinked tears from my eyes, struggling with the implications. "Please give them my thanks."

Giving the only thing I had to offer, I sang most of the way through our last evening together, until Diego and Sarina retired to the teepee.

Later, in the closeness of our bed, with the warm glow of lantern light playing on his skin, Troy looked at me for a long time. Silent. My fingertips roamed over the rough stubble on his face, the smooth curve of his shoulder. They skipped around the wound beneath the bandage, and fell down the rest of his arm to his hand.

"Shelta, I know I'll have to let you go one day," he finally said. My heart dropped, and he saw it. "No." He gave a shake of his head, his smile soft. "Don't fear it. It's your path. I have you now, and when you leave, your memory will bring me joy. I know it won't be the last goodbye. We will see each other again."

A tear ran down my cheek, my throat too tight to speak. I cupped his face in my hand and kissed him, hoping he was right.

We made love with astonishing tenderness and underlying need, intertwined in body, mind, and heart, as if we drew the love out of our souls and wove it into each other. I imagined it threaded through time and space, as well.

In the quiet that followed, in the warmth of his arms, I settled into myself, bones humming with contentment. And my mind, saturated with the magic we'd created, slumbered in a rare sea of trust.

Chapter 34
Falling Through Ice

BEING A MOTHER was like becoming a butterfly but never getting past the messy process of metamorphosis. I sat on the hard wood floor in the kitchen and held my head, elbows digging into my legs, stomach threatening to revolt.

Troy found me slumped against the hand-carved cabinet. Holding six-month-old Brendan in one arm, he knelt and put a hand on my shoulder. "Shelta, are you alright?"

"Yes." Nope. Not even a little bit. "I just don't feel very well."

"Are you—" His hair framed his face as he tipped his head, eyes searching mine. "Are you with child?"

"I think so. Is there any bread?" I stared at crumbs I needed to sweep and wished for scones, or crackers, or any number of convenient food items left behind when I'd charged through the World Tree and gone back in time instead of forward.

Troy helped me to the table. The hearth fire crackled, warming me despite the chill February wind howling beyond the walls of our one-bedroom oasis.

Another kid. Stupid, stupid move. I should've been more diligent with the herbs Sarina had said would keep me from getting pregnant. She'd told me to take the tea every day. I hadn't. I'd have two children to care for the next time I got swallowed by a wormhole—if the babies even made it through. Now, more than ever, I needed to find a way to stop the time travel. And I didn't know how. The thought made me shiver despite the heat from the hearth, drawing Troy's gaze as he warmed bread and broth.

Trust, Shelta. He sent a wave of calm through the connection we shared, that bridge between heart and mind. His presence settled me, as did the food, and I slipped into the illusion of security. His steadfast love lulled me into a sense of peace, despite his having a price on his head, despite the violence of his previous life that had found us here only a few months ago.

I tried not to think about the men I'd killed, or the way the gunfire echoed in the music the mountains sang for weeks after. Now there was only the cold song of winter, of dreaming and waiting.

B'alam had told me I was here to learn to trust. I did trust myself, a lot more than I had when I'd fallen into Troy's world, but it was hard to trust what came next. My dreams were increasingly filled with dragons and stormy seas.

My doom unfolded on a perfect, glittering winter day when the sky was a bright canopy of blue, the trees and mountains adorned with snow.

Troy held my coat as I slid my arms in for a late morning walk. Leather and fur enclosed Brendan and me in soft warmth. My plaid bag weighed on my left shoulder and rested against my hip, jammed full of snacks and a flask of water. I wore a blade in each boot. As always, Troy wore his pistols and slung a rifle over his shoulder.

We followed a route that hugged the borders of the meadow and did a gentle loop through the forest, Damien the wolf-dog padding along ahead of us. The woods were alive with birds trilling over the crunch of our footsteps, the rhythm of Troy's breath behind me, and the soft play of wind in the trees.

At the apex of the hill was a lookout where the whole of the valley spread out below us. We stopped, and the world went quiet. Brendan napped, warm against my chest. Damien roamed around, sniffing at the snow. Troy was a pillar behind me, holding me as I leaned into him for a rest. The glory of the mountains overwhelmed me, triggering mommy hormones and sending tears down my cheeks.

Troy stepped around to face me. "It is that beautiful, isn't it?" He smiled, and kissed my tears away.

I laughed. "Yes. It's perfect."

I took in the shape of his face, the affection in his eyes. Finally, to Damien's delight, we began to walk again.

As was my nature, I started singing. My soft song wove gratitude between the twitter of birds and whisper of branches. Troy held my hand, the path wide enough to walk side by side, as we approached one of the biggest trees in the forest.

A tree I was always careful not to touch.

As if in defiance of that perfect moment, I turned my ankle in an uneven patch of snow as we passed the tree. My hand shot out on instinct to catch myself from falling, even as Troy moved to steady me, and my fingertips grazed the bark.

That was all it took.

The worlds shifted and searing light eclipsed my vision, making my insides spin. Chaotic music incinerated me from within. I felt myself falling as if through ice, Troy's grip on me melting away.

I fought it, tried to reach back, extended my whole being toward Troy. I kicked and swam as if I were drowning. I could grasp nothing, do nothing—but he spoke within me one last time, his words penetrating the smoke of dissolving reality.

Live well, Shelta, Troy said, his voice fading, *and know that you are loved.*

PART III

CRONE

CHAPTER 35
ROCKS AND WAVES

MY FEET HIT GROUND and the bright light vanished, leaving me momentarily blind. The crash of ocean waves accosted my ears and frigid air bit at my nose, chasing away the phantom smell of smoke. Icy spray hit my face in droplets, saltwater on my lips. I backed toward the shadow behind me, a cliff that curved toward the water to become a sheer wall that ran into the sea.

The World Tree had abandoned me at a dead-end at the edge of a long strip of beach.

My heart was an anchor cast carelessly into my throat. "No, no, no," I chanted to the twilight sky. My eyesight adjusted, helping nothing.

At least Brendan was still at my chest. I sucked a jagged inhale in denial of the inescapable vastness of the sea, absently noting that this was the first time I hadn't landed in a forest.

"Not this. Not now." I turned to the rock, and shivered at the sight of a carving that cemented any doubt of what had happened. "No," I whispered again.

My fingers traced the shape of a mighty tree chiseled into the cliffside, roots like knots intertwining with stars depicted above. My breath shook, drowning in the rising tide of defeat.

"Goddess!" I shouted. She didn't answer. What could she tell me that hadn't already been said? It was my path. I had to keep evolving.

My upper lip lifted into a sneer. Bitterness burned in my blood. Fine. I didn't want to talk to her anyway. Nothing would reconcile the loss that seared through me. Furious, I let out a roar that tore at my throat.

Over and over, I'd been ripped away from everything I loved. I'd lost Killian, and now Troy. I had a baby to care for, another on the way, and the World Tree stranded me at the edge of the world?

I sank to my knees in the coarse sand and sobbed. Brendan began to wail, and I didn't have it in me to console him. I just let him cry.

The waves were like the breathing of the world, the water the tears of the gods. Surely whatever powers were watching wept at this. How could they not?

Tears mingled with the spray drenching my face and beading on the leather of my coat. The cliff pushed my wailing toward the water, a wild sound from the deepest part of my soul, and the moody wind ate up my moans.

There was only the grief, the sky, the rock, and the sea.

I pressed my forehead against the roots of the tree carved into the cliff, whispering "No" again and again.

And then there was a shift inside, a change in the music of my grief.

"*Please.*" My voice scraped. Ragged. Desperate. Like a mantra it pulsed from my lips. "Please. Please. Please." I didn't know what prayer to say, nor who I was praying to at that point, for there was no hint of the goddess.

Brendan started hiccupping. The small bulge of my belly was a part of Troy, mine to bring across the threshold of the worlds.

I took a long breath, and pinned my hope on the only thing that would make this remotely worth it. *Please let there be dragons here. Let this be the last time I'm at the mercy of the World Tree. May the next jump be my own doing. My choice.*

I wiped my face with my hands and smeared tears over the tree in the rock. Sorrow seeped from my fingertips in sacrifice. Spite. Defiance.

The tide was coming in, narrowing the beach to a thin ribbon of land. Time to get moving. I made my way over slippery pebbles and wet sand that shifted beneath my boots.

Twice I had to stop to catch my breath. Eventually, the beach widened into twenty feet of safety between rock and waves. A little farther, when the land spread fifty feet between the sea and the cliffs, I stopped to nurse Brendan, eat an oatcake, drink from my flask, and take note of all the familiar things that had come with me, and all the things that had not. I wished dearly for my guitar.

Fatigue numbed the intensity of loss. Survival was my primary concern now.

The stars were the only light, the moon barely a crescent in the sky. I continued along the coastline, face half-frozen, and wondered if the ocean would rise up to claim me.

After what felt like forever, when I was assessing the shore for a place to curl up and rest, the wall of rock ended and the beach receded into a sheltered harbor with long boats at anchor. Beyond, windows glowed like beacons in the night, smoke from their chimneys making a scent that reminded me of Troy's cabin mingle with the sea air.

I imagined him at home without me, sitting by the fire, Damien curled up at his feet, whisky bottle nearby. He might have faith that we'd see each other again—and I'd make it happen if it was the last thing I did—but that didn't stop the loss. I knew without a doubt he'd be as heartbroken as I was.

After tripping over my feet, I sank to my knees for a rest, breath puffing translucent white in the darkness as I stared at the village. I hated asking for help, but I needed shelter, and soon. The chill wind snuck beneath my collar, my skirts damp and heavy.

Finally, I forced myself up, and, step by dragging step, made my way into the settlement. I followed a path that wound through stone and wooden structures with steep roofs, the flicker of fire through windows tempting me with warmth. Laughter came from one house, people going about their lives on that cold, starry night.

I was going to have to knock on a door. My nerves were shot, so tired I almost didn't care. I stumbled every few steps, picking out the house that seemed the friendliest. Its arched entrance was welcoming, the home's windows glowing bright.

Mess that I was, I pushed my hair back from my face, brushed as much sand as I could from my coat, stamped my feet, and shook out the bottom of my skirts. Then I knocked three times and took a step back.

The door opened to reveal a handsome woman with a wide face and deep-blue eyes. I did my best to smile, and said, "Hello."

She saw Brendan peeking out from beneath my coat and the desperation in my face, and ushered us inside. "Hello. Come in. Make yourself warm."

She spoke with a thick accent I couldn't place. At first, her words were hard to understand, but something rang in my ears like a distant song, and the language made sense to me. It was the same as I'd sung in Duart.

An ancient tongue.

My stomach dropped. How far back in time had I gone?

She steered me into a chair with large hands, then headed to the kitchen on the other side of a long counter. I loosened my coat and took Brendan from his wrappings. When my savior returned, she had two earthen mugs, and settled into the chair across from me.

"Thank you." I took the tea, hoping she understood me.

She cocked her head like my words were foreign. Like she was trying to figure me out. Staring at the light-green brew, I reached into the place in my soul that was made of music. Whatever magic I possessed; it was in song. Sound. I willed myself to speak the language.

"It smells good." Honeyed steam in my nose, strange words on my tongue. "My name is Shelta." No last name. Time had stripped me bare. All that was left was Shelta.

"I am Ola." She smiled. "Do you know where you are?"

I shook my head slowly. How did she know?

"You are in Nóregr."

It didn't register at first, but my foggy brain put together the boats I'd seen outside the village, the make of the cottages, and the cold of the sea. "Norway?"

"Norway," she agreed. "Our village is the tribe of Thorson. My brother, Nikolas, is our chief."

I sipped my tea. I didn't dare ask the year. Not yet. My ears rang, the weight of time heavier than ever. All I could think of was the legend of Gillean, who went to Norway to become a god and befriend a dragon.

The tea warmed me. Ola made happy faces at Brendan, her face creasing as she grinned, hints of grey showing in her brown hair. Brendan cooed back, and after a few minutes I let her hold him. He hooked a hand onto the reddish-brown wool of her dress and didn't let go.

Memories of found mothers dropped through my mind. I pushed them away. This woman couldn't be more than ten years older than me.

"I'm sorry I tracked so much of the beach into your house." Every word made me stretch into the magic of music. Language had become a new instrument to learn.

"You are welcome here. Relax." She had this serene look about her, like she was at peace with my presence for some reason beyond sheer hospitality.

I went to the entrance to take my boots off. Turning my back to her, I slid the dirk into my purse, and hung my coat on an empty peg. Bone-weary, I returned to the fire, where she handed Brendan back to me.

"Come." She stood, her command kind. I followed her around a corner to a small room that held a narrow bed, a simple table, and a wash basin. "Sleep." Her fingers played with the end of her long braid. "There is time for talking in the morning."

"Thank you." Tears gathered in my eyes as she let the curtain fall, the heavy fabric sweeping the floor. I didn't have to explain myself. Not yet.

Quiet surrounded me. Dark enveloped me. I tucked Brendan into the bed and proceeded to strip my sandy skirts off, berating myself for not wearing pants like a sensible person. Hanging the heavy wool skirt and layered petticoat over a chair back, I remembered putting them on this morning. I'd wanted to feel pretty, to have fabric swishing around my legs on my walk with Troy, dressing up for a stroll in the snow. Just for fun.

With a groan, I collapsed on the bed. I drew a cover over my body, made sure Brendan was safely tucked where he could breathe, and surrendered to a heavy sleep.

In the morning, I wandered out to the sounds and smells of breakfast: the crackling of wood in the hearth-fire, meat sizzling on a pan, steam rising from a pot on the counter.

"Drink," Ola said by way of good morning, handing me some sort of herbal tea.

I took it, not about to argue.

She was taller than me by a good eight inches, with a broad brow and thick hair bound into a braid that fell most of the way down her back. She surveyed me from the kitchen with blue eyes framed by dark lashes.

I sipped my tea, and sat at the table when she indicated I should do so. When she put a plate of sausage, coarse bread, and thick butter in front of me, I almost cried. "You wonderful woman. Thank you!"

The spiced sausage and fresh bread were heaven in my mouth.

Ola laughed at my enthusiasm. She took Brendan from my arms, not asking, simply doing what was needed. I got that from the start—it was her way to take care of what was necessary. Friendly, strong-willed, and commanding. She reminded me of a cross between Killian's brother, Wallace, and Sarina. The thought made me grin.

"You smile!" She flashed a brilliant smile of her own at me, her teeth straight and all present in her mouth. "That is good." She nodded, weight moving from one thick leg to another as she bounced Brendan, turned her happy face toward him and made him giggle.

A thread in the tangle of tension inside me pulled itself free. I chewed a bite of sausage, and met her gaze with effort.

"You had a hard night," she said, matter of fact. "But you will be all right."

She didn't ask where I'd come from, and I didn't offer the information up. When I finished eating, she gave me back my baby and told me to sit while she puttered in the kitchen.

Over the course of the morning, I watched her do half-a-dozen chores in that space that was obviously her domain. She fed the fire, ground flour, made bread, began a soup, and turned milk into the beginnings of a soft cheese.

It seemed so remote, this village on the coast. Isolated. I knew in my gut I'd dropped a long way back in time.

I could only hope that meant there were dragons.

As I swayed Brendan, the front door opened. There was no knock, just a blast of wind and cold that cut abruptly off as the door shut. A strange quiet hit me, the entrance filled with the bulk of a big man made bigger by his thick coat.

Ola introduced us in her matter-of-fact way. "Nikolas. Here is Shelta."

It was dark in the doorway where he stood. The intensity of his shadowed gaze made the hair on my neck stand on end. I turned Brendan slightly away, trying to keep the fear from my face. Ola had said something about Nikolas the night before. Her brother. The chief.

He had his sister's dominating presence, except fiercer, unquestionably male. There was no smile beneath his beard.

"Will you come with me?" His tone made it clear I was expected to accept the invitation.

Ola waved me off with the back of her hand.

Okay, then. I wrapped Brendan to my chest, pulled on my coat, and stepped into my boots. As I followed Nikolas out, I slipped a dagger into my pocket, and put up my fur-lined hood.

Chapter 36
At the Edge of the Sea

NIKOLAS WAS SILENT until we reached the edge of the ocean. We turned right on the long strip of beach that curved around the bay, away from the cliff where I'd appeared the night before. There was no greeting, no preamble. In a voice that rumbled like a wave, Nikolas dropped the question I didn't know how to answer. "How did you come to be here?"

I opened my mouth and failed to speak, losing the thread of magic that let me treat language as song. What could I say to this massive man?

He had a wild edge, long hair blowing in the icy wind. His eyes were a piercing, stormy blue, and I couldn't hold his gaze. Beyond the sheer mass of him was an underlying intensity that told me he was capable of absolutely anything.

A real live Viking.

Was I far enough into pagan times that my story would indicate the work of the gods, or would I be condemned by superstition?

The only lies I could conceive of were poor ones, and I didn't think he'd buy anything less than the truth. I wouldn't survive without help. My life and that of my children depended on the charity of these people.

Specifically, this man.

"My tale is strange," I said, finding the thread of language again. "I'm afraid you won't believe me. I can hardly believe it myself."

Nikolas stopped walking and fixed me with eyes that matched the ocean. "Do you know what 'Thorson' means?"

"Son of Thor?" I guessed, stating the obvious.

"Indeed." Nikolas spoke with conviction. "Myself and my kin are descended from Thor. I can trace my lineage back seven generations to the seed of the god and his love for a mortal woman. Your tale, however strange it may be, cannot be more so than the history of my family or the things I have seen."

Pagan times indeed. If a goddess had spoken in my mind, why wouldn't Thor be real? I had no right to doubt the improbable. Hopefully, Nikolas would return the leap of faith.

He waited, his fierce gaze making me feel like a warrior under his command, rather than a displaced pregnant mother, afraid and alone. I tried to imagine myself on the field with Clan Maclean. Safe. Respected.

"May I ask a question first?" I needed some context of how far back I'd traveled. "What is the year?"

"The year—the way the Christians count it, is that what you're asking?"

I nodded.

"Seven hundred eighty-nine." He frowned. "I believe. It's been eight moons since I had that bit of news."

I nodded, dizzy, willing myself not to fall to my knees in the sand again. A thousand questions related to the era rose in my throat, but I swallowed them.

"Alright." I took a deep breath. Here goes. "Yesterday, I unintentionally fell through a portal between worlds. This has happened my whole life. I've lived in many different places and times, and I don't know why."

Nikolas looked out to sea. I turned my gaze to follow his, repressing the nervous chatter that wanted to pour out of me. I needed to keep my mouth shut until I had an indication of how he'd react.

He didn't respond for a long time, and I slipped down the steep slope of sorrow. I thought of how alone Troy was, how he would suffer the hurt in his quiet way. The time I'd been given with him had been even shorter than what I'd had with Killian, and being ripped from both of them was too much to bear.

The worst part was I'd known it would be bad, and I'd let myself love them anyway.

Waves rolled and crashed, approached and retreated, singing the ocean's song of fathomless power. I swayed as I stood, keeping Brendan content and trying not to shatter in the fragility of my emotions. I did not want to go to pieces in front of this man.

Nikolas looked from the dozing child at my chest to my ungloved hands wrapped around my son, and eventually to my waiting eyes. "Did you have a husband?"

Tears welled up instantly. My voice scraped, just shy of breaking. "Two loves in two worlds." None of my other lovers compared, not even Evalynne. No one understood me like Killian and Troy.

It meant something to my oh-so-heavy heart when his expression pinched toward compassion. "That is a sad tale. But I see that you speak honestly."

First time I met Troy, he'd sat on his splendid horse and asked if I would speak truthfully. I'd said yes, and that was that. My mouth tugged into a smile, thinking of Troy looking up at me from beneath the brim of his black hat.

Nikolas's hard features transformed, like brightness shining off the cold sea. "Perhaps the story is not all sad."

I shook my head. "No. It's full of love."

"Good." He'd been facing the water. Now, he turned toward me, and it took willpower not to take a step back. "The sea heard you. Last night, when you came through the World Tree."

In that moment, I had no doubt he was descended from a god, his gaze penetrating clear through me. "Do you speak with the sea?" I asked. What kind of abilities did Nikolas claim as a seventh-generation son of Thor? Could he speak mind-to-mind, like Troy?

"I can ask and listen. I am shown visions or given a favorable wind."

He began to walk along the water again, and I paced him. Our footsteps crunched over the rocky shore in rhythm.

"Ola felt you come through at twilight," said Nikolas. "She asked me to watch your way."

Whatever that meant. "You knew where I came from?"

He nodded. Like falling through time was no big deal. "Twice I thought I would have to come down from the rocks to assist you."

Did that mean he'd been above me on the cliffs, or was he watching remotely with god-like powers, able to appear from the sky like his namesake out of lightning and thunder?

Enough. My imagination was running wild. Surely, he was more mortal than that.

"You wanted to let me make it on my own?" I thought of how many times I'd stumbled. "Yet you asked me where I'd come from anyway, having seen my less than graceful entrance."

I was defensive, but too tired to be properly angry. He'd seen me lose control. Fall to my knees. I had thought I was alone in my torment, afforded privacy to let the emotions go. He probably thought me weak, a helpless woman. I narrowed my eyes, hating the vulnerability of my out-of-control life. All I wanted was a way to control the time travel and get back to Troy, back to Killian. Maybe I could go back and forth, spend my life with each of them in turns. If I could find that red dragon…

Nikolas didn't react to the edge in my words, calm as the horizon. "I wanted to see if you were brave enough to speak the truth. I do not know from whence you came—from what world or time or adventure. I know only that you traveled, and the World Tree allowed you to do so. It is the calling of my blood to assist you, such as you are."

Such as I am.

We moved on; footprints stretched behind us in wet sand. I had no words, no song to offer. He seemed content to walk along the arc of water. Slowly, to the soundtrack of the sea, the mess of nerves below my heart began to unravel.

Nikolas stopped and turned to face me. The size of him, the intensity of his presence framed by ocean and sky made him all the more god-like. "You and your children will be cared for, world-weaver. Perhaps we can help you understand something of your nature."

That caught me. I leaned forward, yearning to make sense of it all. But there was that other thing he'd said. "Children?"

"You are with child, yes?"

"Yes, but how do you know?" My belly had only just begun to bulge.

"I know." He touched his brow.

The ocean rolled and the clouds moved, ever-changing. Salt scented each breath. The Viking before me stood steady like stone, still amidst the infinite kaleidoscope of reality.

"What—" I shook my head, tried again. "Do you know what's happening to me?"

He watched the sea. "I know pieces of the whole only, not the full revealing. There are legends of world-walkers, star-travelers, and those who traverse time. I will tell you what I can."

Nikolas placed one heavy hand on my shoulder, and lifted the other to the ocean. His touch sent a spark down my spine and through my bones, like soft lightning. Above the crashing waves, perhaps a hundred feet out, an apparition formed out of saltwater spray. An enormous tree grew, branches reaching to the clouds, roots to the ocean floor, thick trunk spiraling. Constantly changing.

"The World Tree is the axis upon which the universe spins." The resonance of his words coaxed ancient songs from wherever my music came from. "It connects every realm: each possibility a branch, each reality a leaf. Its roots are eternity."

With a twist of his hand, the clouds opened, and the sun shone through the sculpture of water. Each droplet sparkled, colors dazzling, making me gasp.

"The trunk is a conduit that allows some to pass through." Nikolas held it a moment longer, then closed his fingers and turned his fist palm down. His hand slid off my shoulder.

The water fell and the vision vanished. The clouds brought themselves together, dimming the light of the sun to a wash of grey. The waves came in as they'd always done.

"The celestial ones," Nikolas continued, "those who came from the stars, can transcend the limits of time and space. As can gods who are of the stars. And then there are a rare few mortals who walk between the worlds. World-weavers." He flashed his eyes to mine, bright like the sky he'd revealed when he'd parted the clouds.

"By your presence, Shelta," he spoke my name for the first time, "each world you touch is woven more closely to the others. You bind these different times and places. The separation between them becomes less defined, bridged by your coming. Influenced forever by your heart song." He stopped, tilting his head as if the last words weren't his. "What this means, I do not know."

I looked past Nikolas to the ocean. Brendan slept, warm and comforting against my chest. The water made its crashing music and the wind pushed in gusts. I stood there a long time, trying to process what he'd said, and failing.

Turning, I brought my gaze to his. "I don't know what to make of it, but thank you. Perhaps someday I'll understand."

"It will come in layers." He smiled, wisdom in his weathered face.

I studied him as he looked out to sea, standing like a pillar of stone, intimate with the elements of water and wind. After a moment, I took a step toward the waves.

Eyes closed, I let the music of the land seep into me. The ocean's vibration rippled through the shoreline, up the hills, and into deep-rooted mountains. I sensed the songs of waterfalls and rivers, of rain and distant shores. Opening more, I touched the low, fluid song of the fjords. The soaring, sheer rise of land from beneath the water. It sounded within me as a compelling roll of drums and chanting voices in mysterious harmony.

This was new; I was able to hear nature's music so clearly. My ability was growing. Either that, or I'd gone so far back in time that the consciousness of the land hadn't retreated from human contact. Maybe it was my proximity to Nikolas. Whatever it was, it confused me, a song that rose to fill me with silence. Demanded I listen, but not sing.

So entranced was I, that I didn't notice the approach of the sea until it swirled around my toes. I scrambled back a few steps.

"She wanted to say hello." Nikolas grinned. "She likes you."

I shook water off my boots. "She?"

"The ocean." His words held reverence. "The mother. The goddess."

The goddess. Of course. She was behind everything.

Chapter 37
Children

WE WALKED BACK to the village in silence, my head filled with the constantly changing music of land and sea and wind. But we didn't go to Ola's cottage, like I thought we would.

Nikolas stopped before a larger house with ornate pillars, a roofed archway above the few stairs and small porch, and an oversized door with a hammer carved into dark wood. Intertwining designs covered the hammer, and runes were etched into the frame around the door. The roof peaked high and sloped steeply down like most of the other buildings, but this one was taller than the rest. I wondered how many generations had lived beneath its eaves.

"This is my home." Nikolas led me up the stairs and pushed the door open. "You are welcome here. Please come to me if you need anything."

"Thank you." I followed him inside. The interior was as beautiful as the outside; every post, beam, and cabinet finished in exquisite detail. It was also occupied.

Three pairs of eyes stared as Nikolas closed the door behind us. There was a boy of ten or so by the hearth, eyes blazing blue. He stopped in the middle of feeding a log to the fire to gape at me. When he saw me looking back, he continued his task.

Two girls with dark-blonde hair regarded me with a mix of caution and curiosity from the kitchen; one around twelve, and one younger, perhaps six.

Nikolas got as far as, "These are my children—" and was interrupted by Brendan, whose quiet waking-up sounds had escalated into a wail.

I smiled over the sound of my screaming child. "I need to feed him."

Nikolas showed me to a room that must've belonged to his daughters, and I sat on one of their beds as Brendan sucked fiercely. It hurt, and I tried to get him to settle, to be gentle, but he was ferocious in his feeding. I looked around to take my mind off the ache.

The room was sparse, but lovely. A cloth doll lay on each pillow. There were child-sized swords and shields, a few books, and a large dragon carved into the wall opposite the window.

My fingers traced the dragon at my neck, a thrill of rightness clicking somewhere in my soul.

The dragon on the wall soared over a narrow sea, mountains to either side, and I lost myself in the details of masterfully carved stones and scales until Brendan backed off. I knew he would need to pee, and soon, so I hustled from the room, out the front door, and stood near a bush to the right of the stairs.

Just as I was maneuvering Brendan out of his diaper, Nikolas came out.

"Is everything—" He broke off with a snicker as warm liquid splashed my face, my little boy squirting away before I'd had a chance to turn him.

I remedied my mistake, baby piss dripping off my nose. There wasn't a damn thing about motherhood that was glamorous.

Nikolas was still laughing when Brendan stopped and looked proud of himself. I pulled out a cloth, wiped my face, and dried off my son.

"I'm sorry." Nikolas grinned. "I caught you off guard."

"It's fine." I eyed my child. I couldn't be mad at him when he smiled so brightly, but my cheeks burned with embarrassment all the same.

Three heads pulled away from the window. I had an audience. Wonderful. Head down, I busied myself tucking Brendan back inside his wrappings.

Inside the house, the eldest girl brought me a bowl of water and a rag. The children were introduced, oldest to youngest, as Frøya, Leifr, and Dagný.

"Lovely to meet you." I said, and dabbed my face with the damp cloth. The girls giggled.

"We don't often have visitors from afar," explained Nikolas.

"Oh," I said.

"Oh," said Frøya, copying me.

"Oh!" said Dagný, delight in her young face. "Oh!" She bounced on her toes.

Leifr was too proud to engage in such silliness. He eyed me warily as I took a seat on a long, fur-covered bench, baby on my lap. Brendan gazed from one person to another, enjoying the attention. I smoothed his dark hair.

"Can I hold him?" asked Frøya. When I hesitated, she added, very matter-of-fact, "I held Dagný when she was a baby."

Hesitantly, I handed Brendan over, not dropping my hands until I saw how surely her small arms supported his weight. She rocked him, looking down as if she was a mother herself.

Of course, the younger girl wanted to hold Brendan as well. Nikolas made Dagný sit next to me with Brendan on her lap, while Leifr hovered, aloof. I smiled at him, trying to make eye contact. He took a step back, either afraid of me, or not wanting me to be there. My smile faltered, and I looked back to Dagný and Brendan.

Nikolas cocked his head towards his son with an inquiring gaze.

"Örlendr," spat the boy in accusation, eyes narrowed as they swung toward me.

Outsider. I flinched as the meaning hit home.

Nikolas growled words that translated slowly through my fog of sorrow. Leifr stood still, fists clenched. Father stared down son, face hard, eyes dark as deep water.

"I apologize," said the boy in a forced tone.

"For what?" I asked.

"He called you a foreigner," Nikolas said.

I gave a shrug. "He's right. I am."

Leifr looked at me straight. Like he hadn't expected me to admit to it.

Nikolas shook his head. "That may be so, but I will not have you called such in my home, or by my kin." The look he gave his son said, *Is that clear?*

I took Brendan back from Dagný and looked to Leifr. "My child is an outsider, too, but he doesn't know it. I hope he grows up feeling like he belongs somewhere."

Hadn't meant to say that. I smiled to make light of my words, unwilling to let the catch in my throat turn into tears.

Leifr's face softened, his gaze on the child on my lap. "I apologize," he said again, this time with a bow of his head and sincerity in his voice.

"It's alright."

"May I hold him?" asked Nikolas, gesturing toward the baby.

I lifted Brendan, and watched the corners of the Viking's eyes crease as he took my son with a father's ease. The baby fit in a one-armed hold, Nikolas's large hand cradling his head. He used his free hand to tickle Brendan, making him laugh.

"Oh!" said Dagný.

"Come." Frøya took her sister's hand and towed her to the kitchen, where they'd evidently been preparing lunch.

Leifr stood back, watching Nikolas. There was a hint of awe in his face, as if he were seeing his father differently. I could tell how much the boy adored him and wanted to be acknowledged. Nikolas saw it too, and drew him in, under his free arm. Leifr put two of his fingers in Brendan's tiny hand.

"You see how strong his grip is?" Nikolas asked his son. "You were like that. So strong, even as a baby." Leifr stood up taller, looking back and forth from his father to Brendan.

Frøya called Leifr to help bring lunch to the table, and soon I sat with Nikolas and his children, eating with one hand, Brendan on my lap. Nikolas focused on his oversized portion of fish stew and flat, dense bread. The children shot me curious looks between bites. I leaned forward to eat without spilling it on Brendan, who swiped out with his hands, nearly tipping the bowl over. After he'd almost succeeded twice, I gave up and sat back, bouncing my son.

Frøya pushed away from the table and came around to me, taking Brendan into motherly, twelve-year-old arms. She walked a few steps away, and started rocking him, saying, "Come, now. Let your mother eat."

I took a bite of soup and wondered if it was normal for a girl that young to have such an air of responsibility.

"She mothers us all," Nikolas said quietly. "Their mother died shortly after Dagný was born. Frøya has been the woman of the house since she was seven."

I swallowed my food, thinking of Killian and Charlie with sorrow like a trickle of ice water being poured down my back. "I'm sorry."

"It has been many years. We do well together." Nikolas smiled at his son, who'd looked up at the mention of his mother. That explained the boy's aloofness.

It didn't explain the incessant sense of familiarity growing as I spent time with Nikolas, nor my impossible instinct to run away and live like a hermit. Maybe I could've done it before kids, but now that I was a mother, I was dependent on others. I needed this man's help, just like I'd needed Killian and Troy, but I couldn't survive another loss like that.

A little while later, Nikolas and I walked back to Ola's, our footsteps crunching an uneven beat on the rocky ground. He spoke more freely, without his children listening. "It's amazing what they can do," he said. "Frøya would stand behind me and stroke my hair after her mother died, having seen Brynja do the same. She is a healer, like Ola. Comforting comes naturally to her."

"It must have been hard." I imagined what they'd gone through, him with three children, one an infant without a mother. I'd only ever had foster mothers. Some had loved me, and I'd been crushed to lose them, but they'd never been mine. I'd tumbled through time as an orphan.

I could only hope my children escaped that fate.

"It was hardest on Leifr." Nikolas lifted a hand. "As I grieved, he was afraid he'd lost me as well. Frøya took on caring for all of us. It helped her, I think, but she was young to step into such a role."

The wind blew from behind, carrying the smell of wood smoke and cooking as it pushed us along the street. I spotted the cottage where I'd slept last night, and Nikolas said, "You will stay with my sister. She is the medicine woman of our village."

"Thank you." Those two words never seemed good enough, and now I had no guitar to play, nothing to offer in return for food, shelter, and their kindness. I was, once again, at the mercy of charity. Somehow, I'd find a way to help, to contribute; I wouldn't be a burden.

When we reached Ola's door, Nikolas asked, "Would you walk with me again tomorrow?"

I smiled. "Sure. That sounds nice."

He nodded, spun on one foot, and strode off toward the far side of the village, where I glimpsed a large open shelter and what looked like the hull of a ship beneath. When I entered the cottage, Ola was behind her wooden counter as if she'd never left the kitchen.

"You return." She lifted sharp eyes to me. "You did not fall into the sea, after all."

"I got my feet wet." I hung my coat and slipped off my boots, which had dried by Nikolas's fire.

She went on chopping something aromatic with a small knife.

Fatigue hit me hard. I ducked behind the curtain to what seemed to be my new room, and snuggled into the bed with Brendan.

My thoughts were a barrage of questions when I closed my eyes, heart sore.

Eventually, I drifted into a muddled dream state in which Nikolas's children told me how to hold Brendan, constantly taking him away from me and telling me I wasn't doing it right. Killian stood behind them in his green kilt, shaking his head as I tried to communicate but couldn't speak the language. Nikolas's late wife appeared, glared at me and called me Örlendr, while Nikolas was nowhere to be seen. I heard hoofbeats, but there was no Troy. Wingbeats, but no dragons.

I woke feeling out of control, terribly alone, and more fatigued than before. I couldn't escape, not even in sleep.

When I returned to Ola's kitchen, she thrust a cup of tea into my hands. "Drink."

I did. It was hot and soothing, whatever she'd brewed for me.

"Better?" Ola asked, coming over to sit and hold Brendan.

I leaned into the thick fur that covered the chair, and gave the polite answer. "Yes." Maybe the tea helped, but a storm of emotions still waited like an undertow to pull me away.

"Nikolas told you that you are received here." She nodded, agreeing with herself, and smiled at Brendan, who had a fist wrapped around her braid. "How is it, when you travel the World Tree? What is it like?"

I held my cup with both hands. "It doesn't take much time, if you can measure time while being transported through it. Mostly there's a tremendous spinning, chaotic music, and a blinding flash of light. Every other time, I've gone through a tree. When I came out here, there was only a carving in the rock."

Ola rocked Brendan. "The place where you emerged is ancient. Known to the gods."

I raised an eyebrow. After seeing the vision Nikolas conjured from the water, I was ready to believe just about anything.

"Certain places bring the worlds closer together, thinning the veil between." Ola's voice carried the wisdom of a crone. I listened intently. "That rock goes down deep into the ocean. It is a bridge."

A bridge. Nikolas had said I bridged worlds.

Head starting to pound, I sipped my tea and tried not to think.

Chapter 38
Dancing Lights

NIKOLAS APPEARED AT the door the next morning as promised. I greeted him with a tight-lipped smile. I didn't want to go walking, I wanted to curl up in bed and take a day off from reality. The wind blew something fierce, howling outside the thick glass windows. But I'd agreed the day before, so I tucked Brendan snuggly in my coat, my cleavage making a tunnel of breathing space. Ola insisted I wrap a thin scarf around my neck.

Nikolas looked like a bear with his fur-lined coat and wild hair. Everything about him was turned up to eleven. The bass of his footsteps reverberated through the ground and up my legs, his presence powerful though he did nothing but walk.

We strode across the center of the village, past a singular ash tree that grew taller than any building. Another reminder of the World Tree. Helpless frustration spawned bitter thoughts in my head as I tried to match his pace. I kept quiet as we walked along the cliffs in the direction of the carving where I'd been deposited a couple of nights ago, a dragging heaviness holding me back.

When Nikolas spoke, the sound of his voice drew me like a magnet. Deep. Warm. Dangerous. "To the gods," he said, "a hundred years is a blink of an eye, and a moment is eternity. Time is a trickster. It is not linear, as we experience it. Neither are our lives, our souls. You and I have individual perspectives, but our souls stretch much farther."

He needed to stop talking about souls. All I could think about were Killian and Troy and the essence they shared.

"Each child becomes a world of their very own." Nikolas dropped his eyes to the bulge in my coat. "Each choice brings infinite possibility."

"Maybe." My fingers curled through the fur in my pockets, my right hand grazing the hilt of my dagger. "I mean, yes, I see what you're saying. But infinite possibility? If that were the case, I could walk through that rock," I pointed down the beach, where the cliff curved into the sea, "and go back where I was before. Given the pattern of my life, that's not going to happen."

He lifted his chin at the edge in my words.

"I'm sorry," I said. "I don't mean to be bitter."

"You have the right." Nikolas looked down. "Your life has not been an easy one."

I shrugged. "Everyone struggles. I'm not usually one to complain—it doesn't do any good. I just hate being so out of control."

We walked for a while, feet crunching on pebbles and stones, before he spoke again. "Perhaps each choice is infinite in possibility because we are, at our essence, limitless. I think we also overlook the potency of simple things."

"Like conversation?" I tilted my eyes up.

Chunks of hair blew around his face, eyes softening as one side of his mouth lifted beneath his beard. "Like conversation. Companionship. We spend this time together, and our souls know each other. Perhaps we have known each other before, in other places."

His words echoed in my head, smashing together like the water churning on rocks not far away.

Our souls know each other.

No. Even if he had Killian's soul inside him, same as Troy, I would not repeat my mistakes. No more falling in love, no more getting close with people I was going to leave. Definitely no more children.

I stopped and looked out at the waves. If we kept going, we'd reach the place where I'd been spit out of the wormhole and split to the bone by grief.

Nikolas stood beside me, steady as a rock, patient as eternity. He didn't touch me. For that I was grateful.

"I'd like to go back." I didn't want to see that carving in the cliff. Anger rose like a tide.

He didn't ask why. We turned toward the village, walking side by side, in silence but for the roar of the ocean and shifting of stones.

When Nikolas followed me into Ola's cottage, I stepped out of my boots and pushed them to the side, hiding the dirk stashed in the right one. I hung my coat, leaving the little dagger in a fur-lined pocket. Neither Nikolas nor Ola would do anything to harm me, but powerlessness weighed on me like its own version of gravity.

Ola instructed Nikolas to hold Brendan so I could have a lie down while she finished preparing the food. Wicked-tired, having seen him the day before with his own children, I handed over the baby and went to collapse on the bed. But I didn't sleep. I listened the whole time to be sure Brendan was safe.

When we sat at the table a short while later, I had a chance to see brother and sister together. The physical similarities were obvious, but there was a presence of something more, the intensity that came with their god-blood.

"Do you have other siblings?" I asked between bites, trying to make conversation. These people didn't talk unless they had something worthwhile to say. Which was rather nice.

"There are two younger brothers," Nikolas answered. "They're at sea. Their families flourish here, with seven children between the two of them."

So, Ola was the only girl. I brought my gaze to hers. "I hope you don't mind me asking, but have you no husband or children?"

She gave a big chested laugh. "No children, no husband. Not for me. The whole village is my family. If I wish to share a bed with a man, or a woman, I do so, but I have no wish to take a husband; no time to raise children of my own when I care for all the children of our tribe."

If only I'd been wise enough to stick to my guns. No husband, no children. I'd have an easier path. I hugged Brendan to me, mother's love mixing with logic's regret.

"I choose this with ease," said Ola. "I have love enough in my life. I am seer, healer, village mother. That is my path."

She was so at peace with her role. I fidgeted, at peace with nothing.

Nikolas focused on his plate. It held twice as much food as mine. I wondered what it had been like for Ola, growing up with three brothers descended from a god. I guessed she'd had her own advantages.

"Did your abilities develop when you were children?" I asked.

Ola made a sound in her throat, nodding. "I remember being before I was born. I remember the spark and pull into the body, being inside our mother—everything. There was always knowing for me. And healing. Our mother would not have lived to birth my brothers if I had not healed her even as I was born."

My eyes went wide at that. "Is your mother still alive?"

Ola shook her head. "Our parents sailed to their rest together, ten years past."

Sailed to their rest. What a sweet way to say it. More like they went out on a boat and never came back.

Nikolas put down his fork. "My knowing is of nature, of the elements. The ability to interact with the world around me, being able to converse, to ask and shape—those things came early. I had to learn to control my emotions so I didn't call a storm every time I was upset as a child."

"Oh, my." I could only imagine what that must've been like.

"Ola helped." Nikolas inclined his head toward his sister. "She was only two years older, but she helped me realize how important it was to consider others, to harness the power given to me."

Finished with my meal, I pushed back and bounced Brendan, eyes on Nikolas. "Do all your children have abilities like yours?"

Ola's face rounded with pride. "Frøya begins her formal apprenticeship when she comes of age in a year."

Nikolas nodded. "Yes. And Leifr has the gift of the elements, like me. Dagný's ability is with animals. You should see her with the horses."

I thought of Troy and his horses, and smiled through the sadness.

Brendan made small cries, asking for attention. "All this talk of other children and no mention of you, my love?" I stood and rocked him. "You, my dear, are the son of Killian Maclean, heir to the chief and descendant of Gillean, ancient king and dragon friend. You have the strength of his blood in your veins, the love of two fathers, and the ability to melt hearts with those eyes." Brendan glowed with such compliments, and I suppressed the need to cry. All I wanted was Killian. Or Troy.

"And he is a traveler of the World Tree." Nikolas stood an arm's length away, looking down at my son. "You are no ordinary child, little one." He tilted his gaze to me. "Dragon friend?"

My fingers went to my necklace, and his eyes dropped to my throat. "Yes. There was a great statue of a dragon in the gardens. The dragon was the protector of the clan."

Nikolas looked out the window, toward the sea. I glanced at Ola, who winked at me and returned to her kitchen domain.

In a low voice, Nikolas said, "Dragons live in the hidden places of the fjords."

My mouth hung open, a full-body flush making me hot. Real dragons! Here.

He saw what it meant to me. "Perhaps we should take a voyage sometime."

"I would like that." My words rasped out, barely above a whisper.

I couldn't get the idea of real dragons out of my mind. Neither Ola nor Nikolas mentioned them as the weeks stretched by, and I didn't push, since sailing into winter storms didn't seem like a good idea. But my gut told me dragons were a crucial piece of the puzzle, and waiting was infuriating. I was so close to finding them.

As small as the village was, it didn't take long until I'd shared a smile or an awkward greeting with seemingly everyone. Ola had a steady stream of visitors in her cottage, and sent me on chores like fetching water from the well or collecting eggs from the hens in the communal chicken coops. Some people avoided me. They'd take the long way around so they didn't have to pass close by. Daggers in my boots, I walked like I would down a city street. Like I belonged there. Like I wasn't desperately out of place. Like anger and regret didn't eat me from within.

The short days were growing longer, the sun rising a little higher above the horizon. One day, as I walked with Nikolas, bits of blue sky showing through breaks in the clouds, I couldn't hold back any longer.

"You mentioned voyaging into the fjords," I said. "When is the best time to do that?"

Nikolas gave his version of a grin, subdued. "Not for a while yet."

I looked down, nodding. Impatience eating at me.

"What is your urgency?" asked Nikolas.

My fingers went to the dragon at my neck. "I think they're the key to controlling the time travel."

He made a sound low in his throat. "Perhaps. Part of the key. I imagine most of what you need is inside you."

I stopped and stared at him, my jaw hanging open. "How do you know?"

His mouth tightened. "That is usually the way of things. Anything sought without must also be sought within."

We walked for a distance without speaking, the gentle crash of waves and rhythm of our footsteps like a soundtrack. I floated on an island of questions amidst a sea of sorrow.

Then Nikolas stopped and spoke in a hushed voice. "Do you hear that?"

I shook my head. He placed his hand on my back, gazing out to sea. A current of warmth seeped through my layers. My focus followed his, and a song snuck up on me.

Dolphins! I knew the sounds from a brief foray into marine biology in my teens. Nikolas's presence was a tremor of power, lending me his ability to hear them. I could almost see them swimming, leaping and playing in the constantly moving water.

In that trance-like clarity, with strange music in my blood, my inner vision burned bright. The place where he touched me was like a sun in my mind. Part of me wanted to run. And a primal part of me wanted more. Wanted him.

I stiffened. Nikolas took his hand away. The buzz of magic faded, leaving an odd sense of loss.

"Thank you," I whispered, the corners of my mouth tugging into something that wasn't quite a smile.

"You are welcome." There were questions in the creases around his eyes. Shades of blue dancing. What I saw in the black at the center scared me more than anything else. Killian. Troy. They were there, in his eyes.

Need ached in my core, a magnet pulling me closer to him, but all I had to do was recall the searing pain of loss, and I wanted nothing to do with Nikolas or anyone else.

Late one night, as I was about to head to bed, Nikolas barged in the door with his face aglow. "Come see!"

"Do you ever knock?" I asked, going to my coat.

"Knock?" He shot a mischievous glance at Ola, who gave a belly laugh and wrapped a scarf around her neck.

I shook my head and followed him out, tucking Brendan at my chest. When I looked up, my breath rushed in with understanding.

The sky was alive with dancing light: green, blue, purple, and shimmering gold. I'd never seen the Northern Lights like this, so vibrant.

Ola stood not far away, head tipped back to the sky. Neighbors on all sides emerged. Children ran through the streets, laughter like falls of glitter through the murmur of awed voices.

"Do you see?" I whispered to Brendan, who'd been drifting off to sleep before we ventured into the crisp air.

Brendan made happy sounds, grabbing my scarf and directing it into his mouth. Then his gaze shifted upwards to the sky. He reached straight up, as if he could take hold of the dancing color and bring it in for a taste, eyes wide, his mouth a perfect little circle.

"He sees them." I gave Nikolas a wide smile.

He moved to stand behind me as I looked up.

I could've leaned into him—wanted to, the nearness of him like a gravitational pull—but I resisted it. Stayed in my own space.

"What does it feel like for you?" I asked, quiet, over my shoulder.

His slow inhale drew my breath into time, and I swayed, the top of my head almost grazing his chest. My body yearned to give into the warmth, to give in to the illusion of safety.

"It's like soft lightning," he said. "A thousand liquid gemstones. The sky is joy and wonder and play. The sun reaches into the night to make rainbows." I could hear him frown. "I don't know how to tell you what it feels like."

I shook my head. "You just told me. You're a poet, Nikolas, did you know?"

He laughed at that. I loved the sound, deep and easy. Seductive.

We were the last ones standing outside by the end, waiting until the painting of light dimmed and faded into stars on velvet black. Brendan slept, breathing evenly against my chest.

Nikolas turned to me and smiled—not his usual half-smile, but an innocent, relaxed grin. He clearly loved what we'd witnessed, and he'd chosen to share it with me.

I sought answers to my questions in his eyes, but none were given. Instead, his guard went up again.

"Good night, Shelta." He gave a small nod.

"Good night, Nikolas." The magic that danced in my chest dissolved into the uncertainty that never really left, and the unyielding yearning for dragons.

Chapter 39
Songs in Hiding

TWICE MORE, NIKOLAS came to get me to watch the Northern Lights together. Then, one night I heard voices in the streets and headed out the door to see the night skies alive. Nikolas wasn't there. My feet took me down the road to his house, where I found him standing with his children.

Nikolas flashed a smile. "You missed me?" he asked lightly.

"I did," I admitted, hating myself for playing this game with him but unable to stop.

Time stretched out as he looked at me, arms crossed at his chest. Light danced across his face and in his eyes, which seemed to sear into my soul.

Needing a respite from the intensity, I tilted my head up and took in the colors. When I glanced back at Nikolas, he'd returned his gaze to the heavens.

I sat on the front steps and wrapped my arms around Brendan, unable to be so close to this man who sparked such conflict in me. My child looked up, sometimes at my face, sometimes at the sky.

After a few minutes, Dagný sat down and leaned into me. I put my arm around her without thinking, and the way she settled in, I couldn't withdraw.

We watched the bright dance in the sky together, Nikolas standing with his arms around Leifr and Frøya, me holding his youngest daughter and my son.

The longer I stayed there with his family, the more painful the ache inside became. It was too natural, too easy. I could be at home here.

But it would be a lie.

I tried to enjoy the moment while keeping a measure of detachment. The girl who leaned against me did so out of convenience and amiability, not love. The man who stood before me cared for me because he considered it his duty. They were my friends, not my family.

As the lights faded from the sky, Dagný fell asleep with her head in my lap, breath coming in even waves. Nikolas scooped up the sleeping girl, and asked, "Would you like to come in?"

So quiet, his words. They shouldn't have made my heart flip over. I shook my head. "Thank you, but no."

His eyes narrowed, but he wished me good night and ushered his children inside. The hammer-crested door shut with a thud that echoed in my inner emptiness.

Standing beneath the darkened sky, with no one else around, I fought the flood of loneliness and tried to find my connection with Killian through the presence of his child, who slept at my breast. All I felt was his absence. Neither was Troy there to soothe me with words spoken in my head or love sent heart-to-heart.

I had to be strong enough to survive this alone.

Instead of going to Ola's cottage, I walked out to sea. Over-tired, tears streamed down my face. I didn't care. A lone figure on the sand, I let the sound of the waves crash through me.

The ocean consoled me, the vast expanse helping me let go of my own story. Before the greatness of the sea and sky, I was insignificant.

It occurred to me, as the waves made their music, that I hadn't sung since I'd entered this world. I'd shunned that part of myself.

I needed to go sing in the forest. There, no one would hear me. And if the World Tree took me again, so be it. There'd be no one for me to grieve.

The next afternoon, after a quiet walk along the shore with Nikolas, a subdued mid-day meal with Ola, and a short nap with Brendan, I packed myself up and headed to the woods behind the village. The hilt of the dirk was a hard comfort in my palm, the fur lining of the coat pocket warm around the rest of my hand.

As I entered the forest, I didn't care if I fell through to another world. The night before had left me empty, more determined than ever to keep to myself. I didn't tell Ola where I was going, just that I'd see her later. She likely knew, anyway, seer that she was.

I marched into the thick forest without looking back.

What a wonderful thing, to touch the trees without fear. I side-hugged a big trunk, leaning myself and my children into it, forehead on bumpy bark, and broke a little at the love that welled up for the trees. I'd admired them, hated them, and feared them throughout my life, but never this flow of deep connection. Recognition.

Tears streamed down my cheeks as the music of the forest came through me, a mighty chorus of individual voices. I bathed in the resonance for a long time, breathing with the tree, its inhales and my exhales a symbiotic symphony.

I greeted as many trees as I could, after that. Brendan giggled when I let him touch a branch, and let out a squeal as he discovered that the points of pine needles were pokey. Eventually, the easy motion of my walking lulled him to sleep.

Opening my awareness, I basked in the music of the forest until a song formed in my mind. It started as a melody without words, riding nature's layers of bass and harmony. The birds sang their trills; the earth hummed its deep resonance. I let my voice soar through it all.

I'd forgotten how much I needed to sing, as if part of me had been hibernating in the seaside winter. Giving over, the music in my spirit awakened.

The land around me was doing something similar. Coastal rains had replaced the snow of deep winter. Green moss and small plants refused to be discouraged by the cold. I sang to them, my voice a caress of acknowledgement.

I could love nature. She wouldn't mourn me when I left, and she would be wherever I landed. The song became my nurturing, my way of being in a relationship without having to hold back.

It lasted a long time, but eventually my singing ended, my body grew tired, and I reluctantly made my way back to the village. I ducked in Ola's back door and accepted a cup of tea, retiring to a chair in front of the fire. The child within gave a kick.

"How was the forest?" she asked, a knowing look on her face.

I resisted the urge to roll my eyes. Living with the village seer afforded zero privacy. It would be hard to grow up with Ola as a mother, always knowing everything.

"It was wonderful," I said. "Like coming home."

She nodded, and I reconsidered. Maybe it wouldn't be so bad to have a mother who understood you like she would. I didn't have to explain why the forest felt like home, Ola's smile told me she knew.

I had a sip from my mug. "What do you put in the teas you give me?"

"Sometimes it is one thing, sometimes another." She invited me into her kitchen and showed me raspberry leaf, mint, nettle, and rose hips. "I make the tea with these," she said, "and something more."

"Something more?"

"From here." She pointed at her heart, then to each palm.

I brought the mug to my lips again, drinking more of Ola's magic brew.

I went back to the woods the next day, and the day after, and the day after that, escaping to the forest whenever it wasn't wet out. Brendan brightened when he got to connect with the trees, and singing with them satisfied my soul.

I saw wildlife tracks—some that I recognized and some I did not—as well as human footprints. Likely hunters.

My forest excursions were the only time I sang, other than quiet lullabies to Brendan. Before, music had been my way to earn a living, and had allowed me to give something back to Killian and Troy.

Here, I wanted to hide. If I sang for these people, they would *see* me. I couldn't share myself like that. I would give them no reason to love me.

Every time I'd fallen hard for someone, it had been my music that made them want me. The last time the Northern Lights had danced, the way Nikolas had looked at me was dangerous. I could give him no reason to press—it'd be too hard to resist him if he decided to pursue me. He already occupied my thoughts and made my body come alive, too much like Killian and Troy.

These people didn't need my music. They were better off without it. I kept my secret safe in the forest, until one day, as I rode out the end of a song about dragons, I rounded a corner and stopped mid-note.

Two men stood, mouths open, staring at me. Both had bows and quivers of arrows, knives at their belts. Out to catch dinner. One spoke rapidly, telling me how much he enjoyed the song with a cracked-tooth grin.

I greeted them with the barest words, one arm wrapped around Brendan, the other hand on the dagger in my pocket. Heading off the trail, I sought an escape route through the brush. My head spun. Gripping the dirk tighter, I forced myself to stay still, not to run.

They got the hint that I didn't want company, and walked on down the path. My secret was out now. It took little time for news to spread through the small village.

A bolt of remembrance shocked through me, echoing B'alam's words. *Without love you will become lost, and your heart will despair.*

No. Seer's advice or not, I couldn't allow myself to love Nikolas. I wouldn't be the cause of grief for him or his children. They liked me, but they didn't love me. I hadn't given them cause to do so.

Besides, Nikolas hadn't reached out to me beyond his generous nature as a friend. He didn't touch me, except those two times. There must be a reason.

My feet took me to the edge of the forest. I went left where I should've gone right to head back to Ola's, and skirted the village, seeking the sea, walking blindly for a long time.

When I reached the wall of rock and the carving of the World Tree, I realized I'd run back to the place of the beginning, and a fool's hope blossomed in my heart.

Could I find my way back? I would gratefully return to my clan of Macleans, or my mountain homestead with Troy.

I touched the carved tree in the rock, salt on my lips from the ocean air, and pulled all my focus to Troy. I imagined the cabin, the tree that had deposited me here, willing myself to travel to that time and place. I saw Troy's face, could almost sense his presence in my mind. I crooned a song I knew he loved, inviting the spinning, the feeling of falling through.

Invoking whatever magic made the World Tree work, I left off the song and whispered, "Goddess, please. Take me back."

Nothing.

Not even a little pull. The waves went on crashing; the cliff towered above me. I glared at the rock, then tried a second go, this time with all my will bent on Killian. Reaching deep, I sang the song the castle gave me, what felt like ages ago.

Nothing again.

I slid to the sand, defeated.

Knowing I needed to get back to the village before the tide came in, I forced myself up with a groan. What I really wanted was to lie down beneath the grey sky and let the ocean wash me away.

But it wasn't only my life at stake. I had a responsibility I'd avoided for a reason. I'd screwed myself over, having children. I loved Brendan, had love for the one in my belly, but they weighed me down. I'd promised myself I wouldn't become a mother, and I did anyway. For the love of a man who was worlds away.

I was still a good distance from the village when I looked up to see Nikolas. He stood in my path, arms crossed, immovable as the cliffs. I made my way to him, there being no other option. Defenses up, I looked at his chest, unable to meet his eyes.

"Shelta." Nikolas reached a hand out. "Has something frightened you? Have we done something to turn you away?"

The kindness of his words scraped through me. How could I tell him? I was terrified by how I felt about him, and being discovered in the forest by two men who clearly thought I had talent scared me to my core.

I shook my head, eyes down. "You've shown me only kindness. I just—I wanted to go back." My voice cracked. I took a step away from him, turned toward the ocean and dragged a hand across my cheek to stop a traitorous tear.

Brendan cried, despite my attempts at consoling him. I was a horrible mother. Not at all the right person for the job. What had I done?

Nikolas stepped toward me. I could feel him move like the shifting of earth.

I took a half-step away, and he stopped.

"Will you not let me help you?" His words were a whisper from the sea.

I met his eyes, pulled by the care in his voice. He'd raised a hand to touch me, which was what I wanted—needed—most. The one thing I could not allow.

My happiness wasn't worth putting this man and his children through the grief they'd known when Nikolas lost his wife. I'd abandoned Killian and Charlie, abandoned Troy. I was helpless to stop it.

My heart sat in my chest like a chunk of lead. Shaking my head, I looked away.

"Shelta." There was hurt in his voice, and I hated myself for being the cause of it. "We want you here. You are welcome here. Will you not allow yourself to belong with us?"

Cracks ran through the walls of my heart and splintered whatever light shone within. My throat constricted. "I'll just disappear one day," I said. "If it happens like it has before, it will come at the height of my happiness, and everything will be stripped away."

"And so you will not reach for that happiness."

"How can I?" I laughed it off, trying to assure him he shouldn't worry about me; that I wasn't worth the trouble. "I've abandoned so many adopted families, Nikolas, so many I've come to love. I leave them to grieve and wonder what happened to me while I start over again. And again. And again." My voice cracked. I dug the hole deeper. "Now I have two children to drag through this mess of a life. I had no right to become a mother." I cursed inwardly as tears started tracking down my cheeks.

I tried to turn away but he caught me, brought his arms around me, hugging me from the side so he didn't squish Brendan. The same way I'd leaned into trees in the forest. Fear made me want to push away, but I couldn't. I was drowning. I needed his touch.

"Shelta, you protect no one when you deny happiness." The bass of his voice vibrated into my chest.

Pain ripped through me. What a horrible thing I'd done, giving into Killian's dream of having a child.

"Stop." Nikolas whispered in my ear, his beard brushing my cheek. "I am not my sister, but I feel what you're doing. It hurts you, and it hurts your children."

Downward spiral in full swing, I was caught in it like a whirlpool, regardless of the arms that encircled me. They could never be mine, anyway.

He tilted my head up, made me look into his eyes. They belonged to Nikolas, to Killian, to Troy.

I was too far away—could reach none of them. Alone.

"Come back." Nikolas lured me with his voice, and with something deeper. "Swim to the surface, Shelta. I will help you."

And he did. He reached inside, almost like Troy, but not the same. I floated, as if the element of water rose through me, pushing me up. The steadiness of earth grounded me. The fire of sunshine shone through the cage of my chest even as clouds covered the sky. My breath deepened, magically infused with the scent of lavender and mint.

Nikolas had one hand at my back, one behind my head. Eyes closed, waves of elemental caress washed through me. Inhale. Exhale. Hold on tight.

I gasped, and Nikolas withdrew. I would've fallen if he hadn't held me. *Goddess, what am I supposed to do?*

She didn't respond. Evidently, I needed to save myself. Dread pulled at me like an anchor, countering the magic that made me tingle.

Nikolas lifted my chin with his finger, and he was Killian until I opened my eyes, braving the beauty of his. "Thank you," I said. "I'm sorry."

"Why are you sorry?" he asked.

"For putting you through the trouble." I fondled the hilt of the dirk in my pocket, a comfort safer than the hands on my shoulders. "For Brendan, for the child within."

"Not yourself, though?" His brow furrowed.

I gave a pained smile and turned my head. "What I feel doesn't matter."

"Do you truly believe that?"

I did. I wanted to disappear from existence, but I had children. I had to take care of them, and I was doing a crummy job of it. My throat squeezed too tight to answer, but Nikolas got the message.

He took a step back and ran his fingers down my arms, under my wrists. I let go of the dagger, giving him my hands. Mine were small and cold, his huge and full of warmth, full of life.

"Shelta, you need to know this." His words were infused with the strength of the ocean. "What you feel matters more than you can comprehend. Your happiness reverberates through worlds. Your sadness does as well. When your heart is heavy it weighs on the hearts of many, not only your children."

"I don't want that!" I protested. "I don't want that responsibility."

"But it has been granted to you." He squeezed my hands gently. "And that kind of power is given only to someone who can create unsurpassable beauty. *There is magic in you.*"

Killian's words again. I looked to the sky. He thought me a legend, but I was a mess.

"What are you afraid of?" Nikolas asked, entirely too gentle.

My fingers went to the dragon at my neck. I wanted to let myself love him, let myself belong to him, to this place. But

I could never belong. How could I reconcile that? Eyes wet, I met his gaze.

"I'm afraid to be ripped away again." I choked out the words. "I've been searching for a way to control the time travel my whole life, but I keep getting sucked through the World Tree. I need to find dragons, Nikolas, to see if they're the key. I'm afraid of losing my children as I travel, of being powerless and alone until I die."

"You're not powerless." His voice scraped low. "And you're not alone. I'll help you find the dragons. We'll find the answers you're looking for. A few more weeks, and we can sail."

He held me again, stroking my hair. It took a long while, but our breathing came into time, ebb and flow in cyclical symmetry. I breathed in while he breathed out. His inbreath became my outbreath.

That did it, finally. After what felt like forever, as the sun was going down and the tide was coming in, the walls inside crumbled and I gave up the fight. Brendan had to be hungry, but he'd stopped crying. The one in my belly gave little kicks of encouragement.

We walked together in silence, back to the village, the ocean a constant companion. I knew I couldn't call this place home. I wanted to, really, but I didn't trust the twists of time to let me put down roots.

Nikolas seemed to read my mind. "It is home for now. Let that be enough."

He delivered me safely to Ola's cottage, gave me a smile and left. There was no further touch, but I was grateful for what he'd given, out on the strip of land between sea and stone, even if it was as risky as it was healing.

"Drink," Ola said, handing me one of her reviving brews. And that was all. She didn't mention the ordeal, though she surely knew what I'd done.

I'd tried to make the World Tree take me back. And it wouldn't. But Nikolas had promised to help me.

CHAPTER 40
SWORD AND LIGHTNING

NIKOLAS AND I continued our daily walks by the ocean. Today, Ola volunteered to watch Brendan. She assured me I would not be falling through the World Tree anytime soon, and that I needed to walk without always carrying a child. I left him there, trusting her god-blooded wisdom, and relished the freedom.

I also made sure we walked away from the carving on the other side of the bay.

The waves came in like they always did, the sky in layers of grey. If I blinked out of existence, at least I knew Brendan would be well cared for. He'd have a family and probably a more normal life than any I could give him. Maybe he'd be better off without me. Unless he got sucked through time alone.

I pushed my morbid thoughts aside, and asked Nikolas, "What kind of voyage are your brothers on?"

"They lead an expedition far to the west." He lifted a hand toward the horizon. "The ships carry goods for trade and arms for war, depending on what they find."

I recalled tales of Vikings who were basically pirates, but on a grand scale, considering they settled land far and wide.

"The Vikings in the history I know were fearsome." I shot him an apologetic glance. "There were accounts of Norse men invading and killing indiscriminately." He certainly looked fierce enough to fit those historical images, but I knew him as a kind man and a loving father.

"It is the way of some." He frowned. "Not my preference. I think it is better to learn from those we meet, to come as merchants rather than conquerors. We trade, explore, and share knowledge, but sometimes we are met by an army. Often, there is no choice given, and we are always ready for war." His voice rumbled with the hint of a growl. "When those who wish to conquer land on our shores, we do not send many survivors home."

His fierceness triggered a memory, and I saw Killian sparring with Wallace, ruthless determination in them both. A reckless thrill swept through me.

"I'd like a sword." The words came out as a command, and I tried to soften them. "Would it be possible to find one for me?"

Nikolas looked at my belly. I was about six months along, round and awkward. Killian would never have let me train pregnant. "You have wielded a sword before?" asked Nikolas.

"I have." A sword and a gun. The crack of Troy's rifle echoed with the memory of killing to defend my home, my family. Nikolas didn't need to know about guns, but I told him about my time on the training field with Clan Maclean.

Sticking my hand in my pocket, I pulled out the sgian-dubh and turned the rosewood-handle toward him. "That's the little one," I boasted.

Nikolas raised his eyebrows, blue eyes sparkling. "Where is the big one?"

I bent over and took the dirk from my boot.

His cheeks rounded as he examined it. "This is an exquisite blade. I didn't know you carried daggers all this time."

"I didn't mean for you to know." I returned the dirk to its sheath.

"Of course." Nikolas straightened. "We shall fetch you a sword when we return."

Without Brendan at my chest, I was able to look down and see my growing belly. I wasn't exactly in fighting shape. "I don't know how much I'll be able to do with a sword right now," I admitted, "but I'd like the feel of it in my hand. To remember the way the blade sings."

"Since you've mentioned song…" He smiled, changing the subject and throwing me off-kilter. "Two of my men said they met you in the forest some time ago, and that you were singing with the voice of an angel."

I said nothing. Kept walking. I'd been so fragile that day, had dreaded the requests for music that I thought would come, and thought I was off the hook when they didn't.

"You've held yourself back from us." His words hit me like an accusation. "Here you are, carrying unseen blades and a gift of music."

He stopped walking. I made myself look at him. It was like the first day: Nikolas framed by endless sea and dynamic layers of cloud and sky. His steel blue eyes matched the ocean, locked on mine. "Are you ready to share your gift with us, Shelta?"

I drew a salty breath and wished dearly for my guitar. "Honestly, I'm not sure that I am."

He crossed his arms. "The men who saw you that day, they thought they may have frightened you."

"They did. But it wasn't their fault." I started walking again, needing to move. His gaze was too intense. "I spook easy."

"You wish for something." It wasn't a question.

"What do you mean?" I cocked my head. I couldn't hold his gaze, but didn't want to stop looking at him. Couldn't have him, wanted him anyway. Story of my doomed life.

"You feel you are missing something that would help you sing. What is it?"

I stopped in my tracks. "I thought Ola was the seer."

His eyes were deadly serious. "I see clearly enough, when the subject is dear to me."

That sent my heart racing. My mouth hung open. I shut it without having spoken anything. Finally, with a catch of emotion in my throat, I said, "My guitar."

"What is that?"

"It's an instrument. Like a lute or mandolin." I didn't know if they had anything like it here. I hadn't dared to hope, having only seen pipes and drums played occasionally in the village. I took up a stick and drew the shape in the sand, so he could understand.

"Can you craft one?" he asked.

I shook my head. "I wouldn't have the first clue how to work with the wood, or how to make the strings, for that matter."

"If you had this instrument, would you share your song with us?" He started off again.

I fell into stride with him. "Yes."

"What does it change, that you would sing with it and not without?"

We walked in silence for a while before I knew how to answer. "The music from the instrument supports my voice.

I can play the guitar and not have to sing. And it creates a physical buffer between my body and anyone listening. It's like a shield. I don't feel as exposed."

He said nothing. We passed the edge of the cliff band and came into the bay before the village. But instead of turning toward the nearer side of the settlement where the houses were, he kept our path along the sea until we reached the far side of the village.

Winding through the road between structures, Nikolas brought me to a sturdy log building I'd never seen before. It was tucked in the back corner, behind the blacksmith and a large covered shelter where people were working on two different boats. A guard stood at the door of the long building, and another at the corner with a watchful eye on the threshold of the woods.

Opening the thick door, Nikolas gestured for me to enter. I thought back to the first time I'd stepped into the armory at Duart Castle, Charlie taking me to Rodric for daggers. But instead of a wiry master of arms, a stocky woman stepped out of the dim and into the light coming through the door. She eyed me with general suspicion, then nodded to Nikolas.

I studied her, surprised to find a woman there. Well-armed with blades and an axe, with a long scar down one side of her face, she looked capable of going to battle at any moment.

Nikolas told her why we were there, and the woman gave me an appraising look. It wasn't interest in her eyes, but calculating assessment. She turned and disappeared into the dark recesses of the building. Sounds of shifting metal filled the silence.

"Gunnhildr," Nikolas said with a gesture in her direction.

A good name for the matriarch of the armory.

She returned with three unsheathed swords and laid them on a table that held various weapons and a sharpening stone. Without a word, she handed me the first, hilt presented.

I reminded myself I'd held a sword many times before. Stepping back, I swung it twice, shook my head and returned it to her. The weight was wrong for me.

We repeated this twice more. The third sword was better than the rest, but not as easy to handle as the one I was used to in Scotland. Here the swords were broader—more primitive and less graceful—though I had a feeling if I saw the locals wield them, they'd prove effective enough.

Gunnhildr scowled at me, scooped up all three swords and turned her back on us without a word. Nikolas smiled, seemingly amused.

Returning with her deep frown, Gunnhildr brought me a very different sword. She showed it to Nikolas and gave him a look of some significance.

He nodded once, and she poked the hilt my way.

This sword's craftmanship was far superior. The grip was wrapped with dark leather, soft to the touch, but thick, with no tears or catches. The double-edged blade was narrower than the others, slightly wider than an inch, the metal brighter than the swords she'd brought before. I squinted. It had runes written along its center.

I stepped closer to the door for light, and my breath caught as I saw the pommel—a dragon cast in metal, almost an exact replica of the one on my necklace.

The weight was perfect, the balance beautiful. I nearly laughed at the swing of it, the rightness, but I didn't want to offend the large woman watching me. I pressed my lips together in a smile instead.

"We've found a match, then," Nikolas said, eyes twinkling. He thanked Gunnhildr.

She gave a huff, walked away, and came back a moment later with a leather scabbard. Surprising me, she smiled with her ice-gray eyes, and barked out a string of words I tripped over. "The sword carries with it a legend," she said. "Written in the runes."

I nodded in acknowledgement, then looked to Nikolas. "What do the runes say?"

We walked outside to see the thin lines more clearly. Nikolas looked at me for a long moment, then spoke, reciting the runes from memory. "It says, 'The one who wields this sword is a dragon friend, and exists outside of time.'"

My mouth dropped open. A legendary sword. It vibrated in my hands as my gaze moved over the etchings.

I started walking, sword sheathed, at a loss for words. At the question in my gaze, Nikolas led me behind the village, along the path between the buildings, and into the trees. We stopped a few minutes into the forest in a circular clearing.

"Let's see, then," Nikolas gestured with a twist of his wrist.

Heart pounding, I unsheathed the sword and went to the center of the space. Both hands wrapped around the leather grip, I pointed the blade straight up. A posture of prayer. Unbidden, in my mind's eye, light streamed through me from the center of the sky to the center of the earth. The sword became an extension of that light in my hands.

I began a dance, a slow, deliberate run-through of the technique I'd learned from my training in Scotland. Killian's presence waited at the edge of my awareness, like he was watching me.

My heavy coat and round belly weighed me down, center of gravity changed by the baby. Carefully, I found my balance, moving as if in slow motion. Thought dissipated. All I knew was the sword; the swaying, stepping, and swinging.

A sense of liquidity linked each movement with the precision of a ballet. I thought I could see a glow around the blade, around my hand. The spirit of the sword introduced itself to me like a new instrument. I lost time, given over to the music of motion.

There came a shift in key and pace. I wound moves together. Slowly one moment, with speed the next. The blade sang through the air—a soaring, otherworldly sound—like it relished its escape from the dark confines of the armory, out playing in the light of the world.

Spinning, I staggered to a stop in the center of the clearing, blade pointed down. A shiver of energy surged through the hilt, traveled along the blade, and shot like a lightning bolt into the earth. The blast echoed in the quiet. Smoke rose from a scorched patch beneath the tip of the sword.

Breathless, I asked Nikolas, "Did you do that?" Conjuring weather was much more his kind of thing.

"I did nothing but watch," he said, voice trembling as it crossed the space between us.

"Did you—could you see it?" My whole body vibrated.

Nikolas bent to retrieve the sword's sheath, and came toward me. "I saw a woman dance with a sword. I saw flame and lightning weave the dance." He handed me the scabbard, eyes bright.

My breath came in deep drinks, heart beating hard enough to rock me. I sheathed the blade with hands that shook.

"The sword is yours," Nikolas said formally. "It appears I brought it here for you, as it could belong to no other."

"Thank you." I lifted my gaze to his with effort. "Where did it come from?"

I sensed the stone in him, the depth of the sea, the infinite capacity of the sky. "I acquired it in a world beyond this one."

"You—" My head dropped toward my right shoulder. "You've traveled through worlds?"

A breath. Nikolas moved half a step closer.

"I have gone beyond the veil into a different realm." Every word landed like an intimate admission. "I spent what felt like a fortnight in the company of the elves of light. When I returned, three years had passed for my people." He pushed hair away from my face, his touch sparking a vision of a glittering world. He'd gone into the realm of the fae.

He'd seen another world. Been tricked by time. I wasn't alone.

The strength left my legs. Nikolas was with me in an instant, slowing my descent to the ground. I sat in a heap of leather and fur. He crouched down, concern in his eyes.

"I'm fine." A lie. I closed my eyes, dizzy, the baby kicking. In a controlled fall, I curled up on my side with one arm under my head, one hand on the sword.

Nikolas sat behind me, warmth in his touch. His words wound into a chant. "Slow your breathing, Shelta. Feel the earth beneath you. Feel the trees around you, green and healing. Feel the ocean beyond—the pulse of the waves, the current of vitality it carries."

I saw each vision he described. With effort, I smoothed my breath as he wove the elements. I tasted thirst-quenching rains, floated in skies filled with stars and dancing color.

And then Ola was there, saying, "Drink." Something warm and spiced. She asked Nikolas what had happened, her tone sharp.

He shrugged his reply. "She is not used to wielding lightning, that's all."

"Where's Brendan?" I'd left him with her.

"He's with Frøya." She squinted at me. "You will be fine."

After a minute, they helped me to my feet, one hand still wrapped around my sword. Brother and sister walked me back to the village, Nikolas with a hand at my back the entire way.

After nursing Brendan, I went down for a nap. When I woke, I was still dizzy.

Nikolas was gone when I emerged from behind the curtain. Ola was in the kitchen, with Brendan's cradle on the table. I brought him into my arms and sat in a chair, facing her.

"So, now you wield lightning and dance with swords." Ola tossed the words out lightly.

"I'm not planning any of this," I said, still unsure what had happened.

"No, no." She brought plates of meat and flatbread for each of us, then returned with cups of broth. "But now you have this part of you."

"I guess." I chewed a bite of bread. "Do you know what happened?"

She tilted her head side to side. "I saw the power of the sword, and something you have—an ability to attune.

Together they make the lightning. It isn't one or the other. For someone else, the light would not come through. The spirit of the sword would not awaken."

"Will it happen every time I hold the sword?" I cut a piece of meat. "Will I get used to it?"

"Yes," she said, answering both questions at once before tearing off a large bite of flatbread.

We ate in silence. I'd tried to do the dishes enough times that I knew Ola wouldn't let me, so I just leaned back and admired my son after dinner. It blew my mind how fast he was growing, nearly eight months now. He loved the attention. I stopped playing peek-a-boo with him when I realized Ola was staring at me.

"What?"

"He cares for you."

I said nothing. She wasn't talking about my son.

"Nikolas." She tapped her fingers lightly on the counter. "He only shares his gift with family."

My pulse cranked up.

"This is not the first time he has done so for you." Ola nodded, answering her own question. "And you care for him, I see it. So, what are you afraid of?"

It was the same question Nikolas asked me two weeks ago, when I was caught in despair between the cliffs and the sea. "I don't want to cause him grief, or for the children to feel abandoned the next time the World Tree takes me."

"You don't think they would grieve you now?" Her eyelids dropped halfway down.

I shook my head. "Not in the same way. Not as intensely."

"He is afraid to scare you away, and you are afraid to let him get close." Her laughter was a deep, soul-satisfying sound. A crone's cackle.

Chapter 41
Into the Fjords

MY DREAMS TOOK on new strength that night. The red dragon's brimstone breath warmed my skin and the bass of his voice stirred my soul. His golden eyes shimmered, hard scales shining crimson and garnet beneath my hands.

I wished I could remember the things we discussed, the dragon and I. Something about my new sword. I wished I'd had the presence of mind to ask his name, but I hadn't, and the dream was all but forgotten by breakfast.

When Nikolas showed up for our mid-morning walk, he checked with his sister to see if I was well enough to go.

"Really?" I eyed him, speaking before Ola could. "You ask her and not me?"

"My apologies, Shelta." He bowed his great head, chunks of dirty-blond hair falling into his face. "Are you feeling up to a walk today?"

Not really. All I wanted to do was sleep, but I needed to move so I didn't turn into a soft, weak woman whose purpose in life was to care for her children. That was okay for some.

Not for me.

I shoved my feet into my boots and lifted a heavier-than-normal coat with sore arms. Tilting my head up to Nikolas, who towered in the doorway, I said, "Shall we?"

I caught the look he shot his sister over my head, but ignored it and made my way out into the wind. Thanks to Frøya and Dagný, who were looking after Brendan while Ola did her thing, I had freedom to move.

We didn't talk of children or swords as we crossed the space between the village and the ocean. As usual, Nikolas said nothing until we reached the sea. I'd grown accustomed to striding with him, falling into beat with his footsteps, listening to the way we walked in time with the chorus of nature.

We turned right at the water, but instead of following the curve of the bay, we went toward the boats bobbing in the harbor, a few of them moored to a long dock.

Nikolas stopped at the start of the wooden boards and slid his hand to the small of my back, making the hair on my neck rise. I followed his gaze over the water to where several massive ships rode the swells, anchored, and wondered how many ships his brothers had out at sea. It looked like there were enough boats here to evacuate the entire village and their livestock.

Nikolas led me across the dock, his fingers warm around mine. Holding hands? This was new. I sucked a breath, unsure if the heat that bloomed in my chest was attraction or the power that pulsed through him.

We stopped before a ship with a dragon's head on its bow and wings on its sides. Nikolas lit up, glowing in my vision. He squeezed my hand, rainbows in his blue eyes, and looked from me to the ship, as if inviting me to see it through his power.

From the mast to the boards of the deck, the dragon ship shone in my sight. The wheel sat in a sphere of energy that encompassed the vessel, including a half-submerged cabin with protective runes carved in its door. A trapdoor to below decks glimmered near three rows of benches with openings for oars.

"This is my ship," Nikolas said. "Mine in ways the others are not. Those ships," he gestured to the others, "they belong to us all."

He let go of me, and the glow faded, but didn't quite disappear. Nikolas ran a hand over the crest of the wing on the hull. "This ship was my design, one I dreamt."

"It's beautiful," I breathed, my fingers going to my necklace.

He spotted me as I climbed up the ladder. Too near, he walked the deck with me, pointing out details, running his hand over the rail with obvious love.

"Did you build this yourself?" I asked.

"Yes." Pride shone in his eyes. "It took many years. Come." He grabbed my hand and pulled me to the stairs on the side of the cabin. The contact made me giddy.

When we reached the ship's wheel, he all but wrapped my hand around one of the handles. I laughed at his eagerness, teasing with my words. "You're excited about this."

"I am. I've been waiting months to show you." The sincerity of his smile caught in my heart like a fishing hook.

"Why show me now?" I turned to face him, my back to wheel. "Why did you wait?"

"I waited out the weather." His eyes told me that was only part of the story. "Spring comes, and I'm called to go sailing."

"You could've shown me before, though," I said, not taking the hint. "This is gorgeous! And you made it,

Nikolas, you've been—" I stopped, realizing the words applied to myself as much as him. "Hiding from me."

One of his eyebrows twitched upwards, his head tilting for a single nod. "Indeed. And yesterday you danced with lightning."

"It was mostly the sword." My hands twisted behind me to grab the spokes of the wheel, something to hold onto while I faced this man who was larger than life.

"No." He shook his head, eyes darkening. "I've wielded that sword. *I can call lightning from the clouds* and the sword's powers did not come alive for me. It was *you*, Shelta. Dragon friend."

I opened my mouth, half-expecting my heart to jump onto my tongue. When no sound came out, he went on. "I made this ship to explore the fjords. The weather is fair, and provisions are prepared. We could leave with the tide tomorrow."

"Yes!" This was my chance to find the dragons. Of course, I'd be stuck on a ship with Nikolas. I was all but sealing my fate.

He grinned, and launched into the rest of the tour, showing me the space below with a primitive galley, storage for provisions, and crew quarters in foul weather. When we walked down the few stairs and through the runed door to the captain's cabin, it reminded me of Killian's room in the tower.

Nikolas had brought me into his private space, and it was gorgeous, with a seascape carved into the wall behind the bed. I'd had no idea what he was capable of as a craftsman. No idea what he was capable of, in general. "Did you carve this yourself?" I asked to stop my mind from spiraling out of control.

"Yes."

"And the dragon in the girls' room, did you carve that, as well?"

"Yes." Intimacy. Vulnerability in his eyes.

I couldn't hold his gaze. Crossing the small chamber to a window, I looked out over the water at the curve of the bay, the sloped lines of steep rooftops, and the bare branches of the great tree that stood in the center of the village. Aware of Nikolas's eyes on me, I willed my breath to come more slowly, but my hand trembled.

With hesitation, I turned and ran my fingers over the frame of the bed, hugging the port side of the hull. When I finally forced myself to face him, I knew we'd reached the end of whatever game we'd been playing, giving each other distance.

From this point out, resistance was futile.

With a treacherous sense of surrender, I said, "It's beautiful, Nikolas."

"Thank you, Shelta." His voice rumbled low. Humble. Close.

My breath caught, and I backed toward the door, taking the short flight of stairs to the main deck. Nikolas followed, right behind me. Knowing I'd have to face my fears, and soon, I flashed a quick smile to let him know I wasn't running. Not far, anyway. "Tomorrow?"

He clasped his hands behind his back, giving me space. "Tomorrow at dawn."

It was still dark the next morning when I heard the fire come to life and the sound of pots being moved around, Ola brewing something in the kitchen. I nursed Brendan and got dressed, praying that we'd find dragons and I'd figure out a way to get back to Troy and Killian. Anticipation made me jittery as I emerged from the room and tied the curtain back.

Ola presented me with tea, and a basket of sausage rolls.

"You really are amazing," I told her, halfway through my cup of tea.

"The crew will take to you easily when you arrive with these." She gave me a wink. "Tell them I send my blessings for the journey."

"I'm sure they'll appreciate that." I dipped my head. "Thank you, Ola, for everything."

She took my cheeks between her hands, kissed my forehead, then wrapped me—and Brendan, bound to my chest—in her village-momma arms. "Blessed be," she said, and cocked her head, like she was listening. Her next words came across worlds. *"Live, Shelta. And know that you are loved."*

Troy's last words to me. I blinked away tears, but was given no time to dwell on it, as the door opened with a gust of wind and Nikolas stepped through, his children behind him.

He gave his sister a bear hug, gathered my belongings, and we strode toward the sea while Ola headed to Nikolas's house to be with his children. My stomach did flip-flops the whole way, while the child within danced and poked. Brendan offered up garbled commentary on the different start to our day.

Nikolas and I crossed the dock, saltwater slapping at the posts, our footsteps dull drumbeats. The dragon ship bobbed gently, with the warm glow of lanterns reflecting in the water and the deck alive with a small crew getting ready for departure.

We stowed our things in the cabin. When we emerged, climbing the steps to the deck, I brought Ola's breakfast treats. Not only did I have food to offer, the basket gave me something to hide behind. Me and my children, shielded by breakfast.

The crew of four included two women, and two men. The men were the ones who'd surprised me in the forest. Brothers, as it turned out. Agmundr and Arnþórr. They were exceedingly kind, thanking me for the sausage rolls, and I made an effort to remember their names. The women were Nora and Alexandra, wearing breeches like the men, while I wore a wine-red hand-me-down maternity dress beneath my fur and leather coat.

The ship took on a glow when Nikolas slipped his hand around mine. I looked up to see the energy swirling in his eyes. "Are you ready?" he asked.

Would I ever be? "Yes." Hopefully my smile showed my excitement, not the trepidation. Not that I could fool him, this man who touched me and made everything glimmer.

Nikolas brought me to stand near him at the helm. The women raised the full, square sail, and the brothers untied the ship from the dock and hauled the ropes in, lanterns casting golden light across their backs.

The deck tilted beneath my feet. I clung to a rail, standing beside Nikolas, who had both hands on the wheel. I spoke quietly to Brendan, pointing out the way the clouds shone pink beneath a dome of deep indigo.

The crew rowed us out, the tide pulling the ship willingly. The sail billowed, and the oars were brought in, the lanterns extinguished. The ship picked up speed in a hurry.

Once we cleared the bay, Nikolas turned us to the north, and we sailed with the land to our right and the open expanse of ocean to the left. Boards creaked and water swished against the hull. At the back of my mind, I heard the ship singing.

The sun crested over the mountains as Nikolas showed me the edge of the island upon which the village was settled. "There are thousands of isles along this coast," he said. "Some are not as nice as ours, others are home to friends. Some are so large they seem like the mainland until you sail around and realize you've gone in a circle."

His quiet laugh made me smile. Sunlight reflected off the water and illuminated the island in shades of green and brown. Further inland, snowy peaks blushed gold. I held Brendan so he could see the wind-filled mass of sail and the crew moving about below us, their faces shining with love for the sea.

Nikolas was in his glory. He stood, feet wide, hair and beard blowing in the wind, hands on the great wooden wheel. I studied the set of his jaw beneath his beard, the crinkle in the skin around his eyes, the bump at the top of his nose. I was on an expedition into the fjords with an actual Viking. Without a doubt, I'd paid a high price to be here, but the potency of the moment wasn't lost to me.

Nikolas turned his head toward me, mouth curling like he knew I'd been staring at him, and he liked it. I gathered my courage, trying to think of something to say that didn't betray the quake and quiver of my heart. "What do you feel when you sail?" I asked quietly, so no one else could hear.

He looked at me a long moment, then sent his eyes forward. "I feel the tide. The depth and mood of the sea. I hear stories the wind brings, tales of places far and near. I feel the expanse of the sky, ever-changing, and the presence of rock and earth below."

Magnetic—his presence, his power. I wanted to touch him, but I did no such thing. I kept my feet planted wide and surfed the constant rocking.

Nikolas lifted one hand from the wheel, palm up, toward me. "What do you feel, Shelta?"

I moved closer, telling myself it wasn't because of his beckoning gesture, but because I didn't want to be overheard. "I feel the singing of the ship. The wood vibrates with the thrill of knowing its purpose and being able to serve it. I feel the way the water flows around the hull, the strength of the sail as it takes the wind." My voice didn't shake, but it was a near thing. "There's a connection between the ship and its captain. It's like a fine piece of harmony, music that is not complete without one or the other."

His eyes changed, as if the Northern Lights came to play in ocean blue. I swayed, unused to the rocking of the sea and thrown off by the shift in his gaze.

He slid a hand behind my back and pulled me close, gently turning me to face the wheel, where he guided my hands to the handles, big fingers wrapping around my own. Fire blazed through my blood in a flood of heat and longing.

He'd placed me into a circle of belonging; the energy that ran between the ship, which was as a living thing, and its creator, whose body pressed close against my back. I all but heard him speak in my mind.

You belong here, with me.

We stood that way for quite a while, until the intensity of touching Nikolas was too much. Moving my hands beneath his was enough. He stepped back to release me. Not trusting my voice, I gave him a smile and made my way down to the main deck on unsteady legs that had nothing to do with the rolling of the ship.

I spent much of the morning sitting on one of the rower's benches with Brendan in my lap, leaning against the railing and looking out at the splendor of the scenery. We passed rugged coastline with remarkable speed, salty wind blowing through my hair, every opening of ocean between islands a mystery.

Around mid-morning, Nora came to sit with me and asked if she could hold Brendan. Her weathered face lit up when I handed him over. Streaks of gray highlighted her braids, which Brendan thought were wonderful toys.

I moved my hand to cover a yawn, and looked up to see Nikolas coming down the stairs. Nora slipped away. Apparently, Alexandra was first mate. She stood behind the wheel, eyes squinted against the sun as it climbed above clouds that peppered the sky like islands did the sea.

Nikolas offered his hand and helped me to my feet, then proceeded to guide me toward the cabin with a hand at my lower back, Brendan in the crook of one arm. "Go and rest," he said, handing my child over. "It will be some time before we turn into the fjords."

He closed the cabin door behind himself and left me there. Ola had probably sent him with instructions to make sure I had a nap. Footsteps thudded up the few stairs, his retreating presence a reverberation in my mind. I placed the child in his cradle, secured to rings in the wall with rope so it wouldn't slide with the rocking of the ship. Off came my boots and coat. I crawled into the furs and collapsed, reminded of the first time I'd slept in Troy's bed, pregnant with Brendan, newly ripped away from Killian. It seemed a lifetime ago.

Now Troy's child waited in my womb, and I rested my head on Nikolas's pillow.

The motion of the ship lulled Brendan to sleep, my sleeping angel in his bed of fur and handwoven baby blankets. I set aside my confusion and let the sea rock me into the land of dreams. The dragon was there again, but I was too tired to fly with him. He let me rest against him, beneath his gilded wing, with the bass of his heartbeat and the slow bellows of his breath.

Hand on his scales in a dream as real as waking, I sang to him. I reeled my dragon in with the strength of my soul. No more waiting. No more falling through time.

I'm ready.

Chapter 42
Giving Over

WE REACHED AN INLET that evening, at the end of a long fjord. The sun disappeared behind steep mountains and left us in shadow. Anchored, sail lowered, water sloshing against the hull, Nora cooked up a hearty stew and fresh flatbread on the small iron stove in the galley. The scent of meaty broth thickened the air, as did the wood smoke that vented out the side of the ship.

As twilight descended, one of the brothers brought out a wooden pipe and started playing, his song echoing off the cliffs. I retreated to the steps of the upper deck with my music under lock and key.

Nikolas stood with his back to a rail, head tilted, eyes half-closed, gaze on me. When Brendan started to fuss, I took the stairs down to the cabin. Nikolas followed. He closed the door behind us with a scrape and a click, enveloping us in quiet.

I sat on the bed and brought a shawl over me to nurse Brendan while Nikolas lit a lantern and stowed a few things that were not yet in their places.

When he saw I was nursing, he asked, "Do you want me to leave?"

I shook my head, and a smile rounded his cheeks. He bent to put my boots out of the way, and stood to hang his heavy coat over mine. Then he sat in the cabin's one chair, the warm glow of lantern light on his face.

"I can sleep here at the door," he turned a hand toward the floor, "or on the deck if you wish. The bed is yours."

Too many things tumbled through my mind, the child a distraction. "Give me a minute?"

"Of course." Nikolas leaned back, legs stretched out, ankles crossed.

Brendan fell asleep at my breast. Once he was in his cradle on the floor, tucked in safe and warm, I stood in front of Nikolas, who got to his feet. Close.

"Nikolas?" Apprehension flooded my blood like a drug.

"Shelta." He brushed my arm with his fingers.

"I want you to stay." There. I'd said it.

"I would hold you," he slid a hand to my waist, "but I cannot promise to stop there. Two things drive me beyond self-control. One is love." He tipped his head down, fingers on my neck, the edge of his palm touching my cheek.

My heart beat unreasonably loud. "And the other?"

"Battle." His voice was gruff.

Right. Viking. Of course.

"We can take things slow, if you need." He slid a hand over my belly. "But I don't hold back with love, and I need to know if you can handle that." His gaze shone with raw desire. "Is this what you want?"

Terrified, I gave the only honest answer I had. "Yes."

He made a low sound in his throat and wrapped himself around me. His kiss was a passionate storm. It contained the rumble of thunder, the shockwave of lightning, the unfathomable depth and current of the ocean.

And his kisses, they did not stop.

I was on my back on the bed when I finally pushed away. Panting, I held a hand up.

He relented, giving me space.

"A little slower," I laughed.

Nikolas grinned, almost bashful. "I get carried away. I told you." He propped himself up on one elbow, wrapped his fingers between mine and turned my hand so the back of it rested at his chest, above his heart. "I have wanted this, yet I didn't know if it would be granted, if you could allow it. You seemed so fragile, Shelta. I didn't want to frighten you, only to shelter you."

I trembled. Tried not to show it. "Thank you for giving me space, and still being there for me." I took my hand back, then carefully traced the features of his face. My fingers swept over the thick length of his hair. My heart beat like a rabbit about to flee. "I'm still frightened," I admitted.

"What do you fear?"

"I'm afraid of getting so close to you, to your children, that it would hurt you the next time I'm pulled into another world. I don't want to be the source of more grief."

He laughed a little, leaned his forehead down to mine. "Your fear is how others will feel because of you?" He kissed my jaw. "You can only control your feelings, your choices. Others will have whatever experience they choose. And I choose you, Shelta." His eyes searched mine in the lantern light as if he were tapping into my soul.

I smiled through the fear, knowing I was doomed any way I played it. "Thank you."

Nikolas fit himself behind me and held me like he'd never let go. I gave him my weight, leaning into his warmth. It was wonderfully right, and desperately wrong.

If the goddess was behind all of this, either she was unnecessarily cruel, or she had a bigger plan than I could fathom.

CHAPTER 43
STANDING STONES

THE NEXT MORNING, I stood on deck with Brendan wrapped to my chest, the eagerness emanating from the dragon in my dreams still swimming in my blood. Wherever we were going today, it was significant.

Beside me, Nikolas spoke low, lifting his chin toward the end of the inlet, where a river raged through a crack in the mountains. "We walk into that canyon."

"Okay." I was as ready as I'd ever be. "Let's go."

A dark wooden rowboat with a trinity knot carved into the stern was lowered to the water. Nikolas told me it was the first boat he'd made, and the symbolism wasn't lost to me. Three men, three worlds, three loves. Maiden, mother, crone.

With Brendan at my chest, I made my pregnant way down, slow and careful. Nikolas followed with the grace of a big cat. Alexandra handed a heavy pack to him, then my lighter one, to which my sword was strapped. As we pulled away, I waved to the crew, not knowing if I'd see them again. If I found my dragon, would I go to Killian right away? Could I leave Nikolas now, even if I had a way to return?

Nikolas was armed with a sword and hammer hanging at his belt. He caught me looking at the rectangular head of bright metal. "I'll show you more closely when we reach a resting point," he said. "Then you can have the story as well."

I nodded, swimming in anticipation. If we were on our way to the dragons, I didn't want to wait any longer.

Goddess, please. I'm ready. No more blind falling through time. Let me find my dragon.

She didn't respond, but the song around me changed, as if the water was listening. As if the mountain turned its attention our way.

Nikolas rowed us through the current of outflow from the river, headed toward the bank to its left, using the force of his will as much as the oars. Magic seeped through me like a sparkling fog, a cascading song barely sung. As we cleared the mouth of the river, I got a distinct feeling that we'd been *allowed* to cross.

When we ran aground, I stepped out, boots on shifting pebbles. Tall crags rose to either side of us. Nikolas pushed the boat above the tide line, then took up his massive backpack, piled with furs for an overnight trip. He carried enough for both of us. I had my plaid bag of necessities and some extra food, the sword in its sheath across my back. Brendan's gaze was drawn to the hilt sticking up past my shoulder.

With Nikolas a stride behind, I traversed the uneven ground—river on the right, steep rock on the left. Mist draped the narrow strip of land between.

Two giant rocks stood guard at the entrance of the canyon with a third stone above, making a towering doorway. I touched the damp rock as we crossed the threshold, fingers tingling as magic seeped into my skin.

We followed the water along the lush canyon floor. Birds chirped and the river gurgled, every sound echoing up the cliffs like secrets of fractal worlds. Sunlight filtered through the chasm's opening.

Maybe twenty minutes in, as we rounded a corner, a spike of fear made me freeze.

The carving nearly took the strength from my legs. High up and huge, a deeply-etched tree sprawled across the canyon wall on the opposite side of the river, its roots a symmetrical knot at eye level. A single tap root ran into a crack in the wall that disappeared into the river as if it were drinking the water.

Nikolas took my hand, warming my fingers. "This is one of the oldest anchors in the World Tree."

"I'm glad we're on this side." My voice was barely audible above the rushing water.

One side of his mouth curled up. "You can access the power of these points without touching them."

"How?" The word was a whisper in the mist. I'd only been trying to figure this out my whole life.

"By coming into your power." He squeezed my hand, and drew me on down the trail.

Fear gripped me as we passed the carving. I couldn't take my eyes off it. The Tree's power pulled at me. We rounded a corner, leaving it behind, but I could sense it like an undertow in the song around me.

When we reached a second carving, I slowed, wary. A spiral wrapped around a wide boulder in our path. We had to cross it to continue.

"Stand at its center," Nikolas said.

I shook my head in slow motion. "I don't know if that's a good idea."

"Shelta." Nikolas tilted his head down and kissed me, assurance flowing from his lips to mine. He held my face, eyes as blue as the distant sky. "Stand at its center. See what you see."

If I had to get to the end of this canyon to find dragons, and it meant walking over this rock… I stepped onto the boulder. The apex of the stone was the heart of the spiral, wide enough for one person, the carving worn from others who'd come there before me. "Is there a second spiral beneath the stone?" I asked Nikolas, seeing it in my mind.

His eyelids dropped to half-mast, mouth curling. "Yes. It travels in both directions. Imagine yourself within the spirals, one above your head and one beneath your feet."

I closed my eyes and did so, seeing a golden sphere of light around me, rotating slowly on a vertical axis. The connection below anchored into a star at the earth's core. The connection above plugged into the heart of the galaxy. Standing within it, energy traveled through me.

"You're glowing," said Nikolas. Killian's words in a different world.

He was right. A radiance shone from my body, strong and bright near my skin, fading as it reached the edge of the rock.

"Remember this," he said. "Remember this vibration, this light."

I closed my eyes and concentrated on the pulsation that ran through the light. It had its own kind of music. Once I'd memorized it, like a song, I lifted my gaze to Nikolas.

"Ground yourself when you wield this power," he warned. "Within that spiral you harness earth and sky, fire and flow. It's a lot of energy for a human body to take."

My breath stretched out through the dancing, honey-colored light that went through me, through Brendan, through the child within. A sense of completion clicked inside.

That was enough.

Tingling, I stepped down to the trail on the other side, staggering several strides away. I turned and looked at Nikolas. Steadied myself. He gave a nod, and focused on the stone.

He started glowing as soon as he stepped onto it. When he stood at the center, I had to squint against the flame surrounding him. A pillar of light shot through him, crackling and humming like a choir of wild faeries. The hammer at his belt sparked, and, for a heart-flash of time, a god's presence, like distant thunder, rumbled in my bones. I sank energetic roots deeper into the ground, rocked by the force coming from the spiral stone and the man at its center.

When Nikolas finally opened his eyes, they glowed vivid blue against the gold. He moved forward slowly, a crease between his brows. For a moment, his mouth hung open, then he set his jaw and stepped off the rock. The storm of light faded.

"Wow." I was glad he stood a good pace away. He seemed to take up a lot of space.

Nikolas let out a slow breath. "That was different."

"Really?"

"Indeed." He tilted his head. "And it had to do with you."

"How so?"

He was quiet so long I wasn't sure he'd answer. Finally, he said, "My namefather knows your mother. She gave me her blessing, as did he. I'm not sure what it means yet, but that was—a lot of energy. They were present for you, as well, just more gently. They gave only what you were ready to receive."

"Thor knows my mother?" A desperate, disbelieving hope rose in my chest.

His eyes were like blue-green portals. "Yes. The goddess, Brighid."

The sound of my breath blended in with the river. A rightness clicked in my consciousness, but my rational brain wasn't on board. "You mean like the goddess is mother to all children, right?"

He shook his head side-to-side slow, only once. "The goddess Brighid is your mother, Shelta. Of that I am sure."

"How do you know?" There was no way. I was not the child of a goddess. I was a lost, random creature of creation who fell through wormholes, had a supernatural musical ability, and an affinity for dragons.

Then again…

"I know," said Nikolas, "because she told me as she blended her power with Thor's. I have communicated with him before. I trust him. She came with Thor, and he named her."

"I've heard her in my head before," I murmured. "She called me her daughter then, but I thought she meant it on a broader scale."

He took a step toward me. "You are the daughter of a goddess."

"Who's my father?" I asked.

He shook his head. "That I don't know. A mortal, I'd guess."

I didn't want to touch Nikolas. Didn't want to believe him, even if something deeper told me he spoke the truth. I turned and continued on the path in a daze.

Goddess? I ventured, reaching for her in my mind. *Brighid? Mother?*

There came a whisper in the sound of water rushing over rocks. *Wait, my daughter. Now is not the time.*

Dumbstruck, buzzing within, I put one foot in front of the other and went upriver on the narrow path. Nikolas walked a pace behind, his footsteps in beat with mine.

Eventually, the space widened. We came around a bend, and the view opened up.

A large mound dominated the center of a valley, standing stones shining in the sun. Anticipation shivered through me. I turned to face Nikolas with his pack piled with furs, and asked, "What is this place?"

"This is a convergence of four mountain ranges," Nikolas said. "Two valleys cross. A sacred site was built here ages ago." He pointed at the giant stone arches at the top of the hill.

I bounced, trying to calm Brendan, who'd begun to fuss.

He gestured to a fallen stone nearby. "Let's rest and have some food. We can make the climb in a little while."

Good plan. I made my way onto the giant rock to nurse my son. Nikolas laid out the furs, then unwrapped honeyed flatbread and sharp cheese. Brendan tried a little cheese, but was more interested in sampling the grass that grew near the rock, and fragments of the stone itself.

Nikolas brought out his hammer and stood it on its head, handle facing up. I didn't touch it, but Brendan had no such inhibitions, grasping the handle with his little hands, patting the hammer's head. Knotwork adorned the chunk of bright metal and wound around the thick wooden grip.

"Its name is *Fornvéur*." Nikolas nodded to the hammer. "'Ancient Protector.' It is older than these rocks, made of stardust and metal not of this world. The handle is wood from the World Tree." My eyes went wide, and he smiled. "It was a gift from Thor to the lineage he created here."

I wondered about the aftereffects of breeding with a god. "Does your family tend to live longer than most people?" Would I live longer? I still couldn't believe I was the daughter of a goddess.

"Yes." He sat straighter, eyes sharp on mine. "And those of our lineage are bound to the god's purposes: protecting the realm, keeping the secrets of the World Tree, and fealty to the sacred fire of love."

The sacred fire of love. He took my hand and lifted it to his lips, then wrapped my fingers around the thick handle of the hammer. His hand circled my own. Energy vibrated up my arm and into my spine in an infusion of strength.

"*Fornvéur* serves the sons and daughters of Thor." Nikolas spoke low. "Its powers change to meet the need of each generation, each bearer of the hammer."

I closed my eyes and tuned in. The weapon's song was concentrated at the head of the hammer. The shaft sent out flowing light in my inner vision. It carried the force of transformation, and the potency of explosive, thunderous power. I wanted it. Wanted it to help me control the time travel.

I believe in magic, Shelta. I think it runs in your blood, and in mine. Killian's voice echoed through my soul as the hammer sent a blast into me. Magic was the only word that fit.

My eyes fluttered open as Nikolas lifted my hand from the hammer. He helped me to my feet, and moved behind me, spreading my fingers with his own, our arms wide. The energy of the hammer dissipated through my legs into the earth, and out my fingertips, making me shiver.

I turned toward Nikolas, lightheaded.

"There are other items of inheritance." He slid my hands onto the belt at his waist.

My fingers found large gemstones on each side, hidden beneath flaps of leather. "Diamonds?" I asked. They glowed golden in the sun, yet intuition told me they'd turn blue-silver in moonlight.

He put his hands on mine. "Not quite. They are from the Realm of the Gods. They act as conduits for energy and fortification."

I lost myself in the blue of his gaze. His eyes said, *Feel*.

A dancing current traveled up my arms and into my heart, out through my blood. For a fleeting moment, I understood all of the mysteries of existence. I glimpsed the Heart of the World Tree without being sucked into it.

Nikolas touched my wrists and I let go, bringing my hands away from the belt. The depths of his eyes held the spiral of galaxies, dark blue and vibrant. "That energy you can keep," he said. "The lightning it is best to release. Do you understand?"

I took a deep, involuntary breath, magic coursing within. "Yes."

Somewhere, gods existed. Did they watch us? Did they know what I sought? If this man could carry instruments this powerful, I could control the time travel. Maybe I could even do it without dragons.

Once we started climbing the hill, I was glad we'd stopped for a rest. The trail crept at a steady incline. As we passed beneath the first gate, a low-pitched *whoomp* made the hair on the back of my neck stand at attention. My vision crystalized as I followed the path in its clockwise spiral, winding around and around, up and up.

Each valley was a vision of grandeur. Rivers flowed in from the east, north, and west, feeding the one that went to the sea through the canyon to the south. Trees darkened the slopes. Scattered clusters of early wildflowers bloomed yellow and orange in south-facing meadows.

I kept my feet moving until we reached the top. There, on the mostly-flat space at the crest of the hill, stood three concentric circles of stones. Each boulder was massive, the smallest at least nine feet tall and three feet thick.

Entrance pillars towered before us, with runes engraved into the capstone. I stood, mouth agape, as Nikolas read the message. "'Come with care. Know thy purpose. Find thy heart.'" He turned to face me. "What is your purpose, Shelta?"

That I knew. I'd been after it all my life. "To find a way to navigate the World Tree—in control, not helpless to fate. And to know why I am the way I am."

His dipped his head in a sideways nod. "What about your soul? What is your soul's purpose?"

"To sing." My voice caught in my throat. "To love."

"Your life is a tapestry of music, the World Tree, and the mystery of the goddess. Mine is made of wind, waves, lightning, and stone. My path is carved by the hand of the god."

"God-Goddess." Oneness. Creation and creator. I reached out with my mind and felt a brush of omniscient presence as the wind blew my hair.

"We enter here as exactly that. You the goddess, I the god." Nikolas smiled at the child at my chest. "You, little Brendan, are the limitless potential of creation." He kissed him on the forehead, and took my hand.

Thus, we passed between the pillars.

The vibration hit me immediately. Bass notes dropped through the earth at our feet. The music told me the stones were buried deep, each twice as long as what showed above ground. Most of the slabs were taller than Nikolas by several feet, though some in the inner circle were smaller, a couple of chunks broken into legs for a wide alter.

The air around the stones shimmered. Magic deepened its grip on me.

We spiraled clockwise through the outer ring, into the middle one. As we walked, harmonic tones shifted and aligned like we were moving through an acoustic kaleidoscope.

At the center, a circular stone capped the apex of the hill in a floor of white. Nikolas placed his pack on the ground, and laid a few furs down. I let Brendan loose and stretched, in awe of where we'd come.

After a sip of water and a rest, Nikolas retrieved a small pouch from his bag. He beckoned me to the altar in the east, where he brought out a small disc of wood with a six-pointed star in flowing, intertwining lines. I recognized the symbolic meeting of god and goddess—the triangle with its point at the top representing the masculine, the downward-pointing triangle representing the feminine.

Next came a tied cloth that contained herbs reminiscent of Ola's kitchen. Nikolas sprinkled them around the edge, and I smelled the green of mint and sweetness of lavender. But when he slid an exquisite piece of labradorite from the pouch, I breathed out a disbelieving "Oh!"

It was gorgeous. I'd never seen a piece with such vibrant colors. But what got me in the gut was the fact that it was the same size and shape as the crystal I'd brought through several time jumps. Nikolas turned at my intake of breath, and showed me the stone, its face aglow with green and gold, blue and purple, reminding me of the Northern Lights. I handed it back to him and went to rummage through my purse.

My hand closed on the velvet bag of crystals. I brought out my own piece of labradorite, and handed it to Nikolas. They were nearly a pair, though the fire in his was more vibrant.

Then again, mine was from worlds away.

He raised thick eyebrows, mouth a circle beneath his beard. "Beautiful. Would you part with it? I'll give you this in return. You'll be adding something of yours to the offering, that way."

"Definitely." I made the trade.

Nikolas kissed the iridescent crystal and put it in my hand. It pulsed warm. Sentient. The labradorite I'd given him went at the center of the offering, on the wooden star. Then he took out another small, thin cloth, and unwrapped it to reveal dried flower petals. He held it toward me. "Would you make the outer circle?"

The little package tingled in my palm. With reverence, I arranged petals around the edge of the mandala—pink and blue, yellow and red. It was enchanting. Lovely. I didn't realize I was humming until I stepped back to admire what we'd made.

Struck by a possibility, I retrieved my sword from our things, unsheathed it, and placed it on the altar, above the mandala. Would its power help me call in my dragon?

Nikolas swept his fingers down one of my cheeks. "For what do you wish?"

Doubt flooded in. I wanted to stay with him. I wanted to see Killian and Troy again.

"What is in your heart?" Nikolas asked softly.

"I wish for this love to endure." The yearning was overwhelming. I gripped the altar to steady myself. "I want to understand why the World Tree has taken me so many times. I wish to travel at will, to return to those I love, and for a dragon to help me."

I wanted to stay with Nikolas and never be ripped away. I wanted to give myself over, and know he was truly mine. But that meant longevity, some kind of promise I could count on in the face of uncertainty. Marriage wasn't enough. It had to be something more, something lasting.

Nikolas took my hand, and led me to the center of the smooth white rock set into the top of the hill, about eleven feet in diameter. Brendan kept himself entertained on the furs to one side, chewing on a bit of leather.

My focus narrowed to Nikolas, all his attention on me. Man and god at once. Pulled into the black of his pupils, I felt his soul lock into my own.

An all-encompassing current connected us, magnified by the power of the stones and the convergence of the valleys. Nikolas placed my left hand on his chest, covered it with his right hand, then put his left hand above my heart. I automatically wrapped my fingers around his. The link deepened, soul-to-soul, heart-to-heart.

"I claim you," Nikolas said in a deep, carrying voice. It moved through me like an underground river. "I claim you in this realm, and every other, so long as you want me."

His words reverberated through the stones and earth, the power instant and infinite.

"I am yours as you are mine." He wove his words into existence itself. "I will my soul to find you, to love you, anywhere we meet in the branches of the World Tree. This love knows its way through time and eternity."

I swayed, blood in my ears like a choir of waves. It was all I could do to breathe.

He brought me in, arms around me. "Know me, Shelta, whomever I may be in each life, each reality. Find me. Trust me. Let yourself love fully. I will not hold back."

Killian and Troy were there in that moment, and as my eyes pricked with tears, I understood. This moment stretched through the tangled web of time. The vow he made now had already been fulfilled in my past. A promise already proven.

Something hard and broken inside of me blasted apart.

I fell to my knees on the furs, shattered fears blowing away in the wind that came over the hilltop. Nikolas lowered down to the stone to face me.

"Thank you." I whispered the words through tears. I'd never thought love could reach so wide, could be so sure and free. He brought me into his lap as Troy had done. As Killian had done.

Killian, who had prayed to Brighid, asking for love at the roots of the World Tree. Was I the child she'd wept for? Was my father the one she'd turned into an oak that reached through dimensions?

"This is your son," I said, gesturing to Brendan. "And this child is yours." I placed his hand on my belly. "I've known you before, loved your soul in other times."

He held my eyes with his. "I knew you were mine when you entered this world. Yet you came with so much grief, shrouded—so afraid of love. I feared you would not be able to see what was clear to me from the start. You are my match, Shelta."

I swallowed, three men taking up space in my heart. Nikolas. Killian. Troy.

With Brendan beside us, we wrapped around each other in what felt like the center of the universe. Eyes closed, I leaned my head against his chest, and surrendered to soul-deep intimacy.

CHAPTER 44
THE PALM OF THE GODDESS

THE FULL MOON ROSE at the far side of the valley above a narrow peak, creating a silhouette like a cat's eye until the moon crested the point and made its way into the star-speckled sky.

As beautiful as it was, it was hard to be patient. I could taste the knowledge of how to control the time travel, but the secret wasn't mine yet. My dragon hadn't come. What did I have to do to call him, to make him real?

The stones gave off low harmonies, humming through the hill so gently I almost forgot they were there. The floor of white rock beneath our furs surrounded us like a shield, and the bond between Nikolas and me twined through my blood. We leaned against each other on a bed of fur and wool. Brendan slept in a nest of blankets and sheepskin; silver light glowing on his face like the child had his own magic.

Beyond the canyon passage, where the spiral stone lit up with the energy of gods, the World Tree sent its taproot down. I sensed it running up the river, spreading through the valley, and stretching to the hill. And in the inlet beyond the mouth of the river, four people waited, on a boat built by the man whose soul loved me in three worlds.

"What's your ship's name?" I asked Nikolas.

"LófiDanu." The skin around his eyes crinkled. "It means the palm of the Mother Goddess. When I sail, I feel as if the ship is her hand, the wind her breath, the water her will."

"That's beautiful." I tried the name, a new sound in my mouth. "Why didn't you tell me before?"

"You never asked." His mouth twitched in the moonlight. "It is sacred, a name like that, a secret that must be sought to be given. Tonight is perfect, as we await the goddess."

As we await the goddess. Had I sought the secrets of the World Tree long enough to crack open the key?

We fell into silence as the moon climbed higher, and I drifted, my head on his shoulder, his arm around me with a heavy sense of safety that let me relax to my bones.

When the moon was at its apex, I opened my eyes to find the stone around us shining as if it were another source of moonlight. The same luminescence came from Nikolas and myself.

Trust I'd always aimed for but never fully felt thrummed through me. It was time.

Trust is the key, said a silvery voice like starlight in my mind.

Goddess. Mother?

Yes, Daughter. Her consciousness was wide as all the worlds, but she said no more. I sensed her attention move to the man at my side.

"Do you hear her?" I whispered to Nikolas.

Galaxies gleamed in his eyes. "Yes."

My grin turned into a gasp as energy moved in a plummeting path of light from the sky, through us, and down to the planet beneath. Standing, I stepped off the furs, away from Nikolas and Brendan. Bare feet on glowing rock, the wool of my skirts brushed my ankles. Every star in the sky blazed, as if the heavens looked down with other-worldly eyes, witnessing.

You have our attention. Brighid's voice whispered through my chest. *More than one god watches you now.*

No more waiting. *Why have I tumbled through time all my life?*

I birthed you through the World Tree in hopes that you would find your way back to me, but you landed in a world I didn't intend. Her disappointment was a shadow in the sparkling night, a confession that even goddesses make mistakes. *I helped you the best I could along the way. When you answered Killian's call, you found your path home.*

Home to Killian, or home to you? Home was a shaky concept. Not a place, a sense of rightness. And I'd never thought of my appearance before Killian as an answer to his call. Had I done such a thing without knowing? Didn't the goddess orchestrate that magic?

Home to me, home to your loves, home to yourself. I may have pulled a little, but your choices led you to your truth.

How can I love the same soul in three different men?

Brighid's answer came with a soft breeze that played in my hair. *You sang it into being, at your wedding with Killian. Time isn't linear. Your souls are drawn to each other. But even as a spirit's essence can exist in multiple timelines, each human experience is different. Sharing souls doesn't make them the same men.*

Fair enough. Before I thought about whether it was wise, I asked, *Who was my father?*

Hesitation. Old grief bled into my mother's words. *That is a story for another day.*

Right. Other gods were watching. Sorrow pulled at my throat, but I had more important questions. *How can I be finished falling through time without warning?*

That is what tonight is about. Her reply was like a cascade of cool water. A lifelong burden lifted. *The gods have agreed to give you that power, if you accept the responsibilities of a world-weaver.*

Always a catch. *What does that entail?*

Many things. Mainly, that you agree to be a benevolent force in whatever worlds you choose to visit. The answer was loaded. Vague. *You are a weaver either way, but if you agree to use your abilities to bring harmony, I can grant you the power you wish for. Your music brings beauty, Shelta. It brings joy. Love. In that alone, you have already woven light into the tapestry.*

I probably should've asked for the fine print, but it didn't seem forthcoming. Didn't matter. As long as I could travel the Tree at will, I could be with my family. I'd figure out the world-weaving thing as I went. *Yes. I agree. How do I control the time travel?*

Find peace in the storm of your mind. Seek the place of balance. To control your world walking, you must accept the energy of the World Tree. Bond with it, rather than rejecting it. I will help you.

I stood silent. Listening. Riding my breath into the balance she spoke of. It was easy enough with a goddess threading her consciousness through mine, on sacred ground. I sensed a tendril of the World Tree beneath me. I could see it in my awareness, even with my eyes open—a bolt of knowing that connected with something in my soul.

Far below the hill, a rainbow pulsed through a vein of crystal like a deep root. Shards of it shone in the rock upon which I stood, and I knew if I turned on the current, the root of the Tree would connect beneath me. The white stone currently functioned as a shield. I reached into its resonance, wondering if I could replicate it to shield myself...

Nikolas watched me, Brendan beside him. This was my family. This was my chance to learn how to stay with them, forever, but if I tapped into the World Tree, what was to stop it from sucking me in?

I want this power, Goddess, but I can't risk losing my son.

Did the mountains sigh, or were the gods laughing at my mortal demands? At least they weren't all talking in my head.

The same essence that threads existence together ties your family together, Brighid replied. *To access your power, you must surrender to the current, and claim it as your own.*

Could a shockwave be soft and loving? I yielded to the force that coursed through me as the goddess planted a seed of power at the core of my being, mighty as a fully-grown dragon, connected to the World Tree.

A vortex of color engulfed me in all of time and space at once, the workings of the universe in energy form. A rainbow of impossibly bright hues danced with brightest white and darkest shadows, its song a symphony of wonder.

Music burst from within. My voice filled the valleys with a raw, thick sound born in my soul. I shaped notes without words, without thought.

I gave of myself, wholly. Sang for my freedom.

On instinct, I used the song to call my dragon, seeing him clear in my mind. The wordless music swirled into the sky, and the stars brightened. When I rounded into a final refrain, the last notes like stardust that faded slowly into the listening black, the energy of the World Tree ebbed.

"I feel like I could fly," I whispered to Nikolas, spreading my arms out. The back of my neck tingled as I looked up and saw an unmistakable shape moving toward us.

A crimson dragon approached, shimmering with the light of the moon.

I howled my elation into the night. Nikolas laughed soft, love and wonder in the sound.

The dragon came closer. The red of his scales glittered in the moonlight, glowing from within like starlight fire. He was far too big to land inside the circle of stones.

If you want to ride him, you need to rise up to him, said the goddess.

Bending my knees, I took hold of the power that coursed through me, and jumped. My body shot into the sky, all my will bent on getting as high as I could, completely trusting the dragon to catch me.

He came up beneath me like he'd done so many times in dreams, but his scales were hard and real beneath my hands. I hooked my legs on the ridges of his shoulders, above his great wings. A wide spine rose behind me like a seat.

His wings stroked the air and carried me higher, ascending toward the moon. Below, Nikolas gazed up, Brendan safe at his feet, surrounded by circles of stones.

I opened my mind like Troy had taught me, and asked the dragon, *What's your name?*

The sublime connection that melded with his answer was a piece of my life that had always been missing, finally fitting into place. *Eirian.*

I shivered. The name echoed in my bones.

Will you help me get back to Killian and Troy? I asked. He'd been in my dreams all this time; he must know how much I needed to see them again.

Yes. A single word to bring such joy. *You will see them again. I will take you there.*

Tears streamed down my face, saltwater on my lips. I'd see them again. We were a family, linked through time and space.

Eirian's flight was a dance of freedom, his emotions melding with mine. I reveled in his wildness. My hair whipped back, but I didn't feel the cold. The stars burned so brightly that I reached up a hand as if to brush them, waving to the gods who watched.

We soared over the valleys, spiraling high enough that I spotted the *LófiDanu* anchored in the inlet. Did the crew see the dragon glowing against the sky?

I didn't notice the passing of time until the moon was near the horizon, and Eirian glided back toward the circle where the white stone's glow had begun to dim. Sensing it was over, I leaned forward and hugged the dragon's neck. He hummed, a resonance of belonging that thrummed through me.

When we passed over the stone where Nikolas waited with Brendan, Eirian dipped a wing. I slid off, trusting the magic of the night. Trusting the power that coursed inside me. I landed on the earth near the altar as if I'd dropped from a few feet instead of fifty.

But I didn't want Eirian to go.

We will meet again. The dragon's words were a song of their own. *You are in my heart, and I am in yours. If you call me, I will come.*

I will call you, I promised.

He circled once, then shot across the sky like a star.

The offering on the altar was gone. In its place, shimmering below my sword in a wet web of early-morning dew, was the ghost form of a dragon.

When I joined Nikolas on the soft furs at the center of the space, he threaded his fingers through mine. Brendan slept like an angel at our feet.

I stood, speechless, as the moon descended beyond the mountains and the glow faded from the night, dawn creeping in. My mother's presence retreated, but the seed she'd planted within me remained.

I was no longer lost. I knew who I was.

Daughter of a goddess. Dragon friend. Soul-bound with the descendant of a god.

And now, I was a world-weaver.

Whatever that meant, whatever the future held in store, I would see Killian and Troy again. That's all that mattered. After tumbling through time my entire life, wishing I belonged, I'd found my way home.

~

The adventure continues in
DRAGONS IN THE WEAVING,
Which launches Shelta's story
Into the Realm of the Gods.

Read on for the first chapter…

Chapter 1
Storm and Sword

THERE WAS NO END to the beauty of the fjords. Sun-kissed clouds stretched pink and gold across a sky of deepening blue. Gentle winds filled the sails, pushing the dragon ship through a colossal cradle of steep mountains and flowing water, with a god-blooded Viking at the helm.

Breathtaking though it was, I couldn't stop thinking about what had happened last night.

The oath. The goddess. The watchers in the stars.

The dragon.

I'd flown with Eirian, and he'd promised to help me return to Killian and Troy. I'd been too drunk on magic to ask how, but I'd find a way.

The vow Nikolas had made went beyond the bonds of any one world. Already proven.

We'd woven our souls together.

He glanced down from his spot at the ship's wheel, his beard half-concealing his smile. I sat in a nest of furs on the deck with baby Brendan in my lap, who was busy gnawing on a wooden spoon. The weightlessness of the night before had left me sore from the strain of being pregnant and the long journey to the stone circle at the convergence of valleys.

Love shone in Nikolas's eyes as he looked at us. He recognized Brendan as his own, like Troy had. The confounding part was how true it was, even if the child's dark hair and eyes were Killian's. Worlds away.

My mind tripped over the bending of time.

Nikolas relinquished the helm to his first mate, Alexandra, and came over. He kneeled next to me, his big hand dwarfing mine. "Are you alright, Shelta?"

"Tired." I shrugged it off. "Where are we going?"

Instead of answering, he touched my temple, and a map formed in my mind. An aerial view of the fjords showed the ship headed along an illuminated path toward a narrow channel.

"You see?" Nikolas dipped his face down, close to mine.

"I do. And what will we find there?"

"Dragons." He cracked a roguish smile.

"Eirian?" I whispered his name. My dragon. The one I'd sought my whole life.

"Likely." Nikolas rubbed his thumb over my knuckles, the bass of his voice rumbling in my ribcage. "Dragons possess an essence not so different from our own. We each have souls made of stars."

"Souls made of stars?"

His beard gently scratched my cheek as he snuck a kiss. "Didn't you see it last night?"

My breath caught at the glacier blue of his eyes and the gravity of memories spinning through me. "I saw the glow, but that was the magic of the stones, right? The moon, the offering, the goddess?"

My mother was a goddess. How long until that felt normal?

Nikolas ran a hand along his belt. He didn't wear his hammer, but the gems on either side sang, fully charged, as did the crystals in the pouch nestled in my right pocket. When I took my sword from the altar this morning, it had vibrated in my hand.

"Nature's energy amplified what you already are," said Nikolas. "Your essence. Your star-self."

"Like, a real star?" I lifted a finger toward the sky.

"What do you think the stars are made of?"

How absurd would the science I knew sound to him? "Big balls of chemical elements burning in space, mostly?"

He shook his head. "They are conscious beings of light, Shelta. Each and every star."

I held my tongue. Maybe he was right. The gods had looked down on us last night, no question in my mind. The goddess and her kin. Our kin. I looked at Brendan and tried to wrap my head around his being Brighid's grandchild.

Nikolas spoke near my ear. "We believe that when a star arcs through the sky, a child is being conceived. A star may become a human, or a tree, or a cat. Or a dragon."

Or a dragon.

The thought of Eirian made my blood sing, reaching into the realm of destiny.

That night, as the ship slipped through the fjords, a tremor of urgency ripped through the darkness, rocking the boat and shaking me awake. I gripped the bedrail, checking for Brendan, who was still strapped in his cradle, bolted to the floor.

Nikolas launched out of bed and grabbed his boots, which were across the room from where he'd left them. "Ola calls." His voice scraped low. "Raiders were sighted on their way to the village. Stay here."

I nodded, watching him leave, the ship already turning as he called the elements to his need. Seer that she was, it didn't surprise me that Ola could reach her brother telepathically, but what a wake-up call. My stomach churned, thinking of the village with its steep-roofed homes and central tree, of Ola and the children Nikolas had left in her care. Of all the families who lived along the sheltered bay.

Would the raider's ships sail past the cliff carved with the World Tree?

The deck rang with the crew's footsteps. Water rose beneath the ship, and a gust of wind came up behind us. The boat tore through the water. We sailed away from the dragons, away from my chance at seeing Eirian.

If a ship could fly, that is what the *LófiDanu* did. We emerged from the fjords into the open sea and a frenzy of waves. Wood groaned as Nikolas drove the ship to its edge, and anxiety gripped me in a storm of its own. Forcing myself to breathe slowly, I closed my eyes and prayed.

The baby inside kicked hard, making me wince. Pushing back with the flat of my hand, I sang quietly to myself, to Brendan, to my unborn child. Nothing like a lullaby in the midst of complete chaos.

Eventually, I got dressed, and sat in the chair beside Brendan to wait out the storm.

Through the wood, past the wind and pounding water, I heard Nikolas bellow to the crew. The ship slowed. I peered out the cabin's small window, daggers heavy in my boots.

From what I could tell through a sheet of rain, we were coming into the harbor. Long before we reached the docks, Nikolas dropped anchor. The force of the ship dragging to a stop threw me to the floorboards next to Brendan's cradle. Heavy steps sounded on deck, and the rowboat splashed into the water.

I got to the window in time to watch the rowboat surfing a swell. Nikolas stood with one foot on the bow, sword and hammer drawn, the crew behind him.

Lightning crackled. Then, they blurred out of view.

I could see nothing more than moving shadows through streaks of rain and the splash of seawater. I stepped back from the window, retrieved my dragon sword, and sat down in the cabin's chair.

Brendan slept fitfully while I paced the small space, sat again, and paced some more. The ship rolled in the raging sea. Occasionally, the sound of screaming carried over the water with the distant clang of metal on metal. It was hard to tell if my nausea was from being pregnant, deep-set dread, or seasickness.

Just keep breathing.

Footsteps on the deck made my skin crawl. Nikolas wouldn't be back already. Had someone come to pillage?

I squeezed the grip of my sword, swaying with the ship. Heavy steps thudded on the stairs. Then the cabin door flew open.

Lightning flashed, shining on the whites of a man's eyes. He didn't expect me.

Not about to waste my chance, I lunged forward. He brought his sword up, and I hustled to keep him from entering the cabin, steel ringing against steel in the small space. The boat tipped, and I stumbled, arms rattling as I blocked the brute strength of his strikes.

Drops of water flew off his hair, splashing on my face. He roared, pushing forward, forcing me to give way. Bracing myself, I put all my focus on my sword, and it came alive in my hand, sparking as it collided with my attacker's.

Seeing an opening, I ducked, drew my dagger, and plunged it into his ribs. The sickly sound of blade meeting flesh slid beneath his garbled cry. As he fell, I pushed him back, onto the stairs. Blood ran warm over my hand.

Another raider strode toward the cabin, with two more behind. I pulled the dirk free from the man at my feet, slammed the door closed to hide my son, and clambered up to the main deck, where I had room to let loose the full fury of my sword.

Lightning crackled along my blade in tune with the roar of the storm. I let it direct my movements, putting all my energy into the deadly dance. With a slash, a bolt jumped from my sword to one of the men, who fell in convulsions. His comrade, a large man with shaggy hair, snickered as my coat came open, exposing the cleavage of a nursing mother.

As my attacker's sword slammed against mine, a sharp pull in my abdomen made me cry out. My arms shook as the blade carried itself through the air.

The weapon was the leader. I just held on.

When the man came close enough, I drove my dagger into his belly. He fell to the deck with gut-wrenching moans. Letting go of the dirk, I gripped the sword's hilt. The last man rushed forward, growling.

Thoughts dissolved. There was only the blade singing. Clanging. Clashing. It was in its glory, electrical current running through every movement. My opponent lunged, slashing through the leather of my coat, drawing blood from my right shoulder and a yelp of pain from my throat.

A sudden flare from my sword blinded us both. Trusting the dragon blade, I swung out. A muddled moan and thick thud made me stagger back, squinting. I'd slit his throat.

He died slowly, and it hit me like a fall from a great height. I'd killed. Again. This time it was up close and personal, not a rifle at a removed distance. Blood on the deck. Blood on my hands. My right coat sleeve was soaked in red. Rain splattered my face. Thunder roared, and flashes from the clouds illuminated the fighting on shore.

Lightheaded, I stumbled across the tilting deck and grabbed the rail, over which I lost whatever food was left in my stomach.

My sword glowed dull at my feet, as if waiting for the next fight. I turned my gaze toward land and pressed a hand to my shoulder to try to stem the bleeding.

I wasn't that far from the village. The faint light of dawn grew steadily brighter, and I was able to pick out Nikolas among the figures in the fray. He lifted his hammer to call a bolt of lightning, which he sent through the five men in front of him. They fell, only to be replaced by ten more raiders. The villagers were severely outnumbered.

Nikolas swung his hammer and hurled it into the closest man, creating a shockwave that crumpled those nearby. His hammer never stopped moving, and the thunder rolled on. I leaned on the rail, unable to tear my eyes away.

Adrenaline kept me standing when I needed to sit down. Badly. My breath came shallow. The fighting was desperate, villagers and elements pitted against a small army. Another wave of sickness came, and I retched over the rail though there was nothing left inside.

What could have been a lifetime or only moments later, the rain stopped, the wind calmed, and the waves receded to a gentle roll as the sun rose over the mountains to the east.

Nikolas strode, tall and swift, through the bodies in the street toward his home, only now able to check on his children. I sank to the bench beside me, wrecked.

Vision blurring, I tried to get back to the cabin, back to Brendan, but I only made it halfway. I fell to my knees in slow motion, catching my weight in my hands to protect my aching belly, and rolled to my side.

As I joined the corpses that lay on the deck, the suddenly-bright morning faded to black.

Get your copy of *Dragons in the Weaving* and read on…

Author's Note

In the process of creating a fantasy where alternate histories and parallel worlds exist, I've taken many liberties. For instance, my portrayal of Duart Castle and the legends of Clan Maclean are mostly made up. The Nwetaka tribe is also a fabrication, as the Shoshone would've been the Native residents of that area of Wyoming had this tale taken place in our actual history. Even so, I've tried to represent each human and historical element of this story with respect. It is my intention as an author to explore imagined possibilities in ways that inspire hope and an awareness that we are all connected: people, nature, and the cosmos.

ACKNOWLEDGEMENTS

Writing is a solitary endeavor, but it takes a community for a book to become something extraordinary. To my family, especially my mother, and everyone who has encouraged and supported me on this journey, thank you!

Special thanks to author and editor Stephanie Diaz, who read the messy first drafts of this story many years ago and helped me learn how to write. To Kat Turner, D. Lambert, Elysia Lumen Strife, Rebecca Fryar, Nina Castle, Jenna McKinley, Rhonda Kay, Halla Williams, and John King, you're amazing and your feedback helped make this book shine! To Sir Lachlan Maclean and Alison Canham from Duart Castle, thank you for your blessings on this book. One day, I hope to travel Shelta's path to meet you.

Lastly, I want to extend my gratitude to *you*, the reader. Without you, this story would be nothing but lonely words on paper. I hope you enjoyed Shelta's adventure, and that it came to life in your imagination.

About the Author

Leia Talon writes fantasy and speculative fiction with romantic elements. Her lyrical approach is influenced by a lifetime of turning emotions into poetry and songs. She lives with her family in the mountains of British Columbia, where nature sparks her imagination to run wild.

The overarching universe of *The World Tree Chronicles* opens with *Shelta's Songbook*, a standalone collection of Shelta's poetry and short stories, complete with love letters from an immortal. Shelta's story continues in book two of ROOTS AND STARS: *Dragons in the Weaving*.

Connect online:

www.LeiaTalon.com
Twitter.com / LeiaTalon
Facebook.com / LeiaTalon
Instagram.com / LeiaTalon

The World Tree Chronicles

www.ingramcontent.com/pod-product-compliance
Lightning Source LLC
Chambersburg PA
CBHW020005120726
47903CB00004B/1139